Rosalind R. Cuschera

Journey from San Rocco

Rosalind A. Cuschera

Dedication

For my beloved parents, Donata and Rosario Cuschera,

Zia Domenica, Zio Cesidio, Grace Cipriano,

and all the special people who inhabit the pages of this book.

May it be a welcome legacy to my children, Joseph and Denise,

and my grandchildren—Cody, Chase, Devin, Owen and Spencer.

Acknowledgements

A special thank you to my cousins, Rosario and Madeline Cushera, who piqued my interest in genealogy, and to my sister, Kathy Vissa, who shared it.

A debt of gratitude is especially owed to A. Carter Jefferson and my fellow classmates at the University of Massachusetts' Osher Lifelong Learning Institute (O.L.L.I.) in Boston, as well as to many family members and friends for their encouragement and support.

...these three remain:
Faith, Hope and Love —
and the greatest of these is Love.

1 Corinthians 13:13

CHAPTER 1

The Fatal Spark—October 1918

The night passed quietly. The constant shelling had ceased. Light broke gently over the Austrian battleground, causing some movement in the foxhole. Antonio Leonardi stood guard. He stretched his tall, muscular body, making as little noise as possible. Carefully, he removed his dusty helmet and passed his fingers through his clipped black hair, rubbing his head in a single motion. Lifting his canteen, he splashed the precious little water onto his unshaven mustached face, smoothing the liquid off with his now-bedraggled scarf. He replaced his helmet and resumed his watchful position.

The trench smelled of dampness, dysentery, and death. Antonio saw rats scampering along the ditch. *Like us,* he thought, *rats in a hole trying to escape the light.* His only compensation was having his friend, Guido, by his side. They had grown up together and fought side by side, sharing rations and hope. Their bond, stronger than brotherhood, was built on memories, pain, terror, and faith that the war would end soon and they would return home to their families, together.

Antonio's thoughts drifted to the day he'd left to join in a war that few were enthusiastic about fighting. Each town was committed to providing men to join the war, and Antonio's turn came in its second year. Rumors about serious shortages of equipment, doctors, and ammunition proved to be true. Without grenades in the early part of the war, some Italians were forced to throw rocks when their ammunition ran out and frequently collected arms from the fallen after a battle. Countless wounded were left unattended, and transportation problems occasionally caused severe shortages of food and water. *All this misery,* Antonio thought, *just to gain land through the high mountains that bordered Italy and Austria. Land, that in truth, was a series of desolate, rocky ridges, often covered in snow and ice.*

Antonio shifted on a section of log pressed into the side of the trench which provided a makeshift seat to avoid sitting on the cold, muddy earth. As the sun rose, his comrade Guido stirred, coughed, and groaned as he stretched out legs cramped from burrowing in the damp earth. Antonio smiled at his hometown friend. "*Buon giorno, mio fratello.*" Guido looked

1

at his friend, nodding a greeting. "People say the war is almost over. One more strong attack on those Austro-Hungarians and they should be finished. So why are we still here, Antonio? Everybody wants more of something—more land, more money, more power. If we kill each other, who will benefit?"

"I'm ready to go home to my family," Antonio replied. "Caterina wrote the new baby is a handful, like me." He laughed. "I can't wait to see my new bambina. She's almost two years old now." His mind tried to picture the new baby, but instead filled with the image of his wife, Caterina, a dark, fierce beauty—a classic Mediterranean woman, full-figured with soft curves. Caterina had the most provocative walk of any woman he had ever met. Although not very tall, she walked with confidence. She commanded attention, and basked in it.

Antonio's thoughts were interrupted by Guido's shifting into a kneeling position. He watched Guido straighten out his uniform, and settled himself to scan the horizon for any activity. The stillness in the trench and on the field, still littered with dead bodies, filled Antonio with a cold dread. He forced himself to forget his surroundings and think about Caterina.

He remembered her chocolate-brown eyes, which had a piercing, knowing quality that could show warmth and a mischievous humor. He dreamed of burying his face in the thick black hair that curled softly down her back. In public, she wore it braided into soft, full rolls that crowned her sun-kissed, olive face.

His Caterina could be a terror at times, but he loved her too much to take offense at her occasional temper tantrums. He recalled the time he repaired shoes for their neighbor, Magda Cedrone. The woman was embarrassed; she had no money but needed the shoes for her children.

"No charge," Antonio said. "It's a Christmas present."

Caterina was livid at his generosity, and perhaps a little jealous, too. She threw all the shoes from his cobbler's shop out the door into the street, shouting, "Here, be the grand patron to everyone! Why not? Your wife and children can always eat the leather!"

That woman, she could draw a crowd, but he loved her deeply and passionately and told her often, mostly in notes hidden in their bed. Although the war separated them, his letters and cards faithfully testified to his love and loneliness for her.

His children, though, were his greatest blessing; Paolo, his intelligent, serious son, and the two girls, Geneva, who always greeted him with squeals of delight and pleas for bouncy shoulder rides, and Dina, his sweetest, most loving child. The new baby, Loretta, was still a mystery since she had been born while he was in the army. Caterina's letters assured him that she looked like him, and was just as playful, cheerful, and energetic as her father.

Antonio roused from his musings. "One more day, Guido, and we'll be rotated to the rear for a rest."

Guido reached into his jacket and pulled out two crushed cigarettes. After reshaping them, he searched for a dry match and offered one to his friend. "One last luxury," he said.

Antonio gratefully accepted it and bowed his head as his friend lit the match to the cigarette. A thunderous shot broke the quiet. Guido froze as the body of Antonio, his friend, his brother, fell across him.

CHAPTER 2

Cold Reality—January 1919

Graciella was carefully balancing her water jar upon her head when she saw the parish priest, Padre Alberto, rushing across the square. She watched him turn and climb up the bank of stone steps leading to Caterina's house. She rushed after him so swiftly she nearly dropped the stone jar. As the priest paused at Caterina's door, Graciella lowered the jar, set it on the lower step, pocketed her head cushion, and ran up to the priest. He turned and sighed deeply. His eyes and bowed head told her that he had bad news.

"Antonio was killed by a sniper," he blurted out.

"My God, no! Oh, my God, no!" As she attempted to compose herself, Graciella waited for him to knock on her friend's door. Then she stepped forward, following him into Antonio's cobbler shop.

Paolo had opened the door. Seeing the priest, he bowed reverently and ran for his mother. Caterina came into the room, wiping her hands on her apron before removing it. She felt somewhat agitated that the priest chose to come in the middle of the day. She had just fed the children and was gathering clothes and linens to be washed at the town's laundry basin. It would be crowded if she delayed much longer, and the day was growing colder. She bowed to the priest and gestured for him to come into the sitting room.

Suddenly, Caterina saw Graciella approaching her with open arms and a tearful face. Caterina stepped back, and in a choked voice said,

3

"*Pieta Dio, Antonio morto.*" Then her legs failed her as she crumpled to the floor. The priest rushed to catch her, but only managed to grip her large sleeves as she collapsed.

Paolo yelled out, "Mama! Mama!" as he tried to squeeze in between the priest and Graciella. Dina, hearing his screams, dropped the plate she was drying and ran into the sitting room. Paolo was now turning his attention to Padre Alberto. "Why are you here? What did you do to my mother?"

The priest, with Graciella's help, lifted Caterina and gently seated her on a nearby chair before turning to Paolo. He put his slender, delicate hands on the boy's shoulders and said, "You must give strength and courage to your mother. I'm sorry, my son, your father was shot and died of his wounds. He was a brave soldier and an honorable man, Paolo. You should be proud of him."

In the corner, Dina was sobbing loudly, gasping for breath.

Caterina, still dry-eyed, looked at Padre Alberto and said, "Will honor and bravery feed my four children?"

Graciella looked around the room and asked, "Where are Geneva and the baby?" No one replied, so she searched the small kitchen and the single bedroom. No children. She stopped and heard voices coming from the garden behind the house. When she opened the kitchen door, she saw Geneva teasing the baby, Loretta. The girls were squealing with happiness in their play. Graciella kissed them, picked up Loretta, and took Geneva by the hand, leading them into the sitting room. Loretta struggled to get down and scampered to Dina while Geneva rushed to her mother and snuggled up to her side.

Padre Alberto touched Caterina's shoulder. "We must pray..."

Caterina pulled away and said, "Please Padre, my children and I need to be alone." She lowered her head and began to cry. After a short time, she said, "Thank you for coming, but please go, please."

The saddened priest nodded and murmured, "Of course, my child. When you are ready, I am here to help you pray to our almighty God for comfort." Padre Alberto blessed her and each of the children before he left.

Graciella, who was not certain whether Caterina wanted her to leave as well, went into the kitchen. She saw the basket of unwashed clothes, took it, and left quietly. After washing the clothes, she returned and hung them in the garden on drying racks, hoping to catch the last rays of sunlight.

Caterina and the children were still in the sitting room. Paolo was standing by his mother. Geneva was kneeling on the floor with her head buried in Caterina's lap. Dina sat on the floor holding Loretta, who was fidgeting. Graciella took the baby from Dina's arms and carried her into the bedroom. She changed and washed the toddler and brought her into the kitchen. Giving her a piece of bread, she said, "Eat, my sweet one," as the child gnawed hungrily.

Graciella realized that she had not been home since early morning. Her mother-in-law would still be looking after the children, having undoubtedly learned the news from villagers. She would retrieve her water jar if, pray God, no one had stolen or broken it. She would need the water to make a good soup full of vegetables and maybe a little *pastina* for her friend and the children. Hopefully, her mother-in-law would have made fresh bread today for them to share.

Graciella approached Caterina to tell her she would be back soon.

Caterina looked up, and then threw her head back, screaming, "Antonio, Antonio, why you, why you? What will happen to us? Brave, honorable death—for what, for whom?"

The children, startled out of their soft moaning, turned wide, frozen eyes toward their mother. Caterina's tears flowed in anguish. Deep, guttural sounds of pain and anger escaped her throat as she rocked back and forth in the chair. Graciella, crying again, put her arms around her friend, held her as tightly as she could, and murmured, "My dear friend, I'm so sorry, I'm so sorry. God be with you, *bella*."

CHAPTER 3

One Medal for One Life—March 1919

Two months later, Antonio's few belongings, a citation, and a medal were sent to the family. Supported by her children, a few of Antonio's relatives, and her good friend, Graciella, Caterina went through the motions of receiving the citation and medal from the town's mayor, but she felt somehow distantly removed from the ritual as well as from those who came to mourn her husband's death. Many of their neighbors who attended the ceremony stayed to offer their condolences.

As he was leaving, the mayor shook Caterina and Paolo's hands and patted Dina, Geneva, and Loretta on their heads. "Courage, my dear woman. Your husband died a hero, and we, his countrymen, are proud of his valor."

"Pride is hard to digest, mayor, when your children are hungry."

Next, Antonio's friend, Guido, came to her. As he hugged her, he wept and uttered words of sympathy. "*Mala fortuna, mala fortuna,*" he repeated.

Caterina looked at him and tried not to show how much she despised this simpleton whom fate had favored.

People continued to crowd their small house, and Graciella, as usual, came to her rescue and fed the horde that had come to eat and reminisce.

Looking at her neighbors, Caterina thought how strangely detached she felt from these people. *What did they understand? Today they are here; tomorrow I will be alone with my children and a dirty house.*

When the people had gone, and the children had finally fallen asleep, Caterina went quietly into her corner of the bedroom and sat on her bed. After a few minutes, she knelt on the floor and pulled out a flocked velvet box from under the bed. Antonio had sent her a gift from Vienna when he was stationed there. The box had originally held two pretty coffee cups for the quiet nights they would share when he returned. Now it held only memories—letters and cards from Antonio.

Over and over, she read her favorite card, which pictured a lovely bouquet of French violets surrounded by handmade lace. Antonio was such a sentimentalist, and so open and fun-loving, that he sometimes exasperated her with his foolish playfulness. But this card was different. It was a deep, heart-wrenching declaration of his love and desire for her, a desire that would never be fulfilled because of the sniper's bullet that had stilled her Antonio's adoring heart forever.

What future has a widow with four children in this small town? Caterina wept, overwhelmed and consumed by bitterness. *Why did my Antonio have to die, and Guido, that* buffone, *live?*

CHAPTER 4

The Face of Grief—May 1919

"Mama," asked Paolo, "when will they send Papa home?"

"He rests with the other soldiers, my son," she said, "but we will find a place to honor him." Although Antonio's body was buried in a foreign grave, Caterina had his name etched on the Leonardi family stone so that she and the children could visit him in memory. Finding the time to visit the cemetery between caring for the children and her job of cleaning the church was difficult and stressful. Money was scarce, but flowers for Antonio seemed a necessity to her. Caterina left the flowers and leaned on the row of stone burial vaults, rubbing her hand back and forth over the etched names.

Her thoughts drifted to a morning when she was young and sure of herself. A small smile crossed her lips as she remembered Antonio's quiet, shy proposal.

"I want to marry you, you know, and be with you always."

"Marry?" she said, "I'm too young to leave my family." She laughed at him. Then, seeing his troubled face, she smiled and gave him a quick kiss.

He grabbed her hands and said, "I will love you forever!"

She remembered taunting him, "You'll love me forever?" She laughed again, "Antonio, you say it so seriously. Love should be happy and playful," she chided.

Then he grabbed her waist, lifted her in the air and spun around so fast that they both fell into a nearby flower garden. She was shocked at first, but he laughed so hard she started to laugh, too. Remembering, she laughed and pressed her face against the cold stone.

Finally, her thoughts drifted to that fateful day that Antonio, appearing taller and even more handsome in his grey-green uniform, had to bid her and the three children good-bye.

From the moment it was determined that he was to go to war, she had begged him, "Don't go. For the sake of your family, please, Antonio, don't go."

He had held her, kissing her face, and said, "I must go, *bella mia*. Let's enjoy the time we have together. You know that my heart and thoughts will always be with you and the children."

That last night he made love to her with such tender care and gentleness that she trembled, once again reliving those moments of passion and devotion. "Promise me that you will return," Caterina had begged. "Promise me." "I'll do my best," he had whispered. "You and the children are my life. I'll love you every moment that I breathe, and if God will it, I'll love you through eternity."

For the first time in their marriage, she experienced total surrender of herself in love and desire for him that last tremulous night. As fate would have it, she conceived Loretta during those final days of loving Antonio.

As reality set in once more, Caterina's smile faded and she began to cry. Sobbing with grief, she stood staring at the flowers which rested in the mounted vase. Then, one by one, she began pulling them out, slowly at first, then grabbed the remaining flower heads, stripped the petals and leaves, crushed them in her hand, and violently threw them to the ground.

"Forever, forever, I'll love you forever!" she screamed. Caterina fell to the ground, and when her anger and grief were spent, she rose up, turned her back to the stone, and walked home.

CHAPTER 5

Bless the Little Children—October 1919

The children, dealing with their own grief, became a heavy burden for Caterina, and she was often short-tempered with them. Paolo, ten and the oldest, became more introspective. Most days he was away from home seeking small jobs to provide money for the family.

"Paolo, all these jobs. I don't want you to neglect your schoolwork. I know you want to help, but ignorance is a far greater poverty."

"I know, Mama. I don't really miss much school. My teacher lets me leave a little early if I tell him I have a job. He has been much kinder to me since Papa died."

"Are you telling me that your teacher is encouraging you, and not insisting that you must be in school?"

"No, he wants me to study and be in school, but knows I must work, too. He gives me my papers to study at night after I finish my job."

"My son, no wonder you always look so tired. Why didn't you tell me you were staying up late to study?"

"Don't worry, Mama. I'm not too tired, and I like being able to help you."

Caterina, tears misting her eyes, hugged her valiant son. "Promise me you will not take a job if you're too tired or if you fall behind in your studies. Promise me now."

"I promise, Mama."

Dina took refuge each morning at church, praying. The rest of the day she often cried softly over her sewing. The sanctuary of prayer seemed to provide some solace to her. Now that her father was not off fighting in the war, but home with God, she talked to him in prayer.

Papa, is it beautiful where you are? Do the angels sing for you every day? You sing so well, Papa. Do you sing, too? Can you see me and hear me?

Papa, I miss you so much. Mama tries to be brave, but I hear her cry sometimes when she thinks no one is in the house. She cries late at night when we're supposed to be asleep. Do you hear her, Papa? If you do, can you make her less sad, and not mad at everyone, too?

Noticing that Dina was crying over her sewing again, Caterina said, "Dina, how can you see your stitches if you are constantly crying. Your father's death affected all of us, but if we all sat down and cried every day, this house would be a *lavabo* and the women of the town could wash their clothes here."

With this curious image in mind, Dina started to smile. Caterina took the edge of her apron and wiped Dina's face. "My crazy girl—first you cry, then you grin like a monkey. There, you are so much prettier when you smile, and people will want your company if you are not a gloomy girl."

"I'll try, Mama."

Geneva, age five, and three years younger than Dina, constantly clung to Caterina's skirts, burying herself in their long, deep folds.

"Geneva, please go out and play. I can't walk when you're always in my shadow."

"I don't want to go out! Everyone's at school and Loretta is sleeping. I could buy some lemon *gelato*, if you give me money."

"You know we have no money for *gelato*."

"We never have money for anything! My friend, Alma, her father always buys her *gelato*. He didn't get himself killed in the war. Why did Papa? He should have hidden better!"

Caterina shook her head. "Geneva, please go find your friend, Alma, and play until dinner time. I must bring Loretta to Graciella's house, and then go to work. The entire church must be cleaned and polished. I don't have time or energy to argue with you. Go now." Caterina kissed Geneva's head and pushed her toward the door. Geneva made a pouting face and left, leaving the door open in her departure. Exasperated, Caterina murmured, "Why did you desert me, Antonio? Life is too hard without you."

Even, the baby, Loretta, now two years old, seemed to be rebelling against her. Graciella had taken care of the baby the weeks after Antonio's death, and Loretta seemed to have developed a bond with her that she lacked with her mother. Graciella often took Loretta so that Caterina could cook and clean for Padre Alberto and earn a small living. Now, when Caterina approached the baby, Loretta would run away and hide under the bed or behind a chair. She would struggle defiantly whenever Caterina pulled her up into her arms.

One day her frustration was so great she began chastising the baby as she struggled to hold her.

"Why do you resist me? Does my black dress frighten you? You never fight off Graciella. Do you love her more than your own mother? What is it, my child? Are you angry that your father is gone? At such a tender age could you, like me, sense an uncertain future?"

CHAPTER 6
The Proposal—November 1919

When the letter arrived, it caused a small stir in the town. Several neighbors followed the postmaster to Caterina's house. She held the letter, looking at the postmark—America. *Who would write her from America?* Antonio had relatives there, but she barely knew them, and they had already sent their condolences and twenty dollars in American money. Carefully, she tore the envelope open and pulled out the two sheets of paper. Her neighbors drew closer.

"Who sent the letter from America, Caterina?" One asked her, "Did they send you any money?"

"Give me a chance to open it," she said.

When her family and a few friends first heard of Antonio's death, letters came every so often, mostly from her sister, Vittoria. But for the past few months, she had received little mail, and rarely from America. She looked quickly at the letter. *What is this foolishness,* she wondered, *someone's idea of a stupid joke?* She refolded the letter, and chided the curious onlookers.

"Please leave me to my own business." Caterina turned and closed her door, sat down, unfolded the letter and reread it.

"Mama," said Dina, "people just want to be nice. Why are you always so rude to our neighbors?"

"They're not trying to be nice, just nosy," she replied.

The letter was written by a man named Umberto Fabrizio, who had left her town more than twelve years ago, around the time she was preparing for her marriage to Antonio. Her recollection of him was a bit vague, but she thought that he and his brother had gone to America to seek their fortune, after their parents died in an accident. He wrote that he had become a stone mason in America and married an Irish girl, and that they had four children before she died of influenza. He had a large house, a good business, several good wagons, and a motor truck.

In a strong, artistically beautiful handwriting, Umberto had offered his condolences for Antonio's untimely death and then, shockingly, invited her to come to America. "Life in America is not as hard as in our small town," he wrote. "My family and I would welcome you and the children and, together, I believe we could build a good life. I encourage you to write as soon as possible, and if you accept my proposal, I will make all the arrangements for us to renew our acquaintance, and you can inspect your new home and meet my children. If you agree to marry me, we will marry soon after your arrival in America. If you do not wish to marry me, I will pay for your return to Italy and we will part old friends."

Caterina was stunned. She folded the letter quickly and put it in her pocket. *He must be crazy,* she thought. *He barely knew me, and I can't remember his face from his brother's.* She dismissed the letter and began to prepare the evening meal. Later that night, while trying to sleep, she thought of it once again. Antonio always wrote her letters, perhaps it's a sign. The letter haunted her. *Is this fate, some miracle to save her and her children from endless poverty?* Umberto Fabrizio was her countryman and perhaps could give her and the children a life without worry or want. She frowned, wondering if she could cope with more children when her own occasionally overwhelmed her. Well, she reasoned, if he was rich, they could hire a housekeeper like other wealthy American people.

I can't believe he could be serious, she thought again. *What kind of a man proposes to a woman he barely knows? I must be out of my mind to even think about it. We could live with my sister and her husband. No, I won't take charity. Why doesn't he find another Irish or American wife? Maybe he's homesick and wants an Italian family. He could be lying to me, but Antonio's family in America might know him and I could ask them.* For weeks, her mind constantly carried on arguments with itself, an obsession she could not escape.

Over the next few days, her mind drifted to the letter's proposal as a possible solution. There were few other choices. She finally reasoned with herself that if she did not like him or had a bad impression of her new home, she could return to Italy, and destiny would be her guide. Her younger sister, Vittoria, married only two years, had begged her repeatedly in her letters to come north and stay on her husband's farm. She promised that Pietro would give her and the children a small home and some land, and they could grow enough food for themselves as well as to sell at the local market. There would always be a home and work for her and the children. They would be together. Her husband, Pietro, was a good man, Vittoria pleaded. He would love the children and be like a father to them.

Caterina thought of her two brothers, Lorenzo and Vincenzo. Both had been wounded in the war and were slowly recovering. Her brothers had families of their own and were also in dire straits. Like her, neither wanted to accept charity and each was determined to get back on his feet and provide for his family. Lorenzo's wife was very ill, and he had the added task of caring for her and their two children, although his daughter, Maria Elena, was a great comfort to him and his wife.

Caterina's only other choice was to return to her home town and live with her two maiden aunts. Zia Marianna and Zia Magdalena were so old and, in truth, were even poorer then she, although they taught sewing and lace-making. She knew her family would be loving and supportive, but her life and that of her children would be a daily struggle with little hope of a comfortable and successful future.

Reviewing her options, Caterina saw her whole family surviving from day to day for their existence and sustenance. Now that the war was over, the country was dealing with unemployment, political unrest, and economic hardship. Wounded men, suffering both physically and emotionally, filled the towns. Italy may have been on the side of victory in the Great War, but the people, land, and political structure had suffered devastating consequences. Caterina reasoned that America was a big country. People always spoke of men who left for America to make their fortune. Umberto Fabrizio was such a man. He had made a good life, he wrote. He had a successful business, a house, wagons, even a motor truck, as well as four children. He had enough money to send for a new wife and family.

When she first considered Umberto's proposal, she jokingly told Graciella that their former neighbor had become rich in America and had written to invite her, Caterina, to become his wife. Graciella did not laugh as Caterina expected. "Money can't heal a broken heart or provide happiness for everyone," said Graciella.

"Money will put food on the table for my children," Caterina heatedly replied. "Money will give them an education and a good life."

"Please think hard about this, my dear friend. You are struggling, yes, but we're all struggling. Your family, your friends, your neighbors will not let you starve. We love you, and will help you and the children as best we can. Don't make the mistake of selling yourself and the children for a promise of a good life from a stranger in a strange country."

"Graciella, if I didn't know you better, I'd believe you are envious. I could have a comfortable life, while you count pennies every day."

"How can you say that after all we have been to each other? I'm not envious. I wish you every blessing. I can't understand how you can abandon your family and friends for someone who you barely know. Perhaps he is not rich, but wants a wife to serve him and care for his children. Think, Caterina, what you are doing. This is not moving to the next town as when you married Antonio, a man you fell in love with. This is marrying a stranger from across the sea. You will be alone there with no family, no friends."

These discussions raised a tension between them that neither had anticipated. Despondent, Caterina believed that God, like Antonio, had abandoned her. *Perhaps if I could pray like Dina*, she thought, *I would recite, "Do not abandon me, Lord, My God, do not go away from me! Hurry to help me, Lord, my Savior." God knows I could use a savior right now.*

CHAPTER 7

The Decision—December 1919

Caterina wrote her sister first, to tell her of the letter from America; not to ask her advice, but to announce her decision. She thanked Vittoria and Pietro for their kind offer of a small house on their farm, but she wanted this opportunity to travel to America and possibly marry a rich man who was originally from their town.

She wrote her brothers a light-hearted letter telling them to be happy for her.

"The children and I are traveling to America. I am going to marry an old friend and neighbor, Umberto Fabrizio, who has become very successful. He is a widower, but I feel certain the children will become good friends with his two sons and two daughters. Please don't worry about me. I am very excited about my future and hope that good fortune will also fall upon you and your family."

Caterina knew that her brothers were not in a position to help her, and she wanted them to be at ease with her decision. Her letter reflected an assurance to them, and a confidence, perhaps more for herself.

Her sister and both brothers wrote her immediately upon receiving her letters. Vittoria was adamant that this was a mistake. "Caterina, you must not go to America to marry this man. Who is this person? Does he still have family in Italy? Have they contacted you and told you about their relative? Why did he marry an Irish woman? Does that mean there are no Italian women in his town? If so, who will you have for friends?

You will not be able to converse with anyone. No one will be able to help you if you or the children become ill. How can you trust him to care for your children? Perhaps his children are so horrid he needs a wife to care for them."

Vittoria closed with, "Please reconsider this decision. I have written Vincenzo and Lorenzo that they must convince you to stay with your family. Mama is very old and sick. She may die soon, and you will never see her again. Come to our farm and stay with us. You would make us very happy, and Paolo, Dina, Geneva, and Loretta would have a happy life surrounded by a family who loves them. Please write me and tell me you are coming to the farm."

Lorenzo wrote himself, while Vincenzo's wife, Luisa, wrote for him. Both letters asked similar questions. Who was this man? Why did he propose to her? Why did she accept? What about the children? Are they satisfied with this arrangement? Vittoria, Pietro, and Mama want her and the children to live with them. Why are you not accepting their invitation? What about our mother? She may not understand very much since her stroke, but how could Caterina leave her mother, sister, and brothers to cast her lot with a stranger in America?

Caterina sighed as she reread the letters. *Why did everyone have to be so pessimistic? Why couldn't they see that I am going to America to make my fortune just like so many men from our town and other towns did? My brothers and sister have their own troubles, I can't depend on them. I will decide my own life.*

She then wrote Umberto that she accepted his proposal. They would need new clothes and shoes for America. She wanted them to look their best, but had little money to spare.

Within a month, he wrote back and enclosed a bank draft and instructions to a local attorney to provide her and one child with travel tickets and money for America. He explained. "For now, it is best that you only travel with one child, possibly the youngest, and if we marry, perhaps we could take one or two months to prepare our home for the older children. Then we will return to Italy together and bring your children back to America as a family."

Caterina was flabbergasted! She was to leave her children? There must be a mistake. What would her family think if they knew she was leaving her children behind while traveling to America to marry this stranger? She would ask the attorney. Perhaps if she did not spend too much money to ready herself, or if they took a cheaper class on the boat, they could all go together.

CHAPTER 8

The Arrangement—January 1920

She called on Attorney Donato Cardello the next day. "Signor Cardello, I need to speak with you about the arrangements proposed by Signor Umberto Fabrizio of America."

He was not surprised to see her so soon, since Umberto Fabrizio included the conditions of the arrangement along with the necessary bank draft and specific travel dates and instructions.

"I have received all the information, Signora Leonardi. Please sit here," he said, indicating a narrow, wooden chair. Cardello retreated to his desk and waited for Caterina to settle herself. Caterina looked around at the sparsely furnished office which included three chairs, a table, a long bookshelf with worn books, and a small stand which held a water pitcher and several glasses. Signor Cardello had a gentle face with dark, bushy eyebrows and a smooth shaven chin that was topped with a full mustache. His eyes were fixed on her with a concerned look. He reminded her of her father.

"Is there any possibility that I misunderstood Signor Fabrizio?" she said. "His letter said to bring only one child, possibly my baby, Loretta. Surely he did not intend that I leave my other three children behind? Please tell me it was a misunderstanding," she pleaded.

Cardello sympathized with her, but Fabrizio was his client. "No, Signora, that is the understanding. I believe he felt that it would make it easier for you to reacquaint yourselves. A baby, of course, needs its mother, so the child must accompany you. If you decide to marry Signor Fabrizio, then I'm certain you both will return for the other children."

"How can I leave my children? What will happen to them? Who will care for them? What will people think?" Caterina lamented on, hoping to win over Cardello's support.

"Signora, calm yourself. I agree that the conditions are not very agreeable. As I see it, you have two choices. Refuse Fabrizio's proposal—tell him to find another American wife. But if you accept his arrangements, you can call for your children as soon as you settle in America. If I may say so, you are a beautiful woman and will, undoubtedly, charm him. How could he refuse you after the great sacrifice you will have made going to America for him?"

Caterina thought about this statement and agreed to herself that if she made this great sacrifice, Signor Fabrizio would probably deny her nothing. *Antonio could never deny me anything,* she thought to herself. *This man will appreciate my understanding and want to care for me, too.*

Attorney Cardello rose from behind the large wooden table which served as a desk and sat next to Caterina. He took her hand in his and held it. Looking into her eyes, he said softly, "Umberto Fabrizio is most likely having a difficult time caring for his own children, his business, and making plans for your future together. You should think hard on the matter— perhaps discuss it with your family or a good friend. If you decide to go to America and need my help, I will arrange for Paolo to enter a military school and Dina and Geneva to be cared for by the nuns at a church orphanage, on a temporary basis, naturally."

Caterina looked at Signor Cardello's pleasant but reserved face. *What could he be thinking of me? Following the wishes of a stranger? Putting my children in orphanages? Please, don't let me choose. Tell me what to do,* she thought.

Caterina abruptly got up from her chair. She ran to the door, then stopped and pulled out the latest letter from Umberto, which contained his photograph. He was a very handsome man, with thick silver hair that still showed streaks of black. He appeared very distinguished-looking in a dark suit, white shirt, and striped cravat, looking more like a business person than a mason. She could not see his eyes, since his head was turned and he seemed to be gazing at something off in the distance. She stared very hard at the picture, then hung her head and cried silently.

Cardello returned to his chair behind the desk, leaving Caterina to sort out her decision.

Caterina thought of her children. Paolo, with his bright red hair, pale skin, and brown eyes, which seemed foreign compared to his parents' and sisters' darker countenances. He had her sister, Vittoria's, warm nature, but was quiet and deliberate in all he attempted—a perfectionist. When Antonio worked in his cobbler's shop, it was Paolo who shined the shoes and neatly tagged and stacked them for his father's customers. He was an asset with his good manners and eagerness to help. Being the oldest and only son, he took on an attitude of responsibility and dependability. Caterina took pride in her son's contributions to the family, but she relished his unique coloring, which made her preen—her peacock among the mudlarks of the village children.

She thought of Dina, her little nun, who was shy and reserved, yet had a sweetness that endeared her to people. A pretty girl with large dark eyes and hair, Dina was her homebody—sewing, helping with kitchen work and ironing. Sewing was Dina's passion. Along with knitting, crocheting, and mending clothes, Dina liked to draw flowers and other designs, which she duplicated on linen with needle and thread. She was the religious one, always stopping by the church and lighting candles for her father. It was disconcerting at times to hear her mumbling and realize she was praying while sewing. Caterina believed in God, but felt all this praying was fanatical.

Geneva was her princess. Now six, she loved imaginary games and pretended she had beautiful clothes and many servants to order about. Flighty and moody at times, Geneva had a gamin look to her, with a pert nose, almond-shaped eyes, and wispy brown hair. Unlike her other children who could be self-sufficient, Geneva demanded constant attention. Not very helpful with housework, Geneva would play with the baby, using Loretta as one of her subjects. Caterina worried about Geneva's mean streak. At times, when she tired of playing or watching the baby, she pinched the child or took the stuffed stocking Loretta liked to gnaw on. This resulted in loud wails from Loretta which brought Caterina or Dina running.

Thinking of Loretta pulled at her heart. She looked so much like Antonio. Those eyes that seem to look at everything at once, flashing about and sometimes looking right through a person. Loretta was strong-willed and curious as a monkey, never sitting still. Now two years old, she scampered and hid when Caterina tried to take her hand or pick her up. *Even when I nursed her,* Caterina mused, *she would pull and twitch so much I'd be constantly sore. She is usually calmer with Graciella, and seems to laugh more for her. Perhaps I appear too stern, but I've felt no joy since Antonio left for the war and then was killed. We had no time together with this child. I know I resented his leaving us only months before her birth; perhaps she sensed it. When we travel to America, I will have more time to be at ease and can perhaps build a stronger bond between us.*

Cardello had sat quietly. Perhaps he understood that the silence between them would help her to sort out her feelings and come to a decision.

Caterina turned, wiped her eyes, and returned to the chair. Cardello reached across the table and patted her hand while nodding his large head. Caterina spoke again. "Where is the military school for Paolo? Is it a good school? Paolo is bright, but it must not be too strict, because he's such a sensitive boy, and not too wild, because he's a quiet one."

"The military school is in Rome and highly regarded," Cardello assured her, before she could ramble on. "For the girls, the Sisters of

Charity orphanage is a lovely, peaceful school located outside Naples."

"The nuns, Dina will like them, but Geneva is too high-spirited and a bit undisciplined—she will find it hard. The girls will miss their brother, especially Dina, who is so close to Paolo. With his placement in Rome and theirs in Naples, they will not be able to see each other until I return to take them to America. America, our best chance for a good life, lies in the home of a man I barely know," she finally conceded to the attorney.

"Your husband, Antonio, was a well-respected man in the town and a war hero," he assured her. "His children will be looked after properly."

Caterina left heavy-hearted but somewhat reassured by Attorney Cardello's promises to arrange a temporary solution for her children. She should write her sister, but she knew Vittoria would be against her leaving the children under any condition. Wasn't she critical of the whole proposal of Caterina going to America to marry a man they knew nothing about except he was rich and came from their town? Vittoria was content to be a farmer's wife. Caterina wanted more for herself, and for her children. She felt confident that Umberto would fall under her spell and she would be able to manage him, his house, his children, and build a new life—a comfortable life in America.

But first, she must go to America to seek their fortune.

CHAPTER 9

The Children's Lament—January 1920

Caterina had planned to take Loretta, since she was the baby, but Geneva was devastated with the news that she would be separated from her mother, even for a short time. She cried unceasingly.

Paolo and Dina were shocked at their mother's announcement and pleaded that she not leave for America. They were happy, they assured her.

"I will work hard to earn more money to help you, Mama," pleaded Paolo. "Zio Pietro and Zia Vittoria want us to come to the farm. We would truly love the farm, and we could be together. We can be happy again, especially with Zio and Zia and Nonna. They love us. We can visit grandmother every day and help her into her chair and read stories to her. I would help with the animals and raise so much food we could eat forever, and even have enough to sell and make lots of money," he pleaded.

"America is a wealthy country," Caterina countered. "We must sacrifice our being together for a short time, for a wonderful life in America."

Their pleas, arguments and tears could not dissuade her, now that she had made up her mind.

True to his word to work and help the family, Paolo was on his way home from Tocci's butcher shop. Unexpectedly, he saw Dina leaving her friend's house.

"Dina, Dina, wait for me!"

Turning, she began to smile, but seeing Paolo, she gasped, "What happened to you? You're covered in blood!"

Shaking his head, Paolo grimaced, "I've been working for the butcher. He gave me five hundred lire for unpacking the meat and putting it on trays. He said I did a fine job—very neat and organized—and I could come back anytime to work for him."

"Will you go back there again?" asked Dina. "You look awful and you smell bloody! How can you touch those poor, dead animals?"

"It was awful!" Paolo agreed. "At one point, I thought I would be sick, but I kept holding my breath when I was in the market, and only breathed when I was outside unloading the truck."

"Mama will be so upset when she sees your clothes," Dina whispered. "The blood will remind her of Papa—I know it makes me think of Papa."

"Maybe I can change in the garden and leave my clothes in a bucket of water to wash later."

"Do that, but I'll wash them or they'll never be clean."

As they walked, Paolo was greeted with a few curious stares, but hurried along before anyone could stop them to ask questions.

"Paolo, how long do you think Mama will be in America before coming back for us?"

"Not long, maybe two months," he guessed.

"Geneva said she was going to America first because Mama would never leave her."

"No, Loretta's the baby. She must go with Mama."

"I think Geneva wants to go to America because she said we will be rich and she will have lots of pretty dresses and shoes."

"We will also have two new brothers and two new sisters, Dina, and they may not like sharing their papa or their home and money with us," responded Paolo.

"Do you think they're nice children? Will they like us? Do you think Mama will like her new husband as much as Papa?"

"No, she still loves Papa, but she's worried about us and I think she's only marrying him because she's frightened of raising us alone."

19

"But we have each other," Dina said. "We aren't alone. We have Zia Vittoria, Zio Pietro, Nonna, Zio Lorenzo, Zio Vincenzo and their families, the aunts, and we have Graciella too!"

"I know, but Mama wants us to be safe and not poor. I have tried to tell her we want to stay here with our own family and friends. I can help. I can learn to be a cobbler like Papa, and we can open the shop again, but she won't hear of it. She's determined to go to America, marry that man and bring us all there, too."

Crying, Dina said, "But I don't want to leave Papa! If we go to America we'll never find Papa's grave. He'll be here alone with no one to visit him or talk to him, and we'll be across the ocean—far, far away."

"Well, since Papa is in Heaven, we can talk to him anytime," Paolo said. "When we go to America, we will bring some of Papa's things— maybe his medals and, of course, the Italian flag, and we can make a new memorial to Papa there and visit it whenever we want."

"I suppose," said Dina, then added with a smile, "You always make me feel better, Paolo. Do you know how old the Fabrizio children are?"

"Mama said the oldest girl, Ava, is fourteen; Umberto, named after his father, is thirteen; Luca is eleven; and Lena is nine."

"Maybe we can be friends since we're almost the same ages as Luca and Lena," Dina said.

"I wish we could write them and see if they want us to come. Then we'll know if we can be friends."

As they neared the house, Paolo took off his bloodied shirt and ran through the house to the back garden. Dina saw Geneva playing with Loretta and their rag dolls.

"Why doesn't Paolo have his shirt on?" Geneva asked.

"He got it dirty working for the butcher and doesn't want Mama to see it." Dina said. "I'll wash it for him after he soaks it for a while."

"Mama will have a fit if he ruins his shirt. We are not rich Americans yet, you know."

"I don't want to be a rich American," said Dina. "I want us to stay here and be happy. I don't think we are too poor. Mama works and Paolo works sometimes and we can sew our clothes and grow food in the garden. I don't want to leave Papa or our relatives. They love us and said they would help us. Why must we go to America? We won't know anyone and maybe the Fabrizio children will be mean to us. Maybe Mr. Fabrizio will beat us or not like us! I will never call him 'Papa,' never!"

Startled by Dina's vehemence, Loretta started to cry. Dina picked her up and fiercely hugged her.

"If you squeeze her like that she'll only cry more," Geneva warned.

Dina kissed the baby and began to play with her, wiping away both their tears.

"I think going to America is a good idea," reasoned Geneva. "What choices do we have? I don't want to be a farmer like Zia Vittoria, or even a seamstress like Mama's old aunts. I want to be rich and beautiful—maybe an actress or at least a fine lady. I loved Papa too, but he got himself killed and left us without a father. We need a father to care for us and buy us presents and give us sweets and have fun again."

"Fun, that's all you think about—having fun, and pretty dresses and sweets. Suppose our new Papa and his children don't like us? Suppose they live like rich people and they only want us as servants? But you didn't think of that, did you?" Dina taunted. "Maybe instead of being a little princess you will be treated just like Cinderella, with no American fairy godmother to help you."

"Oh, you're just 'the little nun'—that's what Mama calls you—just because you want to stay here and spend your whole life praying to Papa and going to church. "Well, I don't, and neither does Mama!" Geneva shouted.

"How can you forget Papa so quickly? He loved us and Mama," cried Dina.

"I loved Papa, too, but children need a father to take care of them," Geneva retorted.

"Papa, Papa," chattered Loretta happily.

Dina and Geneva laughed.

"See, Loretta needs to have a papa, too," Geneva said triumphantly.

Dina kissed Loretta and whispered, "I'll tell you all about our papa someday."

Paolo returned after washing himself and changing his clothes. "Are you two still arguing about going to America?"

"Yes, same thing—now Geneva wants to go, and I don't and neither does Loretta," Dina said vehemently.

"We can talk about this forever, but Mama has made up her mind she is going, and you know how stubborn she can be," said Paolo.

They stopped then, as they heard the front door open. A tired-looking Caterina came into the room. She paused and regarded her children. "The meeting is over. We are going, now get your chores done before dinner." She said it quietly, but there was sternness in her voice.

21

CHAPTER 10

An Unpopular Conclusion —
February 1920

For the children, it was still not acceptable. Paolo's sense of orderliness wanted to honor his father by reopening the cobbler's shop, thereby keeping his father's memory alive. Caterina again rejected this request. She felt that since he was only ten years old, he was too young to learn the trade and he should aspire to a more prestigious position in life. Paolo loved his mother, but he saw her as too high-strung and impetuous. He continued to try to persuade her that it was foolish to leave their country so that she could marry someone whom no one knew.

"What about his children? Umberto Fabrizio has two sons and two daughters. Suppose we don't like them and they don't like us? Will the bigger children bully us?"

He tried to reason with Caterina that while she was in America, he would be in a military orphanage. "I have a mother—I am not an orphan. Would I be required to march and use a gun?" he asked. "The only positive thing is I might wear a real uniform with shiny buttons and a hat, but leaving Italy, I will lose my friends and I won't be able to talk to anyone or understand them when they speak to me. No, I am the man of the house now and you should respect my feelings, Mama," he argued. But the man of the house was also a young boy, and tears sprang from his eyes. He covered his face and cried until he was spent. Then, taking a deep breath, he told Caterina, "Mama if you will not listen to reason, and I don't like the man or his children, I will just find Papa's relatives in America and live with them until I have enough money to return home to Italy."

When her mother spoke of moving to America, Dina was heartbroken. She felt they would be leaving her father. In her heart, Antonio's body was returned home and buried in the family plot. Dina visited the church each day after school and lit a candle for her father. She told her mother that she loved sitting in the darkened church and talking to God about her father. "Mama, when I'm in the church, I pretend that Papa is sitting next to me. I tell him all about school, about our family, and anything else that happens. I told him I was afraid of leaving our home and going to America, too. Mama, how can you think of marrying another man? Don't you still love Papa? I will never love anyone like I love Papa. The only boy I love is Paolo, and also Zio Pietro because he is funny and always kind to me. Do you remember how Zio Pietro bowed to me at his wedding to Zia Vittoria, and asked me to dance? Even though I was six, he picked me up and danced me all around the courtyard. It was so much fun! Later, he twirled me in the air and said I was the prettiest dancer at the wedding, next to Zia Vittoria."

Dina asked her mother many times if they could live with her aunt and uncle, but Caterina always said, "I'm not a farmer and neither are you." Caterina knew that her no-nonsense attitude and somber, black dresses intimidated Dina at times, but Dina would take her stand that she didn't want to live with the nuns without her family to go home to at night.

Geneva's initial reaction was anger. "Why did Papa get shot?" she would demand. She didn't want Caterina to go to America. She cried, "I will hate being an orphan, and the nuns will be too strict. All the children must wear the same clothes, and the dresses will be ugly! The nuns will cut off all my hair. My friend, Alma, told me so." She cried that the man who wanted to marry Mama might be mean and ugly. "His children," she continued, "will make me do everything because their papa is rich and we are not."

On other occasions, she cried and asked why Loretta should go to America with her mother while she had to wait in a terrible orphanage. "If you must go, Mama, please let me come with you and see the rich country first. Loretta is just a baby and will be so much trouble for you."

After weeks of strong lobbying, Geneva had convinced her mother that she was not as strong or independent as her siblings; she needed Caterina. When Caterina told her that she would be coming with her to America instead of Loretta, Geneva's attitude changed. She gloated to her siblings that she would see America first because Mama needed her. She would be Mama's companion. A baby was not a good companion; that was why her mother wanted her. Secretly, she felt her mother must love her best to choose her over the other children.

Finally decided, Caterina wrote her elderly aunts and asked if they would care for the baby. Geneva would travel with her to America; Paolo would enter the military orphanage in Rome, and Dina would be put in a religious orphanage close to Naples. It was settled.

CHAPTER 11

Visit to San Lorenzo—March 1920

The two years without Antonio had been very hard. Four months ago, she had received a proposal of marriage from Umberto Fabrizio, and in another two weeks she would travel to Naples with the older girls before departing for America. Dina would be brought to the nuns and Geneva would board the *Regina Italia* with her for America. Umberto had sent her two second-class tickets and some money. She and Geneva would leave Italy on April 19, 1920. It would take two weeks to reach their destination: Boston, Massachusetts, United States of America.

Attorney Cardello was to take Paolo to Rome to the military orphanage a few days before Caterina and the girls would leave for Naples. Two weeks before they were to embark on their separate journeys, Caterina had left the three older children with her faithful friend, Graciella, and took Loretta, now a toddler, to her maiden aunts, Zia Marianna and Zia Magdalena in her hometown of San Lorenzo.

Caterina had last seen her aunts at Vittoria's wedding three years ago. They looked much older now. The three women embraced with tears flowing, and the aunts kissed her and Loretta over and over. Her aunts still wore the ethnic dress of the region, a long black skirt, white blouse with shawl, an apron, and a small, starched kerchief pinned to their hair. Caterina noticed that Zia Marianna's hair was completely white. She must be close to seventy by now, she thought. Magdalena's iron grey hair was thick, coarse, and abundant, and her kerchief had difficulty covering it. Zia Magdalena belied her sixty-four years. Her quick movements, slender straight frame, and sharp intense demeanor contrasted with Zia Marianna's soft, slightly rotund body and gentle nature.

"You two talk while I prepare the coffee, some sandwiches, and maybe a few dried figs from our garden. The figs were beautiful last year," Marianna chatted. "You will see, they will be beautiful again this year. You must come to see them and bring some home to the children."

Caterina wondered how her elderly aunts traveled over the rough cobblestoned lanes and up the series of stone steps through twisting alleyways to their old cell of a house. Thinking of her younger days, spent visiting the aunts who taught her to sew, filled Caterina with nostalgia. She observed the large candle encased in a wire basket which hung from the ceiling. During her last visit, a few years ago, she noticed her aunts would take one of the rickety chairs, put it on the table under the candle, and do their sewing at night. She was sure they would eventually go blind, or at least fall off the table and break their necks, but they seemed contented with their lot and never complained about their primitive abode.

"The house is the same," said Caterina, "but there seems to be more light in the kitchen."

"Yes," replied Marianna. "Our wall cracked, and a neighbor pushed out a hole and made a new window for us. Wonderful, wonderful light," she sang.

Magdalena took Caterina's hand and pulled her toward the small, rustic table, seating her on one of the old, rickety chairs. Caterina noticed the beautiful handmade lace tablecloth which her aunts made and only used on special occasions. Fingering it, she said, "I still treasure the lovely tablecloth and napkins you both gave to me for a wedding present."

Both aunts were very talented seamstresses. Along with sewing, knitting, crocheting, and lace making, they also taught these artful skills to young girls in the surrounding towns. An ancient loom rested in the corner of the house. It had been retired some years ago from its task of weaving cloth. The aunts could not afford to have it repaired, and truthfully, were really too old to include weaving along with their other lessons. Besides, young women today wanted to buy pretty material from the large cities like Rome or Naples, or possibly Milan if they had family there.

Well, she thought, *a few months in the care of these loving women will not harm Loretta. She is too little to realize how primitive her surroundings are, and my aunts will smother her with affection and homemade* biscotti. *If they can get her to hold a needle, they probably will try to teach her to knit,* she chuckled to herself.

Caterina put Loretta on the floor to toddle about while she sat with Zia Magdalena at the worn table. From the pantry, Caterina heard Marianna's sudden sobs mingled with the clanging of the coffee pot.

Jolting her from her musing, Zia Magdalena fiercely grabbed Caterina's wrist and cried, "My child, what can you be thinking? To leave this baby—your children—for a man we only vaguely remember, is insane!"

Zia Marianna came to the table with rattling cups, plates, and the ancient coffee pot and confirmed, "Yes, yes, that is it, your grief has made you crazy!"

Caterina lowered her head and shook it in silent agreement. "You're right, there were days when I thought I would lose my mind, but when Umberto Fabrizio offered me and my children new hope for the future, I felt that all was not lost."

"My child," Magdalena insisted, "you have a family, people who love you and will always care for you. No, we are not rich like your suitor, Umberto, but we manage, and your mother and sister would be at peace if you would live with them. Vittoria's husband, Pietro, is a good man, and you and the children would not go hungry on his fertile farm. Perhaps in time, when they are well, your brothers would be able to help you, too."

"And the girls," Marianna chimed in, "could return to us in a few years, and we would teach them to embroider and make lace which could be sold in the large cities. Dina already has a talent for the art and would become a good teacher in time."

Magdalena begged her to reconsider. "It's not too late to write Umberto and tell him you can't leave your home and family ever."

Marianna cried, "We are old, *bella mia*, and once you leave to live in America, we will never see you or the children again."

"Please understand," Caterina told them, "this is a rare opportunity to better my life and my children's lives. If I refuse, I feel certain this chance will never come again to us. I had a wonderful eleven years of marriage to Antonio, but he is dead, and the children and I are alive and need to look to the future!"

Caterina spent two days with Loretta and her aunts before leaving. She held her child almost constantly during her stay. In her waking hours, she tried to appear confident in her decision, but the night before she left her aunts and Loretta, she cried so deeply into her pillow she felt she would smother herself. *Am I demented leaving my children even for a short time? Can I bear the pain of being without all my children, my baby, even for a few months?* Guilt filled her when she reflected on the burden she was placing on her elderly aunts. *Loretta is a handful. These poor old women will be heavily taxed to care for such an active child, even for a few months. God help me, I hope I don't kill them,* she thought.

Before dawn, she forced herself to rise and wash away her tears. She resolved to stand firm on her plans. She would be in America in a month. If everything went well and Umberto and his family were suitable, she would marry right away. She would then have her new husband, arrange for their return to Italy to reunite with her children, and bring them to America. Caterina reasoned that within four months, no more than six, she and her children would be together again and traveling to America— their new home—their new family. She kissed and hugged Loretta good-bye, and turned to kiss her aunts. "I will see you again soon, my dear ones. Watch over my child until that day." Hesitating, she said, "God be with us all."

When Caterina arrived home, another letter from Vittoria awaited her.

"What has possessed you to make such a decision? Pietro and I are heartbroken that you and the children are moving to America. How can you marry this stranger? This is a mistake. I feel it. You must not go. You wrote that this man has children of his own. How can you trust him to care for your children as he does his own? Lorenzo and Vincenzo agree with me. Mama is old and not very strong. If you go to America, she may not see you or the children again. Is this man more important than your own family? We pray that you will come to your senses and join your family."

My sister, Vittoria, may be the youngest, but she was always strong, determined and direct. I will write her again and promise to visit them all soon, thought Caterina. *When I return for the children, we will all visit my mother, brothers, and sister. It will not be necessary to tell them that I travel with only Geneva for now. No, they wouldn't understand. Frankly, I'm not sure that I fully understand Umberto's reasoning.*

CHAPTER 12

The Departure—April 1920

It was the last pilgrimage. All of them walked to the cemetery, leaving flowers, uttering their silent prayers, and saying their good-byes to Antonio—husband, friend, and father.

Walking back home, they stopped at the new War Memorial being built in the town center. Antonio's name was to be carved into the memorial along with the names of the other war casualties of the town. Paolo picked up a small piece of marble which had been chiseled from the stone. He squeezed it in his hand and, taking out his handkerchief, carefully wrapped the stone and put it in his pocket. Standing tall, Paolo saluted his father's name posted on the temporary stone slab.

Dina knelt on the soft ground and whispered, "Papa, I miss you so much, and I always will. Please be close to us wherever we go. We love you, Papa."

Geneva laid the flowers by the tablet and said, "I know you want us to be happy, Papa. Mama and I will go to America and then Paolo, Dina, and Loretta will come, too. Be happy for us, Papa. I forgive you for dying and leaving us."

Paolo touched the stone and, holding back his tears, said, "When we go to America, we will have a special memorial just for you, Papa. I hope you don't mind, but I am taking your war medals and cobbler's knife with me to Rome, and then to America, so I can think of you everyday."

Caterina brushed away the silent tears. In her heart she prayed, *Antonio, forgive me for leaving our home. I know you would want what is best for me and the children. I will return soon and bring all the children to America. Be at peace, my love.*

As they walked through the town, many neighbors and friends came to wish them well. Some said they were very fortunate to go to America; others gave them a sad nod, a handshake, or a farewell kiss. Saying goodbye to Graciella was the most difficult of all. Their relationship had been tense since Caterina had confided to Graciella her decision to leave for America and remarry. But when Graciella learned that Caterina was leaving her children behind, the friendship became estranged. Graciella had still helped care for Loretta and tried to maintain a warm, loving relationship with the children during those final days. They loved this kind, generous woman. She was like a sister to Caterina, a dear aunt to the children, and a friend to all of them.

"Please come back soon, write me often while you are away. Selfishly, I hope you don't like the Americans and will come home to us," Graciella said. Her eyes were red and puffy, and she was fighting back more tears as she embraced each of the children. Graciella looked at Caterina, and after a slight pause, hugged her old friend. They held each other a long time, then after final kisses on the cheeks, they parted.

Padre Alberto came to bless them on their journey and give them each a gift of rosary beads. "Keep God in your hearts and pray every day to his Blessed Mother, and they will protect you, my children." He made the sign of the cross on each of their foreheads and patted the children's heads. He took Caterina's hands and, squeezing them hard, he said, "Be strong, my daughter. Do your best for your children and pray that God will guide you."

Attorney Cardello was at their home waiting to accompany Paolo to Rome. Caterina had decided to delay his leaving until the day they would all depart. She felt it was too difficult to say good-bye twice to their family and friends, and the children would only brood about after Paolo's departure.

In her last letter, her sister, Vittoria, begged Caterina to come north to visit her and their mother before leaving for America. If Caterina was not able to come, then Vittoria would come to see her before she left. Caterina knew that her sister would once again beg her to stay in Italy, to come live with her, her husband, and their mother. Their mother, Benedetta, had suffered a stroke several years ago, and was unable to speak or walk, spending her days sitting in her chair lost in her own private world.

Caterina wrote back that she, the children, and her new husband, if she decided to marry him, would visit her mother, Vittoria, and her brothers upon her return from America. In any case, she would rather that Vittoria take care of her husband and their mother. Caterina would write her as soon as she arrived in America and let her know her impressions of the country, Umberto Fabrizio, and his family. She would also let her know when she would return for a visit.

Attorney Cardello and the driver he hired to take Caterina, Geneva, and Dina to Naples were patiently waiting by the front door. Paolo looked at the portly man who was well-dressed in a dark suit, cravat, and black felt hat. Caterina caught her son's apprehensive gaze at his companion. She was disconcerted at seeing Attorney Cardello's somber attire. *He looks like he's going to a funeral instead of accompanying my son to the military school,* she thought. *As if the poor boy isn't shaken enough.*

Cardello would drive Paolo north to Rome, and the driver would travel south to Naples to bring Dina to the orphanage known as Institute of Santa Maria Della Grazie. He would then proceed to the pier to help Caterina and Geneva board the ship to America.

"Signora, I wish you every happiness in your new life in America. Be assured I will look after the children until your return. Please remind your new husband to write me his wishes, and I will dispatch them immediately." Cardello then gave a formal bow, kissed Caterina's hand, and bowed to each of the girls. Placing his hand paternally on Paolo's shoulder, he instructed him that it was time to leave.

Paolo rushed to his mother and hugged her so fiercely she nearly fell back. He kissed her and pleaded, "Soon, Mama, soon."

Paolo hugged Geneva and, always the big brother, warned her, "Don't get into trouble on the boat. Try not to fall overboard. Try to be sweet to our American family; make them like you!"

Nodding, Geneva hugged and kissed him good-bye.

Dina's face was horrid—red, wet, and grimacing painfully. She threw her arms around him and wept on his shoulder. It was too much. Paolo started to cry; then hurriedly he kissed Dina and, turning to Cardello's small carriage, shouted over his shoulder, "Write me every day—don't forget."

Dina watched the livery drive out of the town and down the mountain road. Her mother took her hand and silently led her to their waiting carriage and driver.

CHAPTER 13

The Road to Rome — April 1920

Paolo sat quietly beside Attorney Cardello, who tried to stimulate a conversation, but the boy rarely spoke. The only response was Paolo's shrugged shoulders or nodding head. "Be brave, my boy. Before you know it, your mother will be back to take you to America. This military school may be an interesting experience. You'll make friends, learn many important lessons, and be a strong, disciplined person, which will be valuable in later life." Cardello thought to himself that this young boy already seemed to have an inner strength that belied his gentle nature.

Paolo sat transfixed, staring at the road ahead, his thoughts torturing his heart. *How could my mother leave me? How could she choose a stranger over her own children? If she really loved us, she would never leave us, not for all the money in the world. Didn't I love you enough, Mama? I tried so hard to keep us together. Please come back, Mama. Please come back. I need you, Mama. I'm so scared to be without you.*

As they approached the outskirts of Rome, Cardello decided to take Paolo on a short tour of the Eternal City. "Rome is the most beautiful city in the world, Paolo. You will undoubtedly have the opportunity to see her vast wonders. Let me show you some of the most fascinating and beautiful sites you will ever see. And history—nowhere in the world does any other country compare with Italy's magnificent history."

"Yes, thank you, sir," Paolo replied.

Traveling the ancient Alpine Way, they passed a number of early Roman ruins as well as beautiful, tall cedar trees. Their first stop would be the lovely gardens of Tivoli which was east of Rome. As they walked toward the villa built by the Emperor Hadrian, Paolo took a deep breath, and the sweet, moist air filled his lungs. He had never seen such a beautiful villa and garden. Flowers in ancient stone urns intermingled in a maze of lush green plants sprinkled by beautiful fountains of water which seemed to come from hidden springs and ornate carvings. As they walked the gardens, Paolo began to experience a peace he had not felt since his father died.

"Did you know that a Cardinal named Ippolito d'Estes created these water works?" asked Cardello.

Paolo shook his head. "This is the most beautiful garden I have ever seen!"

Cardello nodded in agreement and they walked in silence.

Beginning to warm to this genial man, Paolo asked, "Signor Cardello, why do you think my mother wants to leave Italy? Does America have beautiful villas and flowers like Tivoli? My mother said it's a rich country. Do you think Signor Fabrizio lives in a villa?"

"I don't know if he lives in a villa, but no country is as beautiful as Italy—remember that," Cardello said, as he ruffled Paolo's carrot-red hair.

After enjoying their lunch of bread, cheese, a few dried tomatoes, and a small bottle of wine—which Cardello allowed Paolo to share—they continued their drive into Rome.

"What I wish to show you, my boy!" Cardello said. "Rome has so many fantastic treasures, but time is short. We will see what we can en-route to our destination."

Their first stop was Porta San Paolo and the Pyramid. Paolo looked admiringly at the castle-like building with two large vaulted openings, which stood in the foreground of a large pyramid.

"That is Caio Cestio's Pyramid, a burial monument of 12 B.C.—a wonderfully preserved monument of ancient Rome," pointed out Cardello.

Continuing to drive north, Cardello drove toward the Ancient Roman Forum and directly ahead on their left lay the ruins of the Colosseum. Turning left, Cardello drove along the Via dei Fori Imperiali, pointing out many of the structures of the Roman Forum. "Look, my boy, here in the foreground is the Temple of Venus and Roma, and behind that is the Basilica of Maxentius, and behind that is the Temple of Antonius and Faustina."

"What are those arches to the left and those straight ahead?" asked Paolo.

"To the far left is the Arch of Titus and in front of that, those columns, is the Temple of Castor and Pollux. Let us drive a little further and you can see the Arch of Septimius Severus, the Column of Phocas, and the Temple of Saturn."

"How do you know the names of all these ruins?" asked Paolo.

Cardello laughed. "Once I was a student here in Rome. Did you know I even considered becoming a priest? I think I wanted to be a priest so that I would stay here forever. But—well, my family sacrificed so that I could be a lawyer, and my parents had my lovely bride picked out for me when I returned home. So I honored my parents and left this fascinating city to meet my obligations to my family."

As they continued driving, Cardello pointed out more ruins, several impressive fountains, and finally an imposing white structure.

"What is that?" asked Paolo, pointing to the structure.

"That is the Vittoriano, a beautiful monument to Vittorio Emmanuele the Second. This building commemorated the unity of Italy. It is built totally of white marble and is dedicated to our current king's father. Today, Italy is in an economic crisis. People are unhappy about the many railroad, industrial, and postal strikes. Our king does not live in a palace today. No, Vittorio Emmanuele the Third is a modest and, perhaps, a wise man who prefers to live in a private house and not a royal palace."

Paolo liked this kind man. He was so well informed, and Paolo felt less frightened of this massive city.

"The school is not too far away. We will see more of the city at another time, I promise you. For now, you don't want to be late and miss your supper or the opportunity to meet some new friends," concluded Cardello.

CHAPTER 14

The Soldier School for Boys—April 1920

Cardello consulted a piece of paper he had in his pocket. Soon they turned into a narrow road and a large square building with small, barred windows loomed in front of them. Paolo shuddered, thinking the school looked more like a prison.

"Signor Cardello, do you know how long I have to stay here?"

"Not very long, my boy—perhaps a few months. Then your mother will be back for you."

Cardello drove across the large courtyard and left the carriage close to the entrance. He took Paolo's hand and they walked together to the massive wooden doors which held a large metal knocker.

After he banged the knocker several times, a porthole opened, and an elderly voice demanded, "State your name and your mission."

"I am Signor Donato Cardello and I am here with a new student, Paolo Leonardi of San Rocco. We are here to see Major Ravasini, I believe."

The door was opened by an elderly man who wore a grey uniform. Not speaking further, he bowed and held the door open, beckoning them to enter. They followed the man down a dark corridor and were shown to a wooden bench which lined the wall. The old man held up his hand and said, "Wait here."

Cardello and Paolo sat. Almost immediately, a large man in full military dress stood before them. He looked middle-aged, and Paolo noticed his left sleeve was empty.

"I am Major Ravasini. Good evening, Signor Cardello. This is your charge, Paolo Leonardi?"

"Yes, Major, we are pleased to meet you. I hope you don't mind our coming this late, but I wanted to show Paolo some of Rome's magnificent sights," Cardello explained.

"We were expecting the young man earlier, but we will make allowances due to the circumstances." Major Ravasini turned to Paolo. "Your father was killed during the war, and you expect to stay here temporarily while your mother is arranging to remarry in America, is that right?"

Hesitating, Paolo finally uttered, "Yes, sir."

Major Ravasini pursed his lips, but said nothing further to Paolo. Turning to Attorney Cardello, he said, "Since the hour is late, you are welcome to join us for supper, and we may be able to accommodate you for the night. We eat in ten minutes."

"Thank you, that is most kind. I would be pleased to stay, and would appreciate being able to rest before returning home."

The major nodded, turned and walked down the corridor. Cardello and Paolo followed. Paolo was still carrying his bag when the major turned to him and said, "Leave your things. Rocco will take care of them for now." With that, the elderly man reappeared and took Paolo's bag and turning to another corridor on their left, shuffled slowly and quietly away.

When Major Ravasini entered the room, there was a muffled noise as approximately twenty tables of boys stood up. Paolo looked at the boys. There were about sixteen to twenty at each long table, and each boy wore a grey uniform. Each stood up straight with his arms by his side. Most looked about his age, although he noticed that at the back of the room, several tables held very young boys flanked by boys who appeared to be several years older.

Paolo had a feeling of panic. He wanted to run as fast as he could back to Signor Cardello's carriage and beg him to take him home. *Help me, Papa. Help me to be brave! Don't let me be afraid and dishonor you.*

Guiding them to what was obviously the staff table, Major Ravasini directed each of them to a seat. Paolo steeled himself and sat down, not looking at anyone. The room quieted down considerably as soon as the major stood at his seat.

"Men, this is our newest student, Paolo Leonardi. He will be with us for a time. He will be assigned to Platoon 6."

Supper consisted of heavy brown bread, a thick stew of vegetables, and a few strings of chicken meat. The boys' tables held pitchers of water, while the staff table had bottles of a light wine. Paolo, who was hungry, was surprised and grateful for the hearty meal.

Cardello noticed that the boys ate in silence and conversation was also limited at the staff table.

Dinner ended and Major Ravasini stood up. The boys followed suit and began to march out, table by table. A somber-faced young man, perhaps thirteen years old, snapped to attention in front of the major. Addressing the youth, Ravasini said, "Lead Corporal Durante, accompany Leonardi to his barracks."

Saluting smartly, Durante replied, "Yes, sir."

Ravasini turned to Cardello. "You may wish to offer your good-byes now."

"Could we have a few minutes alone, sir?" asked Cardello.

"You may stay here for a few minutes. The corporal and our steward, Rocco, will await you both outside the door," the major replied. "I recommend you do not leave the boy with any sentimental concerns."

When they were alone, Cardello placed his hands on Paolo's shoulders. Paolo was suddenly frightened again. Major Ravasini's words and the environment appeared cold and foreboding.

"Please don't leave me here, Signor Cardello."

Looking directly into Paolo's face, Cardello said, "Have courage, my boy. I hope to see you again, but if your mother and new father come for you themselves, I may not. I will try to visit you again, though. Remember, I promised to show you Rome. Whatever your fate, Paolo, always remember that you are an Italian! Perhaps we are a poor country in raw materials, but we are rich in character. The human mind, heart, and soul can expand more in Italy than any other country, I am certain of it. We are a land that produces great saints and great sinners—men of genius and nobility, as well as tyrants. You have inherited a great cultural past and spirit of freedom of will. Whatever your destiny, my boy, I believe you will be strong and honorable and always do the right thing with gentleness and humility. God be with you. I will write you soon to see how you are getting on here at the school. If you need something, please let me know. As soon as I hear from your mother or new father, I will let you know their plans."

Paolo fought to hold back the tears. "I want to be brave like my father, but I'm afraid, Signor Cardello. Please tell my mother to come for me soon. Please."

With moist eyes, Cardello gave Paolo a strong hug, almost crushing the boy in his embrace. Then he put his hands back on the boy's shoulders, gave him a slight shake, and led him to the door.

The next morning at six o'clock sharp, Rocco came to Attorney Cardello's door. He knocked and entered carrying a tray with a cup of coffee and two hard rolls. Cardello drank the coffee and ate the rolls gratefully. Rocco waited, and after the attorney finished his breakfast, Rocco accompanied him to the huge entry, and in this case, exit doors. Cardello sat in his carriage, took one last look at the school, blessed himself, and drove off.

CHAPTER 15

To Naples and Beyond—April 1920

With a heavy heart, Dina took one last look at their little town nestled in the hills. To her left, the church steeple rose high and solitary, while clustered up the mountain were the homes of friends and neighbors. She could not actually see her home anymore, but she knew it would sit there empty until her father's cousins, the Salvanni family, moved in during the next week.

The carriage bounced along the steep country road, swaying left and right at each bend. Their bodies seemed to be leaning forward as they descended the steep grading. Frightened, Dina prayed silently, *Please God, if we must die, let us die here at home rather than in a strange country.*

Geneva squealed with delight whenever the carriage made a sharp turn. "Isn't this exciting, Mama? I can hardly wait to see Naples—it must be a beautiful city. Do you think the boat will be big? Will we be able to walk around, or must we sit all the way to America?"

Caterina smiled at the childish questions. "The boat is like a whole town sailing on the ocean. You will have room to walk, sit, sleep, and, I pray, you don't fall in the water," she said.

Dina looked at them. They both looked happy and excited about traveling to America. *Why are they not crying when they were leaving their country? Why are you not crying, Mama, at leaving three of your children? Please, dear Jesus, don't let me hate them. Give me patience and help me understand that Mama wants a good life for us. Please help me, Jesus, to be strong for your sake, and for Papa,* she silently prayed.

When they approached the city, the driver, who had not spoken much during the trip, finally said to Caterina, "Signora, the Institute of Santa Maria Della Grazie is about thirty minutes away. We must find La Strada Santo Donato."

When the driver mentioned the location of the orphanage, Dina's stomach felt leaden. She thought to herself that orphanages were undoubtedly dark, dreary places where the laughter of children was never heard. Only the meanest of nuns were there, she felt certain. Dina hoped that there were at least a few windows, and that only kind and interesting nuns would be teaching at her school.

Caterina, who was experiencing feelings of guilt as well as anticipation, tried to hide her emotions from her daughters. She looked at the beautiful countryside and smelled the sea as they entered Naples. She and Antonio had talked about visiting Naples when the children were grown. Antonio had read about Naples' history and regaled her with stories during many of their quiet nights together. Now she was finally going to see Naples, but only to leave one child here while she departed her beloved country with another.

The large wagon seemed to ride much more smoothly as they traveled the city streets. Naples was grand, and beautiful buildings lined large open squares. People, small carriages, large wagons, and even motor cars were everywhere. An impressive building appeared in front of them, over six stories high, with vaulted windows and a massive doorway supported by large white columns.

Dina was quietly taking in all the sights, but Geneva was jumping up and down, asking, "What's that? What's that?"

"This is Piazza Sante Ferdinado, and that is the Sante Carlo Theatre next to the Galleria, which has many stores and offices," replied the driver.

As they drove along, the driver spoke again. "Here at the end of Via Toledo is the Mercatello Arch, which they now call Piazza Dante. See the large statue there of the great poet, Dante Alighieri, who wrote *The Divine Comedy*? My son, who has an education, has read it." His pride showed in his voice.

Dina felt breathless as she looked at the tall statue, which was surrounded by a black metal fence. A few people were leaning against the fence looking up at the statue. Behind the statue was a long building that had a central open portal with an arch that was higher than the main building. It was topped with a large clock. The roof on each side of the arch was flat and open, with great statues interspersed between the carved railings. Dina wondered if they were saints or soldiers. Some appeared to be angels.

As they drove through the city, the driver pointed out the magnificent Cathedral of Naples. "Someday you should see the Cathedral, Signora. There are many beautiful frescoes, and the Chapel of the Treasure is adorned with many, many silver statues. St. Gennaro, the patron saint of Naples, has a special chapel. Many miracles have taken place at the two urns which hold the liquefied blood of the saint, which in itself is a great miracle."

Dina was in awe. Someday she would see the Cathedral and visit St. Gennaro's Chapel and the urns of blood. She shivered just thinking about it.

Finally, the driver announced, "Ah, here we are, La Strada Santo Donato." Ahead of them was a long building with a continuous row of open porticos. To Dina's surprise, it was quite lovely. The carriage stopped before the large high arched door. It was situated at the end of the long row of open arches that were supported by smooth marble columns, beautifully sculptured at the top. Never in all her imaginings did Dina picture such a building as an orphanage.

Even Geneva was impressed.

"Are you going to live here?" she asked in awe.

"This was once a hospital for rich people," reported the driver. "After the war, it was given to the Sisters of Charity, under the protection of St. Vincent de Paul, for an orphanage and foundling hospital."

They all disembarked from the carriage, glad for the opportunity to stretch their legs. The driver led the way and rang a large bell which hung from a thick rope beside the massive doors. Dina stayed back and walked over to the end of the open arches. She poked her head in as far as she could to see the courtyard. To her right, she noticed a smaller door which seemed to open to the main entrance, but looking left, she gasped to see a long corridor of stone tiles and walls dotted with carved stone benches and urns with lovely fragrant flowers. Everything seemed so clean; she was certain that no one ever walked on the tiles or sat on the benches.

Caterina, coming up behind her, pulled her over to the door. "This is a good place. I think you will like it here," she confided. "There is nothing to be afraid of with the nuns."

The door opened so quietly that they had not noticed the nun standing at the threshold. "May I help you?"

Caterina, caught off guard, stammered, "Yes, Sister, yes." Pushing Dina in front of her, she said, "I am Caterina Leonardi, and my daughter, Dina, is here to stay with you for a short time while I travel to America. Attorney Cardello wrote you of our circumstances, I believe." "Yes, we have been expecting you." Looking at Geneva, the nun asked, "Who is this child?"

"My younger daughter, Geneva. She will be traveling with me," Caterina said softly.

The nun nodded, and turned to Dina. "I am happy to meet you, Dina. I hope your stay with us will be pleasant," smiled the nun.

"You'll find her a quiet and religious girl, Sister." said Caterina. She's a good child and a willing student."

The nun bowed her head in acknowledgment. "I am Sister Lauria, Dina. I will be one of your teachers. I'm sure you would like a few moments to bid your mother and sister good-bye." With that, the nun directed the driver to bring Dina's bundle of clothes, books, and few possessions to a small anteroom.

Caterina spoke first. "See, it will not be too bad. The nuns are very kind and this is a beautiful place. You will make many nice friends here, and before you know it I will be back for you."

Dina's eyes were staring at the stone tiles of the floor. Small splashes of tears began to dot the tiles. Her throat was so tight she feared she would choke to death. She tried to say something, but she couldn't force out the words she wanted to say.

Caterina pulled her into her arms. "Please, my child, try to understand. I don't want to leave you, Paolo, and Loretta, but I must find a new life for us. It will be for only a short time. You will see. Take courage, be strong, for my sake and for your own." Holding Dina tightly, Caterina kissed her head, then each teary eye and wet cheek. "*Bella mia*, please understand."

Geneva came to them and put her arms around both Dina and her mother. "I promise I'll think about you every day, and when we are in America together, I'll let you have anything you want, I promise, Dina."

"Don't leave us, Mama." Dina choked as she spoke. "Please, please, let's go home. Please Mama, if you really love us, you'll take us home."

Caterina pulled away. "If I really love you? Don't you see that I must make a future for us? Dina, my heart is breaking. I don't want to leave my children for even a moment, but I have no choice. I will not make my children farmers who work on someone else's land. You will see, this is for the best."

Dina was shaking her head. She couldn't understand why this was happening to them.

Caterina put her arms around Dina, squeezed her and kissed her head. "You will see, this is all for the best," she repeated. "Kiss your mother and sister now. We will be together again, I promise you."

Dina threw her arms around her mother and held her tightly. Caterina was forced to disengage herself; she gave Dina a final flurry of kisses, took Geneva's hand, and then called for the nun.

Dina could not move. She watched her mother and sister leave with the driver. After the door closed, she vomited all over the clean stone tiles.

The driver brought Caterina and Geneva to a small guest house close to the harbor. They would spend the night there, and early the next morning, the driver would take them to the ship and carry their trunk on board before leaving them. Settled in their room, Caterina and Geneva finished the last of their bread, cheese, and water before retiring. Geneva fell asleep almost immediately.

Caterina, restless, went out onto the small balcony of their room. The only light in the street illuminated the monument to those who had fallen for Italy's independence and national unity. There was a bronze statue symbolizing Victory; four lions rested on the pedestal, symbolizing the four revolutions. Although the square was called Martyrs' Square, she hoped that the statue to commemorate independence was a sign of her own life of new-found independence.

CHAPTER 16

Shipboard Shenanigans — April 1920

Ocean travel did not suit her, Caterina grudgingly decided. During most of the voyage, she was so sick that she was convinced that she would die and her body would be thrown into the sea for burial. "*Ce mal essere; io morire!* (what anguish; I'll die!)," she moaned.

Geneva, on the other hand, relished the trip. She skipped around and chatted endlessly with everyone she met.

"Have pity on your dying mother," Caterina often wailed. Geneva was always so cheerful that Caterina was tempted at times to drown the mischievous child for some peace.

Their cabin was tiny and Caterina felt claustrophobic. The narrow metal bed had a thin padding which didn't cushion the tossing of the boat. Geneva felt as if she was being rocked to sleep, but Caterina held fast to the edges of the bed, praying that the rocking would stop. Having to share the toilet and shower with other travelers was terrible. Caterina was often sick and she felt embarrassed; she occupied one of the few toilets day and night.

What little amusement there was came from Geneva. Because Caterina was too sick to restrain her, Geneva rambled all over the third-class section of the ship. One evening she regaled Caterina with the story of an elderly woman who was going to live with her son in America. Her son had done well, and not knowing what an appropriate gift for him was, the mother decided to bring some of her homemade sausages. Because she feared robbers on the boat, the woman wrapped the sausages around her waist and under her dress. That day, some boys had seen her sleeping on the deck, and decided to play a prank on her and steal her sausages. They crawled under her dress, cut off pieces of the meat with a knife, and ate them. When the woman finally awoke, she discovered that many of her sausages were gone. She sent up a howl, running about the boat and screaming. "Robbers, robbers, they stole my sausages. Robbers, robbers!"

Geneva reenacted this scene for her mother's benefit, hopping up and down, waving her dress and repeating the call to alarm. Geneva rolled on the bed convulsed with laughter, and Caterina had to laugh, too.

"Imagine," Caterina said, "anyone wanting to eat sausages that were buried under someone's clothing for over a week! I hope those boys got a good bellyache!"

Choking with laughter, Geneva said, "Oh, Mama, that lady was so smelly. I bet the boys did get sick eating those old sausages."

Geneva continued to be a handful. Often, between bouts of seasickness, Caterina would search their section of the ship for Geneva. Once she found her standing on top of a storage unit, her hair and dress blowing in the wind. "Geneva, be careful! Get down from there before you fall into the water!"

Geneva laughed, saying, "But this is fun, Mama! I'm pretending to be the statue at the front of the boat."

"I swear, Geneva, I will tie a short rope around your feet and fasten it to a pole so you won't fall in the ocean."

Geneva, laughing, skipped away again.

During their fifth day at sea, there was a heavy rainstorm followed by strong winds. Caterina had severe bouts of nausea followed by strenuous vomiting. She wanted to stop the ship and hopefully signal a fishing vessel to take her and Geneva home. Returning to her cabin, she saw that Geneva's bunk was empty. "Geneva, where are you? Don't hide from me. Geneva, Geneva, come out right now." Caterina began to panic. She looked under the bunk; no Geneva. Then she pulled open the tiny closet, but Geneva was not hiding there. *Oh, that child! Where is she now? Please, please, Mother of God, let her be safe.*

Caterina wrapped her head and shoulders in her black shawl and began her search. She asked a steward as he rushed down the hall, "Please, have you seen a small girl with brown hair and wearing a brown dress with white at the collar?"

"No, sorry—there are some people in the Community Room. You can check there."

"The Community Room, where is that?"

"Go down this corridor and turn right, then left at the fourth corridor. It's down the flight of stairs to the right. There will be a small sign reading, 'Community Room—2C', above the door."

"Thank you, thank you. Right, then left at the fourth corridor and down the stairs, thank you," Caterina repeated. She prayed as she ran down the narrow passageways.

As she approached the room, music and singing could be heard. Caterina peeked into the room, not wanting to disturb a possible celebration. The noise was deafening, and she tried calling out to one or two of the celebrants. "Hello, hello." No one turned to her, so engrossed were they with the entertainment that Caterina went unnoticed. Well, she must go in and search or ask someone directly—celebration or no celebration. Entering the room, Caterina noticed groups of people talking, drinking, and enjoying the afternoon, despite the occasional rocking of the ship. A few musicians with guitars, accordions, and one or two harmonica players entertained the rowdy crowd. Caterina saw a group of women sitting on a bench enjoying the music. She would ask them about Geneva. As she walked across the room, holding onto tables, chairs, and a pole or two, she stopped occasionally in an attempt to keep her balance.

Suddenly, there, across the room, was a group of men drinking and singing. Balancing on the shoulders of one of the men was Geneva! Caterina looked on in horror as the man lifted his glass and Geneva took a drink of what appeared to be wine.

Running across the room, leaning on people to keep her balance, Caterina yelled, "Geneva, Geneva, stop that!"

Not hearing her mother, Geneva continued to giggle between sips. Caterina came upon them with such force that Geneva slipped backwards, leaving her legs dangling on the man's chest. The wine glass crashed to the floor.

Caterina began pulling Geneva's legs while the man tottered back and forth. Geneva finally slipped off onto the floor. The music stopped, everyone turned to the commotion. After a long moment, everyone heard Geneva's shrill laugh. "Eee, that was fun, do it again!"

Caterina pushed the men aside, grabbed her giggling daughter's arm, and pulled her onto her feet.

"Mama, I thought you were sick. Are you better, now?"

"You're the one who is going to be sick. How could you drink wine from the glasses of these dirty men? Have you lost your senses? They may be diseased. Do you want to die of some terrible sickness on this God-forsaken boat?"

"But Mama, I was only having fun. I'm tired of staying in the cabin and watching you get sick."

Caterina looked at her daughter, and sensing defiance, lifted her hand and slapped Geneva's face as hard as she could. "I've been half out of my mind looking for you."

Geneva fell to the floor, curled into a ball, and let out a piercing shriek.

People started to pull at Caterina, and everyone was talking to her at once. Caterina screamed, "Enough! Enough! I will take my daughter. Step aside!" Pulling Geneva up, she dragged her out of the room and back to their cabin.

Later that evening, Geneva tried to appease her mother. "Mama, I'm sorry you got so mad. I just wanted to have fun. I like to have fun, but I love you, Mama. Please don't be mad anymore."

Caterina took her child's face in her hands, shook her head, and kissed her cheeks. "Sleep now, my child. We both need our rest for the days to come."

CHAPTER 17

Introduction to Umberto—April 1920

A few days before they reached port, the sea became calm, and Caterina was finally able to sleep. She dreaded arriving in America feeling ill and looking pale and languid. A few days of rest and the ability to hold down her food would allow her to look and feel better before meeting Umberto Fabrizio and his family.

She had just the right dress, hat, and necklace to wear. They were black, of course, except for the soft, grey beads. Caterina had made the dress and hat herself. The basic dress was made of a stiff cotton which her mother and sister had sent her. A neighbor had a large piece of sheer black material which felt soft and rich. The woman's husband had brought it back from the war, but it was not practical for everyday use. Caterina offered to trade one of her beautiful handmade embroidered tablecloths for the material and was pleased when the neighbor agreed. The dress had a high neckline and puffed sleeves at the shoulders. She used the sheer material as an overskirt with gathered pleats down the front of the new dress. Caterina created the final touch of elegance by making the sleeves tapered and sheer from elbows to wrists.

Her hat was large and made of stiff horsehair, and a large pin secured it to her hair.

She would carry black gloves and a small beaded purse which held a slip of paper with the name of the pier, the gate number where she was to meet Umberto, and, in case of an emergency, his home address and a few American dollars. She would make the best impression she could on this man. Her future and that of her family depended on it.

After coming through customs, Caterina and Geneva stopped to collect their belongings and find a quiet spot to wait. In about an hour, Caterina heard her name called. She looked around and saw two men approaching. One looked like Umberto Fabrizio, wearing the same suit that was in the picture he had sent her.

"You are Caterina Leonardi?" the man who looked like Umberto asked.

"Yes, yes. This is my daughter, Geneva. You are Umberto Fabrizio, yes?"

"Yes, and this is my friend, Giorgio Marini."

Signor Marini tipped his hat and shook her hand, saying, "I'm very pleased to meet you, Signora."

Umberto took Caterina's hand and leaned over to kiss her cheeks. Caterina smiled, a bit uncertain.

"You had a good trip?" he asked.

"Well, truthfully," Caterina responded, "the ocean was not very calm or enjoyable for me, but Geneva liked it very much." She pulled her child forward to meet her prospective new father.

"How do you do," said Geneva with a curtsy. "Mama was very sick, but she's better now."

"Oh, how terrible for you! Come now, we will have a nice ride to my house, and Giorgio's wife, Gemma, has cooked dinner for us."

The Port of Boston was crowded, and people seemed to be rushing about. Umberto held her arm and guided her through the fray while she clung to Geneva. Giorgio was pulling the trunk with both hands and doing his best to carry on a polite conversation.

Finally, Umberto pointed out their carriage. Behind the carriage was a motor truck upon which Giorgio loaded the trunk. "Giorgio knows the city well. Perhaps the child can ride with him and he will fill her with stories," said Umberto.

Caterina hesitated. "Oh, well, perhaps Geneva should come with us.

She doesn't know Signor Marini and may be frightened if we are separated."

"Giorgio is a good man. He has six children of his own. He tells funny stories and loves to amuse the children. She will be fine. You and I need a chance to talk and get to know each other better."

Geneva was not happy with the arrangement. "I want to stay with you, Mama."

Giorgio pulled out a chocolate bar and said, "Please, pretty young lady, ride with me. I came a long way to meet you." He made a silly face and pretended to cry; thus Geneva instantly liked him and took his hand.

The motor truck with Giorgio and Geneva pulled out first, followed by the carriage with Caterina and Umberto. Before long, the truck was far ahead of them, since Umberto was driving slowly, letting other carriages move ahead of them.

"Well, I must say, you are a lovely woman, Caterina. Your photograph doesn't do you justice. Even Giorgio says you are beautiful," complimented Umberto.

"I was very impressed with your photograph and especially your artistic handwriting," Caterina countered. "Do you draw pictures or paint?"

"As a stonecutter, I design all my work on paper before creating a monument of stone. I entertain my children with a few drawings on the holidays."

"My children, Paolo, Dina and Loretta, were very upset when I had to leave them in Italy. Are your children anxious about me?" asked Caterina.

"Anxious? Perhaps a little, but they need a mother, and having more brothers and sisters will be good for them. Besides, I need a woman."

Something uneasy stirred in Caterina when he said this, and for the next hour she remained quiet. She felt suddenly unnerved, but it was probably just a frank comment, and not meant to sound so crass. She tried to focus on the ride, to capture her impression of America as they drove along.

Umberto broke the silence. "We are almost home. Let me show you the quarries where we get the fine granite for the monuments we build." Turning down a dirt road, they traveled along until they climbed to the summit of a large stone pit. "That is the stone we harvest to build good granite monuments," he said. "Come—let's get out of the carriage so you can see it better."

Holding Umberto's arm, Caterina ventured forth to the edge of the massive quarry.

"See the ropes?" he asked. "That is where we lower ourselves down, chisel out the stone we want, and secure it to those pulleys for hauling to the wagons. Then we bring the stones to our shop and begin carving and polishing them. When people need a gravestone or a statue, we make the final designs they choose, chisel the information or design, and deliver the stone to its final resting place. My shop is close to the house; let me show you some of our work before we go home."

Caterina would have preferred to go directly to the house, but felt it would have been bad manners to tell this man that she was too tired to tour granite pits and monument shops. He was obviously very proud of his work, and wanted to tell her about himself. She was worried about Geneva, though, and feared the girl would be frightened to be among strangers.

Caterina pleaded, "Perhaps you could show me your shop tomorrow. My daughter is waiting, and does not know your friends or family. She is only six and may be frightened if I'm not there."

"My shop is near the house. We will be only a few minutes. She will be fine."

They drove for about ten minutes and Umberto pointed out an impressive white house with a large yard and fence surrounding the corner lot location. The house was on a busy street and a trolley car passed its front door. "Up the street, you can walk to the church, Santa Lucia, the first Catholic church in the area, built by the Italians who first settled here. My shop is around the corner."

They continued up the street, past the house, and Umberto turned down a gravel road. At the end was a large gray shed surrounded by gravestones and statues of every size. Most were already polished and carried beautiful carvings of flowers or religious subjects—the Sacred Heart, the Blessed Mother, or praying angels. Umberto stopped the carriage and helped Caterina down. They walked among the stones, and finally he unlocked the shed and guided her in. The air hung heavy with stone dust, and blocks of rough stone stood alongside wooden tables holding various chisels and other carving tools.

"Let me show you the office. It is much cleaner there," Umberto said as he placed his arm around her shoulder and showed her into a room, which in the early evening had only a dim, filtered light.

Caterina suddenly felt uneasy. "Very nice, but we should be going. Geneva will be worried about me."

"She can wait a little longer. We need to get to know each other a little better."

Caterina stiffened. Suddenly she felt frightened. He was leering at her.

"We need to go now!" she said, pulling away from him.

"No, not yet," he said. Before she realized what was happening, his hand was squeezing her breast. Then he pulled her forward, forcing her head with his other hand. His hands felt like the granite he carved.

Caterina began to struggle. "Stop, stop. Don't do that—don't touch me like that!"

His arms surrounded her, and she felt his mouth roughly pressing against hers. She tried to push him away, but his steel grip held her tight. Caterina's arms were pinned to her side. She couldn't breathe and silently prayed: *Please, God, help me. Make someone come, please God, make him stop.* Her thoughts were wild—*would he crush her to death?*

Umberto relaxed his arms, and his hands roughly roamed over her body. With one hand, he pulled off her now crushed and disheveled hat while his other hand pulled up her skirt and began to grope her. She tried to pull away; she beat on his arms, his face, his back, but his strong hands restrained her. She lurched forward and bit him as hard as she could on his neck. Momentarily stung, he released her and felt for his neck. She took advantage of the moment and ran for the door. He quickly recovered and pulled her back, grasping the necklace she wore. It tore apart, and he lost his grip for a moment.

She grabbed the hat pin off her crushed hat and tried to stab him. Umberto laughed as he grabbed her wrist in his steel hand. "I like a feisty woman, Caterina. You and I will have great pleasure in taming each other," he taunted her.

Caterina started to scream, but Umberto's hand covered her mouth. They struggled and fell across the table, scattering papers, pencils, and drawings. Caterina had never been so frightened or so angry. She fought like a crazed animal, clawing his face and hitting him with every ounce of strength she possessed.

Umberto seemed to enjoy the combat. The more she struggled, the more he laughed. His hands were everywhere. They squeezed her breasts, held her throat, and assaulted her legs and groin.

Caterina was breathless. It seemed the more she resisted, the stronger he became. Finally, he obtained his objective as his body crushed her to the table and ripped into hers. The weight of his body, along with the constant thrusts, almost smothered her. When he finally was spent, he rolled off her and said, "Fix yourself up. They're waiting for us, and I'm hungry for my dinner."

Caterina slid off the table onto the floor. She gripped the edge of the table, crying so hard she thought her lungs would burst.

Umberto stood over her. She cowered involuntarily. He took her arm and pulled her up. "Go in that room. Wash and fix yourself up. Hurry, they're waiting."

Caterina pulled away. "We are leaving. I will never stay here. You are an animal!"

Umberto laughed. "Do you plan to swim back to Italy? You are here now and here is where you will stay. I have invested in a new wife and I think I will enjoy training you."

Caterina washed her face and rearranged her hair and dress. She was covered in dust and her hat and dress were ripped beyond repair. She thought about how carefully she had dressed to impress this beast. *How could she have been such a fool? Her family and friends, even her own children had warned her she didn't know him. The faces of her sister, Vittoria, Graciella, her aunts, her brothers, and her children all crowded her mind. All of them had begged and pleaded in their own way for her to stay in Italy. Her dear friend, Graciella, along with her sister, brothers, and aunts chided her that this man was a virtual stranger to all of them. Their words burned in her heart and mind, but she had been too proud to listen. She was determined to make a good life for herself and her children without the charity of her family and friends.*

How could she have been so foolish?. Somehow she had to find the money to return to Italy. What could she do? She had spent all the money he had sent except for a few American dollars. Her family could never afford to send her enough money to pay for her and her child to return home. She had no friends to turn to who could help her. Her sister and brother-in-law were the only people who could possibly sell some of their land and pay for her return home. No, she couldn't ask it of them. She was ashamed to let them know of her stupidity. She decided to think about it. There had to be some way out of this mess.

Her mouth felt swollen and her body ached in every spot. She could barely stand. Umberto came up behind her. "Enough time. We need to go home. Here, press this stone to your mouth. It will reduce the swelling. I warn you, Caterina, our business is our own. If you don't want to repeat our adventure again tonight, I recommend you smile sweetly and keep our affairs private."

When they arrived at the house, Umberto ushered Caterina into a bedroom. "You rest. I will make your excuses."

"My daughter…," choked out Caterina. Oh, God, she couldn't let Geneva see her like this.

"She's fine," he said. Gemma, Giorgio's wife, is looking after her."

In the quiet, Caterina could hear voices including Geneva's. Thank God she is with others, she thought, and laughing as usual. Reliving the harrowing scenes, Caterina wept with abandonment over her hopeless situation.

CHAPTER 18

Recriminations, Regret, and Reconciliation — April 1920

Caterina leaned against the closed door and then crumbled to the floor. She began to cry again, placing her hands over her mouth to muffle the sound as she sat curled up, hugging her knees. Her mind raced. *What have I gotten into? How could I have been so naive? What can I do now? How can Geneva and I escape and go home to Italy? Who can I turn to for help? I must think, I must think.* A noise behind the door made her stiffen.

"Caterina, dinner is ready, if you feel you can eat something."

Umberto's voice sounded kind and concerned. *Was his concern real, or was that tone for the benefit of his family and friends?* She couldn't respond, but pressed her back harder against the door. She heard him walk away. For the first time, she looked around the room. The light through the windows was waning and she had to adjust her eyes to see the room's contents. Noticing a chair by the bed, she stood up and pulled it across the room to block the door. She walked over to a small table and saw that a pitcher of water, soap, a washbowl, and towels were laid out. On the bed was her hand valise, and her trunk rested at the foot of the bed. Her mind went blank for a moment; then she remembered Giorgio Marini had taken her things in his motor truck, along with Geneva. She prayed that Geneva was all right. *The beast wouldn't hurt a child with his family and friends present,* she thought.

Caterina saw her reflection in the mirror and gasped. Her face was bruised. She was totally disheveled. Her beautiful dress—the one she painstakingly made by hand—was ripped in several places. Her beads were gone, and her hat had a large rip in the brim. She felt dirty, despondent, and disgraced.

Closing the curtains, Caterina lit the table lamp and poured water into the washbasin. She started to undo her dress, stopped, and then pushed the chair tightly against the door to bar it. She could hear people talking and dishes rattling. She thought of her child again. *Geneva should be all right for a while,* she reasoned. *Signor Marini and his wife were still here.*

I must clean myself, Caterina thought. She took her clothes off and scrubbed her body, rubbing it hard to remove all traces of Umberto's heavy hands. She toweled herself dry, pulled her nightgown out of the trunk, and quickly put it on. Taking the coverlet off the bed, she wrapped herself in the warm chenille and sat in the large chair against the door. Again, she drew up her knees and buried her face in her hands. She tried to blot out the terrible attack, but it played over and over in her mind. *What I fool I've been. I was so hungry for a better life, a secure life, that I abandoned my children for a madman's promise. I deserve this pain; God is punishing me. No, no, God knows I only wanted a better life for my children. Umberto Fabrizio is evil; he's the devil. How can I get home? How can I explain what happened? They will blame me; everyone will blame me.*

Caterina heard a noise and shifted in her chair. Pain reverberated through the most delicate parts of her body. *Antonio, my love, I'm sorry. Why did you have to die? What can I do? I'll tell the police. No, they will not believe a foolish immigrant. He is a citizen, a wealthy man from the looks of his house and business. They will believe I tricked him. Help me, God. Help me and Geneva find a way home,* she prayed.

Everyone was seated and waiting in the dining room when Umberto returned.

"I'm afraid this will be a short evening, Giorgio." he said. "Caterina is very tired. She was quite ill on the boat and has still not fully recovered. Please ask your wife if we could eat right away, and I will take a plate to Caterina."

Geneva started to rise, but Umberto stood behind her chair. "Your mother is fine, but very tired. You sit here and eat, and you can say good night to her before retiring yourself. It has been a very long day for you both," he smiled.

"I want my mother," cried Geneva.

"You will sit quietly, have your dinner, get acquainted with your new brothers and sisters, and then you may go to your mother." Umberto was not smiling this time, and Geneva was trapped in her chair.

Umberto took his place at the head of the table. Gemma Marini nervously began serving the food. Noticing that Caterina was not there, she started to speak, but her husband caught her eye and shook his head. She shrugged her shoulders and continued to serve.

"Gemma, please put Signora Leonardi's plates on a tray and I will take them to her myself."

After taking the food to Caterina's door, Umberto knocked gently and said "I've left a tray of food for you, Caterina. Try to eat something." Hearing no response, Umberto left and resumed his position at the table.

"Geneva, these are to be your new brothers and sisters. The big boy is Umberto; next to him is Luca. On your left is Ava—she is the oldest girl—and then we have Lena. You will share a room with the girls, who are anxious to get to know you." Looking at his children, he said, "You will all meet your new mother, Caterina, tomorrow. She is very tired and needs to rest tonight."

Luca started to say something, but his brother pinched him hard and gave a warning look. Luca rubbed his thigh and concentrated on his food.

After dinner, Giorgio and Gemma bade their good nights. Quickly, Umberto slipped an envelope into Giorgio's hand. Giorgio started to protest, but as Umberto slapped him on the back and led them to the door, Giorgio merely shook Umberto's hand in thanks.

"It's time for bed. Ava and Lena, stop by the rear bedroom so that Geneva can say good night to her mother. Then off to bed, everyone," said Umberto.

Geneva knocked on the door. There was no response. She called, "Mama, Mama, it's me. Can I come in? Are you still sick?"

Caterina, remembering her reflection in the mirror, called back, "Mama is very tired. Go to bed, Geneva, and I will see you in the morning. Are you all right, my child?"

Geneva wasn't satisfied. "Mama, are you all right? I want to stay with you," she pleaded.

"No, not tonight—I am very tired. Please be a good girl and go to bed now. I will see you in the morning," said Caterina.

Ava took Geneva's hand. "Come and rest for now. We have a bed for you, and my father wants you to have one of our old dolls," she said.

Caterina was petrified that Umberto would bother her again and was afraid to sleep, but the night passed and Umberto left her alone. By dawn, she was exhausted and fell asleep. No one woke her until it was almost dinner time. Washed and dressed, Caterina left the room.

Geneva ran to welcome her and clung to her skirt. "I like my new brothers and sisters, Mama. They're nice to me, and I have my own bed and a doll to play with."

Caterina looked at her daughter, who obviously was happy with her new family and home. Umberto came in so silently that Caterina literally jumped when he spoke.

"You look rested, Caterina," he said. "I hope you are hungry this evening. My children are anxious to meet you."

Caterina froze. Umberto took her arm and lead her into the dining room. He showed her a chair, and she sat without comment. "Children, I want you to meet your new mother and greet her nicely, so that she will feel welcomed. This is Ava, who is the oldest; next is Umberto; followed by Luca; and finally, Lena, who is the youngest."

Caterina looked at the children. Ava was a full-figured, plumpish girl with a dour expression. Umberto, Jr., whom everyone called Berto, was a pleasant-looking boy, but very large for his age. Luca had a wild, unkempt look about him. His eyes were always darting to his father and then quickly away, as if he didn't want his father to know he was watching him. Lena was tall and slender. She had an odd way of scrunching up her face and hiding her teeth. Of all the children, only Luca was fairly good-looking, if a bit jittery. *Who would wonder*, she thought, *with a father like Umberto?*

The girls gave Caterina a slight kiss on the cheek and the boys bowed awkwardly, each saying, "Welcome, Caterina."

"In time they will call you 'Mama,' won't you children?" urged Umberto.

Caterina looked at Umberto's children and realized they were all frightened of their father. She understood, and thought, *I will never expose my children to this brute.*

After dinner, Caterina said, "Umberto, I am not well and want to retire. Geneva will stay with me tonight."

"Of course, Geneva should stay with you for now," Umberto said.

The next few days were like a dream. Umberto was very courtly. He brought her flowers, left beautiful drawings for her to enjoy, and had Gemma cook wonderful dishes of veal, lamb, and homemade pastas and soups. Caterina and Geneva had never eaten so well. Geneva continued to sleep with Caterina that week. The Fabrizio children were pleasant to them both, and Geneva was allowed to keep the doll.

All week, Umberto was kind, thoughtful, and generous to her. At night, though, she lay awake, reliving the terrifying moments of their first meeting, and clung to Geneva anxiously, as if to ward off overwhelming fright. After a few days, she began to see it as a nightmare that somehow couldn't have happened, but had. Umberto was a totally different person. He never apologized or seemed remorseful, yet he was courteous and showered her with compliments and gifts. Perhaps he had been widowed too long and just went mad with the thought of having a new wife, a new lover. He certainly was a very passionate man, even about his work. He may have regretted his actions, but been too proud to admit it, Caterina reasoned.

On Saturday, a delivery man brought three packages addressed to Caterina. "Signora, these boxes are for you," said Gemma with a smile.

"For me? It must be a mistake. Perhaps there is another Caterina Leonardi in America."

"No, Signora, the address is this house," said Gemma. "Open them."

Caterina brought the packages into her room and laid them on the bed. "I'll open the small package first."

"No, no, open the big box," said Gemma.

"Yes, the big box, first," laughed Caterina. Pulling the string free, she removed the heavy, brown paper from the box. Inside the box, thin white paper covered something blue. Pulling the paper away, Caterina found a dark blue silk dress with long, tapered sleeves, a dropped waist, and a flared skirt.

"Oh, so fine, and so modern!" whispered Gemma.

Caterina held the dress up against herself, then carefully laid it back in the box.

"Open the others, open the others," Gemma said.

"All right," said Caterina, "but where did they come from?" Caterina opened the round box, removed the tissue, and took out a silk cloche hat. It was dark blue and had a lovely pearl pin.

"*Madonna mia*, how fine, how elegant!" said Gemma. "It matches the dress."

Caterina picked up the smallest box, unwrapped it, and took out the most beautiful necklace she had ever seen. Nested against the necklace were matching earrings.

"Pearls, these are pearls!" shrieked Gemma.

Caterina was stunned. "Where did they come from? Who would send such things to me?"

"It must be your fiancé, Signor Fabrizio," said Gemma. "How fortunate you are, Signora!"

Caterina said nothing, but rewrapped the items and placed the wrapped boxes on a chair.

That evening, Umberto asked Caterina, "Did you like your presents?"

"Yes, they were very beautiful. Thank you."

"A beautiful woman should have beautiful things," said Umberto. "I would like you to wear them to church tomorrow."

"I'm not sure they will fit. The hat will be difficult to wear unless I arrange my hair differently."

"Then arrange your hair differently," he said. "You will look very lovely, and I want you to enjoy the presents. Here, try the pearls on now." He handed her the small box.

She found it difficult to open it because her fingers were trembling so much. Umberto took the pearls and stood behind Caterina to clasp them. The mere touch of this man's hands and his closeness still frightened her. She shuddered.

If he noticed, he didn't say anything, but guided Caterina to a nearby mirror so that she could admire the necklace. They were the loveliest pearls she had ever seen. Even the ladies coming off the boat who were in the first-class section did not have such luminous pearls. She lowered her head and softly murmured, "Thank you, they are beautiful."

The children rushed to see the presents, and the girls all asked if they could touch the pearls.

"No, you may not touch them," said Umberto. "They are too delicate for your careless hands."

The next day, Sunday, Umberto took Caterina to the church. After Mass, he remained in the bench and motioned her and the children to wait. The priest came out again, and Umberto took Caterina's arm and led her to the altar. She started to pull back, but he put his arm around her shoulders and whispered, "I will not have people think I am living with a bad woman. You will become my wife today, if you ever hope to see your other children again. It's arranged."

Caterina looked at him. "When will my children come?"

"Soon, in good time. Now, smile for the priest so he will feel he has saved you from living in sin."

Caterina's heart froze and she began trembling. *To marry this man who had raped me the first time we met? Could I tolerate this beast? What can I do? How can I not marry him? I have no money to return home; I know no one here; I'm not even sure I like his children very much. Only Gemma has become a good friend, but I can't confide in her. Her husband works for Umberto, and he can do nothing. I have no other choice. I have made my bed, now I must sleep in it. In the five days since I've arrived, Umberto has been kind to me and Geneva,* she reasoned. *Perhaps he regrets forcing himself on me. He has not touched me since and speaks sweetly to us. He bought presents for me, including the new dress and hat I'm wearing today. Well,* she concluded to herself, *as long as my children are coming soon, I must bear being married to this man. What other choice is there?*

CHAPTER 19

Private Paolo—April 1920

After showing Paolo his bunk, Corporal Durante said, "Leonardi, you have thirty minutes to unpack before the sound of the bell telling you to hit the bunk. Store your things in the locker under the bunk. Reveille is at six sharp. Listen for three bells. Washroom is at the end of the corridor. Have your bunk made, be washed, dressed, and standing at the end of your bunk by six-thirty for inspection. At six-forty-five, I'll escort you to the stores officer, who will assign you a uniform. We eat at seven. That's all for now."

Paolo watched Corporal Durante walk to the last bunk, closest to the washroom.

I have to be strong, Paolo kept repeating to himself. *Only a few months and my mother will take me home—wherever that is.*

Paolo pulled out the metal box under the bed. Putting his things away and undressing only took a short time. The other boys were chatting, undressing, or jumping into their bunks early. Most looked over at him, but no one approached him. Paolo wasn't sure whether he was disappointed or relieved—probably relieved. He didn't know if he could hold it together if anyone spoke to him. Paolo crawled into his bunk, pulled the rough blanket over his head, and tried to shut out the world with sleep.

"A land of great saints and great sinners—tyrants and men of nobility." Cardello's words filled Paolo's restless mind. Images of his father, Cardello, his mother, his sisters, and finally, the stranger who tore his family apart, all drifted through his head.

"Heart, mind and soul can expand more in Italy..." But we are going to America, thought Paolo. *This is our homeland. My father died for our country. My uncles were hurt in the war, too. How can Mama leave our country, our father, our family, us, for some rich man in a rich country? Italy is rich in history—in greatness. What good is being rich if everything you love is left behind? I'm lonely for you and my sisters, Mama. Aren't you lonely for us?*

Strong no longer, Paolo let his tears flow. He buried his face in the blanket and became a young frightened boy of ten who felt abandoned by all those he loved.

CHAPTER 20

Dina's Guardian Angel—April 1920

Dina felt a cool, wet cloth on her forehead. She opened her eyes and saw the nun.

"Feel better? Remember me? I'm Sister Lauria."

"Yes, Sister, I remember you. I'm sorry I got sick all over your nice floor."

"Don't worry. The floor is clean again. I want you to rest for now. Tomorrow you will need to meet with the Mother Superior, Mother Marguerita."

Looking around the room, Dina saw a striking picture of a Madonna and Child. Looking at it gave her comfort. The Madonna sat among clouds surrounded by baby angels caressing the Christ Child, whose head was resting on his mother's shoulder.

"Is that your picture, Sister? It's very beautiful."

"The picture belongs to all of us. It's 'The Virgin with Child' by Sassoferrato. The original is at the Vatican in Rome. I'm very fond of this picture of Our Lady. Rest now. You'll be safe here. Mother Marguerita has given me permission to stay with you. Are you hungry?"

"Yes, a little. Thank you, Sister."

"Good. I'll return with some soup and a nice piece of bread."

Dina was starting to drift off to sleep when a knock on the door startled her.

"Did I wake you, Dina? I'm sorry. Here, eat this good soup and bread. I recommend you break up the bread and put it in the soup. That will make it more filling. And look, here are a few grapes. I hope they are sweet. Eat now, my child."

Dina was thinking about Sister Lauria's calling her "my child." Under the large black veil and the stiff white headpiece she wore, the nun looked very young. She was very slender and not much taller than Paolo. Thinking of her brother brought tears to Dina's eyes. She looked at the Madonna and Child and said a silent prayer that he was safe and not as frightened as she.

"Sister, can you tell me what it's like here?"

"Well, it's like a school you live at. Tomorrow you meet with Mother

Superior. She will tell you which dormitory you are assigned and review the schedule which includes morning Mass. You will attend classes, be assigned chores like sewing, cooking, gardening, and cleaning. The day ends with evening prayers and some free time before bed. It is very important that you listen carefully and learn the rules, Dina, or there may be consequences."

"What are consequences?" Dina asked.

"Well, it may mean more chores, more studying, or self-denial penances. I can't say what, but my guidance to you is to try your very best in all things."

"But how long do I have to stay here? When will my mother come back for me? Do you know, Sister?"

"No, I don't know. Perhaps a little while, but whatever the time, please remember to abide by the rules and schedules. It will be easier and the time will pass quickly," said Sister Lauria.

"Good, you've finished your supper. Tomorrow you will have a new dress and hair ribbon to wear. It's like a uniform that all the girls wear that shows we are all equal, and gives a sense of belonging and community."

"What does the dress and ribbon look like?" asked Dina.

"It's a simple black smock with a large white collar and a white hair ribbon. You will also have two sets of white underwear and black stockings, but you will keep your own shoes until they need to be replaced. You will be responsible for keeping your clothes clean and mended at all times, and your shoes dust free. Now sleep. I'll awaken you tomorrow to meet with Mother Superior."

Dina closed her eyes and said her silent prayers to her father and the beautiful Madonna and Child. She imagined that if she could see her guardian angel, the angel would look like Sister Lauria.

CHAPTER 21

Loretta's New Home — April 1920

Having had no children of their own, Zia Marianna and Zia Magdalena found the task of caring for a toddler challenging and exhausting. They decided to divide the care of Loretta by tasks. Zia Marianna, the elder of the aunts, was responsible for feeding, washing, and dressing the child, as well as telling her stories and teaching her songs. Zia Magdalena, the stronger of the two, took on the job of supervising Loretta, carrying her, chasing her, putting her to sleep, and staying up with her when she was fretful or ill. Together they were a loving, attentive pair of surrogate mothers to the three year old.

The first few weeks, Loretta cried frequently and would toddle around the small house aimlessly, going to each corner, tilting her head, and saying, "Mama, Mama?" in a questioning voice. Frustrated with her search, she would plunk down on the floor and start to cry, "Ella, Ella."

"She's searching for her mother and Graciella," said Zia Magdalena.

Zia Marianna found this heart-breaking. She would pull a chair near the child, and fanning the baby with her skirt, cry back, "*Gioia mia, bella mia*, don't cry."

CHAPTER 22

The Shopping Trip—May 1920

Caterina was adjusting to life in America, but not easily. An early experience of shopping in Boston still caused her to shudder. Umberto had told her he was planning a trip into Boston. Having seen only the harbor and landing pier upon her arrival from Italy, Caterina wanted the opportunity, but hesitated before accepting his invitation—worried about being alone with him. As if reading her mind, he said, "If you don't mind, Giorgio will be riding with us. I have some business, then we can go to the market for some shopping. What do you say?"

Relieved, she said, "Oh, that's fine. Will Gemma come too?"

"No, Gemma will stay home to care for the house and children. We'll go tomorrow, but you need to be ready early."

"I can be ready. Should we bring Geneva? She'd love to go."

"No, leave her home," Umberto said. The older children will keep an eye on her."

By six the next morning, they were on their way in the same truck in which Giorgio had taken Geneva home from the pier. Caterina hesitated before boarding, remembering that terrifying day. As if reading her mind, Umberto said, "Get in, you'll enjoy the trip and I'm feeling generous today."

It was a beautiful spring day. Caterina sat next to the window, saying she liked the air and could see better. That left Giorgio to sit in the middle seat while Umberto drove the truck. After a long, dusty, and odorous ride, they arrived at their destination, the North End of Boston.

"This area of Boston is where my brother, Davido, and I first lived when we came over," said Umberto. "It's even more crowded now, but you'll enjoy the market and shops." Umberto stopped the truck on a narrow side street and helped her out. "Watch your step!"

Caterina looked down at the rotting fruit, vegetables, and horse droppings strewn on the damp ground. Even the carcass of a skinned rabbit lay rotting in the street. Shuddering, she nimbly walked among the debris, holding up her ankle-length skirt, and followed Umberto into a basement coffee shop.

Small tables with metal chairs were scattered around the room. She noticed a counter with high stools, and sighed with pleasure when she smelled fresh coffee and cinnamon bread. They joined two men seated at a corner table. Umberto greeted the men, who tipped their hats to Caterina. A woman brought three more cups of coffee and three sweet cinnamon rolls slathered with butter. The woman smiled at Umberto and greeted him by name. Umberto and the men quickly began talking business about tools which Umberto was considering for purchase. Caterina sat quietly, drinking her coffee and enjoying the fresh, buttery, sweet roll. Concluding their business, the men shook hands and Umberto and Caterina left for their shopping excursion while Giorgio stayed to enjoy more coffee with the men.

As they walked along the bustling street, Caterina was delighted at the pushcarts overflowing with fruits and vegetables—many of which she had never seen before. The men and women behind the carts shouted at the people passing by.

"What are they saying?" Caterina asked.

"They want you to buy from them and are yelling about their produce and prices."

Individual shops featured cheeses, cured meats, olives, pasta, ground coffees, candies, nuts, and barrels of lemon ice. Umberto and Caterina purchased enough food, fruit, and vegetables to fill four shopping bags.

"America is truly a land of plenty," said Caterina. "I've never imagined so much food."

Walking back to the truck, they passed shops with linens, shoes, children and women's clothing, men's work boots, and women's millinery. "All right, a few more purchases, and then we go home," said Umberto. "Here, you look and I'll get Giorgio and the truck, and come back."

Caterina entered a shop which seemed to have everything—linens, clothing, shoes, and material for sewing. She happily chose eight heavy white towels. The sign read "39 cents." She didn't know if this was a lot of money, but she knew they needed the towels. Next she selected two nightgowns for herself and two for Geneva. She then decided to buy two more for Umberto's girls, to avoid problems of jealousy. The cards said "79 cents" for her gowns, and "59 cents" for those selected for the girls. Then she saw bolts and bolts of colorful cloth. One in particular caught her attention—a shimmering pearl grey sateen—a lovely cotton with a satin finish. The card read "90 cents/yard." Not sure how much material was on the bolt or how much each meter cost, she started to unwind the bolt. A man rushed over and took the bolt from her hands.

"How much you want?"

Caterina looked at him, smiled and shrugged her shoulders. She didn't understand what he said.

"How much you want? How much?" he asked loudly.

In Italian, Caterina said, "I don't understand. Do you speak Italian?"

"*Italiana? Quale?* How much?"

"*Ah, quale? Quesda,*" she said, which meant "this one." Why was he asking her which one, when he was holding the bolt?

"*Si, si,* lady. I know you want it, but how much?"

Each time he asked Caterina, his voice got louder and harsher. She started to color and tears misted her eyes. She anxiously looked around for Umberto.

"Do you want it or what, lady?" the burly man asked.

He then turned and called to another man who was at the back of the store.

"Hey, Rocco, the lady don't talk English. Ask her how much of this stuff she wants," he said gruffly, and then he shook his hands in the air and left Caterina.

The man called Rocco came over to her. She had hope now. He had an Italian name. He would understand her.

"*Signora, quante voi?* How much you want?"

Some of it sounded like Italian, but Caterina didn't understand this second man, either. How much, me? Is that what he's asking? She shrugged her shoulders and shook her head, saying, in Italian, "Excuse me, I don't understand."

"Jeez, these people should learn to speak English when they come here," the first man said.

Caterina dropped her items on the counter, and bursting with tears, turned to leave the store.

Umberto met her at the door. "Caterina, are you all right? What happened?"

"I wanted to buy some material and a few other things," she said, "but they don't understand me. That man was getting angry with me."

"Don't worry," Umberto said. "Show me what you want and I'll talk to them."

Driving home, Caterina said, "How will I survive in this country? I don't understand these people?"

"You'll learn to understand, or you can just shop among our people at home," he said.

Fortunately, she and Gemma Marini were becoming good friends. Unable to speak English and unfamiliar with the town, Caterina was constantly frustrated and anxious. With time and Gemma's help, though, she was learning where to shop among Italian merchants, and the familiar people and products helped ease her nervousness in adjusting to this strange country. Although some dialects were unknown to her, Caterina found a large population from her own region of Italy. Most of the Italians were very friendly and asked her about the home country and if she knew any of their relatives or friends. Within a short time, Caterina found herself in a very tight community with little interaction outside their parochial group.

CHAPTER 23

Married Life—July 1920

A far greater adjustment was being married to Umberto Fabrizio. She had married a demanding, autocratic, passionate man. After the wedding, she dreaded each night's encounter. Umberto, however, was more restrained at first and granted her a courtly honeymoon period. Their first few weeks as husband and wife were not unpleasant. He was courteous to her among family and friends, but it became very clear that he expected her to comply with his every suggestion and direction.

After a month of civility, however, he became more aggressive in his lust. At first, Caterina tried to escape mentally by thinking of Antonio. Her first husband's gentle, at times shy manner always initiated their lovemaking. He would tease and coax her, gently stroke her body and whisper sweet, loving compliments to her. Antonio made her feel safe, secure, and protected, like a cherished lover who is enticed into a happy submission.

Umberto's aggressiveness made her feel conflicted and, finally, self-assertive. It became a battle of wills. Their honeymoon ended abruptly in the third week of marriage. Caterina became less submissive and passive, and joined his domineering, imperious style of passionate battles.

"Umberto, please do something about your hands. They are so rough and callous, they bruise my skin," complained Caterina. "Here, I have bought you some nice soap and a cream to use to soften your hands. Use them."

"What's the matter, Caterina? Aren't you used to the hands of a man. Do you want somebody with girlish hands to touch you? When I touch you, you know you are with a man. Did your soldier husband have soft hands? He was a shoemaker, right. Shoemakers have rough hands—or did he cream and perfume them for you?" Umberto chided her.

"Don't you ever mention Antonio to me! He was a gentleman. He knew how to be sweet and considerate—something you will never be. You are like a crazed bull in heat. You don't coax a woman, you attack her."

As if to prove her point, Umberto grabbed Caterina by the neck and, pulling her toward him, fiercely kissed her and then pushed her so that she fell against the bureau.

"An animal, that's what you are. Your Irish wife probably died just to get away from you!" Caterina screamed, as she picked up a vase and threw it at him.

Umberto laughed. "Well, she was not as good a fighter as you, my pretty one."

But Umberto had released a passion in her that equaled his. Caterina felt an aliveness and emotional restlessness she had never experienced before. Some of their battles resulted in one or both of them getting bruised or bloodied, but she seemed to relish the fierce nature of his passions. The consequence of that passion was evident two months later—she was pregnant. This fact caused her more worry about the children she had left behind in Italy. *Paolo, her sensitive, quiet son—how is he adjusting to military school? Shy, sweet Dina, so much like her father—is she happy with the nuns at the orphanage? And the baby, Loretta, does she miss me? Does she even remember me?*

Caterina decided to confide the fact of her pregnancy to her friend, Gemma, on the evening that she and Umberto were invited to dinner with the Marinis. After following Gemma into the kitchen, Caterina blurted out, "Oh, Gemma, I'm pregnant!"

Gemma turned to her friend, smiled, and hugged her, saying, "Caterina, that's wonderful."

"No, it is not wonderful. I barely survived the boat trip here and now I must return to Italy for my children and fight nausea from the pregnancy as well as from the sea. I may die before I ever reach Naples."

"Perhaps if you wait a month or two, you will be over the morning sickness from the pregnancy. The sea is usually calmer in the summer, no?" asked Gemma.

"Yes, late July or early August might be best. I should be feeling better by then, and we can escape the heat here for cool ocean breezes," Caterina said.

Before going to bed, Caterina decided to tell Umberto about the pregnancy and propose the plan to return to Italy for her children. "Umberto, I am pregnant. We need to discuss going to Italy and bring back my children before I am too big and uncomfortable to travel. We should travel in July or early August. I should be feeling better by then."

Umberto, who was checking his pocket watch before laying it on the bureau, stood very still for a moment before speaking. "I don't mind another child, Caterina, but we should wait until after the child is born before you cross the sea again," he said.

"But my children, Umberto! I will need a few months after the birth of the child, and then it will be almost one year since I left them. I can't let them wait a year for my return," Caterina said.

"You can, and you will. They are being well cared for, and I will send some money to the attorney. Signor Cardello will see to their needs. It will be a good experience for them, and they will appreciate you and a life in America much more if they wait a bit," he said.

Caterina looked at him in shock. "If they wait a bit? If they wait in orphanages or at the mercy of my old aunts? How can you say this? You promised to bring my children here if I married you. I want my children!"

"Don't upset yourself, Caterina. I will bring your children here in good time, but not now. You barely have had time to get to know my children or become familiar with living in America. Give it some time. They are fine and busy with school and new friends to even miss you and Geneva." *Geneva and Umberto's children were a handful for her. Perhaps it was best to wait until she felt better,* Caterina mused.

Interrupting her thoughts, Umberto said, "You told me how ill you were on your first sea voyage. Being pregnant will be much more distressing and possibly dangerous for you and the child. And what about leaving our children here? Can I impose on the Marinis to care for our children as well as their own for several months? No, Caterina, we will wait until after the child is born and you are feeling strong enough for another ocean crossing."

"Please, Umberto, perhaps it would be best to go in August as I first suggested. I will be only a few months along, and the sea should be calmer. Besides, it will be very hot and humid here, and the ocean breezes may be more beneficial to my health. I am willing to cross the sea again for my children. After they are here, I promise never to ask to go back to Italy again, if that is what you want. My children should be here with us now, especially with a new child coming," Caterina pleaded.

"No. My mind is made up. I will not risk your health or the child's when it makes more sense to wait. That is my final word on this subject. Let us speak no more of it. I will send a letter and a bank draft to the attorney to look after your children's needs, which are undoubtedly few. You may write the children, your aunts, your sister, or whoever you want to look after them, but you are staying here for now," Umberto said.

Caterina realized she had mixed emotions on the subject. In truth, she was frightened of crossing the sea again, especially when pregnant, but she missed her children and felt a deep sense of guilt about leaving them. What would her children, family, and friends think of her? Umberto left her alone that night as she cried herself to sleep, resolved to write them all and explain her predicament.

Umberto's children seemed nonplused at the news. The girls made a slight grimace, and she thought she heard Luca call his father a "dirty bastard," but was unsure that it meant the same in English as Italian. Umberto, Jr., called Berto, was the only one who put his arms around her and hugged her. He didn't say a word, but he didn't look very pleased with the news either. Geneva was, however, very excited about the new baby. She chattered on about making new clothes and decorating a bassinet for the baby.

"I hope it's a girl. I will have fun with a baby sister. I think I'll make a green dress for her, and Mama, you can embroider little yellow flowers all over it. I wish Dina was here. She would make lots of clothes for the baby. I'll bet Paolo would even make her a pair of soft shoes. When are Dina, Paolo, and Loretta coming, Mama? I miss them. They were always so nice to me. Papa Umberto's children are sometimes mean to me," said Geneva.

"We must wait, my child, until after the baby is born and I am able to travel again—maybe a year. We'll see."

"That's so long to wait, Mama. You'll take me with you? You won't leave me will you, Mama? I don't want to be left here in America with Papa Umberto's children. I want to stay with you and see Paolo, Dina, and Loretta again. Maybe we can see all our family. I miss everybody. Don't you? Promise me you won't leave me too, Mama."

Caterina's heart turned to lead. This child was afraid she would leave her, too. Perhaps Geneva feared she would return to Italy and stay, deserting her as she had her other children. Taking Geneva in her arms, Caterina said, "I won't leave you, my sweet. When we go back to Italy, you will come with me, the baby, and Umberto. We will bring Loretta, Paolo, and Dina back to America. You will see. Calm yourself and be patient, my child. Everything will work out for the best. I promise."

"As long as you promise, Mama, I will wait and just think of the new baby," agreed Geneva.

CHAPTER 24

The Birthday — August 1920

It was August and his eleventh birthday. Paolo had not heard from his mother or sisters, or even Signor Cardello, in almost four months.

Mama must be happy now with her new husband, he thought as he lay on his bunk. *She has forgotten us.* Tears formed, but he quickly brushed them away lest one of the other boys noticed.

The bell rang and everyone climbed out of their bunks, most of them reluctantly. Paolo rose and went through the motions of making the bed, washing, dressing, and standing in formation for inspection.

After breakfast, Corporal Durante told Paolo to report to Major Ravasini's office.

Excitement filled Paolo's head. *My mother has come at last, and on my birthday! Thank you, Mama, thank you. I love you!*

Composing himself, Paolo knocked on Major Ravasini's door. After a brief wait, the major shouted, "Enter!"

Paolo stood at attention and saluted. "You requested to see me, sir?"

The major looked up from his desk. He was impressed with the boy's appearance. He was clean, neat, and stood at attention very well. In the few months he had been at the school, Paolo Leonardi had studied hard and, although somewhat reserved, got along well with his instructors and the other boys. He never grumbled when assigned additional tasks, and had a strong sense of perseverance and perfectionism. *This boy has the makings of a good soldier,* he thought.

"At ease, Private Leonardi. I've received a letter from your mother's attorney, Signor Cardello. It seems your mother is not able to return to Italy for a while. She is having a child and cannot risk the voyage. Your stepfather has sent money to cover any expenses, and there is some indication you may be here until your mother is able to travel, possibly in a year."

Paolo was stunned. He had expected the major to tell him his mother was back and would come for him soon.

The major looked at the boy and saw his shock. "The time will pass quickly, Private. You are doing well here and will make a fine soldier someday."

"Yes...yes, sir. Thank you, sir. May I go now, sir?" asked Paolo.

"You may go, Private. And compliments on your birthday," said Major Ravasini.

"Thank you, sir."

Paolo stood outside the major's office and tried to catch his breath. *One year. I must wait one year?* His stomach and head began to hurt, but he tried to push the pain away. Rushing into the lavatory, Paolo washed his face and drank some water from his cupped hands. He braced himself against the sink with both hands and tried not to think of his mother, but his emotions overwhelmed him.

How could you, Mama? How could you have that man's child and forget Papa and your own children? Why did you let him touch you? Why have you forgotten us? I love you, Mama. I want us to be together. I want to see Dina and Loretta and Geneva and you, Mama—all of us together again. I hate you, Mama, and I hate this baby, but most of all I hate Umberto Fabrizio for taking you away from us. I will never forgive you, Mama, never! Paolo was startled by his own voice echoing in the empty room.

Washing his face again, Paolo steeled his resolve to hate his mother. *Somehow, he would retrieve his sisters, Dina and Loretta, and they would build a life together. Mama and Geneva and the new baby could go to hell!* With that declaration, Paolo stiffened himself and marched to his first class.

CHAPTER 25

Dina's Despair—August 1920

Signor Cardello decided to bring the news personally to Dina. He would like to have seen Paolo again, but it was impossible to make two trips, one to Rome and another to Naples, and he reasoned the girl might take it harder.

An elderly nun answered the door and showed Signor Cardello to the

Mother Superior's office. He explained his mission to Mother Marguerita.

Shaking her head, she said, "Dina will be devastated. She is a good girl, always pleasant and eager to please, a sweet child. But behind her eagerness to please is an anxiety about her mother's return. This news will greatly distress her. I think it would be better to talk to her in the garden. She is fond of Sister Lauria, I'll ask Sister to bring her to us."

Although she enjoyed mathematics, Dina was grateful to leave class since she was having some difficulty with the problems presented in the day's lesson. When Sister Lauria called for her, she asked, "Am I in trouble, Sister? Why does Mother Superior want to see me?"

"No, Dina, you're not in any trouble. Signor Cardello, from your town, is here to visit with you."

"Sister, do you think he has news of my mother and sister? Did he come to take me to them? Shall I get my things ready before I see him so we can go to them as soon as possible? Oh, Sister Lauria, I will miss you, but I'm so excited about seeing Mama, Paolo, Geneva, and Loretta again. Did Signor Cardello say when she was coming? Is she here now, perhaps visiting our town or our family—Nonna, Zia Vittoria, Zio Pietro, and our uncles? Yes, we will need to visit all our family before we leave for America. Oh, Sister, I'm so happy."

Sister Lauria, not knowing the purpose of Signor Cardello's visit, laughed and said, "So many questions. Be patient, all will be revealed soon, and before you start packing, meet with your visitor first."

Signor Cardello and Mother Superior were standing by the small fountain in the garden. Mother Marguerita motioned Dina to come and sit on the stone bench near them. While the nuns remained standing, Signor Cardello took Dina's hand, pulling her gently on the bench, and kissed the top of her head.

"Signor Cardello, I'm so happy to see you. Has my mother arrived? Are we leaving soon to join her? Have Paolo and Loretta seen her yet? When can we go?"

Cardello lowered his head and remained silent.

Mother Marguerita said, "Dina, Attorney Cardello has received word from your mother in America. He is here to tell you what she and your stepfather have written." She waited for Signor Cardello to speak, but he remained silent.

Dina jumped off the bench and said, "You mean my mother is not here? She just sent a letter? Why didn't she come herself?"

Cardello took Dina's hands and, once again pulling her down on the bench, he gently said, "She cannot come for another year, my child. She is going to have a baby and cannot travel for a while. Your stepfather has asked that you be kept with the sisters until they are able to come for you. I'm sorry you are disappointed."

Sister Lauria put her hands on Dina's shoulders, but did not say a word. Tears formed on the young nun's face, but a stern look and gesture from Mother Superior warned her not to show her emotions.

Dina sat frozen on the bench beside a stooped Cardello. "Mama's not coming back. I know it. She has a new husband, a new baby, new children, and Geneva. She is not coming back."

Sister Lauria said, "She will be back, you'll see. We must wait for her to have the new baby, but after that she'll be here to bring you and your brother and sister to America. Then you'll have new brothers and sisters to play with and a new life in a wonderful, new country. Have faith, my dear, and pray the time passes quickly. Have faith and pray for your mother and the new child."

Standing up, Dina said, "Yes, Sister, I'll try to have faith." Before anyone could catch her, Dina suddenly crumpled to the ground.

In the days and weeks that followed, Dina reverted to the quiet, reserved young girl who first arrived at the orphanage. She rarely smiled or chatted aimlessly with the other girls. She spoke when necessary, but always softly, with little inflection in her voice. Sister Lauria observed to Mother Superior, "Dina is not eating very much. Her dress seems too large for her. The girls say she cries at night and often seems to have bad dreams. What can we do, Mother, to help her?"

"Pray, my child, simply pray," answered the older nun.

CHAPTER 26

Loretta's Mixed Blessings—August 1920

Magdalena opened the letter and looked at the bank draft. She read the letter from Caterina several times. It told of her new pregnancy and the delay in returning for Loretta and the other children.

"*Stupida*," Magdalena muttered. In truth, she was not upset at the prospect of having Loretta live with them for another year. She was disappointed at the foolishness of her niece—going to America to marry a man no one knew, leaving her children behind, and now getting herself pregnant so soon. "*Stupida*," Magdalena repeated out loud.

Her sister, Marianna, was playing with Loretta in the square while gossiping with the townswomen. Well, they will have more to gossip about now at Loretta's expense, thought Magdalena.

Marianna returned breathless and laughing at Loretta's antics. "Oh, this child wears me out. She is like a monkey, scampering here and there. At times I thought she would fall into the wash basin."

"Marianna, sit down. We received a letter from Caterina."

"Caterina! Oh, is she coming home? I can't wait to see her and meet her fancy new husband, but I dread having her take Loretta away from us," she said.

"Well, she is not coming back—at least not for a year. She's pregnant," said Magdalena.

"Pregnant? But how can she be pregnant? She just got married," reasoned Marianna.

"Marianna, you are a simpleton. Just because she just got married does not mean she kept her legs together. I'm sure her Umberto wanted a return on his investment. Women are foolish and men are pigs, I tell you."

"But...but so soon!" sputtered Marianna.

"Well, soon or not, it is done and now we must think of Loretta," said Magdalena. Seeing Loretta playing with the cat, Magdalena picked her up and squeezed her in a loving hug. Loretta squealed and fidgeted in her arms, wanting to return to the cat.

"Kitty, kitty, mine, kitty, mine," Loretta repeated.

"Yes, the kitty is yours, my own little pet. Go play with the cat," said Magdalena as she lowered the child to the floor. Loretta, delighted, gripped a handful of fur. With that, the cat let out a yowl and scampered under the bed. Not discouraged, Loretta ran after the kitten and crawled under the bed, hoping to corner the reluctant feline.

CHAPTER 27

A Family's Disappointment— August 1920

Pietro picked up the letter from the postmaster and handed it to his wife, Vittoria. "Your sister has finally written," he said. "Hopefully, she is returning soon to her children, not to mention her mother, sister, and brothers. I never thought Caterina could be so selfish and unfeeling."

Vittoria grabbed the letter from his hand. "Please, Pietro, you know she felt tortured over her decisions. She is coming back soon. I know it. Now, please, let me read the letter. Go tell my mother that the letter from Caterina has arrived. She'll understand." Vittoria tore the letter open and read eagerly until she got to the news of Caterina's pregnancy and delayed return.

"Your mother is napping in her chair. I didn't want to disturb her. Well, when will she be back?" asked Pietro.

"I can't believe it!" cried Vittoria. "She's pregnant and will not be back for at least a year."

Pietro reddened. "A year more for those children—is she crazy? While she sits rich and pregnant in America, her children are living as orphans at the mercy of the government. People here are going without work and are hungry—does she think her children are living in luxury in orphanages? And what about the baby? Your aunts are poor and struggle to keep the baby. We must do something," said Pietro.

"What can we do?" asked Vittoria.

"Get the children and bring them here. We can take care of them until she returns—if she returns," he said.

"Pietro, I know you love the children. I love them too, but they are Caterina's children, not ours. She has a new husband. He has more authority over those children than we do, even if we are their family," said Vittoria. "By February, we will have a baby of our own to care for."

Pietro put his arms around his wife. "Don't upset yourself. I'll write Caterina's attorney to see about Paolo and Dina, and we'll write your aunts again to ask if we can do anything for them. I'll insist that the lawyer tell us how to get in touch with Paolo and Dina and if they can come for a visit," he said.

"Thank you, my dear one. You know I miss my sister and her children. Please let us try to stay in touch with them so that they don't feel alone. I'll write my brothers, too. They are worried sick about Caterina and the children, despite their own troubles," said Vittoria.

"I told your mother only yesterday that Caterina and the children were coming soon. She seemed to understand and smiled," said Pietro. "How can we tell her the truth?"

"Don't say anything. She is happy now and will forget the conversation tomorrow," said Vittoria.

CHAPTER 28

The American Siblings—September 1921

"**W**hat are you doing with my things?" screamed Ava.

Startled, Geneva dropped the box of lip rouge she had found in Ava's underwear drawer.

"Look what you've done, you little thief. It's spilled all over the floor," said Ava.

"I was only trying a little on my face. I didn't mean to drop it. You scared me!" said Geneva.

Ava pushed Geneva aside and tried to retrieve her lip rouge. "It's all over the bureau and floor, you rotten brat!" said Ava.

"I'm sorry, but you scared me," repeated Geneva defensively.

"Oh, it's my fault, you brat!" said Ava. "I'll really scare you if you ever touch my stuff again."

Geneva ran off to find a safe place to hide from Ava's wrath. She spotted Luca working in the backyard on his old wagon. "Luca, Ava is mad at me again. Can I stay here with you?"

"What did you do now?" asked Luca.

"I only tried her lip rouge and she scared me and I dropped it. I didn't mean to, but she scared me," insisted Geneva.

"Yeah, well, maybe you shouldn't touch her stuff. Forget it. Ava's a witch. She gets mad over everything. If she threatens you, tell her you'll tell Papa that she wears lip rouge. That'll shut her up. He'll cream her if he catches her wearing that junk," said Luca.

"Okay, thanks." said Geneva. "Luca, I wonder what the new baby will be. I hope it's a girl."

"Who cares," said Luca. "We don't need more kids. When your brother and sisters get here, this place will be like an ant colony—kids everywhere."

"You sound like you don't want them to come or Mama to have a new baby," said Geneva. "I miss my brother and sisters. You'd like them. They're nice, not like your mean sisters. My papa was nice too. He never yelled or hit us. Your papa is scary. He's always pushing and punching you and Berto. I'm afraid of him," said Geneva.

At dinner, Geneva sat next to Luca. "Hey, that's my seat," said Berto.

"She had a run-in with Ava again today," whispered Luca to Berto.

"Tough. This is my seat. I don't want to sit next to Pa and Ava," said Berto.

Geneva got up and took her regular place at the table. Ava and Lena came into the dining room and took their places. Ava grimaced at Geneva, causing the girl to move her chair closer to her stepfather.

Caterina waited for her husband to sit at the table before bringing out the meal.

"Where were you today, Luca?" asked Umberto.

"I had to fix my wagon, Pa. It needed a new wheel and axle," said Luca.

"Berto had to do your job and his own today. You fix your wagon after work," said Umberto.

"Yeah, Pa, I got lots of time after work. I got to run errands for Ma, help in the garden, and keep these girls from killing each other," said Luca. "Yeah, Pa, I got lots of time."

Umberto picked up his plate of spaghetti and threw it at Luca, hitting him square in the face.

Caterina and Geneva screamed.

"You don't talk to me like that, understand?" said Umberto to Luca.

Luca had involuntarily leaned back and fallen on the floor. He wiped his face with his arm, which also became covered in the thick tomato sauce. Luca awkwardly crawled to the door and ran out to the yard.

"Umberto, he is only a boy. You may have hurt him," said Caterina.

"Quiet! I will deal with my children," said Umberto. Turning to the girls, Umberto asked, "Why are you fighting?"

Ava and Lena shifted in their seats and Geneva started to cry.

"I asked why you are fighting, and I expect an answer," said Umberto.

"Honest, Papa, I wasn't even here," said Lena. "I didn't do anything. Ava and Geneva were fighting, not me,"

"Geneva, I want to know what you and Ava have to fight about. Tell me."

"I was only looking," cried Geneva. "I didn't mean to drop it."

"Stop crying and tell me what you dropped of Ava's that caused this fighting," said Umberto.

Ava looked imploringly at Geneva and her eyes glistened with tears.

Geneva looked at her mother and said, "I only wanted to try her lip rouge. I didn't mean to drop it. Ava came into the room and scared me. I didn't mean to drop it. I only wanted to try a little on to look pretty."

Ava dropped her head and began to cry.

Umberto rose from his chair and stood behind Ava. "So you want to look like a harlot—color your face with paint and parade in front of the boys? Is that what you do, Ava? Answer me!" shouted Umberto as he grabbed Ava's hair and pulled her off the chair.

"It was only a little powder, Papa. I haven't done anything wrong. All the girls wear it. I just wanted to look nice. Geneva wanted to try it and she's only eight. I'm almost sixteen, Papa."

Umberto released Ava's hair. "You will not paint your face or dress like a harlot," he said before grabbing her face between his granite-like fingers.

"Umberto, please," pleaded Caterina. "You're hurting her. Let her go."

Umberto released Ava's face and turned to Geneva.

Caterina froze. "Don't you touch her. She is only a child. She will not touch Ava's things again. Please, leave her to me."

Umberto, still staring at Geneva, said to Caterina, "You will control this spoiled child or answer to me. Do you understand? Geneva, you touch anything that does not belong to you, and you will regret it, I promise you. Caterina, bring me another plate of spaghetti."

Caterina retreated to the kitchen and was trembling so hard she feared she would drop the plate. While she composed herself, she reflected that at least Umberto had left the disciplining of Geneva to her.

Geneva, Berto, and Lena sat fearfully at the table. Although the food nearly choked her, Geneva gulped it down, eager to leave the table and retreat to her room.

Caterina came to kiss Geneva good night and said, "Don't worry. Just behave and it will be better. You must behave, Geneva, for my sake as well as your own," said Caterina. "Sleep now and try to be good."

"I am good most of the time," said Geneva. "They don't like me, Mama. I want my own brother and sisters. Why can't we go home? I don't like it here anymore. We can keep the new baby. I'm sure that Dina, Paolo, and Loretta will like it. I'll be good, Mama, but I want to go home."

"This is our home now, my pretty one. You must try to accept that. Someday your brother and sisters will join us here, and it will be better for you. Just be patient and don't get into trouble. Try to stay on the good side of Ava and Lena. Luca and Berto are nice to you, aren't they?" asked Caterina.

"Yes, but they usually ignore me. Luca talks to me sometimes, but he doesn't like me to bother him too much."

"Well, you have me," said Caterina.

"But Mama," said Geneva, "you are always so busy, and he is always around you."

"He's my husband, Geneva. I must make time for him, but I try to spend time with you too."

"He's mean, Mama. How can you like him? I don't like him."

Feeling frustrated, tired, and conflicted, Caterina hardened her voice as she said, "Geneva, I have tried to reason with you. We are here. This is our home. Umberto is my husband. You must face these facts and learn to change your attitude. You have too much time, I believe. Starting tomorrow, you will have more chores after school to occupy you and keep you out of trouble. Sleep now." Caterina gave her daughter a quick peck on the brow and left.

Geneva cried, "You don't understand, Mama. You just don't understand."

Caterina didn't reply. She closed the door firmly behind her.

True to her word, Caterina kept Geneva busy with household chores after school. On Saturdays, Geneva was responsible for dusting all the main rooms, including her parents' bedroom as well as her own. To avoid further conflict with Ava and Lena, Geneva was moved to a small anteroom which was curtained off the living room. As much as she had hated sharing a room with her stepsisters, Geneva hated being isolated in this small airless space more. She found it difficult to sleep, separated by only a curtain from her parents as they sat in the living room after dinner. She would try to listen to the radio or to their conversation at first, but once or twice Papa Umberto called a warning to her, "You better be sleeping, Geneva." After that, she hid her head under the pillow as soon as Mama drew the curtain, afraid that he would know she was still awake.

Things will be much better after Paolo, Dina, and Loretta come, she thought. *Paolo will help me stay out of trouble, and Dina and I can share a room together. It will be much better then.*

CHAPTER 29

Living On Charity—October 1921

Dina moved as in a trance those first few months. She felt abandoned by her mother and longed for her siblings. She confided her longings to her good friend, Domenica, who understood because she had a brother, too.

"If only I could write Paolo, but the nuns say they don't know which military school in Rome he was brought to by Signor Cardello," said Dina. Seeing Sister Lauria coming out of class, she said, "Please, Sister Lauria, write a letter to Signor Cardello. He knows where Paolo is, and then I can write to him."

"I'm sorry, Dina. I am not permitted to write Signor Cardello or anyone else. Our rules are very strict. All correspondence outside of the convent and school must go through Mother Superior. We are allowed very limited contact with people outside. Even correspondence with our family and friends is restricted to a few letters a year," said Sister Lauria.

Assigned to work in the garden later that week, Dina saw Mother Superior walking along the paths examining the plants and rushed to greet her. "May I speak with you, Mother?"

"What is it, Dina?" asked the nun.

"I would like to write Signor Cardello and ask him for my brother, Paolo's address so that I might correspond with him. Could you please help me? I miss my brother and sisters so much. Please, Mother, help me find a way to contact my brother," said Dina.

"I'm sorry, Dina. I can't give you Signor Cardello's address. If your mother wrote Signor Cardello and requested that he give you your brother's address, it would be permissible for you to write him on occasion."

"But Mother, you could write my mother and ask her to send the address to me. I don't know my mother's address in America, but if you give it to me, I will write her myself."

"Hasn't your mother written you in all this time?" asked the nun.

"No, Mother. She writes to Signor Cardello. When he visited me, he told me that my mother misses me and sends her love. She told him to tell me to be good, to study hard, and to mind the nuns. I'm also to be patient and try to understand why she has not come for us."

Mother Superior closed her eyes and shook her head, repeating, "I'm sorry, Dina. I can't help you. Perhaps your mother will write you soon and you can ask her for your brother's address. I will pray that you and your brother find each other again."

Mother Marguerita touched Dina's head and continued walking along the garden path. Dina wanted to pursue her and plead again for Mother's help, but then she heard "old grumpy" calling her.

"Dina Leonardi, return to your work," said Sister Celeste. "Plants do not take care of themselves. Look at those weeds. Start pulling them."

"Yes, Sister, I'm coming," said Dina.

Pulling the weeds under Sister Celeste's watchful eye, Dina thought about praying. She prayed now because the nuns made her, but secretly she was angry with God. She had always prayed and tried to be good. When her father went to war and then after he was killed, Dina had prayed constantly for God's guidance and her father's soul. She prayed for her family and then God stopped listening. She lost her home, her family, and her friends. Her mother left her to marry a stranger in a strange country, and then broke her promise to return.

"Dina, I asked you to pull the weeds, not attack the plants. Look at what you are doing, you careless child," scolded Sister Celeste.

"Yes, Sister, I'm sorry," said Dina.

"'Sorry' does not put food on our table. Unless you wish to eat weeds, pay attention to the task," said Sister Celeste.

"Yes, Sister."

After the nun walked away, Dina muttered under her breath, *I'd rather eat weeds than the bugs and worms that turn up in our food.*

Most foods, including pasta, rice, flour, and corn meal, were donated to the school by local farmers or the government. In most cases, it was old or surplus food and often infested with vermin. The nuns and students assigned to the kitchen tried to remove the insects and worms, but they seemed more bountiful than the grain. It was both time-consuming and futile to pick them out, so most ended up floating in the various food dishes served. At first, Dina refused to eat. Later, forced by hunger or an over-zealous nun who saw waste as a mortal sin, she tried eating the repulsive food, but most of the time, Dina would gag at the prospect. Whenever anyone objected, the more kindly nuns would remind the children that "we must be grateful for all that God provides and give thanks for all His blessings."

This only added to Dina's grievances against God. To satisfy the nuns, she tried to eat the infested food, but usually gave it to less particular students who could overlook the vermin. As a result, Dina became thinner and more prone to illness.

Sister Lauria, who had a special fondness for Dina, would occasionally save her a small piece of cheese, fruit, or a raw carrot. It was forbidden to show favoritism among the students, but Sister Lauria feared that Dina was too fragile, and her health seemed to be rapidly deteriorating.

The idea of a hungry child was abhorrent to Sister Lauria. She remembered watching her sister, Clara, slowly die from hunger. Clara was only eight when she became ill with an intestinal disease that caused her to vomit any and all food, even liquids. Sister Lauria, whose birth name was Anna, had been holding her little sister, prompting her to try to eat, when Clara died. Although only fourteen, Anna decided to dedicate her life to God and become a teacher. She joined the Sisters of Charity to work among orphans, and she saw Clara in every hungry face. Sister Lauria, now twenty-five, felt old at times. She loved being a teacher and felt God had directed her to her vocation through Clara. Some students, like Dina, made her feel Clara was still with her.

CHAPTER 30

Paolo Joins the Band—
November 1921–July 1922

In November, Marco Antonelli, Paolo's friend and roommate, spoke to Paolo about playing an instrument in the boys' band. "You could play anything you want," Marco said. "Why not try? We will be practicing for the Christmas concert and might even be invited to play for the towns-people on Christmas Eve."

"I've never even played a whistle," said Paolo. "I don't think I have any musical talent."

"Well, you'll never know if you don't try," said Marco. "Come with me to band practice, and I'll talk to Sergeant Amante. He's not a bad person, and he'll help you decide what you could play if you really want to join the band."

"Marco, I appreciate your wanting me to join, but I'm afraid I'll make a fool of myself, and the other boys will laugh when I try to play an instrument," said Paolo.

"They might laugh a little, but everyone has had the same experience. Only a few boys actually ever played something before, and it was usually a harmonica or piccolo, or one of those squeezeboxes. Just try."

"Okay," said Paolo. "But if the sergeant tells me that I am incapable of playing any instrument and I feel stupid, I'll stuff your horn down your throat." Paolo laughed.

After a few experiments with horns, stringed instruments, and accordion-type instruments, the sergeant tried Paolo on drums. Finally, an instrument that Paolo could feel confident about! Banging a drum took some practice but felt comfortable to Paolo. The sergeant seemed pleased, and Paolo was issued a bright red sash, a red cap, a small drum with a red cord that draped around his neck, and two sets of drumsticks. "I'm a musician," chanted Paolo to his friend.

Paolo wasn't quite ready for the Christmas concert in the town, but he diligently practiced and played his drum at all marching exercises.

In April, Sergeant Amante told the boys that they were to be photographed. Everyone was to clean and polish his instrument, as well as his face and shoes. When the photographer came, Marco and his horn were placed in the front row. At first, the drummers were placed in the back, but then the photographer had them come to the front and sit on the floor in front of the horn section. Paolo carefully held his drum between his crossed legs and presented the serious image of a dedicated musician to the camera.

Each boy was given a photograph as a souvenir of their band membership. Paolo wanted to save the picture to show his mother when she came for him. It was already May, and Mama may have had the baby. *She'll probably come in August for my twelfth birthday*, Paolo thought.

"What are you going to do with the picture, Marco?" Paolo asked.

"I could put it over my bunk, but Durante said 'no pictures on the walls' was regulation. I might send it to my sister and make her a little jealous," said Marco.

"My mother will be coming for me in a few months, I'm going to save it for her," said Paolo. "I'll bet my new stepbrothers aren't in a band. I can make them a little jealous, too."

In early July, Major Ravasini sent for Paolo again. When Paolo entered the major's office, he was surprised and delighted to see his old friend, Signor Cardello.

"Private Leonardi, I believe you know Signor Cardello," said Major Ravasini.

"Yes, sir. It's nice to see you again, Signor Cardello."

"Sir, may I ask Signor Cardello if he has heard from my mother?" asked Paolo.

"Signor Cardello has heard from your mother, Private, and has some news for you."

Paolo looked expectantly at the attorney. Cardello stood up from his chair and said, "My boy there is no easy way to say this, but your mother has had her baby, a boy, and is expecting another child. She is unable to come for you at this time. I'm sorry, son."

"My mother is having another baby and can't come now? Is that what you said, Signor Cardello?"

"Yes."

"But when will she be able to come?" asked Paolo. "Will it be another year, and another baby?"

"Private, remember yourself!" snapped the Major.

"But sir, my mother promised that she would come for me and my sisters," said Paolo.

"Not all promises can be kept, Private. Your mother meant to keep her promise, I'm sure, but she has a new life, a new family, and most importantly, a new husband. She is not in a position to make promises any longer. Perhaps in time, after this next child, she and her husband will be able to send for you and your sisters. For the present, your stepfather has arranged that you stay here and continue your education and training. That is all, Private. You may spend the rest of the day with Signor Cardello, but I expect you to resume your duties tomorrow," said the major.

"Yes, sir. Thank you, sir."

Signor Cardello shook Major Ravasini's hand and said, "With your permission, I want to take the boy into town. Have a nice, quiet dinner and perhaps talk. I appreciate your understanding, Major."

"Signor Cardello, please have the boy back in four hours. It's best to keep to the routine and not allow him to wallow in self-pity. It may be that this life is meant to be Paolo's future.

CHAPTER 31

Mothers Are Wives, Too—July 1922

Seeing Paolo's disappointment at his mother's news of a second pregnancy, Attorney Cardello felt a tour of the Vatican City would cheer the boy up. Paolo could only greet the grandeur of St. Peter's Square with a lowered head and a dull stare when encouraged to view the magnificent columns.

"Come, let us find a quiet place," said Cardello. "We will eat; we will talk."

Entering a small neighborhood restaurant, the older man and young boy sat outdoors under the striped canopy in an obscure corner distant from the street traffic. The small square tables were inside a wrought iron fence which held blooming flower boxes all along the row. Crisp white tablecloths and an unlit candle topped each table. Busy pedestrians and traffic vehicles could be seen from their corner. Across the street was a long row of stone steps which led to a church and a square containing a fountain. They ate in silence. When coffee was served, Cardello offered Paolo a cup.

"I haven't had coffee since Papa died," said Paolo. "Graciella, our neighbor and friend, made me drink it. She said that the man of the house always drinks coffee to help him think and make decisions." With a deep sigh, Paolo continued. "I loved Graciella. I loved our home and all our friends. Now, I've lost my father and sisters, and my mother is busy making babies in America." Paolo's eyes misted with tears. He quickly brushed them away and shrugged off Cardello's sympathetic touch. "How could she have forgotten us so quickly, Signor Cardello? How could she forget my father and give herself to that man? She will never come back for us. Two years and two babies—she's abandoned us!"

"Don't be too hard on your mother," Cardello replied. "I believe she had few choices. She was a widow with four children, struggling to support you all. Our country is poor and suffering—no work, political unrest, labor strikes, and food shortages are everywhere. Many men who returned from the war were injured or broken from cruel weapons, gasses, and deprivation that no one had ever seen before. Life became harder." Putting his hand on Paolo's arm, Cardello continued, "Your mother received an invitation to start a new life in a rich country. She felt you would all be well cared for and have a secure future. But Paolo, you know that women are without power and subject to their husbands."

"My mother is strong-willed. She usually gets her way if she wants something," said Paolo.

Releasing Paolo's arm, Cardello said, "Perhaps that was the case in Italy, but now she is in a strange country and has a new husband who controls her destiny, as well as a new and growing family. Your mother's life, possibly, is not the paradise she imagined," Cardello said. "Be patient, my boy. Your mother is a strong woman. She may have her way soon, and you and your sisters will be reunited. I am sure of it,"

"Signor Cardello, one last favor. I want to write my sisters, especially Dina. Could you give me their addresses? I must know if they are well and not too sad waiting for our mother's return."

Cardello looked into Paolo's serious brown eyes, which had a pleading look. "Send your letters to me and I will see that your sisters receive them," promised Cardello as they rose to return to Paolo's school. Once again, Cardello left Paolo with a heavy heart and troubled thoughts.

CHAPTER 32

Creative Hands—December 1922

Sister Lauria rushed into the Chapel and found Dina dressing the Infant Jesus in preparation for the Christmas crèche.

"Oh, Dina," said Sister Lauria, "What a beautiful gown you've created for the Christ Child. Your stitches and the lovely embroidered design are the most beautiful I have ever seen. God has truly blessed you with a unique skill."

Dina smiled shyly and softly whispered, "Thank you, Sister. Do you really think it's nice? Sister Agnessa told me to keep the design simple since Jesus was poor and born in a stable. But He's God, and I wanted to make a special robe. You don't think Sister Agnessa will be mad. Do you?"

"Well, here she comes now," said Sister Lauria. "Why not wait and see what she says?"

A small, slightly stooped nun slowly walked to the crèche. Dina thought that Sister Agnessa must be at least a hundred years old. Her heavily lined face was framed by wire-rimmed eyeglasses that were at least an inch thick. Her face always looked a bit squeezed, as if she were trying to hold up her glasses with her petite but pudgy nose. "Perhaps she won't see all the fanciful stitches," Dina whispered to Sister Lauria.

Nodding to the young nun, who in turn gave a slight bow to Sister Agnessa, the old nun stepped up on the wooden kneeler and leaned over the colorful crèche. All the figures had been created and painted by the students, and Dina had volunteered to make the gown for the Infant Jesus. She held her breath as the little nun peered closely at the garment.

"Dina Leonardi, did you sew this gown?"

"Yes, Sister, I did. Is it all right?"

"Well, I never taught you these stitches or designs. Why did you make these narrow pleats?" asked Sister Agnessa. "And the embroidery, what is that design?"

"Oh, Sister, I just wanted to have a fitted bodice for the Infant's chest, and then let it open to a flare at the bottom for His feet. The embroidery is supposed to be stars, like the one that led the Wise Men to Jesus."

"Yes. Well, who taught you to sew like this?" demanded Sister Agnessa.

"My mother and her aunts taught me, Sister. Of course, you taught me many stitches, too. Are you upset with me, Sister? I only wanted to do something extra special." Dina nervously chewed her bottom lip, waiting for the elderly nun's formidable scolding.

Sister Agnessa stepped off the kneeler and, turning to Dina, walked slowly to her. Dina's eyes glistened with tears as she anticipated the nun's words of rejection and reproach. The nun grasped Dina's hands firmly in hers, and without another word brought them to her lips and gently kissed them.

"*Bella, bella,*" she whispered.

CHAPTER 33

He's My Brother — April 1923

"This is disgusting," said Dina. "I hate all these bugs!"

"You always say that, but you know there are always bugs or worms or other creepy-looking things in the flour," said Domenica.

"Well, why don't people donate food that isn't crawling with stuff that we have to pick out before using it or cooking it?" asked Dina.

"Sister will be back in a few minutes," said Domenica. "Just sift the flour and maybe you can catch the bugs before we make the Easter bread."

Dina started dumping the infested flour into the wire strainer. But black specks sifted through and the flour looked little better than before all the sifting.

"Give it up. Sister will get mad if she thinks we're wasting time," said Domenica. "Just dump the flour onto the board while I start cracking the eggs. Hurry up! Here she comes!"

Sister Celeste was carrying a large jar of anise seeds as she rushed to check the girls' progress.

"Have your two been dawdling? What is this mess of flour all over the floor and counter? At the rate you two are going, we'll have Easter bread for Christmas! Get to your work, both of you. No more talking! Domenica, start crushing these seeds while Dina finishes cracking the eggs. Dina, be sure to make a nice large well of flour and drop the eggs into the center. Then mix the flour into the eggs, keeping your hands in a curved motion as you mix."

The nun turned and began shouting instructions to the other girls who had cooking duties that day. With a final turn to Dina, she said, "Lift and mix, lift and mix—keep it going."

In the dormitory later that evening, Domenica stopped by Dina's bed before curfew. "I had a lovely letter from my brother, Marco. He also sent me a picture of himself and the band at his school," said Domenica. "Here's what he wrote. 'We had great fun playing for the mayor and the other dignitaries at the town's holiday concert. They gave us sweet bread and candy and even an *orangata* drink. It was a good day, and my friend, Paolo, and I each have a coin from the mayor. How are you doing with the old nuns? I'm studying harder and have passed my examinations. All of the band members got a new red sash before the concert, but they made us give them back in case we need them for another concert. Here is a picture of our band which you can keep for me. That's me, and Paolo is sitting on the ground, to the left of the photo. Paolo plays the drum.'"

"Here's my brother, Dina," said Domenica. "See, the one with the funny grin, holding the trumpet."

Dina took the photograph and studied it. "Domenica! Domenica! That boy next to your brother is my brother, Paolo!"

CHAPTER 34

A Day in the Dungeon—May 1923

"Happy Easter, my sweet Dina," wrote Signor Cardello.

"I received a letter from your mother, and she sends her love and warm wishes. She had another boy, so you are blessed with two new brothers. She named the first boy Davido, after her husband's late brother. The new baby is named Lorenzo, after her brother, Zio Lorenzo. Do you remember him? I received a letter from him last month. He is doing well and almost recovered from his war wounds, although he has a slight limp, he says. It will be a long way for him to come, but he hopes to visit you, your brother, and Loretta later this year before the harvest.

Your mother also wrote that your sister, Geneva, constantly asks for you and misses you. Your mother said she thinks of you all often and longs for the day you are reunited. She has not indicated when that might be, my child, but don't lose hope. She will come as soon as she can. In the meantime, she sent the enclosed money for you to buy something special for yourself."

Dina folded the letter and looked at the money, which she had thrown on her bed.

"*Santo mia!* Where did you get the money?" asked Domenica. "Now you can buy stamps, paper, and envelopes to write to your brother."

"My mother sent it. Three years and she sends me a little money to ease her conscience. I wish I could write her and tell her what these past few years have been like," said Dina.

"You should tell her about how hard we have to work and how hungry we usually are. Tell her how strict the nuns are and about the time you got locked up in the dungeon," said Domenica.

Dina closed her eyes and shuddered. "I was awful to Sister Rosaria. I couldn't understand her. She speaks Sicilian dialect and it's hard to follow her. I got so frustrated that I pushed her and told her to speak Italian. Nobody understands the Sicilian dialect."

"Well, how could you know she would fall down and hit her hip on the bench!" said Domenica.

"Sister Marguerita said I needed to be punished by spending time alone and praying to God to help me control my anger. Domenica, I hope you never get sent to the dungeon. It was dark and cold, and I could see only a little light outside the window of the stone wall. At night, they give you one candle, and the walls have scary shadows. Sister Rosaria came to see me and left me some food under the door. But when I uncovered the bowl, I screamed and dropped it on the floor. It looked like snake pieces swimming in a white broth. How was I to know it was a special Sicilian dish—eels in broth! I thought Sister Rosaria was getting back at me. She unlocked the door and started to shake me because I was screaming. She kept saying, 'It's good, it's good—something special for you,' but I never saw an eel before. It looked just like a snake! I was more frightened by the eel than the three days I spent in the dungeon," said Dina. "Yes, I should write my mother and say thank you, Mama, for sending me to a place that puts twelve-year-old girls in a dungeon for misbehaving. A place that feeds you food that is infested with bugs and worms. A place where you must rise at dawn and work all day until you collapse gratefully onto your thin, metal bed. A place where you are isolated from everyone you love. Yes," said Dina. "I should write and thank her."

CHAPTER 35

Minding the Babies — August 1923

"Quiet! Stop crying! I can't stand it!"

Geneva was furiously shaking the wicker basket to quiet a screaming Lorenzo while Davido sat under the sink whining for attention. She stopped rocking Lorenzo's basket and reached down under the sink to lift Davido into her arms. Patting his back, Geneva tried soothing him, but Davido began to struggle, pulling her hair and beating her with his pudgy little fists.

"Fine, then sit on the floor! I don't care if you cry all day. I can't wait for Mama to come home and see what a brat you are."

Davido crawled across the room and, balancing himself on Lorenzo's basket, pulled himself up, whimpering piteously all the while. Suddenly, there was a flash of blankets, basket, and babies, as Lorenzo and Davido tumbled to the floor. Both began to scream in earnest now.

"Oh, no! Oh, no!"

Geneva rushed to pick up the baby and also pull Davido onto his feet. She rocked the baby in her arms as Lorenzo's piercing screams dulled her brain. Davido cried constantly and would not stand up. Each time she pulled on him with her one free arm, he would plunk down on the floor again as soon as she released him.

"Shut up! Shut up!"

"Why are you screaming at the babies? Have you gone crazy?"

Geneva turned to see her mother standing at the door.

"Oh, Mama! They haven't stopped crying for hours! Then Davido pulled Lorenzo's basket over and I was just trying to get them to stop crying."

Caterina took Lorenzo from Geneva's arms. The baby instantly stopped crying and Davido, seeing his mother, got up and toddled over to her, giggling.

"What is wrong with you, Geneva? Why can't I trust you to take care of the babies while I'm out?"

"They're your babies. You should stay home and take care of them yourself!"

Caterina, still holding Lorenzo, and with Davido clinging to her skirt, swung around and slapped Geneva, catching her across the ear.

"Ouch!" cried Geneva. Her hand flew to her throbbing ear.

"You will remember whom you are speaking to," said Caterina.

"But Mama, all my friends are at the festival—even Lena and Luca are there, and I'm always left home to watch the babies. It's not fair."

"They have their responsibilities and you have yours," said Caterina. "Now take Davido and change him before you feed him."

"But Mama, it will be too late to go to the festival if I have to change and feed Davido, and then change him again. Papa Umberto will never let me go if he's home before I'm finished with the babies."

"Well, that's too bad. If you had more control over your tongue, you wouldn't find yourself in these unhappy situations. You're becoming more difficult and rebellious every day, Geneva, and it has to stop. You are much too *insolente* for your own good."

"I wish I never came to America, Mama!" shouted Geneva. "I wish you'd left me with my real sisters and brother. I hate this family, and sometimes I don't like you, either, Mama."

CHAPTER 36

My Sister, My Friend—August 1923

"Paolo, you've read that letter about a hundred times. Nothing my sister writes me is ever that interesting. She always writes the same boring stuff—'I did this, I did that, Dina made this, Sister said that'—same old stuff. What's so great about your sister's letter?"

"That's just it, Marco. It's a letter from Dina, a nice long letter telling me everything that's happened to her. I haven't seen or heard from her for over three years—three long years. Truthfully, Dina is my favorite sister. She and I were good friends."

"Friends! With your sister? My sister is okay, but I don't think of her as a friend—more like a self-appointed sergeant. All her letters ask if I did this, or did that, what kind of food we eat, how is my school work going, am I brushing my teeth, am I combing my hair and washing regularly? The girl thinks she needs to oversee my life!"

"That's funny, Marco. Is she really that bad?"

"Busybody enough, if you ask me. Well, she's not too bad. Just misses me, too, I guess."

"I've written Dina three letters back, but haven't told her yet about my going into the Army."

"Well, we're almost fourteen, so it's time, I guess. Major Ravasini said once we reach our fourteenth birthday, we must join the regular Army. I'll be fourteen this month," said Paolo.

"I have to wait until November. It would be great if we were in the same unit."

"Wouldn't that be great? My only problem is that once I'm in the Army, my mother won't be able to take me to America until my service time is over—four years. I'll be eighteen and a man by then. Maybe her new husband won't want me then because I'll be grown up and able to take care of myself," said Paolo. "Marco, I'm writing my sister, but I'm not going to tell her about the Army yet. I'll tell her in the next letter, so don't say anything to your sister, Domenica."

"Don't worry, I won't tell her anything. She'd tell Dina for sure. Girls can't keep anything to themselves, especially Domenica. If girls were in the Army, they'd probably talk the enemy to death," pronounced Marco.

CHAPTER 37

The Peach Thief—June 1924

"**S**anto Antonio! What have you done to your dress and stockings, Loretta?"

Loretta examined her dress and lifted the skirt to see the tears in the hem and the large hole in her best stockings.

"I'm sorry, Zia Magdalena. I had to climb a tree to get the peach stones."

"What are you talking about, child? Were you stealing peaches again from Signora Coletti?"

"Well, I needed the peaches to get the stones. Now we can grow a tree, and I promise I'll never steal her peaches again."

"And I suppose you didn't eat the peaches, huh? Just took the stones?"

"I needed to eat the peaches, Zia, because the stones were inside!"

Magdalena leaned over and placed her hands on Loretta's shoulders. "First of all," she began, "you must not steal from other people's trees. If you want a fruit, ask Signora Coletti. Second, we can't plant a peach tree or any other tree. We have no land for fruit trees. Our tiny garden barely meets our needs for vegetables and herbs. A fruit tree takes too much room to grow."

"Signora Coletti won't give me any peaches," complained Loretta. "She always chases me away from her trees. I hope she gets a bellyache from eating all that fruit."

"Well, then don't take her peaches! And look at the tears. Your stockings will show a long line when I repair them. You can no longer wear them to school. This dress—I don't know how many times I've repaired the hem, the sleeves, or replaced the buttons." Unbuttoning Loretta's dress, Magdalena said, "You must be more careful of your clothes, Loretta. We have no money to buy new material every week. Now, take off the dress and stockings so I can repair them. *Mama mia!* What a child, just like a monkey!"

Zia Marianna entered the room, and seeing her, Loretta burst into tears.

"I'm sorry, Zia Marianna, I'm sorry," wept Loretta.

"*Bella mia*, why are you crying? What has happened?" The older aunt hugged Loretta and repeatedly kissed her head, murmuring soft words of comfort. "G*ioia mia, bella mia,* don't cry," said Zia Marianna. "We are here for you."

Interrupting her, Magdalena said, "Oh, stop that! She was stealing peaches again from Concetta Coletti and ripped her dress and stockings in the process." "Oh, my child! Is that all? I thought you were hurt," said Marianna. "Don't cry, *gioia mia,* we can fix the dress and I'll speak to Concetta about the peaches. I'll bring her a piece of lace and she'll be satisfied."

The next morning, seeing Loretta still in bed, Zia Marianna gently shook her. "Wake up, my sleepy head. You'll be late for school."

Clutching her head, Loretta moaned, "Oh, Zia, my ears hurt so much. I don't think I can go to school today. It hurts to hear people talking. Please, may I stay home and rest?"

"Oh, dear, this is the third time this month," said Marianna. "Magdalena will be upset if I let you stay home again. But if you are ill, you must rest and get well. Poor child, I will warm some oil and find a soft piece of cotton to place in your ears. You'll feel better soon."

"Thank you, Zia. You are so sweet to me. I'm sure I'll feel better later."

Marianna prepared the earache remedy by saturating small pieces of cotton in warm olive oil. When they were ready, she carefully placed a ball of cotton in each of Loretta's ears.

"Oh, that feels better already, Zia. Thank you."

Returning from her teaching rounds, Magdalena bustled into the kitchen and began preparing the noon meal. "What is this? Loretta is home from school, again?"

"Oh, the poor child had an earache this morning," said Marianna. "I put some oil in her ears and she has been resting peacefully, poor child."

"Oh, yes, and when the children return from school, she will have another miraculous recovery and be scampering out the door to play," said Magdalena.

"You are too hard on the child, Magdalena. She is suffering. An earache is very painful for a child."

"Earaches, bellyaches, headaches—all seem to disappear when school lets out," said Magdalena. "Then Loretta feels so much better and needs fresh air and exercise. Marianna, the child has cast a spell on you. Well, today there will not be any sudden cures." While the child slept, Magdalena took her clothes and hid them away, leaving Loretta only in her nightshirt.

Later that day, as children beckoned Loretta to come out to play, a glum little girl sat in her nightshirt watching them through the window

CHAPTER 38

Family News—October 1925

"Mama, a letter from Italy! Open it, open it!"

"Geneva, did you leave the babies alone in the yard?"

"Yes, but they'll be okay. Davido's digging in the dirt, and Lorenzo is watching him."

Caterina put the letter into her apron pocket and rushed out to the back yard. Lorenzo, nearly three, had fallen into the large hole dug by four-year-old Davido, and Davido was happily covering his little brother with dirt. "Thank God he didn't cover his face!" cried Caterina.

Geneva pulled Davido away while Caterina dug her hands into the dirt and rescued Lorenzo from his spontaneous burial.

"Up, up!" shouted Lorenzo. "Up, up!"

Kicking to free himself from Geneva, Davido shrieked, "Renzo dirty, Renzo dirty!"

"Take the boys and wash them, Geneva, and see that you don't let them drown in the tub!"

"Yes, Mama, I'm sorry," said Geneva, as she carried the struggling boys into the house.

Caterina watched her leave and uttered a deep sigh. Feeling the letter in her pocket, she walked to the stone bench Umberto had made for her and sat down to read it.

The letter was from Signor Cardello. She scanned the first part of the attorney's letter in which he sent his regards, and so on, until her eyes stopped abruptly.

"Please do not be alarmed," the letter continued, "but Paolo has had a slight mishap and required a short stay in the hospital. During one of the mock training battles, a comrade tripped and pierced Paolo's left arm with a bayonet. Your son required a few stitches, but there appears to be no serious damage to the arm, and he is doing fine now."

Caterina looked up and, beseeching heaven, prayed, "Oh, God, protect my son. Don't let him get hurt again. Make him well. Please, God, watch over my Paolo." She picked up the letter again, and continued anxiously reading.

"On a happier note, I visited your aunts, and Loretta is doing very well. She has grown into a lively little girl and loves to play pranks and tell funny stories about the neighbors and her friends. Loretta told me that she was made to wear a black ribbon on her white communion dress to honor her late father. Not happy with this, she cut a piece of lace from the altar cloth at the church and quickly stitched it over the black band. When the children returned for the communion breakfast, the priest had some heated words with your aunts. They have their hands full, but they obviously love her, and Loretta seems happy. Marianna appeared very frail to me, but she and her sister, Magdalena, insisted they are both well.

"The nuns report that Dina studies hard and is an accomplished needlewoman. She is a very devout child and constantly prays for her brother and sisters, and all of you, of course."

Caterina folded the letter. Four years, she thought, four years! Where did they go? Paolo, now sixteen, was in the Army. Dina, fourteen, was still the "little nun" she remembered. And eight-year-old Loretta, the child who hid from her and clung to their neighbor and friend, Graciella, seemed to echo Caterina's own youthful exuberance and willfulness. "I did what I had to do!" said Caterina aloud, and stuffed the letter back into her pocket.

CHAPTER 39

A Wedding in the Family—*April 1926*

"Stop fidgeting, Geneva," said Caterina. "If you don't stand still, I'll be pinning this dress to your skin."

"I can't help it, Mama. This is my first wedding. I love this dress! Can I see? Can I see?"

Caterina rose from her knees and took the pins out of her mouth. "All right," she said, "look at yourself and then we can get on with the fitting."

"Oh, Mama, it's lovely. Don't you love the color?" asked Geneva.

"Yes, blue is very pretty. Now, Geneva, get back on the chair so we can finish before Papa comes home."

"Yes, Mama, but it's not just blue, it's periwinkle blue! Isn't that lovely—periwinkle blue, periwinkle blue!" gushed Geneva. "Don't you just love the name and color?"

"Lovely, now stay still," said Caterina, "or it will be polka-dotted with crimson red."

"Well, look at the little girl, all dressed up. You're almost as pretty as your mother, Geneva." Caterina looked up to see Umberto.

"I'm not a little girl," said Geneva. "I'm twelve, and I'm going to be a bridesmaid in Ava's wedding. I'll be the most beautiful and elegant bridesmaid in the wedding, I'll bet."

"Humph, such foolishness," said Umberto. "What is wrong with just going to the church and getting married without all this fuss? It was good enough for me, and for you."

After Geneva left, Caterina said to Umberto, "Times are different. Your daughter will have a special day that will give her memories for a lifetime. Don't spoil it for her or the other children."

"Money wasted, that's what I say. Money wasted on foolish things to impress people who used to spit on us," said Umberto.

"Ava and Salvatore are a new generation. They have Irish friends, and Salvatore's aunt is Irish, so it can't be helped. We had to invite them to the wedding," said Caterina. "Your first wife was Irish. If you hate them so much, why did you marry her?"

"Why did I marry Maura? When my brother and I came to this country," said Umberto, "we lived in a dirty, crowded, cold-water flat near the docks in Boston. We couldn't find jobs because the Irish had all the jobs. You could feel the hate and animosity they felt for Italians whenever you looked for work or went into a store or tried to find a place to live. When we found work, they tried to cheat us in our pay. My brother, Davido, was beaten up by a drunken mob on his way home from looking for work. They told him that Italians were no better than niggers, and if he knew what was good for him, he would go back to Italy."

Umberto paused and looked at Caterina, who had tears in her eyes. Shaking his head, he continued his story. "Well, I got a job in the quarries. I was treated like the dirt I wore every day, but I was determined to stay. Maura's father, a big, ugly Mick, was the foreman. I saw her when she brought his lunch one day. Not a pretty girl—big-boned and plain like her father. I decided that marrying this Irish girl could work in my favor, so I flirted with her, away from her father, of course. Three months later, we were married, and I got a better job and a raise."

"Umberto, that's a terrible story," said Caterina. "Did you love her?"

"Ha! Love! What a foolish sentimentalist you are, Caterina. I married her to survive. I had a better job, we made a home, I gave her children, and the status of being a married woman. Did I tell you she had an uncle who was a priest? He refused to marry us. He was a bigger bigot than his brother. I said, no matter, we would have a civil ceremony, and that shocked the good Father into consenting to marry us."

90

Caterina looked at Umberto and quietly asked, "Why did you marry me?"

"My dear Caterina, isn't it obvious? I needed a mother for my children and a woman for myself—and you are doing a wonderful job. If you would stop lamenting about your other children, it would be almost perfect, my dear." Umberto squeezed her face and left the room.

Bastardo, Caterina whispered under her breath.

CHAPTER 40

A Family Death—March 1927

"Benedetta has died," said Magdalena. "Vittoria wrote to tell us that she died quietly, sitting in her chair as the babies played at her feet."

Marianna, suddenly uneasy on her feet, reached for the table's edge and lowered herself on the nearby bench. Rushing to her, Magdalena said, "*Dio mio*, are you all right? I'm sorry, I shouldn't have told you so bluntly. Marianna, say something!"

"Oh, I'm upset, but I thank God, Benedetta is at peace," said Marianna. "Poor Caterina, she will be deeply saddened by her mother's death, and now she will never see her again,"

"And whose fault is that? She should have gone to see her mother before going to America. Vittoria is right. Caterina did a cruel, heartless thing to leave her family, especially her children, and marry a stranger in America. She left the burden of care for her mother with her younger sister. Poor Vittoria had to care for her invalid mother, a husband, and now three sons. And what about this child?" continued Magdalena. "She was a baby—a baby. Loretta has grown up these last seven years not even knowing her mother, or her sisters and brother. What a disgrace!"

Marianna's face was covered with tears and her small, rotund body shook with grief.

"Marianna, please, you will make yourself ill. I weep for Benedetta, too. She had a good life—the blessing of four children, a good husband, and beautiful grandchildren. Everyone loved her, but you know how terribly the stroke affected her. Be at peace; she is with God now."

Marianna nodded and tried to rise from the bench. Magdalena gently took her sister's arm, lifted and embraced her. The sisters clung to each other and wept over the loss of their sister until both were exhausted.

Running through the door, Loretta stopped short to see the two old aunts sitting quietly at the table. Both women had tear-streaked faces and puffy eyes. Zia Marianna was shaking her head from side to side and Zia Magdalena had her arm across the older sister's shoulders. "Is everything all right? Are you sick, Zia Marianna? Did I do something wrong? Did something bad happen?" asked Loretta. "Why are you crying?"

Magdalena rose and pressed Loretta to her. "We had sad news today, child. Our sister, Benedetta, your grandmother, has passed away. She was old and very sick. You didn't know her. She lived with your Aunt Vittoria."

"My grandmother died? But I never saw her. Why didn't Mama take me to see her? Promise me that you and Zia Marianna won't die for a long, long time," pleaded Loretta.

"We will all die when God wants us. But I'm too stubborn, so God won't want me for a while yet," said Magdalena. "So don't worry yourself, my child."

"But Zia Marianna is so sweet and older than you. Will God want her soon?"

Magdalena smiled, "Yes, Marianna is sweeter and older than me, but I'm determined enough to keep her for now."

Loretta hugged her aunt and then rushed over to Marianna and kissed her.

"Oh, my child, my dear child," said Marianna. "God has blessed us with you. Every day you have been with us has been His gift to us."

"Well, some days are better gifts than others," Magdalena tartly replied.

They all laughed, and Loretta turned and kissed each aunt in turn again.

CHAPTER 41

A Daughter's Regret—April 1927

The news was broken by Vittoria's husband, Pietro, in a letter to Caterina.

"I'm deeply saddened to write and tell you of your mother's death. She was a good and loving woman, even to the end. She loved seeing the boys each day and delighted in watching them play. She would sit in her chair, and although she rarely moved, her eyes were always bright and she smiled often at the children and their antics. She died peacefully in her chair while the boys played on the veranda. Vittoria is too distraught to write; thus I am the bearer of this sad news.

"We have written the aunts and your brothers. As their mother, we feel it would be best if you wrote to Dina and Paolo about their grandmother."

Visions of her mother sleeping in her chair filled Caterina's mind. She whispered a silent prayer. *Mama, forgive me for not coming to see you. Please, please believe me. I thought I would be back to see you again. I couldn't face Vittoria's anger for leaving my children and you. I feared I would lose my courage and any hope of a better life for us. Mama, I'm so sorry.*

Her guilt turned to anger at her sister and brother-in-law. *Of course, I must tell the children myself. What would they think to hear about my mother's death from their aunt and uncle? Vittoria and Pietro would let them believe that I don't care about them. They won't tell them that the reason I have not sent for them is that emigration to America from Italy has stopped. They'll make them believe I don't want them. Vittoria has always been jealous of me because I was my mother's favorite child. Vittoria had no children when Antonio died, that's why she wanted my children to come and live with her. She was jealous that I had four children and she had none.* Caterina closed her eyes and tried to dispel the anger and resentment she felt toward her sister, as her thoughts took a more introspective path.

Perhaps I am resentful of my sister because she was fortunate. She married a man who had property, and lived to give their children and themselves time together. Perhaps I feel regret that Vittoria took care of my mother while I was the oldest and favored child. Perhaps I'm angriest because she was, after all, much wiser than me, mused Caterina.

CHAPTER 42

A Momentous Decision—July 1928

"Dina, are you awake?"

Dina opened her eyes and looked at her friend, Domenica. "I'm awake now."

"Oh, Dina, I've been praying and praying and I now know for sure that I want to be a nun. Have you decided to speak to Mother Superior about becoming a nun yet?"

"No, not yet," said Dina. "I was hoping you would come with me and we could both tell her."

"Won't it be wonderful to be nuns together?" said Domenica. "That way we can stay together as friends forever. I think I want to be a teacher to the younger school children."

"I want to teach older girls how to sew, and especially teach embroidery," said Dina.

"Shush, stop that talking," said Sister Adela. "You know the rules."

Dina ducked her head under the thin blanket. "Please, God, make me a good nun who remembers the rules."

The next afternoon, Dina and Domenica were assigned to work in the vegetable garden.

"You know, Domenica, I love working in the garden. It's one of the places I feel happiest and most at peace with my life. Maybe I could be a farmer or teach gardening. I could teach how to make preserves, too."

"No, if we want to be together, we both have to be school teachers," said Domenica. "I'll never see you if you're a farmer. They might even send you to a farm where there isn't a school."

"You're right. I love sewing, and after school, I could always work in a garden at the school, like we do now."

"The tomatoes are so high, Dina," said Sister Lauria. "You have a natural talent for gardening."

Dina smiled at Domenica and winked. Domenica smiled back, shrugged her shoulders and turned back to her work.

"Sister Lauria," said Dina, "could we talk to you?"

"Of course, girls, but only for a few minutes," the nun said. "I can't interrupt your work for long."

Dina nodded and said, "Sister, Domenica and I are already seventeen, and we would like to speak with Mother Superior about becoming nuns. Could you ask her if she would see us?"

"Why, Dina, Domenica, how wonderful!" said Sister Lauria. Have you both thought and prayed about this decision? It is not an easy life, and you will have many sacrifices to make during your life as a Bride of Christ. You will be taken away from your families, you may be sent to a remote region or another country to do God's work. You will, of course, give up having your own children someday, in exchange for ministering to all of God's children. And you will need to take a vow of poverty," Sister Lauria said, looking at Dina, who had a habit of meticulously recording every lira she received, loaned, or spent. "Obedience without question is also demanded," continued the nun. "Can you girls live up to this expectation? It is very difficult at times."

"Yes, Sister, we think we can. We even know what we want to teach," said Dina.

"Dina, did you hear everything I said? Some decisions are not yours to make. The Order may want you to be nurses or missionaries or serve other nuns as cooks or laundresses."

"Oh," said Dina, "I didn't realize that you couldn't choose what you want to do."

"Making the decision to be a nun is generally the last decision you make on your own," said Sister Lauria. "Besides, Dina, your mother may still come for you and bring you to America. If you're a nun, you may never see her again, or at least not for many years."

"Sister, I've waited eight years for my mother. She has written so many excuses for not coming, or for our not going to America on our own, that I don't believe I will ever see her again," said Dina. "And forgive me, Sister, but sometimes I don't care if I ever see her again."

The nun started to rebuke the girl, but bit her tongue in silence. She could forgive Dina her anger when she thought of the pretty woman who had so easily left her child a decade earlier.

"I'll speak to Mother Superior and ask her to see you both. God be with you, whatever your life," said Sister Lauria as she left them to their gardening chores.

A week later, Domenica was summoned to see the Mother Superior, Sister Marguerita. The nun spoke with her for over three hours, questioning her and telling her about the choices and sacrifices one must make to become a nun. "Domenica, I know you and Dina are good friends, and Sister Lauria has told me that Dina also wishes to become a nun. I must tell you that close friendships between nuns are strongly discouraged. There are no assurances that you will be together as teachers or any other occupation decided for you. We become a Bride of Christ and have allegiance only to Him and to our Order. We love our fellow sisters as we love all of God's children, but we do not, cannot bond with anyone other than God, the beloved Bridegroom. Do you understand?"

"Yes, Mother, I understand," said Domenica, but she felt a sadness in saying it.

Dina met with the Mother Superior a week later. The same process of questioning, probing, and clarifying the life and expectations of entering the convent continued for hours. The girls waited another two weeks before being summoned by the Mother Superior again.

"Dina, I have given some thought to your request and Domenica's, and have decided that you, Dina, will stay here to teach sewing and embroidery while preparing for the novitiate, and Domenica, you will be sent to our convent in Bologna for advanced education to prepare you for teaching academic subjects. Some time apart will help prepare you both for the solitary life of a nun." The nun looked at the girls and could see the disappointment in their eyes. "Domenica, you will leave at the end of the semester. I will write your guardian and you may wish to write your brother. I will give you the address of the convent in Bologna which you may wish to share with your friends before leaving," Mother Superior said more gently.

Dina felt a painful stab in her chest. In her mind, she thought, *why does everyone I love have to leave me?* But she replied, "Thank you, Mother."

CHAPTER 43

Love in Bloom—May 1929

"Stop, Mario, you're messing up my dress. My mother will shoot me, if my stepfather doesn't kill me first!" Geneva pushed the handsome young man away and straightened her dress, smoothing out any wrinkles.

"Give me a break, Geneva; it's been three months since we started going out together. Be a little nicer to me, huh?"

"If I'm any nicer to you, you'll have to marry me," replied Geneva.

"Maybe I will marry you when you're older," laughed Mario.

"I'm sixteen—that's old enough to get married."

"Well, I'm only eighteen," said Mario, "and I'm too young to settle down."

"I can't stand living with them anymore, Mario. I need to get out on my own. My stepfather has a terrible temper and hits everyone—even my mother. She jumps to please him and watches me like a hawk. My stepbrothers treat me like a servant and my sister, Lena, is jealous of me because I'm a lot prettier than her. You think I'm pretty, don't you, Mario?" Geneva coyly asked.

"You're beautiful to me, babe. It's just I don't have enough money to get married, and I just started my job at the shoe factory. It's going to take a couple of years to save enough to marry someone."

"Someone!" said Geneva. "Don't you want to marry me? Well, I won't wait a couple of years!" If you don't want to marry me now, or at least get engaged, I'll find someone else!"

"You don't mean that, babe," said Mario as he nuzzled her ear. "I like you a lot and we have fun together."

"Too much fun for not being engaged," she said as she pulled away. "Find yourself another girl who'll wait, because I won't!" Geneva opened the door of the old jalopy and started walking down the street toward her house. She always made Mario meet her a few blocks away to avoid her stepfather's anger. To him, every woman was looking for trouble and every young man gave it to her.

"Wait, Geneva, can't we still see each other?"

"No, I want to be engaged to marry, or don't bother calling for me again," she said. Smiling, and caressing his face, she said, "Oh, honey, you're the sweetest boy I know. I can't think of anyone I like better than you. We could be happy and have lots of fun. I hate to lose you, honey, I really do, but I need a man who wants me and will take care of me. I wish that was you, Mario." She softly kissed him.

"It can be me! It will be me! Okay, let's get married!" he said.

"Oh, honey, let's tell my folks right now! Be sure to tell my stepfather you're working at the shoe factory, okay!"

"O-okay, but, but don't you think it's a little late? May-maybe they're sleeping," Mario stuttered. "Let's wait until tomorrow, okay?"

"No, they always wait up for me. My room is right off the living room, so they know when I'm not home," said Geneva. "Don't be afraid, we'll tell them straight out," she said, giving him a hard kiss and squeezing his nose.

Umberto was smoking his pipe and reading the newspaper, while Caterina was mending little boys' trousers. Neither one looked up when Geneva and Mario entered the room.

"Mama, Papa Umberto, this is Mario Cardarelli. Mario and I are going to be married!"

Caterina stood up so fast, her chair fell back. "Get married! Are you joking! You're just a child! Who is this boy? He looks too young to get married. Are you pregnant?"

Mario colored, and started to protest, but Geneva reacted first. "Of course not! How can you say such a thing, Mama?"

"Honestly, I hardly touched her!" squeaked out Mario.

Umberto stood up and walked toward the couple. Geneva clutched Mario's arm, while Mario gave an audible gulp.

"So, you want to get married? I suppose you have a job?"

Mario was furiously licking his lips when Geneva gave his arm a shove. "A job? Yes, I have a job at the new shoe factory in Braintree. I work there, you know, making shoes. But...uh..."

Umberto interrupted him, saying, "That's fine. Well, Caterina, it looks like another wedding in the family!"

"But Umberto, she's too young!"

"Nonsense, she's a woman who knows her own mind. It's time she made a new home and future for herself." Turning back to Mario, Umberto said, "Good, so when's the date?"

"The date?" asked Mario.

"When do you plan to get married? What day?" Umberto asked as he turned to Geneva.

"Well, I'll be sixteen this month, so maybe in four months—September—would be the date," said Geneva.

"Four months," said Caterina, "is too soon! Another year at least is more seemly. Why must you marry so soon?"

"September, it is!" said Umberto. "Tomorrow, go to the church and get a date and your mother can help with the dress and all the other arrangements. Good, that's settled! Congratulations, young man, and good night! It's late."

Mario, in a daze, muttered good night and turned to leave. Geneva rushed after him and gave him a quick kiss. "You did it! Don't forget to tell your folks! Goodnight, honey!"

While Geneva was walking Mario to the door, Caterina looked angrily at her husband. "Why did you agree to let them marry? You practically pushed them into a quick marriage. What are you thinking? Geneva is too young!"

"My dear Caterina, Geneva is getting old enough to have her own life. She has been discontented for a long time. Let her go, and our relationship with her will be better, I assure you," Umberto said. "Besides, we have two new daughters to occupy your time. We need the room!"

Delighted, Geneva plunged right into the wedding plans. "I want a white satin gown that shows off my figure, but it must have a long train—yards and yards of lace from my veil. When I walk down the aisle, I want the train to be at least six benches long in the church."

Ava was pregnant again, so she couldn't be a bridesmaid. Geneva had to have her other stepsister, Lena, as maid of honor. Umberto insisted on this, and it was the only interest he showed in the wedding plans. Gloria, her three-year-old stepsister, was to be a flower girl, and Lorenzo and Davido were to be ring bearers. Her two older stepbrothers were not included, since she only had one bridesmaid, her friend, Bianca. Mario's two brothers filled out the party as best man and usher. Umberto, Jr. was in the Army now and would look impressive in his uniform. Luca, not the neatest person, had found a nice girl who had taught him how to dress and behave. He had inherited his father's fiery temper, which was exacerbated by Luca's fondness for liquor.

Mario's parents were not happy about the marriage. They, like Caterina, felt the couple was too young. Besides, they only met Geneva after she became engaged to their son. Mario's mother cried hysterically when he told her, but his father concluded that "at least she's Italian."

Geneva was in a constant whirl over her wedding plans. She insisted that Caterina make her wedding gown, veil, and most of her trousseau. The subject of a long train was a constant theme.

"No, Geneva, you cannot have a veil that is over five yards long. Who do you think you are, the Queen of America? You will not be able to walk, and later, when you try to carry it, you will be smothered in material and look like you are carrying one of those big hot air balloons. No, and that's final!" As for Geneva's trousseau and collection of linens, Caterina outdid herself.

"Oh, Mama, these nightgowns and my honeymoon dresses are wonderful! Oh, thank you, Mama! Do you think I'll ever use all these tablecloths and bed linens?" asked Geneva. "The stitching is so beautiful, I'm almost afraid to let anyone use them. The work is so delicate, I'll probably have you help me wash and iron them."

"That's what you think, my girl. I have two babies, two wild boys, and your stepfather to take care of," said Caterina, "I won't have time to take care of you and Mario too!"

CHAPTER 44

Loss of an Angel—August 1929

There seemed little time for all the preparations before the wedding, and the heat of the summer did nothing to diminish the anxiety of the bridal couple and their families. Caterina, in particular, was feeling overwhelmed with all the planning and work required. She had little free time to enjoy her younger children or to take any daytrips to the ocean where she could relax and revel in the cool breezes and tangy sea air which she had come to love.

One morning in mid-August, Caterina awoke with a start. She realized she was breathing heavily and was covered in perspiration.

"What's wrong?" asked Umberto? "Why did you jump up like that? Are you all right?"

"I don't know," said Caterina. "Do you hear that? Do you hear the baby?" Caterina ran from their bed to the little alcove that was once Geneva's room. With all the wedding paraphernalia, Geneva needed a larger room, and had moved upstairs to occupy her stepsisters' former bedroom. A low, sustained, moaning sound was coming from the alcove. Anita, her baby, was drenched with sweat, tossing and turning in the small crib. "Oh, dear God!" cried Caterina as she felt the child's head. Anita was burning with fever. "Quick, get some water!" she shouted to Umberto who had just entered the room. "Oh, my sweet baby, Mama is here. Mama is here. Quick! Umberto, what is keeping you?"

Umberto rushed into the room and handed Caterina a small basin of water with a cloth floating in it. Caterina quickly began to pull off Anita's drenched gown, fumbling with the tiny buttons. Anita's hazel eyes, once so shiny and quick, now seemed dull and swollen. She moaned pitifully and with great effort. The baby's quick nervous jerks frightened Caterina, and she clutched the baby to her chest, trying to soothe the child's spasms.

"Here, give her to me," said Umberto, as he tried to loosen Caterina's hold on the baby. Umberto carried the baby to the kitchen sink and splashed cold water on Anita's convulsing body. Anita suddenly doubled up at the waist, causing Umberto to almost lose his grip on her.

"Please, get the doctor," shouted Caterina, as she reclaimed her baby from Umberto's grasp.

"Yes, you keep her cool and I'll go for the doctor," said Umberto.

Dr. Messina arrived with Umberto in less than an hour. Anita was listless and Caterina was rocking her and cooing soft pleas through her tears. Dr. Messina examined Anita and shook his head. "She has a high fever and it may have affected her nervous system," he said to a stunned Caterina. "I'll give her something, but you need to keep a close watch over her, and if she convulses again, call me," said the old doctor. "Keep her cool, bathe her every hour to keep the fever down. I'll come back tomorrow, if I can."

Caterina covered the little baby's face with gentle kisses as she continued to rock her.

When Geneva and Mario's wedding day arrived, it was overcast by sorrow. Three weeks earlier, Caterina's baby, Anita, had died of the fever. She was seven months old.

Caterina, grief-stricken, did not attend her daughter's wedding. Geneva, feeling hurt that her mother loved Anita more than her, found this unforgivable.

CHAPTER 45

Letter from Paolo—July 1930

Dear Dina,

I'm so excited! My platoon is being moved back to Rome. I will be stationed near Anzio. There is a fine beach there, and my good friend, Marco Antonelli, writes his platoon is also scheduled to train at Anzio.

From all the stories, Rome has changed a great deal. Mussolini and his fascist movement have taken over the city. Everyone said he duped King Victor Emmanuel III by saying he and his fascists would put down the strikes, but instead they took over the city, burning down buildings and destroying the *Avanti* news presses. Some people say he is a great man, others that he is a brutal madman. One thing is for sure—he likes to distribute his picture everywhere. There are even postcards with his photo everywhere you go. Well, enough of Mussolini!

Do you really want to become a nun? You've been in the novitiate for two years now, so you must be pretty close to taking your vows. To be honest, I'm not surprised, but I feel I will lose you. The Church might send you to a different country to do missionary work. Wouldn't it be ironic if you got sent to America and found our mother?

Signor Cardello wrote me that Geneva got married and is expecting a baby. Can you believe it? I'm almost twenty-one, so she has to be only seventeen—and a mother already!

Our little sister, Loretta, is a spitfire, I'm told. She has more adventures than I ever remember having as a boy. Of course, she was able to keep her childhood longer than us, and at thirteen, she is still a child! Did you hear about the day she convinced her friend, Guiliana, to borrow her father's umbrella? Since it was a sunny day, Guiliana was unsure why Loretta needed it, but gave it to her anyway. Loretta led a band of youngsters, including Guiliana, to a neighbor's garden and proceeded to pick all the figs off the trees. Loretta hid their share in the umbrella and quickly made her escape to Guiliana's house where they returned a fig-stained umbrella. I'll bet they pooped for a week after that excursion! My apologies for being so blunt.

Signor Cardello visited the aunts, and they told him so many stories about our little sister that he said he got a coughing spasm from laughing so much. Zia Marianna is doing very poorly. She is almost eighty, and Loretta is helping Zia Magdalena take care of her.

Loretta presented Signor Cardello with a nice pair of knitted socks. She sells them in the market to help the aunts.

Well, I have my boots, rifle, and gear to clean before bed. Yes, my hair is still a terrible red! I'm putting some hair oil in it to change the color, but it doesn't help much. I'm pretty happy. The army life agrees with me because I like order, and the discipline seems to keep me strong and focused on doing my job. Please write me often and tell me how things are going with you, my dearest "Sister Dina." I miss you. Paolo

CHAPTER 46

Zio Lorenzo and Family—April 1931

"Marianna, Marianna, good news! Lorenzo and the children are coming home!"

Confined to her bed for some months now, Marianna was slow to comprehend Magdalena's news.

"Lorenzo is coming home? Is the war over then? Oh, thank God, he is coming home. Is Stella coming too?"

Magdalena sat in the chair next to the bed and took her sister's soft, withered hand. "No, dear, Stella died in childbirth; Lorenzo and the children, Tomaso and Maria Elena, are coming. They will be here in a few weeks."

"Oh, a few weeks? I hope he comes to see me and brings the children," said Marianna. "Is the war over?"

"Yes, dear," Magdalena said as she gently kissed her sister, "The war is over."

Loretta was excited about meeting her uncle and cousins. She and her mother's brother were named for their town's patron saint. She knew her cousins would be older than she, and flooded Magdalena with questions about them.

"What is Maria Elena like? How old is she? Do you think she'll like me? Tell me about Tomaso. Is he much older than me? When will they be here? Will they live with us? How?"

"Stop, please, Loretta!" Magdalena pleaded. "No, they will live near the school. Zio Lorenzo will work to repair the church. His wife, Stella died, and he is returning to our town with Maria Elena, who is eighteen, and Tomaso, who is fifteen. They will be here in a few weeks, and I'm sure they will like you, my little monkey."

Soon the weeks passed, and Lorenzo and the children were at their door. It was a joyous reunion; everyone laughed and cried and hugged and kissed each other profusely. Lorenzo looked at his Aunt Magdalena. She still had the slender, straight figure he remembered, and the no-nonsense face. She always looked stern, but her eyes were kind, and a small smile would often escape her thin lips. But her steps were slower, her face was deeply lined, and her hair, under the traditional scarf, was a metallic gray.

Loretta liked this family instantly. Her uncle was fun and boisterous when he scooped her up in his arms and hugged her. Tears misted his eyes as he said, "You look like your father. He was a good man, a good husband, a good friend, and a good father. Always remember that."

Although everyone said that her mother was beautiful, Loretta felt a sweet pleasure that she looked like her father.

"This is Maria Elena and this is Tomaso," said Lorenzo.

"Maria Elena! I like your name. You must be the same age as my sister, Dina."

"Yes, I think we're about the same age," she said smiling.

Loretta hugged her. She thought that Maria Elena had the prettiest eyes—large, dark and soft like a gentle doe. She felt an immediate liking for her.

"Hey, what about me?" said Tomaso. "I'm your handsome cousin. Don't I get a kiss?"

Loretta leaned her head up for a kiss and felt Tomaso's hand pinch her backside. As she pulled away, he winked at her. Tomaso is an *amoretti*—a flirt, she thought.

As he greeted Zia Marianna, Lorenzo's tears started anew, but this time, they were tears of sadness. The full-figured, somewhat rotund body had diminished, and a very small, frail, bird-like figure trembled in his arms. He kissed her gently and said, "Zia, I'm home."

"Yes, God is good. The war is over and you are home. Praise be to God!" said Marianna. She clutched his hand and whispered, "Antonio died, you know."

"Yes, I know," he said, "a tragedy."

"Where is Vincenzo? Why did he not come?" she asked.

"My brother is very ill, Zia. He was gassed during the war. His wife, Luisa, cares for him," said Lorenzo with fresh tears. "That is another tragic family. Do you remember their son, Stephano? You remember he was born with a weak heart? Well, Stephano died three years ago. He was only eleven. I thought that Luisa would go crazy. If it weren't for taking care of my brother, I think she would have died along with her son. So much misfortune in one family!"

"Those years were very bad. So much tragedy," said Marianna.

Loretta and Maria Elena saw each other every day. Loretta loved her uncle, a warm, affectionate man who seemed to fill the void she had always felt inside. She imagined that her father must have been just like her Zio Lorenzo. Maria Elena was a quiet, shy girl who doted on her energetic father. She was an excellent cook, especially when it came to baking sweets. Magdalena and Marianna had taught Loretta to prepare vegetables and soups and make a variety of pastas, but sweets, other than fruit and *biscotti*, were rare in their home.

"My father has a fondness for sweets," said Maria Elena. "I always make a sweet bread or cake each week for him, when we have the flour and sugar to spare. Of course, I have to hide some from Tomaso, or he'll eat it all," she laughed.

"Did you love your mother very much?" asked Loretta. "I don't remember mine too well."

"Yes, I loved my mother very much, and I remember your mother and father very well. She was nice to me and he was a very kind man," said Maria Elena. "Once he made me a beautiful pair of shoes. They were so soft and comfortable, I would keep them under my pillow for fear they might be stolen by a thief in the night." She laughed.

"Really? Was my father handsome?"

"Oh, yes! He had black hair and black, piercing eyes. He always had a nice smile under his thick black moustache," said Maria Elena. "I remember his hands. Strong, yet with long fingers that seemed stained, maybe from the shoes he made." She paused for a moment before continuing. "My mother told me once that after my father was wounded in the war, your father sent a beautiful letter to us. He told her to take courage that all would be well, and that my father would come home to us soon. Do you know that we received that letter after we received the news that your father had been killed? My mother cried when she found out, and she saved that letter for years."

"Do you still have it?" asked Loretta. "Can I see it?"

"No, I'm sorry. It's lost. When my mother died..." said Maria Elena, but she couldn't finish her sentence, and started to cry.

Hugging her, Loretta said, "That's okay. I have the letter in my heart now. I don't need to see it. Thank you for telling me."

"You have a good heart, just like your father," said Maria Elena as she kissed Loretta's cheeks.

CHAPTER 47

Dina's Return—October 1931

The chapel has a cold, damp feeling to it today, thought Dina. It was still early, but she knew she only had a few more minutes to pray before the other sisters, postulants, and novitiates would be in for morning vespers. Dina had been assigned to open the chapel, light the candles, and prepare the altar. A cold shiver passed through her, and a sense of melancholy seemed to engulf her.

"Ah, here you are! Good morning, Dina," said Sister Theresa, the Sister Superior for Postulants.

"Mother Marguerita wishes to see you at the school right after vespers."

"Yes, Sister. Is anything wrong?" asked Dina.

"Well, she will need to speak with you. I can't say anything more," replied the nun.

After vespers, Dina walked quickly to the Mother Superior's office at the school. She hesitated at the door before knocking. *What if my mother has returned for me? Will they make me leave? Perhaps she has died, that's why I feel the day is so ominous.*

"Dina? Are you going in to see Mother Superior? Or are you just guarding the door?" asked Sister Celeste.

Dina nodded to the old nun, turned, and knocked on the heavy door.

"Come in," said Mother Superior. "Dina, thank you for coming so promptly. Please sit down. I hear you are doing very well, Dina, and are only two years away from joining our Order. Are you happy, my child?"

"Yes, Mother, I'm happy. I want to be a good nun and pray and work very hard toward that day."

"Well, my child, you may need to set your plans aside for a while. I received news that your Aunt Marianna has died, and you are needed to help take care of your sister, Loretta. Your Aunt Magdalena writes that she is not able to work as much as she once did, and along with their financial problems, your sister, Loretta, needs some guidance and, well, a big sister to watch over her for a few years."

Dina was stunned for a few moments. "Of course, Mother, I would love to see my sister Loretta and my aunt again. I was a very small child when I last visited my aunts. They were kind to care for my sister all these years. Perhaps it's a sin, but I envied Loretta at times," said Dina. "But Mother, I won't be able to leave Loretta for quite a few years—not until she marries—or the slight possibility that our mother may still come and bring her to America. Could I return to the convent then?"

"Yes, if that is still what you want," said Mother Marguerita. "This may be a blessing for you. You will be reunited with your sister, your aunt, and I understand you have other family in the town—your Uncle Lorenzo and his family. He offered to take your sister, but your Aunt Magdalena needs you, I think. It is best you go and assist her in her late years."

"Yes, Mother, I'll go, but how?" asked Dina.

"It's all arranged. Your uncle and his son are coming for you. They should be here by the end of next week. This should give you time to pack and say your good-byes to your friends and teachers," said Mother Superior. Rising from her desk, the nun stood over Dina, and taking her hands, lifted her out of the chair. Embracing Dina, she said, "Go with God, Dina. Always put your trust in Him. He knows where you are meant to be, and what is your destiny. Follow your heart and put your faith in Him, my child."

Dina sat in her tiny cubicle that night and thought about her sister, Loretta, who was three when they were parted—now she was fourteen. With Zia Marianna dead and Zia Magdalena growing old, Loretta still needed a mother—or at least a big sister.

When Zio Lorenzo and Cousin Tomaso arrived, Dina was sitting in the same courtyard where her mother had left her. Sister Lauria, her first friend and dearest mentor, sat with her, and they shared stories of their time together.

"I will miss you, Dina. I'm happy that you will get reacquainted with your family, especially your little sister. Having a family is so important, and you deserve to feel their love again. If it is meant to be, you will return to us. Our destiny is in God's hands. Just trust Him and you will be happy. I believe that," said the nun. "Were you able to say good-bye to all your friends and the sisters?"

"Yes, Sister. I had to write Domenica in Bologna, and she said she will pray that I return soon and we will take our vows together," said Dina. "I also wrote my brother, and he's happy that I will be reunited with my sister and all the other family members."

"Oh, look," said Sister Lauria, "there are two men at the gate now." She rose to open the gate and show the men into the garden.

Lorenzo spoke first. "Dina, I would know you anywhere. You look just like your mother when she married your father." He opened his arms to embrace her, but then hesitated, knowing she had been brought up by nuns and was preparing to enter the convent as well. Lorenzo looked at his niece, smiled, and then lifted her hands to his lips and lightly kissed them. With tears in his eyes, he said, "We have missed you, my dear child. Let us go home now to your sister."

Tomaso was anxiously shifting from side to side, as he awkwardly twisted his hat in his hands. Being around nuns made him nervous. Those long black dresses and the stiff white headdresses and bibs they wore made him uneasy. He felt they could look right through him and gave him the evil eye.

"Tomaso, why are you standing there? Come and say hello to your cousin, Dina," said Lorenzo.

Tomaso smiled weakly, bowed his head several times, and squeaked out, "Hello."

"My son is usually a more intelligent conversationalist, especially with women, than he seems to be able to demonstrate today. My dear, he must be overwhelmed by your beauty."

Dina and Sister Lauria laughed.

"We will have a lot to talk about on the way home. Now, Tomaso, put that wretched hat on your head and take Dina's bag so we can get home tonight."

At the gate, Dina turned to say her last good-byes to Sister Lauria. The nun had tears in her eyes as she gently kissed Dina's cheeks.

"Go with God, Dina."

"Thank you, Sister, for always being there for me from my very first day. I hope to see you again. Pray for me," said Dina.

As the cart pulled away, Dina turned to look back at the abbey and school that had been so much a part of her life. Suddenly, the same sadness she had felt when she left her hometown enveloped her. As she had done that day so many years ago in San Rocco, she stared at the retreating buildings and prayed for the day she would return.

CHAPTER 48

Portrait of a Mother — December 1931

Looking outside, Geneva saw the snow falling into heavy drifts as she gently rocked her child, Bonita, who was now seven months old. Her thoughts filled with the memory of her late sister, Anita, and those dark days in August 1929, the weeks before her wedding. She could still recall every detail, and again experienced the mixed emotions of sadness over the loss of her sister, hurt that her mother didn't attend her wedding, and anger that she apparently mattered less to her mother than the children of Caterina's second marriage.

Hugging Bonita as she slowly rocked her, Geneva recalled the scene before Anita's wake, and how her mother had sat for hours in a daze, not moving from her chair next to Anita's bassinette.

"Mama, you must eat," said Geneva. "Please, you'll get ill. We all loved Anita. Please, Mama, Davido, Lorenzo, and Gloria need you. I need you too, Mama. Eat something!"

Umberto came abruptly into the room. Leaning over Caterina, he said "Caterina, it is time to go," He placed his hands under her arms and lifted her from the chair, pulling her from the bassinette.

Caterina looked at him, bent her head, and slowly walked from the bedroom with him.

Umberto had befriended a new businessman from his hometown, the owner of the first Italian funeral parlor in the area. Meeting them at the door, Signor Nepotino whispered words of condolences to the family. Geneva remembered his eyes, so large, dark, and soulful, and thought they were perfect for an undertaker.

"Did you see that man's eyes?" she whispered to her fiancé, Mario. "They must get that way from looking at dead people." Geneva shuddered.

Mario's parents were seated at the rear of the viewing room, and after giving Geneva a quick kiss, Mario left her to join them. He knew he had done the right thing when he caught Umberto's eye and saw the quick nod his future father-in-law gave him. Mario never experienced Umberto's quick angry temper, but Geneva had told him stories of his fiery wrath against his wife and the older children. Geneva confided in him that she always felt that her stepfather and her mother favored the children they had together over their older children.

Caterina still has a pretty face, thought Mario, and his mother had told him she was one of the most generous people in the town. When new countrymen came, she always gave them a large basket of food and later brought them clothes that her own children had outgrown. Umberto and Caterina were not strong churchgoers, but when the church had a special project or festival for one of the saints, they made impressive contributions. Even though Mario was a little fearful of Umberto, Caterina had always been kind to him, but he noticed she was more abrupt with Geneva, Luca, and Lena, who were still at home, than she was with the younger children. She never mentioned Paolo, Dina, or Loretta, who were still in Italy. Geneva had told him about her brother and sisters and how they had been left behind ten years earlier. Geneva cried when she talked about them, and said she often wished she had been left behind too. Life was very stressful in the Fabrizio household, she confessed.

Geneva remembered that the dignity of the wake had been abruptly disturbed by the sound of running feet. Luca, who looked a little disheveled and was adjusting his tie with dirt-stained hands, had arrived late. He received a cold look from Umberto.

Geneva, nervous about being separated from Mario, quickly grabbed Luca's arm and followed her parents to the casket holding Anita. "Oh, dear God, she's dressed like a bride—a baby bride!" she had whispered to Luca.

The red velvet-lined casket was surrounded by small white roses, and Anita rested on a white satin pillow in a box which resembled more a jewel case than a casket. A garland of baby's breath, intertwined with white silk ribbons, crowned her black curly hair. Anita wore a long white silk dress with a white lace overskirt. Her tiny feet were encased in white satin slippers trimmed with small pink rosettes. A nosegay of miniature pink roses and lace rested in her folded hands.

Caterina, eyes downcast as she was led into the room, slowly looked at her youngest child, who appeared to be sleeping peacefully. "Anita, *bella mia*," Caterina whispered as she bent to kiss Anita's cold face. "Anita, Mama is here." Caterina then began to touch the baby, adjusting her nosegay and smoothing her dress.

"No, no, my dear," said Umberto. "Don't disturb her."

"Disturb her? Don't disturb her?" shouted Caterina. "These are my last moments with my baby and you talk of disturbing her."

"Shush, shush, calm yourself," said Umberto firmly. "You are creating a scene."

Caterina tore herself away from Umberto's grasp. She turned to her other children who stood behind her. "Davido, Lorenzo, Ava, Lena, Luca, Berto, Gloria, everyone, you too, Geneva, come now and give Anita a kiss. No, wait, wait. Signor Nepotino, I want photographs of Anita first. Then I want everyone to be photographed with Anita so that they will remember her."

"Caterina, control yourself," Umberto said. "You are becoming hysterical. If you want photographs of Anita, we can arrange it later. For now, we are here to honor Anita and greet our friends who have come out of respect."

"No, please, Umberto, do this for me, please," Caterina cried.

"Come, sit down," said Umberto. "People are waiting to pay their respects."

Caterina crumbled into a chair. She began rocking back and forth as she moaned softly.

Geneva remembered those photographs of Anita that her mother had taken before the burial. Whenever she visited her mother, Caterina would pull them out and, looking at them, speak of Anita and what a precious child she was.

"Why is it you never had photographs taken of me or the other children, Mama?" asked Geneva.

Caterina looked at her. "But you are here, Geneva. Why do I need to have photographs of you? You are here."

"You know, Mama, you have only a few photographs of Paolo, Dina, and Loretta, and you hardly ever look at them," said Geneva bitterly, "much less talk about them or mourn the ten years since we've seen them."

Caterina dropped Anita's pictures on the table, and with a fierce look, smacked Geneva hard across the face.

Geneva was startled from her recollections by the sound of Bonita's cry. "I will never hurt or abandon you, my baby. I promise."

CHAPTER 49

Luca's Trauma—March 1932

"Pull yourself together, Caterina," said Umberto. "This house is falling apart. The children are running around wild. Anita is gone. You have other children to look after. Get out of that chair, fix yourself up, and get on with it —now!"

Slowing lifting herself from the chair, Caterina looked at Umberto. "You have no heart, and if you do, it must be made of stone like the granite you work."

"You-you tell him, Ma!"

Umberto and Caterina turned to see Luca covered with dirt, his bandaged head stained with blood.

"Luca, what happened?" asked Caterina.

"Who did this to you?" Umberto asked.

"Don-don't worry, Ma. It was jus-just a little ac-accident. I lost my ba-ba-balance and fe-fell in the quarries. I'm okay ex-ex-except for a ba-ba-bastard of a headache."

Caterina rushed to Luca and, removing the dirty bandages, began examining his damaged head.

"Were you drunk?" asked Umberto. "You stupid bum! If you drink on the job, you deserve to get hurt," he said unsympathetically.

"Okay, so-so I had a couple of beers. That damn dust gets in your throat an-and you need to wash it down," sputtered Luca.

"Knowing you," said Umberto, "you undoubtedly washed it down with whiskey, too!"

"Umberto, this looks bad," said Caterina as she washed the blood and dirt from Luca's head. "We must call a doctor."

"Tha-tha-that's okay, Ma," said Luca. "I just need to lie dow-down for a wh-while."

"Ah!" Caterina screamed as Luca collapsed at her feet. "He's bleeding again!"

"Stupid, drunken bum!" spat out Umberto. "Leave him there. He'll sleep it off."

"What devil possesses your soul, Umberto? This is your son! Have you no compassion?"

"I have no compassion for stupid drunks," Umberto replied. "All right, I'll go for the doctor, but Luca will pay the bill!"

Caterina ran to the kitchen for a fresh basin of water and more clean dishtowels.

"Luca, please don't die," pleaded Caterina. "There is enough sorrow in this house."

Luca didn't respond. He seemed to be sleeping, but he lay so still and quiet that Caterina began to shiver as she bathed his face and damaged forehead.

When the doctor arrived, he inspected the cleaned wound which was still oozing blood.

"I'll need to stitch that cut, but we won't know if he has any serious damage until he wakes up."

"Doctor," said Caterina, "he had trouble speaking. He was forcing his words and repeating them. Do you think he cracked his brain?"

"He doesn't have a brain to crack!" said Umberto sarcastically. "He talked like a drunk!"

Shaking his head, the doctor replied, "That could be it, or he may have suffered more serious repercussions. He hit his head pretty hard from the looks of it."

Luca recuperated slowly, but Caterina and Umberto noticed a marked difference in his personality. Luca's previous short temper now became violent as he drank more liquor, more often. Trouble seemed to follow him, fights and verbal outbursts for the slightest offenses, which were usually about the permanent stutter he had developed. Luca's inability to read or write was also a sensitive point. He threatened to kill any man who called him stupid. Of course, the man he most wanted to harm was his father, but his respect and affection for Caterina prevented him from doing so.

CHAPTER 50

Sisters—June 1932

Having her big sister, Dina, back with her was exciting for Loretta at first, but the rigors of living together dampened that euphoria.

Dina had a lovely serene face and a serious pragmatic personality that resulted in her appearing older than her twenty-one years. Loretta, at fifteen, was a sharp contrast to her sister. Where Dina was quiet and occasionally solemn, Loretta sparked with vitality and an impish spirit.

Zia Magdalena, who was approaching her eighties, was relieved when Dina returned from the convent to help raise Loretta and support their little family. She beamed with pride at the exceptional talent Dina possessed in her needlework and lace designs.

"Dina," said Zia Magdalena, "Stella Bergozzi was delighted with the altar cloth you made for her husband's memorial Mass. All the neighborhood women went up after the Mass just to look at it. Simply beautiful and such delicate workmanship—I'm so proud of you, my child."

"Did you like the scarves I made for Regina Rosati's dowry?" asked Loretta. "Regina said they were the loveliest she ever saw."

"Of course, my dear," said Zia Magdalena. "They were lovely. You are learning very well and in time may achieve your sister's level of excellence."

"She is not disciplined enough," said Dina. "Loretta is too much a social being. She is always off with her friends, especially Guiliana, instead of concentrating on her sewing or schoolwork, and even less on her housework."

"I am too, disciplined," protested Loretta. "At least I have friends and enjoy life. You're just an old nun and so bossy—do this, do that, don't do this, don't do that. You're more domineering than even Zia Magdalena!"

Loretta immediately regretted her words. She would never intentionally hurt her aunt, whom she loved dearly, almost as much as she had loved Zia Marianna.

"Zia, I'm sorry," said Loretta. "You weren't that domineering."

"Oh, my dear, I was. You were so spirited, I sometimes worried about you. But you know, I wouldn't change one thing about you," said Zia Magdalena with a smile.

"You can be so tactless, Loretta," said Dina after Zia Magdalena retired for her afternoon nap. Loretta started to protest, but Dina interrupted her. "Have you forgotten you have a sewing class to teach this afternoon? You must do better in maintaining discipline with your students."

"My students are only little girls. Fulvia is the oldest and she's nine," said Loretta. "It's easy for you because all your students are older; most are either married or getting married. Besides, they need to concentrate more on lace-making than my children, who are learning simple stitches and knots," protested Loretta.

"No matter," said Dina. "Discipline and order are important for the students and the teacher. By the way, are you keeping your records up to date and accurate?"

"I'm doing the best I can," shouted Loretta as she ran out the door. She almost collided with some of her students who were about to knock on the door. Muttering to herself, Loretta mimicked, "Records. Are they up to date? Are they accurate?"

Dina kept detailed records of everything: income, expenditures, and types of supplies, with copious notes on their quality, quantity, and cost from various merchants. She kept notes on each student and her work. She was very meticulous in all her habits and expected Loretta to follow suit. She and Loretta argued over everything—school, sewing, cooking, and housework. Dina was a perfectionist; Loretta was not that particular, especially about housework, which she hated.

When Loretta became angry or totally frustrated with her sister, she went to her cousin, Maria Elena. Over time, Dina formed a deep friendship with Maria Elena, and when friction developed between the two sisters, Maria Elena's gentle, mature logic usually kept the sisters living in harmony, albeit sometimes a little strained, but working together.

CHAPTER 51

Paolo's First Love—September 1932

"What's your name?" Paolo asked the pretty girl behind the fruit stand. Paolo caught his breath when he looked at her. Her thick dark hair hung loose off her shoulders and down her back. She seemed to blush when he spoke to her, which gave her skin a soft pink glow. Long lashes framed her green eyes, and she had a sweet smile with small even teeth. He noticed that she was petite, but proportioned beautifully.

"Valeria," said the girl. "Our figs are very fresh. See, the dew is still on the fruit."

Paolo smiled. "You've convinced me. I'll take a bag."

"Green or black figs?" asked Valeria.

"Both," smiled Paolo.

Valeria leaned forward and whispered to Paolo, "The blacks are riper if you plan to eat them today. You'll need to wait a day or two for the green ones."

"Maybe I can buy the black figs today and the green ones tomorrow. Will you be here?" he asked.

"Yes, if you're sure you're coming back," teased the girl.

So started their courtship. Paolo and Valeria had to meet discreetly in quiet coffee houses or in empty churches. Camp rules discouraged the men from fraternizing with local girls.

"My comrades know about us and tease me mercilessly," laughed Paolo. "They say I've changed from a diligent military officer to a day-dreaming private, and it's all your fault!"

Valeria laughed, "I'm glad, as long as you're daydreaming about me. Are you as happy as I am, Paolo? I know you make me happier than I've ever been."

"When I'm with you," said Paolo, "nothing matters but us. I look into your beautiful green eyes and I want to burst with joy. I feel all the bitterness and emptiness of my life is washed from me. When I'm with you, I feel complete and alive, really alive, not just marching through life."

"Oh, my sweet, I wish I could take away all the pain and loss you have suffered," said Valeria.

"You have, more than you'll ever know," whispered Paolo as he kissed her. She fit so perfectly in his arms that it was if their bodies had been molded together.

"Remember," said Valeria, "besides me, you still have your sisters who love you. They say time heals all things. One day you can reunite with them. We will be great friends, and I will invite them to dinner every Sunday."

"See, you always know what to say to make me happy," he said. "And what about your family? When will I meet them? Have you told them about us?" ask Paolo.

"No, not yet. My papa is not too fond of soldiers. He was imprisoned by the Germans during the war, and now he hates Mussolini and his soldiers."

"I'm not fond of Il Duce myself, but being in the military makes it unwise to voice any opinions," said Paolo. "Everybody knows he's a braggart and a tyrant and won't last much longer."

Life was sweet for Paolo and Valeria for almost four months. Then their idyllic time ended as quickly as it started.

"It doesn't matter that I'm being sent to Africa," said Paolo. "I'll be back. Please just promise you'll write and wait for me. Promise," he pleaded.

Weeping, Valeria said, "I can't. Someone saw us together, and my father has forbidden me to see you again. He's the one who reported you to the commander and insisted they transfer you. He still has some friends among the military. Besides, he has arranged a marriage for me, and my mother said I must obey him or he will disown me. Oh, Paolo, I'm so sorry. I will always love you but what can I do?" moaned Valeria.

"Nothing, my sweet, nothing," Paolo said sadly. He took Valeria in his arms for the last time and kissed her with every fiber of his heart and soul.

CHAPTER 52

Seeds of Discontent—October 1932

"Geneva, this feud with your mother is ridiculous," said Mario. "Everyone talks about what a generous woman your mother is—always helping people who are out of work, bringing them food and clothes for their children."

"Oh yes, my mother, who is a saint outside the house to her neighbors and friends," retorted Geneva. "They don't know how cruel she can be to her own flesh and blood."

Mario looked at his young wife with her stylishly curled honey blond hair and her slim, graceful figure. He thought she was more beautiful than the day he married her. Bonita, now two, looked like her and had the same stubborn streak. "Look, I have to go to work. I can't argue with you anymore about this problem," said Mario. "If I don't leave now, I'll be late and lose my job!"

"Go ahead, go! You never have time to talk with me. Your job, your mother, your problems are always more important than me or Bonita," said Geneva.

"You know that's not true," said Mario. "And why do you always bring up my mother? At least I get along with her."

"Oh, yes, mama and little sonny boy get along famously—always stopping at her house when you should be home with me."

"She's always making something special for me. How can I refuse to go over there? My father is sick, you know. She needs help getting things done, and my brothers live too far away to help. Besides, they're both out of work."

"What about when I cook something special and wait for you?" said Geneva.

"You, cook? Believe me, Geneva, there's nothing special about your cooking! I can't believe you never learned. Your mother is a great cook. Of course, we rarely eat there anymore, but whose fault is that?"

"Don't you dare criticize me or compare me to my mother! Sometimes I hate her! If you had any feelings for me..."

"Got to go, bye!" replied Mario as he grabbed his coat and ran out the door.

"And I hate you, too, sometimes for never understanding," shouted Geneva to the closed door.

Later that day, Geneva was surprised to see Ava and her two children at the door. "How well you look, Ava!" gushed Geneva. "Oh, Susie is getting so big, and look at this beautiful baby! Hello, Gina."

"I hope you're not too busy," said Ava. "I just had to get out of the house, and I wasn't up to facing Ma today. Sal's out of work, and he's driving me crazy hanging around the house."

"Thank God, Mario still has a job, but his hours have been cut," said Geneva. "Hopefully the country will straighten out again and there'll be jobs for everyone. So many people out of work. It's scary. But about Mama, I understand completely," said Geneva. "I'm never too busy for a visit. I'll make some coffee and I have some *biscotti* that Mario's mother made."

"How are Mario's parents?" asked Ava.

"Please, I'd rather not discuss them either, especially his domineering mother."

"As bad as that?" said Ava. "Fortunately, I have only Ma to contend with. The last time I saw her, she said I was getting too fat and that girls were nice, but it was better to have boys. 'Boys are stronger for this life,' to quote her."

"Women need to be stronger than men to survive them," said Geneva.

"Well, I don't think Ma will survive my father," said Ava. "I remember all the beatings he gave her as well as us."

"Do you think he still hits her?" asked Geneva

"I don't see them very often, but when I do, Ma usually has a bruise or a swollen lip. I think Luca takes on the old man, and Luca's so crazy now, I think Pa is a little afraid of him."

"Lorenzo and Davido are the crown princes in that home," said Geneva. "Even Gloria is overlooked at times. She's such a sweet, timid child. I think she just stays low and out of the way."

"No wonder, in that madhouse with Pa and our half-brothers always fighting. Ma sticks up for them, though," said Ava. "I feel bad for Lena. She's treated like a maid. She's dying to meet someone and get married, just to get out of there."

"I'm sorry for Lena, too," said Geneva. "I wish we were closer, but I think she resents me."

"Well, Geneva, you're married, you're a mother, you're pretty, and you're out of there. Why wouldn't she resent you?" said Ava.

CHAPTER 53

An Understanding — August 1933

Guiliana knocked on the door of Zia Magdalena's house. When the door opened, Guiliana sighed, dropped her head, and finally said, "Can I talk to Loretta, please?"

"She's busy doing her work right now, but come in for a minute," said Dina. "Why are you all dressed up, Guiliana? Is today your saint's day?"

"No, my saint's day is June 19, the feast of Santa Guiliana Falconieri of Florence. I'm on my way to Santo Rocco's Festival, and my father said I could ask Loretta to come with us."

"Well, that's kind of your father, but Loretta is too busy today," said Dina.

"I'm not too busy," said Loretta as she came into the room.

"Loretta, you know we have several orders for tablecloths that must be done by the end of the month," said Dina. "Embroidering and cutting the designs will take weeks. We haven't time for frivolous festivals."

"Work and pray, that's all you want to do," said Loretta heatedly. "My best friend and her family have invited me and I want to go!"

"I'm sorry..."

"No, you're not sorry," said Loretta. "You never have fun, and you don't want me to have any either. Work, work, work is fine for you, my sister the nun, but not for me! Wait here Guiliana, and I'll change."

Not wanting to be in the middle of another battle of wills between the two sisters, Guiliana said, "I'll wait near the church and meet you there."

"Don't wait too long," said Dina as she closed the door.

The bickering continued until Zia Magdalena came home from her shopping. She listened to the exchange for a moment and then said, "Stop this arguing, now! Dina, you are too strict with the girl. And Loretta, you must speak more respectfully to your sister," said Magdalena. "All right Loretta, you may go to the festival, but be home before dark and stay close to Guiliana and her parents. Understand?"

"Yes, Zia! Oh, thank you, Zia."

"Dina, I will help you meet your work schedule," said Magdalena. "My hands are not very strong, but I will pace myself and the tablecloths will be ready in time."

"You spoil her too much, Zia," said Dina.

Magdalena smiled. "That's what I used to say to Marianna. She is young, Dina. Don't pull the rope too tight or it will break, and you will lose your sister. Loretta is not as disciplined as you or me. She is high-spirited," said Magdalena, "but a good worker. Let her do what she is good at; she likes to cook but hates to clean, so you clean and let her cook. Not all the time, but enough to keep her from getting too discouraged. She enjoys sewing; you prefer design and cutting. Do that and let her sew. She is an excellent seamstress and knits very well too. You, my child, are an excellent designer as well as seamstress and manager of the work," said Magdalena. "Let Loretta do what she does best and your skills will complement the work."

Loretta returned to the room and said, "Dina, don't be mad at me. I'll work extra hard tomorrow, I promise."

Reflecting on her aunt's words, Dina said, "You look very nice, Loretta. The work can wait until tomorrow. Have a good time."

Loretta embraced her sister. "Let's always be friends, Dina. I never thanked you for leaving the convent to come and stay with us. I know you want to be a nun and I will pray that you get your wish, but I hope you change your mind. Is that okay to say?"

Dina smiled and embraced her sister. "All things are destiny and in the hands of God. It's okay to ask God for whatever we feel will make us and others happy."

CHAPTER 54

News from Ethiopia—September 1933

Dear Dina, Loretta, and Zia Magdalena,

My tour of duty in Ethiopia is over, and I will be sent home and stationed in Rome for at least six months, or until they send me back to Ethiopia.

The wonderful news is that I will have two weeks leave, and I plan to come there for a visit. Don't worry about where to put me. I'll sleep on the floor. After almost ten years in the army, I could sleep anywhere, on anything.

Did I tell you I made captain? You needn't salute me when we meet, though. (A joke!)

I'm so excited about seeing you and also Zio Lorenzo, Maria Elena, and Tomaso. What I've wanted to do for a long time is go back to San Rocco, our hometown, and see Signor Cardello, our beloved Graciella, and any other friends and neighbors who might remember us. Since Graciella can't write, I've tried to learn news of her and her family through Signor Cardello. Did you know that her mother died? Her son is in the army and her daughter is now married. Graciella's husband contracted a fever a few years back and has been an invalid. He has a bad heart, and can only work a few hours a day before tiring out. Fortunately, he has Graciella, who takes excellent care of him, according to Signor Cardello. Remember how wonderful she was to all of us, especially to Mama? I hope we find her well. Please say you want to come with me. It will be more meaningful if we all go together. I've been saving my pay, so don't worry about money.

Do you remember my telling you about Valeria? She wrote me several times while I was in Ethiopia. I don't know how she got the letters past her father, but she did. Valeria married the man her father wanted for her. She said he's kind to her and she's expecting a child. I want so much to see her, but know that would be unfair to her and too painful for me to leave her again. I wish I had the courage to marry her at the time, but I had nothing to offer her—no home, no money, and the constant absences of a soldier's life. What woman could resist that? Valeria deserved everything a good life could offer. I'll never forget her and hope she's happy.

Do you remember my friend, Marco? Well, he's out of the army now and getting married next week. I'm going to be a witness along with his fiancée's sister. Maybe there's hope for me, yet.

Oh, I almost forgot the most important news. I met our cousins, Antonio and Dante, in Ethiopia. Isn't that amazing! Zia Vittoria is doing well and her other sons have served their military duty and are now working on the farm with Zio Pietro. Remember how we begged Mama to move to the farm after Papa died? I sometimes wonder what our lives would be like if she did; at least we might have stayed together.

With affection and anticipation,

Paolo

CHAPTER 55

Money is Power—September 1933

Lena was finally getting married. Caterina offered to make her wedding dress, but Lena objected.

"Gee, Ma, it's much more stylish to wear a suit and 'drop-dead' hat with a face veil than a boring old wedding gown."

"'Drop dead hat?' What is that?" asked Caterina. "Young people today have no respect for traditions. Who wants to wear a hat that will make people drop dead?"

"Gosh, people don't really drop dead, it's an expression," said Lena. "Like it's going to really wow them."

"Wow them?" Caterina shook her head. "I don't understand you. What's a 'wow them'?"

"Forget it, Ma. Just tell Pa I need some money to buy an outfit and a lot of new clothes."

Caterina struck her hand to her head. "Now I know you are crazy," she said. "Your father will tell me that there's a Depression. That he has no money. You want the drop dead hat, you ask him."

"Please, Ma," said Lena. "He'll give you money. Just don't tell him what it's for. Okay?"

"We'll see. I don't know," said Caterina, shaking her head again.

"Thanks, Ma," said Lena. "If anyone can get money out of the old man, you can."

Over the next few weeks, Caterina began finding excuses why she needed funds: Gloria dropped the eggs and she had to buy some more; prices at the butcher shop had gone up; many of her staples of flour, sugar, and olive oil had run out; and so on. Begrudgingly, and always with a lecture about the lack of money and the Depression, Umberto gave her a few extra dollars. Caterina would put the money in an old olive oil can she had washed and hidden in the basement. Weeks passed, and she continued to add a few coins or a dollar. Soon the can became heavy and she prided herself on her cleverness. Her satisfaction was short-lived, however.

One evening, Umberto was tinkering in the basement sharpening his tools when he opened a cabinet and, rummaging through it, noticed the olive oil can. "That woman forgets what she buys," he said as he took the can off the shelf. At first he was perplexed, but slowly his expression changed to anger. He slowly wiped his hands of the mechanical grease used to clean the tools, and picking up the olive oil can, he climbed the stairs. The house was quiet. The younger boys had gone off to bed, and Gloria, their eight year old, was sitting on the sofa talking to her doll. Umberto found Caterina in the kitchen making bread for the next day's meal. Her back was to him.

"Aaah," she screamed as the olive oil can hit her hard between the shoulder blades.

"I don't give you enough? You have to steal from me, you ungrateful bitch!" shouted Umberto.

Caterina's pain was so intense she was unable to reply. Before she could explain, Umberto's iron grip fastened around her neck and slammed her against the icebox.

"Please, Umberto, please stop!" Caterina cried. "I can explain."

"What can you explain?" he said as he grabbed the front of her apron and threw her across the room. "That you rob me and tell me lies?"

Caterina grabbed hold of the sink to break her fall.

"Mama! Mama! What's happening?" screamed Gloria, "Stop, Papa! Stop!"

"Gloria, go to your room, now!" shouted Umberto. "Now, I said!"

Gloria, frightened by her father's anger, ran to her room, hid in the small closet, and covered her ears.

Caterina took the diversion with Gloria as an opportunity to run away. She ran into the bedroom, and as she had years earlier, when she first encountered Umberto's violent passion, bolted the door and secured it with a chair. Within seconds, the door frame cracked under Umberto's swift kick. He continued to hammer away at the door with his foot until it smashed open. Umberto's beatings were not rare, but only once before had she felt this much terror.

"You will never lock a door in my house against me," Umberto shouted. "Do you understand me, Caterina?"

Caterina, too frightened to speak, nodded her head. The cries of her young sons reached her as she forced herself to say, "I'm sorry, Umberto. Please let me explain."

As she cowered against the large oak dresser in their room, Umberto calmly sat on the edge of the bed and said, "Go ahead, explain."

Taking a deep breath, Caterina said, "I was trying to help Lena buy a wedding suit and a trousseau. She was afraid to ask you, and … I was too…" Caterina whispered hoarsely.

"So you preferred to steal from me instead of asking me. Is that it, Caterina?"

"I thought you would think it extravagant. I was only trying to help your daughter!" Caterina screamed.

"You don't even worry about your own children, why concern your-self with mine?" he said.

Caterina picked up the scissors from the dresser and lunged at him. "How can you say that?" she screamed between clenched teeth. "I have asked you for years, 'when will my children be able to come,' and you give me excuses."

Umberto caught her wrist and twisted it until she dropped the scissors. "Caterina, I have told you repeatedly they have stopped immigration from Italy. Don't I send money to support your children and your aunts, too? I will not open this discussion again. Do you hear me?" he said as he pushed her away. "Worry about yourself, Caterina. You have grown fat on my generosity. If I had left you in Italy, you and your children would have starved. You would have gone begging to your sister and brother-in-law. Now you are like a patroness to the poor. With my money, you can be good to yourself, the children, and all those people you like to impress," said Umberto with a smirk. "The watch words are 'badare ai fatti propri'—mind your own business."

During the night, Caterina turned her head and looked at him lying beside her. Her entire body ached. How can you hate someone one minute and let them possess you another, she wondered. Possess, that was the word, she thought. She used to tell herself that he might love her, but that was a delusion. What she and Umberto had was an arrangement.

CHAPTER 56

Oh Brother, My Brother—October 1933

This was the day Paolo was arriving. Excited, Loretta slipped out the door while Dina and Zia Magdalena were changing bed linens and polishing their few ancient pieces of furniture. The day before and all through the night, they had been cooking special sauces, making pastas, soups, and baking bread. Loretta had the job of promising bread to Signora Coletti if she would give them some dried peaches and figs. Loretta ran down the wide steps to the street and past the church and school. The old men who were sitting near the post office and tobacconist waved at her as she ran by.

One shouted, "*Piano, piano*—slowly, slowly," but Loretta just waved back and laughed. When she ran by the water fountain, the women filling their jugs tried to ask her where she was going. Loretta skidded around them, almost bumping into Signora Sortini who steadied the large earthen jug on her head and shouted after Loretta, "You break my new jug, you crazy girl, I'll break your head!"

There, ahead of her was her destination—the Corso Gallio Arch. She would climb to the top and from that vantage point would see Paolo coming up the mountain road.

"Loretta, where are you?" asked Dina. "Look at that, Zia, she left the fruit on the table and escaped again. That girl lacks discipline. I'd love to take her back to the convent with me and tame that wild spirit of hers."

"Oh, leave her alone," said Zia Magdalena. "She's undoubtedly gone to meet Paolo."

"Well, there is so much to do here, and she barely remembers him," said Dina. "Paolo and I were always the best of friends. I should be the first to welcome him."

"My child," said Zia Magdalena, "you sound jealous and possessive. Don't forget that you had time with your brother when you were young. Then you were fortunate enough to find each other again when you were in the orphanages. You were even able to correspond through the years. Loretta is just now getting the opportunity to see and know her brother. Be happy you will all be together again for even this short time."

Dina lowered her head and said, "I'm sorry. I was a little jealous. I remember how much Paolo loved Loretta when she was a baby. After Papa died, she was the only one who could make Paolo laugh with all her antics and funny faces. She made all of us laugh, except Mama, who was angry and frustrated with being left alone with four children. Even Loretta was afraid of her. She would always hide when Mama came into the room. Mama had changed so much after Papa died. Paolo always made a game of Loretta's hiding, and she would come out from under the bed or from behind a chair laughing at his playfulness. In some ways, Loretta kept all of us from total despair. She was so lively she cheered us up and made us put Papa's death and Mama's anger aside for a few moments."

Loretta sat patiently, but it was windy and cold on top of the arch. Several people passed below and cautioned her to come down before she fell. Just as the sun had peaked in the sky, she saw him. Yes, yes, she thought, it's a man coming up the mountain road. Loretta slowly climbed down, but it was more difficult coming down from the massive arch than going up. She scraped her hands and legs on the rough stones frantically trying to get down before the man passed her. Breathless, she ran to meet the man and then stopped to wait for him.

"Hello…no, I'm sorry you're not him," said Loretta.

"Well, I'm disappointed. Who were you expecting?" asked the man.

"My brother, but he's a soldier and very tall and strongly built," said Loretta. "He's very handsome, too." Then thinking about what she said, "Oh, I'm sorry. You're very nice looking. I didn't mean to say you weren't."

The man laughed. "Thank you, if that's a compliment, but not quite the Roman gladiator you were expecting, huh?" With that, he dropped his traveling bag and put his arms around Loretta, picking her up and twirling her.

"Put me down, you idiot, or my brother will beat you!" said Loretta.

The man lowered her to the ground, but his arms still encircled her. "Loretta, it just had to be you," Paolo said. "Now I believe all those funny stories about you. Besides, you look just like Papa." His eyes misted.

"Paolo, can it really be you? Why aren't you in uniform? How was I to know? Oh, stupid me, now I see that you resemble Dina, except you hair's lighter and you're probably nicer," she said with a laugh. "You both have nice fair skin, while I must have been left in the sun too long. No wonder she thinks you're only her brother."

"Ha, you should have seen me last month," said Paolo, "I looked like a native of Ethiopia."

Loretta started jumping up and down, kissing Paolo's face and squeezing her arms around his neck.

Paolo laughed. "Don't tell me that now I pass inspection? A few minutes ago, I didn't quite muster up for my baby sister."

"I said I was sorry," said Loretta. "Well, honestly, I thought you'd be bigger. I mean…well, you know, like Mussolini, but very, very handsome."

"Please," said Paolo, "one Il Duce is more than enough for this country."

"Don't you like him? Everybody says he makes the trains run on time and he's building a beautiful stadium in Rome."

"Only to glorify himself, my little sister," said Paolo. "Come on, let's talk about you and not Mussolini."

Loretta looked at this man of medium build and height. His complexion was still very tan, and his hair had the color of sun-bleached almonds. His eyes were a deep brown, and even if he wasn't a Roman gladiator, Loretta mused, he certainly had a Roman nose.

After dinner that night, while smoking a cigarette, Paolo looked at Dina. She looked like their mother. Her thick, black hair tightly pulled back into a chignon, her pretty dark eyes, and her soft complexion, which was lighter than their mother's olive skin, brought Caterina's face to mind. Caterina, however, was not as serious or pensive or soft-spoken as Dina. He remembered his mother as passionate, lively, and quick. Dina was so methodical and introspective that it was hard to understand her at times.

Their reunion was joyous and tearful. Dina experienced it as a catharsis. She had not realized how much anger and loneliness had welled up inside her. Seeing Paolo again was a happy release of all the bitterness she carried for her mother, for her life, and for all her losses. Her need to control her life, to be meticulous about even the smallest things, stemmed from this fear of releasing the pent-up anger she felt. Her trust in God helped to ease the burdens of hurt and desolation. The nuns said that one could only adore God, but Dina in her heart also adored Paolo. He was her blood, her friend, and her hope.

"Oh, I've missed you Paolo," Dina said as she squeezed his hand.

He looked at her, kissed her forehead, and felt the sadness expressed in her eyes. *How fragile and sensitive is our Dina,* he thought. *Loretta, on the other hand, has my mother's spirited nature and olive complexion, but looks like my father with her large, vivid dark eyes and thick eyebrows.* Her hair was a deep chestnut brown, and she wore it loose around her face. At sixteen, she was slender, but had a womanly figure which reminded him of Valeria. Dina, taller than Loretta, was thin and older-looking than her twenty-two years. Thinking of his sisters brought to mind Geneva—the pretty little sprite of their childhood, now a mother. *How had the years treated her? Had she become the American princess she dreamed of?*

CHAPTER 57

Going Home Again—October 1933

During the first week of Paolo's leave, many of his neighbors from San Lorenzo came by to see him. A few older women remembered his visit as a young boy when he and his sisters, Dina and Geneva, had accompanied their mother and father. Caterina had been pregnant then with Loretta, and Antonio was on a brief leave from the war. Paolo thought how strange that both he and his father would return to Caterina's hometown of San Lorenzo while on military leave.

"You won't remember me," said a woman, whose name Paolo did forget, "but I remember you."

"Oh, yes," chimed in another woman. "Remember we called you 'caporosso' because you had such bright red hair."

"Like a candle flame," said the first woman.

Finally, the local townspeople satisfied their interest in visiting him, and Paolo was able to plan their trip back home to San Rocco. Zio Lorenzo and his family planned to accompany them. Only Zia Magdalena refused to go.

"I'm too old to go climbing up and down those mountains," she protested. "I can barely make the many stairs we have in my own village. You all go," she said, "I'll be fine."

After much debate and Maria Elena's offering to remain behind, they decided to leave Zia Magdalena in the care of her neighbor and friend, Signora Coletti.

The morning of their departure, Loretta heard several loud banging noises and opened the door to investigate. There was Zio Lorenzo sitting in a dusty, dented truck that sputtered loudly.

"Where did you get it? Are we all going in that truck? Can I sit in the front?" Loretta was full of excitement and questions.

"My child, today we travel first class!" said Zio Lorenzo. "My friend loaned me this magnificent truck and we are returning to San Rocco in style," he said, bowing to her.

"If you please, Papa," said Tomaso, who was already sitting in the front seat, "this truck is old and dirty. I doubt we'll make it to San Rocco."

"No matter," said Zio Lorenzo, "you have two mechanical geniuses, by way of Paolo and myself, to fix the truck if it breaks down."

Everyone laughed as they climbed into the back of the truck. Zia Magdalena gave them two large baskets of food, a jug of water, and another of wine. She insisted they also take several blankets in case it turned cold.

"Cold!" said Paolo. "Zia, it's late October. The weather is perfect!" But he kissed her on her cheeks and took the blankets with a smile.

The truck sputtered frequently and occasionally stalled, but everyone laughed and took it in stride. As they approached the road which led to town, Dina shouted, "Stop! Stop!" The truck stopped with such force, everyone was jostled.

"What is it, my child?" Lorenzo jumped out of the truck.

"Look, you can see it." Dina pointed up the mountainside.

Paolo helped Dina and Loretta out of the truck. They looked at San Rocco—their beloved hometown. "It's just as I remember it," said Dina in a hushed tone. "Just like the day we left."

San Rocco was a smaller town than San Lorenzo. While San Rocco's village of ancient houses leaned on the slopes of the Apennines, nestled among cliffs, San Lorenzo lay further down in the valley and enjoyed better vegetation for gardening and livestock. Both towns offered a labyrinth of stone distinguished by winding, tiny, narrow streets in covered passages of small squares. The early medieval design had provided both defense and shelter to the inhabitants. Their view was like a postcard. Older homes with red tiled roofs framed the entry into the town. Further up the mountain, the houses seemed to have fewer red roofs and had grey stone exteriors with protruding balconies and multiple green-screened windows. A few clotheslines could be seen here and there. Framing the town was a majestic mountain, green in spots with trees and vineyards, and then barren as your eyes trailed off into the distant mountain range. Silhouetted against the mountain, at the top of the town, was the church, gleaming white with high arches, a dome, and a tower.

"Let's go! Hurry!" said Dina.

Paolo lifted the women back into the truck and jumped in, banging the roof of the cab to signal Zio Lorenzo to go.

CHAPTER 58

Return to San Rocco—October 1933

"Can we go to the church first?" asked Dina. "We should thank God for this return."

"Why can't we thank Him later?" asked Loretta. "He's not going anywhere, and I want to see everything."

Paolo laughed. "It might make sense to go to the church first, since it's at the end of the town. Then we can work our way back and see people and places along the way."

"Leave it to a military man to have a plan," said Zio Lorenzo. With that, Tomaso stood erect and, arm extended before him, began marching back to the truck.

"*Stupido,*" said Lorenzo, but he laughed. Nothing was going to spoil this perfect day.

"I always remembered this church as being big," said Dina. "But it's not as large as our church at the convent." Inside the sanctuary was a nave with the venerated statue of Santo Rocco lying under a vaulted ceiling decorated with plastered friezes, figurines, and gilding. The entire group of them, even Tomaso, took turns lighting candles and kneeling in front of the altar to pray. One by one, except for Dina, stopped at the special side altar for the Blessed Mother and lit more candles in prayer.

"How do you get away with that in the convent?" Paolo asked Dina.

"Get away with what?" she asked.

"Not praying to the Blessed Mother," he replied.

"I do pray to her, but today, here, I don't want to think of our own mother, and I'm not praying for her either," she said.

"Nuns must pray for everyone," said Paolo. "Are you sure you want that life?"

"Yes, I'm sure," said Dina, "but I hope that the three of us never lose each other again."

As they were leaving the church, they heard someone call, "Wait! Wait!" Turning around, they saw Padre Alberto rushing toward them. "Is it really the Leonardi family? Paolo, my boy! Dina—and this must be the baby!"

Paolo embraced the old priest who appeared smaller, thinner, and was now bent with age. "Yes, Padre, this is Loretta—not a baby anymore, as you can see."

They all embraced and kissed. Dina said, "I can't believe you're still here, Padre."

"Well, I've been waiting for the Holy Father to write me and tell me he needs me in Rome, but so far, no letter."

They all laughed. Paolo didn't remember the old priest having a sense of humor. He only remembered the day the priest told them their father had been killed in the war.

"Father, please," said Dina, "there's someone we must see. Is Graciella still here?"

"My child, of course Graciella is still here. Come, we will go to her house."

"We must see Signor Cardello, too," said Paolo. "He has always been kind to us."

"Signor Cardello has been very ill," said the priest. "He lost his wife and son. His son was always sickly—bad lungs. When he died at only twenty-two, Signora Cardello went crazy. She stopped eating, cried constantly, and began muttering to herself. One day she fell from their balcony and died within a few hours," said the priest, crossing himself. "I believe that Signor Cardello's body could not bear the strain. He suffered a stroke after their deaths.

Since Graciella's house was nearby, they decided to see her first.

Graciella had aged considerably. Her hair was streaked with grey, and many of her teeth were missing—probably from malnutrition. She had a habit of covering her mouth with her hand when speaking. The reunion with Graciella left them emotionally spent. They loved this generous woman who had helped care for them when their father died and their mother was lost in grief and despair.

"How is your mother?" Graciella asked tearfully. "Why didn't she come back with you? Is she ill? How is your sister, Geneva?" Wiping her eyes, she continued, "It was so painful to see her leave for America and to lose all of you. You were like my own children. But thanks be to God, you have come back to see your old friend. I have missed you all and prayed for you every day." The girls cried. Even Zio Lorenzo had to leave the room, with Tomaso following him.

"Our mother is still in America and we are still here," said Paolo in a choked voice. Clearing his throat, he continued. "Signor Cardello has been our only contact with her and her new family."

"My God! Can this be true?" said Graciella. "You have not seen your mother for, what, thirteen years! Who has been taking care of you?"

"Well, you remember that I went to a military school, an orphanage really, near Rome," said Paolo. "Dina was placed in a convent school in Naples. Loretta was raised by my mother's aunts in San Lorenzo. Dina and Loretta are living in San Lorenzo now. Our mother took Geneva to America with her."

Graciella covered her face with her hands and began to cry. Paolo put his hand on her shoulder in an attempt to console her. The room became quiet. Everyone fell into their own thoughts.

Finally, it was time to say good-bye again. Graciella covered each one of them with kisses and hugs. Some old emotional pull made them want to stay together, but Graciella had her own family to care for, and they needed to part. Dina and Loretta promised to try to get back to San Rocco again.

Traveling to the outskirts of the town, Paolo found Signor Cardello's house. He knocked on the door. After several minutes, a small woman dressed in the local costume of a bygone era opened the door. She wore a white flat-top hat covered in white cotton lace that covered her grey hair on three sides. Her dress was black, and covered by a white apron embroidered with various designs and flowers all in white. She had heavy black stockings and sturdy black boots that were well worn. Paolo asked for Signor Cardello and was told that he was not up for company and to return another day.

As she was closing the door, Paolo shouted, "Signor Cardello, it's me, Paolo. Please, can we see you? It's Paolo!"

The old woman, startled, stared at him. Then Paolo heard a shuffling noise behind her and a hand pulled the woman away from the door.

"Paolo, can it really be you, my son?" said Signor Cardello. "You are so tall, and look how strong and healthy you are. Come in, come in, my boy."

Paolo noticed that one side of Signor Cardello's mouth was paralyzed. He sat on a special chair with wheels and support bars to keep him from falling out.

As Paolo entered the house, Signor Cardello looked out the door and asked, "Who are these people? Are they with you?"

"Yes, but we don't want to tire you. I just had to see you if you're up to a short visit."

"Come in, come in," said Cardello.

The old man grabbed Paolo's hand and tears flowed from his aged eyes. "I can't tell you how delighted I am to see you, my boy, and you, Dina and Loretta. All of you, so kind to come to see me," Cardello said as he reached for Zio Lorenzo's hand and nodded to Maria Elena and Tomaso.

"What beautiful young women you are, and such a handsome young man," he said to Tomaso. "Oh, it pleases me so much that you have come to see me. Sadly, I haven't heard from your mother and stepfather for a while. Things are very bad in the world today—no money, no jobs. Thank God you are in the military and Dina is in the convent. Only Loretta and your Aunt Magdalena I worry about, because they must be struggling to live." Leading the group into the house, Cardello said, "Come in. Sit. Tell me your news."

Loretta looked around the main room, which was graced with several pieces of dark, ornate furniture. Dina and Maria Elena were shown to a faded settee while Loretta was directed to a matching tufted stool to sit on. A small table set for the next meal nestled in the corner. Since no chairs surrounded the table, Loretta assumed that Signor Cardello was confined to his wheelchair.

With a shuffling walk and a deep sigh, the woman servant returned with a tray of coffee cups and liquor glasses.

Dina spoke first, telling Cardello that Magdalena was very weak. "I have taken a leave from the convent to care for her and my sister. I have a few students that I teach, and we live very simply so we manage if I budget well."

"Oh, Dina can squeeze every drop from a lira, believe me," said Loretta.

Everyone laughed.

"God bless you for that," said Cardello. "Maybe God has other plans for you, Dina. Never give up or lose faith that you have a destiny and He will watch out for you."

When it was time to leave, Paolo lowered himself before Cardello's chair. "I just want to thank you for all your kindness to us, especially your fatherly concern for me. We will always be grateful."

Tears flowed again from Cardello's eyes, and everyone had to clear their throats to say good-bye to their dear friend and guardian.

They saw other friends and neighbors including Guido, their father's comrade; Mr. Tocci, the butcher; an elderly aunt of their father, Zia Alessia; and several former school chums of Dina—Barbarella, Maria, Rosalia, Helena, Nanetta, and Susanna, who were all married and in various stages of motherhood.

A poignant moment occurred when Zia Alessia, a bit confused with age, mistook Zio Lorenzo for her nephew, Antonio. He kindly went along with it, and the woman was happy that her nephew had returned with all his children to visit her.

They walked up and down the narrow streets, past familiar fountains, schools, and marketplaces. The old men still sat in the square smoking, talking, and greeting passersby. Women still carried large water jugs, piles of bread, or sacks of food on their heads in perfect balance. Their father's cousins, the Salvanni family, still occupied their old house, except that the father had died and his son ran the cobbler shop. The house and shop had not changed; Paolo could smell its leather and glue. He absently-minded stroked a finished shoe as his thoughts carried him back to memories of his father.

Before leaving, they walked to the small cemetery and laid flowers on their father's grave and spent time recollecting their own memories of him. Finally, they stopped at the site of the War Memorial where their father's name and those of all the fallen were etched. It was a beautiful large marble stone topped by a winged angel. A thick black chain circled the monument. The town had placed a large black wreath beneath the names, and scattered around the large memorial were flowers placed by other mourners. Loretta had saved a flower from the gravesite and placed it on the ground near the side that faced their old home. Everyone touched the stone as they left.

Paolo, the last to leave, placed his hand on his father's name and felt a cold chill run down his spine. "I still miss you, Papa, but I know someday we'll be together again."

CHAPTER 59

Separation Again—November 1933

The day they had all dreaded finally arrived. Paolo's military leave was over, and he would return to Rome for his orders. Dina asked if they could take a walk together, alone, before he said good-bye to the family.

"Please, Dina, don't worry," said Paolo. "I'll write as often as I can. You must write me, too, when you return to the convent so that we won't lose touch."

Tears were streaming down Dina's pale, slender face. Her eyes, so large and dark, filled with pools of shimmering tears. "I'm so afraid you'll be killed like Papa if you go to some foreign country," she said. "What if they send you to Africa again?"

"It wasn't too bad there," said Paolo. "The people were friendly—well most of them. Besides, if I hadn't been stationed there, I might not have met our northern cousins."

"You always think of the good and ignore the bad," said Dina. "I wish I could always be so sure of happier days. I seem to be locked in the past and my heart feels like a stone most of the time."

Paolo kissed his sister's forehead. "Here, I'll kiss away all your sad thoughts and pray you have a lighter heart."

A smile escaped Dina's mouth and she hugged her brother tightly, wishing to hold on to his strength and confidence. Finally she released him and said, "I've knitted some socks for you and washed and mended your clothes. Wear this medal of Santo Michele to protect you. He's the patron saint of soldiers."

Paolo took the medal and placed it in the pocket of his jacket.

"No, no, wait. You must wear it near your heart," said Dina. "See, it has a pin."

Paolo removed the medal from his pocket and, taking the pin from his hand, Dina pinned it to his undershirt.

"Ouch!" said Paolo.

"Oh, did I stick you? I'm sorry, but it's better to shed blood now than later," she laughed.

"Thanks! I'll keep that in mind."

They walked around the little town in silence for a while, both finding it difficult to speak. A few townspeople stopped them to wish Paolo well and urged him to return soon. They both stopped once or twice to look at the distant mountains which glowed in the afternoon sun.

As they approached Zia Magdalena's house, Paolo turned to Dina. "I want you to be happy, Dina," he said. "Stop worrying about me and take this time to think of your own life. You are the sweetest, kindest person I know. Don't try to be Loretta's mother, be her friend. She's had three or four mothers in her life counting Mama, Graciella, and the aunts. She needs a big sister—she needs you."

"But she can be so wild and spontaneous," said Dina. "It's unseemly."

"Now, I see a lovely, lively young woman who enjoys life and has spirit and determination," said Paolo. "We should all have her zest for life. Come on, you know you enjoy her. I see you turning your head to smile whenever Loretta tells one of her stories about our town characters. Admit it."

Dina laughed, "Yes, she is funny and lively. It's just that the convent did not encourage behavior like Loretta's. She would make a troublesome nun."

Paolo hugged his sister. "You're not in the convent now, and Loretta will probably never be a nun. Enjoy your sister. Enjoy your freedom."

CHAPTER 60

Prosperity—April 1934

With *Pasqua* only weeks away, Caterina was busy cleaning the house and taking stock of the larder in preparation for her Easter baking and dinner specialties. Although most of their friends and neighbors had lost their jobs and were struggling, her husband, Umberto, provided very well for her and the family.

She looked proudly around her kitchen. Her white enamel stove gleamed. *Imagine having two ovens, a warmer, and a stove with four burners for cooking,* she thought. Brightly painted ceramic jars of spices were neatly lined up on the stove's top shelf. A large earthen jar held her cooking utensils and beside the jug were two metal sifters and her favorite paring knife. On the wall were the matchbox holder and the telephone, which was one of the few in their neighborhood. Her handsome wooden icebox, almost as big as the stove, kept food cold and fresh. On top of the ice box was her mortar bowl, pestle, and a coffee grinder. Secured to the edge of a utility shelf were her meat and cheese grinders, which were always spotlessly clean. She looked at her strong, hard-maple chairs and matching trestle table and the brimming china cabinet that gleamed from polishing. Caterina was particularly proud of her fine bone china dinnerware and the etched glasses which were used only for company or special holidays.

Noticing a spot on the polished wooden floor, she reached under the white enamel painted sink, which had a colorful floral skirt surrounding it to camouflage the dishpan and her cleaning supplies. She took a clean rag, moistened it, and wiped the spotted area.

Umberto was generous in allowing her to furnish their home with the best and latest appliances and furniture. But her most prized possessions were a Victor Victrola and their record collection of Italian singers and operas, which Umberto had bought for her shortly after their marriage. She was shocked to learn that he had paid one hundred dollars for the Victrola.

With her shopping list in hand, she put on her coat and hat and waited for her daughter, Geneva, to come by for her.

"Sorry if I'm a little late, Ma," said Geneva. "Mario's mother would not let me go. She talked on and on about how hard Mario works and how little time he has for her!"

"Well, children should visit their mother," said Caterina, "especially if she is alone. Be patient."

"I'm always patient! The most time Mario spends with me is when he's sleeping," said Geneva. "His waking hours are either at work or with his mother. I almost wish he had a girl friend."

"Don't talk foolishness," said Caterina. "He's a good boy and a good worker."

"He's an absentee husband and neglectful father," said Geneva. "I dread having this new baby if I can't depend on him to spend more time with me and the kids."

"You talk to him plain," said Caterina. "Tell him how you feel and that you need him home after work. "I'll talk to his mother, if you want."

"I've tried that, but it doesn't work for long," said Geneva. "He'll hang around the house for a few nights and then Mama will call, and he's off and running to her."

At the entrance to a new dress shop, Caterina said, "Geneva, look at the pretty dresses in this shop. You need a new dress for Easter. Buy one and forget your troubles."

"Well, that deep green one with the yellow scarf would look pretty on me," said Geneva. "Green is a good color for me don't you think?" It's almost nine dollars but Mario owes me a new dress after all the aggravation he causes me," she said. "Paris Shoppe, here I come! I may even buy a coat to spite him!"

CHAPTER 61

A Miscarriage of Marriage — April 1934

Geneva wore her new green dress and spring coat to Caterina's Easter dinner. Fortunately, she was only three months pregnant so the dress still fit, although not for long, she thought.

"Caterina, did you make extra Easter bread this year?" asked Mario. "I'd like to have some for lunch this week. Geneva's not a great baker and this is such a treat. My ma used to make the same sweet bread with the eggs baked in, but since my father died, she has a hard time during the holidays."

"Yes, everyone take home a loaf of bread. "Just be careful not to break the eggs as you carry it."

"Oh, when my husband was alive, I used to do everything," said Mario's mother. "But now, who is there to cook for? I am too old and sick to cook much; just a little for my precious sons when they have time to see me."

"Well, Mario must have a big appetite," said Geneva. "He's always stopping by your house for one thing or another."

Wanting to change the subject, Caterina said, "Did you see the beautiful cassocks worn by the altar boys at Mass today? Did you like the red ribbons around the waist with the new lace tops?

"Oh, yes, so much nicer than the black cassocks," said Mario's mother. "You and the other women did a wonderful job. The boys looked so angelic, like Mario when he was a boy."

"What's so wonderful about boys wearing dresses?" said Umberto. "Church and dresses are for women, not men."

The room fell silent. No one dared to argue or contradict Umberto.

Later that evening, after returning home, Mario said, "Geneva, why do you always make me look bad to your parents? We have been over this a thousand times. My mother is alone and needs help. I'm the only son she can depend on. It's my duty to help her."

"And I'm your only wife, the mother of your children," said Geneva. "What is your duty to me besides getting me pregnant?"

Mario's face reddened. "That's not fair," he said. "I provide a home for you and the kids. I put food on the table and fancy, expensive dresses on your back. Do you know how many people have been let go? I work hard to keep my job."

"I'm not complaining about your work," said Geneva. "I'm sick of waiting for you every night while you visit your mother. You fix her problems but not ours. You eat her dinner and leave ours on the table. You kiss her goodnight, while your children fall asleep waiting for you."

"Do I just toss her aside?" said Mario. "For God's sake, she's my mother."

"And I'm your wife," said Geneva. "Those kids upstairs are your children. Didn't the priest say 'leave your mother and father and cling to your wife?' Didn't he?"

For the next hour, they continued arguing until Mario stormed out of the house and Geneva ran upstairs to their room.

When Mario returned a few hours later, Geneva said, "Why didn't you sleep with your mother?"

She left the bedroom and ran downstairs to sleep on the couch.

Seconds later, he heard the scream. Rushing to the top of the stairs,

Mario saw Geneva sprawled at the bottom, her nightgown ripped and spotted with blood.

"Oh, God! Geneva, talk to me," said Mario. Geneva was clutching her belly and crying, "I'm bleeding, get the doctor. Oh, dear God, I think I hurt the baby."

Mario heard his daughter, Bonita, calling, "Mama, Mama" and Donata, the baby, began crying too.

"Stay there, Bonita," he said. "Mama can't come right now. Go back to sleep."

Mario ran to Caterina's house to use the phone and call the doctor. The doctor said not to move her, but to stay with Geneva and he would come as fast as possible.

Umberto drove Caterina and Mario back to Geneva's house. Mario rushed in first, but froze when he saw Geneva sitting in a pool of water and blood.

Caterina rushed past him and began stroking Geneva's face. "*Bella mia*, don't move. The doctor is coming. Be calm."

"The baby's dead," said Geneva. "I know it, and the kids are both crying."

Don't talk, my child. Here, here's the doctor now," said Caterina.

The doctor quickly examined Geneva and said, "Get her upstairs as gently as you can."

Mario and Umberto carefully lifted Geneva and carried her up the stairs to the bedroom. Caterina ran up ahead of them to arrange the bed, adding more sheets for padding. Bonita and the baby were still crying.

"Mario, you left the children alone?" asked Caterina.

"I didn't know what to do," he said. "Geneva was lying there bleeding and I told the kids to go back to sleep before I left."

"Mario! They're babies!" said Caterina. "What's the matter with you?"

"They're all right," Mario said. "I panicked. I needed to get help for Geneva."

"Enough!" said Umberto. "The doctor is here now. Caterina, we left our own children at home. Take Bonita and Donata to our house for now."

"Mario, you stay with Geneva," said Caterina. "Let us know if you need anything."

"I need to tell my mother what happened and that Geneva may lose the baby," said Mario.

Caterina gave him a long look. "You need to be with your wife," she said. "If you leave my daughter now, you will live to regret it, I promise you!"

CHAPTER 62

Dina's Letter to Domenica— November 1934

To my dear friend and sister in Christ, Domenica,

How I miss you and all my friends at the convent. Our plans to become nuns together will not happen as yet for me. In another year, you will become a true Bride of Christ while I am still in my own personal limbo.

I have had to write to Mother Marguerita that I must stay to care for my younger sister, Loretta, since the death of our beloved Aunt Magdalena.

My heart aches at her passing, but Loretta was devastated with the loss. Zia Magdalena and Zia Marianna were her true mothers. After our own mother went to America, they loved her, spoiled her, and gave her the childhood she was almost denied.

For two months, Loretta stopped eating and would cry constantly. She now has become quieter and more introspective. I fear for her health, since she is so thin and her eyes are sad and shaded. Her carefree enthusiasm has subsided, and I find I miss this quality which I once found so irritating. I told her I would stay with her as long as she needed me and thought this would help her feel more secure.

Knowing how much I wanted to return to the convent, she tried to relieve me of the burden she felt she had become. A young man in our town, Aldo Quintiliani, has always liked Loretta. After our aunt's death, he came over quite often to visit her. He tried to console her with flowers, sweets, figs, and even picture postcards from his relative in Naples.

At first Loretta seemed unaware of his visits; then she found them annoying. Aldo, a gentle, quiet man of about twenty, was not discouraged. He began to invite us for walks in the square, or out for a gelato. Thinking it would revive Loretta's spirits, I encouraged her, and after a few weeks she agreed.

It seemed pleasant enough, and Loretta began to look better and be somewhat calmer and at peace with life. She is a hard worker, and soon she was again crocheting and knitting articles we might sell.

One evening, Aldo came with his parents for coffee. For some reason, I felt there was something on their minds, but everyone chatted easily about the town, the holidays, the weather, and other ordinary subjects. When they left, Loretta took my hand and said, "Aldo wants to marry me. His parents have accepted me, so now you can go back to the convent and be a nun."

"Loretta, you are only seventeen!" I said. "You're too young to marry and you don't even have a dowry."

"I know. Perhaps we can contact Signor Cardello and ask him to write to America. If mama and her husband know I'm getting married, they might send me money for a dowry, and that will free you to be a nun," she said.

I asked her, "Is that what you want, Loretta?"

"Aldo is nice and his parents like me," she said. "You won't have to worry about me. I'll be fine. I want you to be happy, Dina. Please promise me that you'll write me every week. I'll miss you very much."

All I could do, Domenica, was cry and hug her. She was willing to sacrifice her life so that I could fulfill my desire to be a nun. We talked until the early morning hours. I don't think I ever loved my sister more than I did that night.

By morning we agreed that Loretta would not marry Aldo or anyone for now, and that I would remain with her in San Lorenzo.

My grandmother once told me *tutto cossa il destino*, but God has given us free will, so is everything really destiny? For now, Loretta and I share a destiny of being together, working together, loving each other, and waiting for our brother, Paolo, to return safely home to us.

Pray for us, dear friend,
Dina

CHAPTER 63

America Bound—April 1935

"Loretta, there is a letter for you and your sister at the post office," said Signora Coletti. "I offered to bring it, but you or your sister must sign for it."

"Who is it from?" asked Loretta.

"*Che ne so?*" asked Signora Coletti shrugging her shoulders. "It's none of my business who sends you private mail. That's what the postmaster said, a private letter, as if I would tell everybody your business. It's not my concern, I'm sure. But if it's bad news, just remember I'm your friend and here to help."

Loretta considered waiting for Dina to come home before picking up the letter and opening it. She hated the suspense of not knowing who had written them a private letter which sounded mysterious and ominous, thanks to Signora Coletti. Dina would be busy with her sewing group at the church for at least another hour. They were repairing old vestments and altar cloths. Loretta needed to stay home and continue her sewing work for paying customers. Finally convincing herself that the post office might be closed when Dina returned, Loretta set off to pick up the letter.

Although she was impatient to know the contents, Loretta knew she should wait for her sister before opening the letter. This didn't stop her from holding the envelope up to the light to get a hint as to what it contained. All she could see were heavy black lines that blended and left an unintelligible scrawl.

When Dina returned home that evening, Loretta had dinner on the table and the letter propped up against a loaf of bread.

"When did this come?" asked Dina.

"Earlier today." said Loretta. "Open it."

Dina took the envelope and stared at it for several minutes.

"Open it." Loretta pleaded. "It's a private letter. See who it's from and what it says."

"I can't," said Dina. "It may be about Paolo. You open it."

Loretta took the letter from Dina's trembling hands and slowly opened it. With relief she said, "It's from Signor Cardello. He says he has amazing news. We are to be reunited with our mother and sister. We must prepare to settle our affairs in San Lorenzo and plan to sail to America in October. We leave from Naples and we will arrive in America in about two weeks, sometime in early November."

"That's only six months away," said Dina. "What about Paolo? What about our home? What about my plans to return to the convent?"

"Wait, I'm not finished reading," said Loretta. "Signor Cardello's letter says he has petitioned Mussolini directly and asked that Paolo be allowed to leave the military and be reunited with his mother and three sisters. He told Mussolini that Papa was a war hero and that we have been separated from our mother and sister for the past fifteen years."

"Please God, to have Paolo out of the military and safely home," said Dina, "would be wonderful."

"Signor Cardello is wiring us some money so that we can buy what we need for the trip," said Loretta.

"I wonder how much money it will be. He said it will take about six months to file for all the necessary documents and obtain a visa for each of us to travel to America. He said he has lived for this day, and through the grace of God it has arrived. He will write us again soon and let us know when Paolo will join us."

Dina began to cry.

"What's wrong, Dina?" asked Loretta. "Don't you want to go to America with Paolo and me? I won't go if you don't. I don't even remember what Mama and Geneva look like except Mama always wore a long black dress."

"I thought we would never see Mama or Geneva again. Before I take my final vows, I must find peace and forgiveness in my heart," said Dina. "My anger toward Mama is a cross I bear every waking moment."

"You'll make yourself ill," said Loretta, "if you don't let go of this anger."

"I ask God and the Blessed Virgin to help me understand and learn to love her again. My sisters in Christ give me strength and hope that I will overcome this anger that poisons my soul. If I go to America, I may never complete my training to become a nun. My soul might never be redeemed."

"They must have nuns in America. You'll just join a different order and learn to talk American," said Loretta. "That way we can still be together and you can still be a nun. Remember, God is everywhere, even in America. Just think, Sister Dina, an American nun, who speaks beautiful Italian."

"We should speak with Zio Lorenzo," said Dina. "He will guide us in our decision."

"Dina, we must go. We're so poor here. We struggle just to stay in our small house and put food on the table. If our stepfather stops sending money, we will not be able to pay the rent and support ourselves. You will lose your dowry to the convent, and Paolo may be forced to stay in the military. America is a rich country. Our mother and stepfather must be rich to send us money over the years and now to pay for all of us to sail to America."

"If Paolo leaves the military, he can take you to America," said Dina. "I can return to the convent and fulfill my destiny."

"Maybe your destiny is to be with us in America," said Loretta. "Please, I don't want to leave you. If you return to the convent, then I'll become a nun, too, and we can be together."

Dina smiled. "Perhaps Paolo can become a priest and Holy Mother

Church will be our new family."

Before Loretta could answer, there was a pounding and she turned with a start. The door suddenly opened and there stood Zio Lorenzo, Maria Elena, and Tomaso.

"Did you read your letter?" asked Lorenzo. "We are all going to America. Your stepfather is sponsoring us and we leave as soon as our papers are processed. I am going to work for him in America. Who would have thought that bastard would be my *patrone?*"

CHAPTER 64

Return to North Africa—June 1935

Dear Zio Lorenzo,

I am writing to ask you for your help in convincing Dina to go with Loretta to America. From your last letter, it seems you, Tomaso, and Maria Elena will be leaving for America a month or two earlier. If Dina had not insisted on waiting for me, she and Loretta could accompany you, and I would feel more at ease about their passage.

Our campaign in North Africa has ended, but unfortunately, I will not be released from the Army for perhaps another year. As you may have read, the Italian troops and some German soldiers had a strong foothold with Arab support fighting mostly British troops. Rommel's troops fought primarily the French as well as the British. At times, the Ethiopian soldiers were somewhat ahead of us, and caught a number of Italian soldiers. They buried three a day in the sand with their heads exposed. At night, we could hear their screams and when we advanced, found the bodies, but the heads were clean to the skull bones. Enough! You know the horrors of war. I pray I return to my family in one piece.

Forgive me for not immediately offering my condolences on the death of your brother Vincenzo. In truth, I have only a small memory of him. What I remember best is his allowing me to ride on his back as he crawled around the floor on his hands and knees and occasionally rearing up and neighing in a wonderful horse impersonation.

I still mourn the loss of my father, but then I think of Zio Vincenzo. He never recovered from being gassed in the war, and returned home an invalid only to lose his one child, Stephano, who, I believe, was about eleven years old. His poor wife, Luisa, must have died of a broken heart;

she survived her husband by only six months. For some, life is only a tragedy.

You are very special to me, Zio Lorenzo. Please take care of yourself and help my sisters prepare for the move to America. They are undoubtedly a little frightened by the prospect.

To be honest, I, too, have mixed emotions about our reuniting with my mother and her new family. I long to see Geneva and her family and hear the children call me Zio Paolo. But thinking of my mother brings only bittersweet memories and I sometimes have such a deep foreboding of the future. In truth, though, I miss my mother and long to kiss her face and hold her in my arms once again.

After you are settled in America, can I pretend to be that small child that still haunts me? Can I ask you to scout out the situation of my mother's present life and family and report back to me, sir?

With deep affection,
Paolo

CHAPTER 65

The Package—July 1935

The weather was hot and humid, and there was a stillness in the air. Dina, overcome by the heat and her anxiety about leaving her homeland, lay prostrate on the small mat by the open door. Loretta ran into the house, almost tipping over her languid sister. "Loretta, for God's mercy, watch where you're going! Why are you running in this heat? You'll get a stroke for sure!"

"A package, Dina, a package from America!" shouted Loretta. "Get up. We must open it. It's from Mama."

"I'm not feeling well, Loretta. Let's open it tonight."

"No, please. Can't I open it now?" Loretta began tearing open the cloth-covered box. "Mama must have lots of sheets to be able to waste a piece on wrapping a box."

"If you must open it, do so carefully. We may be able to use that material," said Dina as she grudgingly arose from the mat.

"Honestly Dina, you are such a saver. Is there anything you don't keep and reuse until it literally rots?"

"Well, my little *Regina* Loretta, maybe when you are in America you can be the queen who tosses away useful things, but for now, please remember that we are poor, and waste is a terrible sin."

"All right! Here is your valuable piece of cloth. Maybe you can embroider over it and use it for a tablecloth decorated with an address."

"What a terror you must have been for the aunts," said Dina. "You always have a sarcastic reply."

"Well, you're such a fussy old lady sometimes. I can't help myself. If I say I'm sorry, can we stop arguing and open the box?"

Dina took a deep breath, sighed, and sitting at the table, gestured with a wave of her hand to Loretta to do as she wished.

Loretta looked at the wooden tray which had been covered by the cloth. It had thin slats and a wire mesh to hold the sides, bottom, and top together. A small hook released the top of the box and another cloth-covered bundle lay inside.

Dina pointed out a colorful paper that was affixed to the end of the box. "It says 'apples.' The picture looks like a *mela*."

"'Apples' must be *mela*," said Loretta. Our first American word—*mela* is 'apples.'"

The cloth-covered package inside the box was stitched closed. Dina reached over into her sewing bag and pulling out a small pair of embroidery scissors, began carefully snipping away at the package. When she finished, she gently pulled away the cloth enclosure and again gestured to Loretta to continue exploring the contents.

Loretta pulled out a dress with a wide flounce-trimmed neckline. It was a mass of brown, burnt orange, and beige flecks of color. Another dress, also with a wide collar, was a lovely deep green with a pretty yellow silk scarf draped around the neckline. A matching green coat complemented the dress.

"Oh, they are so beautiful, Dina, and so elegant. Do you think they will fit us?"

"Much too bright and fancy for me," said Dina. "You can have them."

"Oh, thank you! I'll save them for our trip to America, but I want to try them on now to see if they fit." Both dresses were too big, and the green and yellow combination did not flatter Loretta's olive skin. She felt disappointed, but when she tried the earth-colored dress with the brighter orange flecks, it looked lovely on her. "They just need a little alteration and they'll fit perfectly."

"These dresses can't be Mama's. They must have belonged to Geneva or one of the stepsisters," said Dina. "Read the letter and see what they wrote."

Opening the large envelope, Loretta pulled out a letter and two photographs. "It's a picture of Mama and her husband." Loretta and Dina held the photo between them and looked at the face of the mother who had been parted from them for fifteen years. Both figures were looking with deep concentration off to the right of the photo. Mama wore a white dress with pointed collar tips and a lacy bib. She had a chain and locket and small earrings. Her abundant shiny black hair was wavy and pulled softly back. Her deep dark eyes, straight nose, and soft small mouth were reminiscent of Dina. But Mama was fuller than Dina, who was gaunt. Their stepfather, Umberto Fabrizio, was a head taller than Caterina. He was handsome with a fair complexion and a full head of graying hair which looked a bit tousled, giving him a boyish look. His deep set eyes were shadowed by his graying eyebrows. He had a full, straight nose and a thick darker hair mustache which rested above large lips that were parted slightly. He wore a dark suit, white shirt, and a dark bow tie. A watch chain showed on his vest.

"They make a handsome couple, don't they?" said Loretta.

Dina didn't answer but continued to silently stare at the photograph as if studying their faces.

Loretta picked up the second photograph. It showed a lovely bride with a three-tiered lace wedding gown and a long sheer lace-trimmed veil which fell from her rose crown and draped in a wide circle before her. She carried a massive bouquet of white roses, each tied with small white ribbons and trailing between background ferns. "Geneva's wedding picture," said Loretta. "How beautiful she looks, and what a magnificent gown!"

As Dina took the photograph, she studied it, and tears escaped from her dark eyes. "We have a beautiful sister we don't even know. She left as a child and grew to be a woman, married, had children, and we've lost all those treasured moments with her." Dina turned the photo over, and it read "Mrs. Mario Cardarelli (Geneva Fabrizio)."

"Geneva Fabrizio, not Geneva Leonardi. Even Geneva has forgotten who she is and that she is Papa's child, not his," said Dina. "Well, I will never take his name and neither will you or Paolo, I'm sure."

Don't be upset, Dina. He raised her. She was only five when she left us. I'm sure she remembers us and Papa. You'll see."

The final packet contained documents to present to the Italian and American governments to process their immigration. Two tickets for the *Italia Rex* were enclosed. The *Rex*, a new ship, was scheduled to sail from Naples on November 6, 1935. Destination: New York City, U.S.A.

CHAPTER 66

Mama's Letter—July 1935

On one of his leaves, Paolo had bought them an intricately carved wooden box which held chocolates. Loretta devoured the sweet confections, but Dina kept the box. In it she retained special letters, her rosary, her crucifix chain from the convent, and their government identity cards. Although it would be a tight fit, she decided this was the safest depository for the tickets and documents sent by her mother. Separating all the papers, she found a letter addressed: "To my Leonardi children." Dina, taking the letter, put the other papers in her box.

"Loretta, Loretta, there's a letter from Mama."

Loretta ran into the room, and tried to take the letter from Dina's hand. "Stop," said Dina. "I'll read."

Paolo, Dina, and Loretta,

It has been many years since we have seen each other and now you are finally coming to America. Your stepfather has given Geneva and me a comfortable life, but I don't want you to think that everyone in America is rich. Many people here are without work, and these are hard times. Your stepfather provides well for his family, but money is scarce. I tell you this so that you will appreciate the sacrifice he has made so that I might be reunited with my first-born children.

You will not come to America as many immigrants do, on an overcrowded ship with poor food and accommodations. You will travel tourist class on a large ship which will have many educated and rich people. Please wear the dresses I sent you which belonged to Geneva, and with your sewing skills, make some suitable clothes for your trip and stay in America. Also, be sure to put the tickets and other documents in a safe place. They cannot be replaced.

I want you to understand that we would have lived like beggars if I had not come to America. Paolo and Dina, you were put in good schools, and Loretta was cared for by my aunts who, I'm sure, spoiled her.

Loretta, interrupting Dina's reading said, "Do you think Mama really believes you and Paolo were in good schools?" asked Loretta. "I guess I was the lucky one to be raised by the aunts, but we were poor, too. How could they spoil me?"

"I wonder if Mama is trying to tell us not to expect too much when we come to America," said Dina.

"Keep reading," said Loretta. "What else does she say?"

Dina continued reading Caterina's letter.

Life is not easy for any of us. My husband can be a very generous man, but he will not tolerate any laziness or disobedience. I tell you this to prepare you for a life of work and duty, not a life of leisure. When you arrive in America, you will find a large family. Your stepfather, Umberto's older daughters are married with children; his first two sons are not married. One son, Umberto, called Berto, is in the Army, and Luca works with his father. Geneva has two girls, Bonita and Donata, and is pregnant again.

My children with Umberto include Davido who is thirteen, Lorenzo who is twelve, and Gloria who is ten. The boys are tall, strong, and handsome of face and full of energy. The girl is pretty but timid. My beloved baby, Anita, would be seven years old now if she had not died of the fever.

I am happy that my brother, Lorenzo, and his family are also coming to America, but I wish you could have come first.

Your Aunt Vittoria wrote me that you may visit her before coming to America. That would be good. She has never forgiven me for coming to America and leaving you behind. She could never understand because she had her husband, a good farm, and a stable life. You can assure her now that I have kept my promise that we would be reunited.

"Sure, Mama," said Loretta. "I'll tell her it only took fifteen years to keep your promise."

"I'm almost finished reading," said Dina. "She talks about Paolo now."

Take courage in coming without your brother, Paolo. He can join us when he separates himself from the Army. Umberto thinks that he should stay with the Army and possibly achieve a high rank. Perhaps Paolo would prefer this, too. He can decide and let us know, but I long to see him again.

While on the boat, I caution you to be wary of strangers, especially young men. Be sure to keep the tickets, money, and documents safe. Make your preparations for coming to America, and notify the appropriate people. Again, be careful of strangers.

Give my best regards to my sister and her family. We await your arrival, Your mother, Caterina Fabrizio

CHAPTER 67

Ciao, Zia, Ciao—September 1935

It wasn't until late September that Paolo received his leave from the Army. Dina was nervous about the delay, since she feared that it would be difficult to see Zia Vittoria and her family during the harvest season. Actually, the timing worked out for the best. The Italian government granted Dina and Loretta a visa; they received a generous allowance from their stepfather via Signor Cardello, and they had their tickets to sail on the *Italia Rex*, tourist class, from Naples. They would sail on November 6, 1935 and arrive in New York City on November 14. They were assigned Cabin 579.

Looking at the formal documents and bank draft, Loretta thought, *finally it was true that they would be immigrating to America. Eight days to a new country, new family, and new life.* The thought was terrifying. Since Paolo would only have two weeks, they decided to spend one week in northern Italy with their mother's family and the remainder of the time visiting friends and family in their old hometown of San Rocco. A neighbor gave them a ride to the train station and they traveled to Rome before changing trains for Milan.

"Well, Mussolini did something right," said Paolo. "The trains are on time and efficient in getting you to your destination."

"Shush," said Dina. "Someone may hear you and report you for criticizing Il Duce."

"I'm giving a compliment," said Paolo. "Not criticizing."

"Well, I agree," said Loretta. "The trains run wonderfully and are pretty clean, too."

Pulling into the Belforti station, Loretta was the first to see the four men standing on the platform.

"Paolo, Dina, look!" said Loretta. "Are they our cousins?"

Paolo ran to the window and began to furiously wave to the men. He lifted the window and shouted, "Dante, Antonio, Zio Pietro, Guido, *ciao, ciao!*"

Waving back, the men began to approach the train. Paolo, Loretta, and Dina grabbed their few bundles and rushed to the train's exit door. After a flurry of introductions, hugs, and kisses, the trio was ushered into a large car which was followed by a well-worn truck.

"We're so happy to be here," said Dina. "I hope we have not put Zia Vittoria to too much trouble."

"Zia Vittoria has been cleaning, cooking, and ordering everyone about for weeks now," said Zio Pietro. "I think she even dusted the feathers of those damn peacocks she insists we keep."

Antonio, who was driving, laughed. "My mother has not rested. She wants everything to be perfect for you." A few miles outside the town of Belforti, Antonio traveled down a small dirt path and into a large cobblestone courtyard. The grand piazza led to a huge rambling house with large columns and a red tile roof. Flower baskets hung off the two second-floor porches and along the veranda.

"Oh, look!" said Loretta. "Look at those beautiful birds."

"Those are the peacocks," said Guido, "that my mother insists we keep. They're pretty, but useless."

"*Grazie Dei, grazie Dei*, you've arrived," said Zia Vittoria. "My precious ones—welcome, welcome. Are you hungry? We eat soon, soon. Come inside! Do you want to wash?" (That was a gentle way of asking if they needed to use the toilet.) Vittoria talked non-stop as she hugged each of them, covering them with kisses, holding their faces, and gazing at them as she gave them a flourish of compliments..

"Enough! You're smothering them," said Zio Pietro. "Come, let me show you the barn."

"Later," said Vittoria. "We eat first; we talk; we rest. They can see the barn, the animals, the farm—everything tomorrow."

Dinner was superb. Homemade tortellini with freshly ground meat, cheeses, and sage were gently served in a light butter sauce. Fresh salami, smoked, dry prosciutto, and creamy cheeses were served on a large wooden board surrounded by slices of crusty, homemade bread.

"This is a banquet," said Paolo. "Everything is delicious and wonderful to behold."

"The chicken is delicious," said Loretta, "so sweet and moist."

"*Coniglio, coniglio*," sang Dante, as his fingers made mock rabbit ears on his head. That's rabbit." Everyone laughed. Bowls of fresh black figs still kissed with dew, grapes, melon, and crisp apples accompanied a sweet, multi-layered creamy cake and the traditional *espresso* coffee. Fruit brandy completed the meal.

"I've never eaten so much in my life," said Dina. "I may burst!"

"You're all so thin," said Zia Vittoria. "Just like matchsticks. You need fattening up."

Loretta laughed as she looked down at her dress where Zia had pulled a handful of extra material. "Look, how skinny you are," she said.

"Well, this dress is a little big," said Loretta. "I made it for America and left room in case I gain weight."

"Come, girls, sit with me," said Zia Vittoria. "The men will go outside for their cigarettes and brandy."

After the men left, taking the bottle of brandy and glasses with them, the women sat in the small salon. Offering Loretta and Dina more coffee, Zia Vittoria sat down and took both girls' hands. "You know how much it has pained me that you were left in the care of strangers all these years. My sister, your mother, thought she was doing the best thing, but her pride directed her to refuse our help. We were not rich then, and even today, life is hard, but we eat what we raise. Letters from your mother have been few, and she says little about herself. Her letters speak of her young children, how well her husband does in his business, and how many people she helps. But on occasion, she writes of her husband's temper and how difficult it is to know his moods. Once she did not write me for months. She said she broke her hand in a foolish accident, but she didn't say exactly how it happened. Another time, she wrote that she and her husband were going to a special festa. She was so excited about it and described her new dress, coat, hat, and jewelry. When I wrote to ask if she had a good time, she wrote back that something happened and she was too ill to go," said Zia Vittoria. "I wrote and asked what happened to make her ill, and she never mentioned it again."

"Well, at least she wrote you occasionally," said Dina. "We rarely heard from her directly. We received most news through our attorney and friend, Signor Cardello."

"Maybe she felt guilty," said Loretta, "and that's why she rarely wrote us."

"No, she had another family," said Dina, "and was too busy to worry about us."

"Why not stay here?" said Zia Vittoria. "We are your family too. When Paolo is free from the military, he can join you here. This is your country. Many people go to America, but many return to Italy. They are not always able to make a living there. Too many people resent immigrants. We can't speak their language or know their ways. They don't understand our ways and sometimes ridicule us, I'm told. Your home can be here with us."

Dina squeezed her aunt's hand. "I truly want to stay here, be a nun, and fulfill my destiny," she said, "but I must bring Loretta to America. She is young and deserves to have an easier life. My mother and stepfather will give her a better life. She'll find a nice Italian boy in America like Geneva did and make her own future in a rich country. When she is settled," said Dina, "I will return to Italy."

"Loretta," asked Zia Vittoria, "do you want to go to America?"

"I miss Geneva and my mother, and America sounds so wonderful. For Dina's sake, though," said Loretta, "I could stay, but Paolo thinks I should go and find my own life."

"Well, go then," said Zia Vittoria. "Perhaps your mother and Geneva need you, too. Perhaps I had hoped for daughters to comfort me. My sons are a blessing—all of them—but you are my sister's children, and I love you and worry about you."

"We promise to write regularly," said Dina, "and let you know how we are doing and what we find in America."

"Oh, please, do write me often," said Zia Vittoria. "I'll cherish every letter from you, and if you want to return, you'll always be welcome in our home."

Their week together was wonderful. They ate heartily and slept late each morning, despite the crowing of the rooster and the screaming of the peacocks. They visited with their mother's uncle and aunt, Zio Pasquale and Zia Teresa, who had recently lost their only son, Franco, to influenza.

Before leaving, Zio Pietro lined them up for a photograph. Dina wore her best dress of cream wool with brown accents; Zia Vittoria, was in black, still mourning her mother; Zia Teresa was also in black, mourning her son; Loretta wore her loose-fitting, large-plaid dress with black sash and collar; Zio Pasquale, dressed in his only suit, leaned on his cane and looked away from the camera; Paolo, handsome in a dark grey suit, white shirt, black tie, and pocket handkerchief, smiled for the camera. In front of the group was ten year old Guido with shirt, knee-pants, socks, and shoes covered in dust. Paolo used the camera to take photos of his robust cousins and Zio Pietro in front of the barn. All the cousins posed with Paolo, Dina, and Loretta for a final photograph before their departure.

Tears, wet kisses, crushing hugs from the cousins, and words of bene-diction from their aunt and uncle enveloped them at their departure. Paolo promised to visit again the next time he got leave. The girls, Dina and Loretta, vowed to write often from America. Zia Vittoria gave them a basket brimming with food, wine, and water for the train trip. She also gave the girls three bolts of material for dresses. "Take this material and show those American people how fine Italian women dress."

Having spent ten days with their northern relatives, their stop in San Rocco was only for a few days. Because they had visited San Rocco a few years earlier with Zio Lorenzo and his family, they felt this visit would allow enough time to visit the people and places most important to them.

Their first stop was Signor Cardello, their closest friend and ally. His health had deteriorated considerably since the last time they saw him. He could barely speak and was permanently in his wheelchair and at the mercy of his housekeeper. During their visit, they all needed to touch him—a hand on his shoulder, holding his hands, and adjusting the blanket that covered his legs. They knew, as he did, that this was the last time they would see each other on earth.

"I did my best," said Signor Cardello. "Pray for me, Dina. I will miss you all, especially you, my dear Paolo, my boy. And I'll miss all the stories of your antics, my sweet Loretta. May you find only happiness in America. Always remember your old friend," he said, "and never forget, whatever happens, that you belong to each other. Together, you will always be strong."

Seeing Graciella was painful, too. She had been like another mother to them when their father died and their own mother was lost in grief and desperation. Graciella had several grandchildren who seemed to adore her. They ran around the house and in and out of the door squealing with delight every time Graciella tried to catch one to introduce them to the visitors. Her husband had died, but her daughter and sons were good to their mother, and she found comfort in her family.

"You will always be like my children," she cried.

A wonderful surprise awaited them in San Rocco. Their father's sister, Anina, who had been living in America, had returned to their hometown with two sons and a daughter. Her husband stayed in America to work and earn money for his family. Anina had become homesick for Italy and her husband's mother was very old and ill. They worried that she would not be able to survive alone, so Anina agreed to come back to care for her mother-in-law until her death.

"Oh, Loretta, how much you look like your father," said Zia Anina. "He was so handsome and so good." She cried and blessed herself. "He died too soon, too soon."

"We're so happy to see you," said Dina. "I had hoped to find you when we arrive in America, but you are here! How wonderful!"

"Well, not so wonderful," said Zia Anina. "I am now a white widow. You know, my husband is not dead, but I am alone. Well, his mother is very sick and old, the poor woman. Could we let her die alone? No, so I came back. My son, Bruno, is in the Army. He will be disappointed he missed you. My other son, Antonio, is working, but he and my daughter, Fulvia, will be here tonight for dinner," said Zia Anina. "She is out shopping now. They'll be so happy to see you."

The evening was enjoyable and their aunt took pains to prepare a nice meal. "Antonio is the quiet one; Fulvia doesn't talk much either, but, oh," said Zia Anina, "you should meet my Bruno. He's the wild one and full of fire, like you, I think, Loretta."

Everyone laughed, and agreed that Loretta was the spitfire in their family group.

"Like your mother, eh?" said Zia Anina. "She was always full of spirit and fire, but my brother loved her very much, you know."

Everyone became quiet, lost in their own thoughts and memories.

Finally, it was time to go, and Zia Anina embraced them several times. "God grant I see you soon in America. But if not me, then my children will return. Stay close. We are your father's family. You have other aunts and an uncle there too—my sisters and a brother. Visit them and my husband."

CHAPTER 68

The Blessings of Friends—November 1935

November had finally arrived and Dina and Loretta were packed and ready to leave for Naples to begin their voyage to America. Saying good-bye to family and friends had been heartbreaking.

Dina scrubbed their home from top to bottom, while Loretta gave away the few household goods they had. Dina took out the carved wooden candy box that Paolo had given them and transferred their documents, money, and ship tickets to her large handbag. Along with her convent rosary and crucifix which she kept in the box, she placed a few treasured photos: one was of their visit with family in Belforti; another was of her cousin, Bruno, in military uniform, which her Aunt Anina gave her; there was Geneva's wedding photo; a photo of their father, also in uniform; several photos of Paolo; a photo of their mother which showed them all after their father's death; a photo of her class at the convent; a picture of her dear friend, Domenica, in her religious habit; a photo of their friend, Signor Cardello; extra copies of their passport photos; and finally, a picture of their sewing class.

When they returned from Belforti and San Rocco, Sister Carmella—who had taken over the sewing class in San Lorenzo—invited Dina and Loretta for a small reunion and an opportunity to say good-bye to old friends and students. Fifteen of their former students, mostly in their teens and twenties, gathered in their best dresses at the local convent.

Sister Carmella instructed the church's caretaker to set up light chairs in the courtyard. With the nun sitting at one end and Dina and Loretta in the middle, the women took seats or lined up behind them for a photograph. Every one of the former students posed with needle in hand, holding a piece of cloth she was embroidering or had completed under Dina and Loretta's instructions. Dina looked at the photo, smiled, and put it in the box.

Noticing she had dropped the recent photo of her mother and stepfather, she decided to add it, instead, to her purse with the documents.

Since they were scheduled to be in Naples a day before the actual sailing date, Dina requested and was granted a visit to the convent to see old friends, especially Domenica, now a Sister of Charity who was teaching there. Mother Superior Marguerita invited them to stay two days to see old friends, talk, and pray about their impending emigration to America.

Although Loretta was nervous about staying in a convent for two days, Dina had never been happier. She noted that the new students wore pretty grey dresses with pert white collars and a belted waist. They looked more like students than orphans, she reflected, thinking of the long, loose dresses she had worn as a child, which had seemed so drab. Some girls even had white bows in their hair and white socks with ankle-strap shoes. Dina thought of the severe bowl-cut hair style and the rough stockings and boots she had worn.

Mother Superior summoned Dina that first evening. At first they enjoyed some pleasant conversation, but then Dina fell silent. She lowered her head and when she raised it, tears streaked her cheeks.

"What is it, Dina?" said Mother Marguerita. "Why do you cry? Are you sad to leave your country?"

"Yes, but I'm afraid I might never return to continue my vocation and become a nun. What am I to do, Mother? I love Loretta and long to see my mother and sister, Geneva, again. But if I go to America, will I be able to continue my training and fulfill my destiny to become a nun?"

"You speak of destiny," said the Mother Superior, "but destiny is not always of our choosing. If God wants you to be a nun, you will reach that goal, but the world needs more than nuns. The world needs good women and mothers who will teach their children to know and love God. The life of a nun," said the sister "is not for everyone. You have had a sad life and feel abandoned by those you loved. Taking shelter in a convent is not a solution to your pain. You are a good and loving woman. Perhaps Our Lord wishes you to start fresh in a new country and to rebuild old ties."

"But all I've ever dreamed of," said Dina, "is becoming a nun."

"Well, maybe you will become a nun in America. You will need to learn English, but perhaps you are meant to minister to the children of immigrants as a teacher. You have a special gift as a needlewoman. Perhaps you can teach others this skill and help them make a living while learning about God. Whatever your destiny," said Mother Marguerita, "God will show it to you. Pray for guidance and He will show you the way."

Not totally satisfied, but unable to know what else to do, Dina sat with her dearest friend, Domenica, to discuss her feelings and concerns.

"You've taken your final vows," said Dina. "Will we still be friends with you here and me in America?"

"Of course," said Domenica. "We will write often. I will always be your friend and you mine, no matter how far we are from each other."

"Thank you, Sister Giovanna, my dearest Domenica."

"Strangely, it will be easier for us to stay close friends with you in America," said Domenica, "than if we were nuns together in Italy."

"I know. Such a cruel rule about not having any close friendships," said Dina. "That was one rule that I would have found difficult to accept as a nun."

The day of departure arrived. Mother Marguerita gave her blessing to Dina and Loretta. Domenica, now Sister Giovanna, led a group of young students who offered flowers and a basket of fresh rolls and fruit to the America-bound women.

Dina was disappointed not to have said good-bye to her dear friend and mentor, Sister Lauria. Earlier in the year, Sister Lauria had been transferred to the convent in Bologna to take up a new teaching assignment. Dina would miss this young nun who was as dear to her as Domenica.

Under the watchful eye of the Mother Superior, Dina and Domenica gave each other a final hug and a gentle kiss on the cheeks. They struggled to compose themselves and their last words were, "write" and "promise."

Somehow, Paolo had secured a pass to Naples and met them at the convent. He wanted to spend as much time as possible with his two sisters. After they passed the convent gate, Dina began to shudder with grief. Paolo put his arm around her. "It's going to be all right. Your friend will write you," he said. "Perhaps the fates will bring you together again."

"No!" cried Dina. "Short of a miracle, we will never be together again."

"Please stop crying, Dina," said Loretta. "I feel like you are doing this for me and I can't bear to see you so unhappy. Let's go home. We'll return the money and tickets to Mama. Maybe they can get their money back."

"Stop it, both of you," said Paolo. "We are going to America. There is where our future lies. You both will get on that ship today and I will follow you in a year or so. That's it. That's the plan."

Both women nodded agreement, and the three of them hugged before entering the ship's registry office. Paolo asked if he could accompany his sisters on the ship, and seeing he was in uniform, the official waved them on and reminded Paolo to leave as soon as he heard the ship's horn for guest departures. During their final hour together, the sisters found their cabin, and walked past the dining room, the reading room, and other sundry facilities on the ship. The *Rex* was a new ship, only two years old, which accommodated about three thousand guests and crew. It was the only Italian ship to win the Blue Riband for the fastest crossing of the Atlantic. "What a beautiful ship," said Paolo. "You should have a very comfortable trip. Be sure to enjoy it and take advantage of all it has to offer."

The bleating of the horn signaling guest departures startled them. Loretta hugged Paolo first and covered his face with kisses. "Come soon, please," said Loretta. "Come soon. Promise me."

"I promise," he said as tears welled in his eyes.

"God protect you until we meet again," said Dina. She clung to him so long that he needed to break away as he kissed her gently good-bye.

CHAPTER 69

The Arrival—November 1935

Unfortunately, Dina and Loretta did not take Paolo's advice. They spent most of their time in their cabin or, when weather permitted, on the deck looking back across the vast sea to Italy. Years later, when asked about the voyage, neither remembered much except that the dining room dishes were beautifully decorated and very heavy, they were served large meals, and their stateroom was clean and had a modern bath.

Back in America, Caterina and Umberto planned to be at the pier in New York to welcome the young women. At home, the older children were charged with caring for the youngsters and cleaning the house to ready it for the new arrivals. Dina and Loretta were to take Ava and Lena's old bedroom. Geneva was home cooking for her sisters and, having just had a new daughter, wanted to stay with her three children.

"So, the old bastard finally let Ma bring her kids here," said Luca. "Good for you, Ma."

Geneva had stopped by to borrow some large plates. "I'm so excited and nervous," she said. "Suppose they don't know me, or maybe my Italian is not as good anymore. I'm so anxious. I can't wait to see them again."

"Where will Ma put them?" asked Lena. "My old room has Gloria in it now."

"Mama said I was going to get Geneva's old room," said Gloria. "It's kind of small, but Mama made new curtains to match the bedspread, so it's prettier now."

"Well, do you think they will like America?" asked Lena. "After all, they come from a small village in the mountains. They'll probably be scared of everything."

"Lena, stop talking and go clean the bathroom," said Ava. "They'll do okay. After all, there are lots of immigrants around. I'm sure they'll make friends and have people to talk to in Italian."

"We can speak Italian," said Luca. "Why can't we be their first friends, Lena?"

"I didn't say we couldn't be friends, but we don't have much in common," said Lena. "I can imagine what they will look like getting off the boat. Black kerchiefs, rough traveling shoes, baggy dark dresses down to the ground, and probably wearing aprons and carrying sacks of clothes," she said with a laugh. Davido and Lorenzo, hearing Lena's remarks, started to put dish towels on their heads and began hobbling around singing, "The guineas are coming, the guineas are coming."

Luca stopped them with a sharp slap across their heads.

"Don't you dare talk about my sisters like that," said Geneva. "I'll have you know they both sew beautifully and have probably more stylish clothes than you, Lena. And Davido and Lorenzo, they are not guineas. They are as good—no, better than you brigands," said Geneva as she pulled the dish towels off their heads. "My ancestors were all artisans and tailors. Why, one of my mother's uncles was tailor to Pope Pius the XII. Your family was all rough neck rock cutters."

"Don't pay attention to them," said Ava. "Those boys are spoiled rotten. If they didn't have someone to fight with or tease, they wouldn't be happy. You two—go wash down the front steps. Now!" ordered Ava. "Go before I slap you again. And you, Lena, get to work and keep your mouth shut about things you don't know, which is a lot." Ava started to usher the boys out.

"Nah," said Davido. "Ma said we can't get dirty." With that retort, both boys took off to the yard to play ball.

"Let them go," said Geneva. "They're more in the way than any help. Here, I'll collect the plates and go home to my children. Call me when they arrive."

157

"They should be home tonight," said Lena. "Pa didn't want to spring for another night in New York."

An old friend of Umberto's met the train which took Umberto and Caterina to New York. They stayed with their friend and his family before being driven to the port authority to meet the *Italia Rex*. Like her own arrival in Boston some fifteen years ago, Caterina took great care with her appearance. She wanted to set a good example of how proper people dress in America. If they recalled a poor peasant mother, well, now they will see that she has prospered and made a good life for them in the end.

"There they are," said Caterina, as she watched two young women approach. But another couple met the girls who were accompanied by another woman, possibly a relative, and they all hugged as a group.

"We will wait here," said Umberto. "They will find us." Eventually, two young women, arms locked together, approached them. One woman, the taller of the two, held a photograph and studied it, surveying the crowd of welcomers.

"Dina," said Caterina. "Dina, yes?" "Oh, you have grown so tall. And this is Loretta? How pretty you look."

Hesitating for a moment, Loretta hugged her mother first, followed by a trembling Dina who whispered, "Mama."

They hugged, cried, and Caterina held each of her daughter's faces and kissed them.

"Dina looks like you when you were young," said Umberto.

Caterina froze for an instant and then said, "How is my little nun?"

"Fine, Mama. I'm not a nun yet," said Dina. "I need more training. Perhaps we can talk sometime about my vocation."

Caterina gave her a hard look. "We'll see," was all she said. "Loretta, you look like your father," said Caterina as she sniffed and looked away. "Same dark eyes, so large and deep." Changing the subject, she said, "And Paolo, he is well? It's unfortunate he could not come with you."

"He is well, Mama," said Loretta, "and looks forward to being reunited with you and us, hopefully in a year or so."

Umberto cleared his throat loudly, shook hands with the girls, and pulled each of them forward for a full kiss.

Caterina noticed that both girls turned their heads so that he only kissed their cheek or the side of their forehead. *Well*, she thought, *I'll have to keep an eye on these two.* "How nice you both look," said Caterina.

"Thank you, Mama," said Loretta. "We made our clothes."

The girls were wearing identical tan coats, softly belted with deep lapels and large pockets. Loretta wore a dark dress with a little lace trim at the neckline and a string of pearls. On her right hand she wore a small gold ring. "Where did you get the ring?" asked Caterina. "Do you have a boyfriend already?"

Loretta laughed. "No, Paolo gave it to me as a present on my saint's day."

Caterina continued inspecting her daughters. Both girls had their hair pulled back, but Loretta's was fuller, softer, and she styled it with a side part. She also wore small gold earrings.

Loretta noticed her mother looking at the earrings, and touching them, she said, "Zia Magdalena gave me these for my confirmation."

Caterina than focused her attention on Dina. Although similarly dressed, Dina wore a plain grey dress under her coat. Her hair was severely pulled back and she wore no jewelry. Caterina noticed that both women had similar dark stockings and stylish shoes. In all, they presented very well, and she was relieved.

On the train ride home, Loretta babbled on about the trip, Paolo, friends, relatives, and finally asked about Geneva and the rest of the family.

Dina was quiet, staring out at the passing landscape. She spoke only when asked a question. All the while she was observing her mother and stepfather. When Caterina excused herself to use the toilet, she asked Umberto to escort her down the aisle of the moving train.

"Well," said Dina, "we must have passed inspection. Our mother didn't criticize our appearance. And Mama certainly looks the plump, rich matron of America. Watch out for our stepfather," cautioned Dina. "He has bad eyes that make me uncomfortable."

"Me, too." said Loretta. "I thought I must look funny since he winks and grins at me whenever I catch his eyes."

Taking Loretta's hand, Dina said, "We must stay together and watch out for each other. Remember, we are strangers in a strange country. Mama and her family are strangers to us, too."

"We must try, though," said Loretta. "Geneva is here, and next year Paolo is coming and we'll be together again."

"Just be cautious, I say." said Dina. "Don't embrace everything all at once. Watch, wait and see how we fit into this new family. Be wise and less spontaneous."

"Oh, Dina," said Loretta. "Don't you feel the excitement, the energy, the youth of this country? I think life will be good here. It'll be fun!"

As they arrived at the house at nightfall, even Loretta's usual high spirits were beginning to flag. It had been a long and emotional day and only one more reunion kept them anxious—seeing Geneva again.

As they entered the door of the large white house, which looked like a villa to them, unfamiliar faces greeted them. Luca, who was now twenty-four, Dina's age, was the first to shake hands, and then kiss them. A full-figured and pregnant Ava, now twenty-eight, greeted them next, introducing her husband, Salvatore, and three children who were half-asleep on the sofa. Next came Lena, now twenty-two, and her husband, Bernardo. Lena gravely shook hands, and her husband nodded his head in greeting. Caterina then introduced Davido who was thirteen and Lorenzo who was twelve. Both were tall, handsome, ruggedly-built boys who looked like Umberto. They were nervously nudging each other. Caterina pulled a sweet-looking young girl forward to meet them. Gloria was ten and a fragile version of her mother.

"We're pleased to meet you all," said Dina.

"Where's Geneva?" said Loretta.

"Here, here, I'm here," cried a voice from the kitchen. "Oh, I'm sorry, we just arrived," said Geneva. "Mario had to put the kids to bed for his mother, and I needed to bring the food myself." A lovely young woman with light brown, curly hair and shiny eyes emerged through the crowd. She held her arms out and hugged Loretta and Dina. The women stood like a statue of the three graces, not moving, not talking, but locked in an embrace of sisterhood. How long they would have stood like that is difficult to know, since Caterina broke the spell. "Geneva, did you bring everything? Is it still warm or do we need to reheat the food?"

Geneva didn't reply, but she broke the stance and began cupping each of her sister's faces in turn and kissing them. Still holding the hand of each sister, Geneva said, "How lovely you both are! I can't believe you are finally here. How is Paolo? Does he still remember me? Loretta, you were a baby and now look, you're a beautiful young woman. You're eighteen now, right?" asked Geneva. "Yes, of course, I'm twenty-two and an old mother with three girls. You will see them tomorrow, and you must meet my husband, Mario. He'll be here soon. His mother will watch the children tonight."

"Geneva, enough!" said Caterina. "You do babble on. Everyone's tired and hungry. Help me with the food. Ava, you look after the children. They can all sit in the kitchen to eat. Lena, you seat everyone at the table and get the wine from the cellar—two bottles. Luca, put Dina and Loretta's bags in their room. Oh, Loretta, Dina, if you need to use the toilet, it is at the top of the stairs. All right, now, everyone settle down and let's eat." After they were settled at the table, including Ava, whose husband replaced her watching the children, they all sat quietly for a moment waiting for Umberto to tell them to begin. Loretta looked at the table. The linens were beautiful, as were the china and glasses. She had never seen such fine silverware, not even on the ship. Geneva had produced huge platters of homemade pasta, roast chicken, and various vegetables. Loretta particularly enjoyed the beef which was pounded thin, stuffed with hard-boiled eggs, and herbs, rolled and cooked in a savory tomato sauce. It made her think of Zia Vittoria and their visit, and she started to cry.

Umberto looked at Loretta and then to his wife.

"Loretta, please don't be so emotional," said Caterina. "It will ruin your appetite."

"I'm sorry, Mama," said Loretta. "I was thinking of Zia Vittoria and all the family we left behind."

With a huge sigh and a sharp voice, Caterina said, "Well, you're here now. We will talk of my sister later."

Caterina looked at Umberto. He gave her a strange look, then addressing the family, he said, "Eat!"

CHAPTER 70

Sister Talk—December 1935

In the first few weeks since their arrival in America, Dina and Loretta became caught up in a social marathon. Each day either people would stop by to see them or they would be escorted to the home or apartment of a relative or *paesani* of their mother and stepfather.

"Must we visit again today?" asked Loretta. "I feel like a monkey on a leash—dressed up and paraded out for people to see. And they all say the same thing!" "Pleased to make your acquaintance," "How pretty you are," "You're so thin—your mother will need to fatten you up."

"Well, we are thin," said Dina, "and I for one like having good food and a lot of it on the table."

"Sweets are what I like best," laughed Loretta, "and fruit like we never saw this time of year in Italy."

Well, if you really want to be a nun, I wouldn't get used to it, Loretta thought. But she silently hoped that while they were in America, Dina would change her mind. Among the more welcome visitors were their sister, Geneva and, her children, as well as Zio Lorenzo, his daughter, Maria Elena, and her new husband. Zio Lorenzo was doing well. Maria Elena had married Guiseppi Cedrone, whom she had met on the boat from Italy. He was a barber and worked with his brother. Maria Elena and Giuseppe, who asked to be called Joe, were already expecting their first child. When asked about Tomaso, Zio Lorenzo shrugged his shoulders. "He never works steady, but has a new girlfriend every week."

"Joe is such a kind man," said Dina, "and he obviously loves Maria Elena very much."

"I think he's so funny, too," said Loretta. "I love the stories he tells and all those characters he imitates that he met on the boat to America. But he's rather old. Twenty years older than Maria Elena. That's ancient."

"Maria Elena looks happy and content," said Dina. "More than I've ever seen her when we were home in Italy. If this man loves her and will take care of her and provide for her, what does his age matter?"

"You're right," said Loretta. "He can't be too old because she is already expecting a baby."

"Don't talk of such things!" said Dina. "Young ladies do not discuss such subjects."

"Well, I think Maria Elena is so happy because she is having a baby," said Loretta. "She has a new inner beauty that shines out—like the Madonna."

"Perhaps, but you should not compare people to the Madonna," said Dina. "In any case, I'm happy we are together again and that Zio Lorenzo lives nearby.

"I miss Paolo, though," said Loretta, "and I know you do because you stare at his picture all the time."

"Do you think he's all right?" asked Dina wiping her eyes quickly with her fingertips.

"Of course he's all right. He plans to go to Belforti for Christmas," said Loretta, "provided they don't cancel his pass and ship him back to Ethiopia a little sooner."

"How do you know that?" asked Dina. "He never told me. Why did he tell you?"

"He wrote Zio Lorenzo," said Loretta, "and Zio told me. He even let me read the letter."

"Why didn't you show the letter to me?" asked Dina. "You know how much I worry about Paolo."

"Because you were out shopping with Geneva and Maria Elena," said Loretta, "while I was visiting Zio and watching the children. You left me behind, remember?"

"Well, I wanted to give Geneva an opportunity to be with us and not worry about the children," said Dina, "but you should have told me."

"I just did," said Loretta. "You're just upset because I knew something before you did."

"That's not true," said Dina, "but I'm the oldest and we agreed to stick together. News about Paolo is very important to me, and it was childish of you to keep it to yourself this long."

"Oh, my heavens!" said Loretta. "Three days—that's how long I've known, and I meant to tell you right away but I forgot."

"You've always been half-headed, Loretta," said Dina. "News that I wish to hear, you forget; and news that is totally useless, you prattle on about. You're such a child!"

CHAPTER 71

Family Holiday—December 1935

As the holidays approached, Loretta and Dina accompanied their mother on various shopping trips as she purchased gifts for her younger children. "I don't buy presents for the older children because you already have everything you need."

Occasionally, Caterina would fill a sack with staples like flour, sugar, a loaf of bread, and a small jar of olive oil, and they would visit a needy family. "Your mother is an angel—a saint," said one woman, "always helping the poor and the sick. My husband has bad lungs and is out of work. Your mother, this saint," said the woman, blessing herself, "helps everybody. May God bless you, Signora Fabrizio. I pray for you every night."

"We must help our own people, no?" said Caterina as she benevolently patted the woman's hand. "When Providence is good to us, we must help each other."

"Thank God your husband is strong," said the woman, "and so good to let you help us."

"Yes," said Caterina. "Umberto sends his good wishes to your husband and you. We do what we can."

"Thank you, dear *patrona*," said the woman. "Thank you for your kindness," and she kissed Caterina's hand.

"Mama," said Loretta, "do you help a lot of people like her?"

"I do what I can," said Caterina. "Many people are out of work these days, and it is Christmas. These people have three children. After Christmas we'll find some clothes to send them."

Dina could not help wondering why her mother never realized what conditions her own three children suffered. *Where were you, Mama,* thought Dina, *with the gift basket of food when we were hungry and eating worm-infested food. Where was the sainted, angelic Caterina then?*

163

On Christmas Eve, Caterina cooked the traditional fish dinner. Loretta, who had developed a passion for good food, stared in awe at the lavish table of seafood. Heaping platters of fried fish, shrimp in a spicy sauce, and fried smelts; squid, transferred from its inky broth, now stuffed and baked with a seasoned breadcrumbs mixture; and finally, homemade pasta, light and fluffy with a rich tuna fish sauce. Vegetables included fried squash, eggplant, and an asparagus platter. Rich desserts of cream puffs, ricotta pie, rum cake, and an assortment of Italian cookies completed the meal.

"Everything is so wonderful, Mama," said Loretta. "Does everyone eat like this in America?"

"I'll tell you that my brother, Davido, and I never saw food like this when we first came to America." said Umberto. "We almost starved that first year. Jobs were hard to get for Italians," he said. "No jobs and no place to live except in crowded tenements with rats and the smell of grease and rot so bad you couldn't sleep."

"That must have been terrible," said Loretta. "Didn't anyone help you?"

"Help? Who helps anybody?" asked Umberto. "Sometimes a *paesano* would share some bread or give you a little soup, if there was enough. Do you know what Davido and I ate our first Christmas in America? Horsemeat! Somebody's horse died in the street, and we were lucky to get there in time to cut a small piece for ourselves. But we survived. When we got jobs, we worked hard, we stayed sober—not like some of those Irish—and we saved our money. Now I don't owe anything to anybody, but I don't forget those days, and neither should any of you."

After dinner, Caterina and Umberto gave their presents to the younger children, who shouted and ripped them open with great ferocity.

"Go ahead," whispered Dina to Loretta. Loretta left the group and ran to their room, returning with three boxes.

"Should I?" asked Loretta to Dina, "or do you want to?"

"Mama, Umberto, Geneva, these are presents from Loretta and me for our first Christmas together," said Dina as she handed the first gift to Caterina and waited for her to open it.

"My," said Caterina, "what a lovely pin. Thank you, my child." Tears filled her large dark eyes.

"Geneva, we made this special for you," said Dina. "We hope you'll like it."

Taking the large box, Geneva put it on her chair to open it. Inside was a beautifully crocheted white bedspread with an intricate design of flowers, swirls, and birds. "Oh, how beautiful!" said Geneva. "This is the loveliest work I have ever seen! I'll treasure it always."

"The birds are doves for love and peace," said Loretta, "the flowers are roses for beauty and contentment, and the designs are for harmony and prosperity in your life."

"Thank you, my dearest sisters," said Geneva. "I'm so happy we are together again. Let's never part. Never!"

"Umberto, this is for you with our appreciation," said Dina, "for reuniting us with our mother and sister."

Umberto took the box and opened it. A small gold lapel pin in the shape of a diamond lay on the silk lining.

"Very nice," said Umberto, "but where did you get the money for all these expensive gifts?"

"Well," said Dina, "from the money you sent us. Since we made our own clothes from material that Zia Vittoria gave us and other gifts from family and friends, we had some money left when we arrived."

"Dina is very good with managing money," said Loretta. "She is very thrifty and we were able to save some of the money, so we decided we wanted to give you, Mama, and Geneva a gift for Christmas."

"I'm sure your mother and Geneva appreciate the gesture," said Umberto, "but in the future, if you have money that I gave you in excess, it should be returned to me."

"Please, Umberto," said Caterina, "it's Christmas and the girls wanted to give us a present."

"Yes, with my money," said Umberto. "Enough said. Time to leave for midnight Mass."

CHAPTER 72

Paolo's New Year's Letter—January 1936

Dear Zio Lorenzo,

I hope you, Maria Elena, her husband, and Tomaso all had a nice Christmas. I had hoped to visit your sister, Zia Vittoria, and her family for the holiday, but Il Duce had other plans for me. Within one week of writing you last, I received orders that my platoon would be sent to Italy's colony in Somalia. Although Christmas was somewhat quiet, all hell broke out by the end of the month. Unfortunately, our bombers accidentally destroyed a Swedish Red Cross unit in Ethiopia.

In some respects, I guess I was fortunate in not getting sent earlier in the year. In mid-February of last year, the first wave of troops returned. By October, our army had occupied Adua, Abyssinia.

Dina must be praying hard, since I'm still in one piece. Many of my comrades were not as lucky. Sometimes the slaughter was brutal, and those who didn't find a bullet or machete succumbed to poison gas. It looks like I'll be here for an indefinite period. Don't say too much to my sisters. Dina tends to brood over my military life, and Loretta is too young to be burdened with war news.

Please tell them I think of them often and hope they are well and happy now that they are reunited with our mother and sister. Truthfully, I hope I make it back to see them again and finally be reunited with all of my family. When I do arrive in America, I know there will be a big family to greet me—my sisters, mother, you, Maria Elena, her husband, and Tomaso—who might also be married by then—Umberto and his family, and all my father's relatives.

I hold this thought, and it helps me get through each day. Who knows, both my sisters may be engaged by the time I get to America. Watch over them for me. Write when you can and hopefully your letter will reach me.

One of the men in my platoon said he met a soldier who knew me, but forgot his name. It could be anyone, but I'm wondering if it's one of my cousins from Belforti. Antonio was stationed here before, so he might have been sent back, too. Let me know if you hear anything from Zia Vittoria.

Stay well, Zio. God willing we'll see each other in America next year. Please tell my family that they are in my thoughts, and yes, in my prayers.

Happy New Year!

Paolo

CHAPTER 73

One of the Family—January 1936

Their status as guests ended right after the holidays. Caterina assigned Dina and Loretta a number of daily household chores. Loretta was responsible for making all the beds each morning and tidying up the kitchen after breakfast. She was also charged with making Umberto's, Luca's, and the children's lunches each day.

Dina washed the floors every day and cleaned the bathroom, which was always a mess after the boys and men left. During the week, she and Loretta dusted, swept, beat rugs, and did the laundry.

This allowed Caterina to do her shopping and cooking, make visits, and spend time with the younger children. Of course, any sewing or mending was given to either Dina or Loretta, including items from their stepsister, Lena, who always seemed to need some alterations for herself and her family.

As to the other occupants of the house, Umberto and the young boys seemed to go about their business with little attention to Dina and Loretta. But Luca was kind to them and tried to help them learn English, as well as run interference with Umberto and the rowdy boys.

Gloria, who became their little sister, was showered with attention and affection by Loretta and Dina. The little girl seemed to blossom; she laughed more, seemed to have more energy, and was better able to stand up to her rambunctious brothers.

Geneva and her children came over often, usually when Caterina was out. Time seemed to fly when they were together. Occasionally, Maria Elena would visit, and the four women relished each other's company. Loretta and Dina became more comfortable with their new life in America. People were kind to them. Everyone seemed to know and respect their mother and stepfather. Geneva and her children were a joy, as were Maria Elena, her husband, Joe, and Zio Lorenzo.

Ava had them over for dinner after the holidays, and it was a pleasant evening. Lena and her husband and son joined them and were friendly, but somewhat reserved.

In late January, Umberto made an announcement at dinner. "Next week, the first of February, you both will start work at a dress factory."

"But how will we communicate?" asked Dina. "We can't speak English or understand what people are saying when they speak. And a factory means machines," she said. "We don't know how to use machines."

"Don't worry," said Umberto. "They'll teach you. Most of the women who work there are Italian, so they'll understand you when you talk. But I warn you, there's not much time for talking when you work."

"But how will we take the streetcar," asked Loretta, "if we can't read signs or speak English?"

"The factory is in Quincy, within walking distance from here," said Umberto. "Tomorrow I will take you both to meet the owner. He will show you how to use the machines and explain the work."

"Umberto, perhaps they should wait a little longer before going to work," said Caterina. "I need them to help me here with the house and children."

167

"They will have time to work and help you," he said. "When they take lunch, instead of wasting time, they can come home and do what they do now."

"How much will we be paid?" asked Dina.

"I believe you are paid for each piece you produce," said Umberto. "However, in this house, all money is turned in to help the family. You are amply taken care of by your family. You will not need any money."

"But—" Dina started to say, when she felt a sharp pain to her ankle. She stopped and looked at her mother who gave her a warning look and shook her head slightly.

Across the table, Luca gave an audible sigh.

"You have something to say, Luca?" asked Umberto.

"No, Pa," said Luca, as he visibly reddened.

"Good, then," said Umberto. "Caterina, find the girls some appropriate clothes and shoes for factory work. Tomorrow, early, we visit the factory. Now, everyone eat."

After dinner, Dina cornered Luca and asked him. "Do you have to turn in your pay to him? Do you get to keep any money for yourself?"

"No," said Luca. "Pa's pretty strict about that. You've got to give him the money."

"But what if you need something?" asked Dina.

"Then, you've got to ask him for money," said Luca, "but I wouldn't recommend it. He's a tight-fisted old bastard. To be honest, I'd go to Ma first. She's more likely to give it to you."

Dina thought about this, and she doubted she felt any more comfortable asking her mother for money than she would be asking her stepfather. That night she dreamt of her father and how warm and generous he was. She knew they must have been poor, but her father never made her feel that they were. He always had a small treat or a coin for her when she visited his cobbler's shop. She remembered his words, "Enjoy, but don't tell your mother."

CHAPTER 74

The Stitchers—February 1936

Factory work was a mixed blessing. Dina and Loretta enjoyed the camaraderie of the other women who worked there, but the sewing machines were a challenge. First of all, they were intimidating, loud, and too mechanical. This, combined with the pressure of doing piece work and being paid for only those pieces that passed inspection, was overwhelming. The women were not allowed to talk to each other during work time, and were given only brief breaks to use the toilet or eat something they brought from home. Loretta and Dina did not have the luxury of using their thirty-minute lunch break to get to know their coworkers, since they had to rush home to do chores and then hurry back to work.

Caterina, seeing their frustration with the machines and their piece-work quota, had an idea. "Your father's sister, Donata, has a son who works as a tailor in Boston. He and your Aunt Guiseppina work at a factory in Boston. On Sunday, we will visit them and see if they can teach you about the machines."

The following Sunday Caterina, Dina, and Loretta paid a visit to Zia Donata and her husband, Zio Franco. Their son, Enrico, had been a tailor for the past three years and had a sewing machine at home to earn extra money. Zia Guiseppina, who lived next door with her brother and two sisters, also stopped by. These relatives and Zia Donata were their father Antonio's siblings who had immigrated to America in 1912.

Enrico had set up two chairs by the machine. He sat in one and placed Loretta and Dina in turn on the second chair. Slowly he described each part in Italian, and as he spoke, made a diagram of the part and wrote a brief description of its function.

"How well you draw," said Loretta.

"Oh, I draw, paint, and do a little sculpting," said Enrico. "But here in America, there is little work for artisans, so I followed my family's profession as a tailor."

"My son," said Zia Donata, "is a genius. He also plays the violin and is a wonderful gardener like his father. He has so many talents."

"My mother," said Enrico, "is very biased. Mama, perhaps you, Zia Caterina and Zia Guiseppina can visit while I teach the girls about

169

sewing machines."

In a few hours, Dina and Loretta were using the machine and doing practice stitches, learning to sew buttonholes, zippers, collars, pockets, and various trims. Both women could load and change bobbins and thread the machine easily.

"*Bravo*," said Enrico. "See, you can do it. Just stay calm, pay attention so you don't sew your fingers, and work a little slower at first until you learn the work."

"Thank you so much," said Loretta. "I feel much more confident about going to work tomorrow."

"Here," said Enrico, "keep the drawings and descriptions and study them."

"Along with all your other talents," said Dina, "you are also a good teacher. Thank you for your help."

As they were preparing to leave, Zia Guiseppina invited them to stop over and see their uncle and other aunts. Dina's impression of them was that they were very different from her father—especially Zio Costanzo.

Later that evening, when Dina and Loretta were alone, Loretta started giggling, recalling their visit today. Zio Costanzo was the obvious king of the house, and his adoring sisters were his handmaidens, fawning on his every word and gesture. He had an imperious air and constantly smoked a smelly stogy cigar as he stood poised and directed his sisters about. The ladies sat at the small kitchen table until he directed their activities.

"Get the cups, Palma; warm up the coffee, Tomasina; more chairs, Guiseppina." Addressing their guests, he said, "Drink. The coffee is fresh. We made it yesterday."

Loretta mimicked her uncle and laughed. "It was awful!"

Dina, joining her laughter, said, "You know, no matter how poor we were, we never served day-old coffee!"

CHAPTER 75

Carnival Money—May 1936

Although Dina and Loretta were making friends at the factory, they had little time to pursue activities with friends outside work. With the warm inviting days of spring, the carnival came to town. Loretta's friends urged her to accompany them on Saturday.

"But I've never been to a carnival," said Loretta. "What do people wear? Will I need to bring something? Should I pack a lunch?"

"No, no," said her friend, Carmella. "Just bring some money for food, rides, and maybe a chance at the games."

"What kind of rides and games?" asked Loretta. "Will there be animals there? I don't want to wear a nice dress and then ride a smelly donkey, and I'm afraid of riding a horse."

"You're funny," said Carmella. "The only animals are two-legged ones, and I'll be looking out for them! If we meet someone nice, he might play some games of chance and win us each a prize."

"I'm not sure my stepfather will let me go," said Loretta. "He says that most of the men in our town are no good."

"Well, don't tell him we hope to meet some nice guys," said Carmella. "Just say you've never been to a carnival and your friends at work want to take you so you'll learn more about America."

"How much money do I need?" asked Loretta.

"Well," said Carmella, "a dollar would be plenty for food and rides. You won't need more than that, I don't think."

"I wish I could ask Dina to come too," said Loretta, "but she's going to be helping our cousin, Maria Elena, whose baby is due in a few months."

Carmella thought that it was just as well that Dina was busy, because she was so serious that she probably would never spend money for anything as frivolous as a carnival, but she said, "Oh, yes, it's too bad. I'm sure she would have enjoyed it."

Friday evening, when Loretta gave her pay to her mother and stepfather, she said, "My friend, Carmella, from work and some other girls are going to the carnival tomorrow. They invited me to come with them, and since I've never been to a carnival, I'd like to go."

"Carnivals!" said Umberto, "Those people are all *briganti*. They rob people blind with their games, foolish rides, and bad food. You'd do better to stay home and help your mother," he said, as he pocketed Loretta's wages.

Later that evening, when Loretta could talk to her mother privately, she said, "Mama, I really want to go. Please let me. I'll do all my work before I go, even if I have to get up at dawn."

"We'll see tomorrow," said Caterina, "after you do your work. But if it's not done, or I think you cut corners, that will be it—no carnival."

True to her word, Loretta, who loved to sleep a little longer on the weekends, was up by 5 a.m. She worked as quickly and quietly as possible, dusting and polishing the furniture, washing floors, and cleaning the stove inside and out. Dina would do the laundry and all the ironing to help Loretta be ready by 11 a.m. to meet her friends. Her final chore was to make all the beds. The younger children were no help. The boys, Lorenzo and Davido, kept running through the kitchen attempting to slide on her wet floor. Then, right after she made the beds, they proceeded to jump up and down on their beds, spoiling her work. Meanwhile, Gloria decided to sleep late that day.

Finally, all chores done, Loretta washed and dressed, choosing a pink dress, a colorful scarf, and her almost new open-toed shoes which had been handed down from Geneva. Fortunately, her thick, dark hair always held a curl, so a quick combing was all she needed.

Caterina was inspecting the living room when Loretta approached her. "I've finished all my work, Mama. Can I go now?"

"You're dressed pretty fancy for a carnival," said Caterina. "Are you sure you're telling me the truth?"

"Of course, Mama," said Loretta. "My friends, Carmella, Velma, Francesca, and all the girls are meeting me in front of the church, and we're all going together to the carnival."

"Well," said Caterina, "don't be late. You know your stepfather wants dinner promptly at five o'clock. If you're not back in time to set the table, I promise you this will be your first and last carnival while you are in this house."

"I won't be late," said Loretta. "Thank you, Mama."

"Go, now," said Caterina, "and make sure you conduct yourself properly and not act too foolish."

"Mama, I need money for the carnival," said Loretta. "Can I have a dollar—or even fifty cents, I think will be enough."

Caterina reached into her apron pocket and handed a nickel to Loretta.

"Mama," said Loretta, "this is not enough. I never ask you for money and every week I turn in all my pay. Please Mama, don't treat me like a small child. Give me fifty cents, at least," cried Loretta.

"Fifty cents," said Caterina, "for the carnival! You must be crazy. Take what I give you and be grateful. That's enough for an ice cream."

Loretta's eyes filled as she looked at the nickel in her hand. "Keep your miserable nickel, Mama."

Loretta threw the coin at her mother and ran out of the house.

CHAPTER 76

Family Conflicts—August 1936

Surviving the record hot days of August, Maria Elena had her baby, a sweet girl complete with a shock of black hair and a rosebud mouth. They christened her Marianna, and a small reception was held in her parents' garden to celebrate.

Geneva, Dina, and Loretta were sitting on a bench watching the children play.

"You look thinner, Loretta, if that's possible," said Geneva. "Are you eating enough?"

"When we first came to America," said Dina, "I thought she would burst from all the food she ate. Now she doesn't eat, she has headaches, and she jumps when you speak to her. I told her she should see a doctor."

"Loretta, is everything all right?" asked Geneva. "Is something bothering you? Don't you like being here in America?"

"I'm fine," said Loretta. "Dina worries too much. I'm just not used to being here, that's all."

"Well, I'm not used to being here either," said Dina, "but I haven't stopped eating or had nightmares and wake up crying like you. Something is wrong—tell me what it is."

"I wish we could go home, back to Italy, back to Paolo and all our friends and family," said Loretta as tears lined her sallow cheeks.

"Did something happen, Loretta?" asked Geneva. "I know about Mama not giving you any money or time to see your friends. Is that it? Or did someone..." She paused and then continued, "Hurt you?"

"Hurt her? Who would hurt her?" asked Dina as she turned Loretta's face to hers. "Loretta, tell me, please, why are you so...?"

"Frightened," said Geneva.

"Frightened?" echoed Dina. "Who has frightened you? Tell us, please."

"I can't," cried Loretta. "I'm afraid."

"Afraid of whom?" asked Dina. "Is it Mama you're afraid of?"

"Yes," said Loretta, "and him—all of them."

"Please, my dear," said Geneva, "tell us what happened. We want to help you."

173

"You can't. No one can." said Loretta. "If only Paolo were here, free from the Army. I dreamed he had been killed and everything was hopeless."

"Don't say that!" said Dina crossing herself. "God forbid you even think of Paolo dying in the war like Papa. No, it can't happen. I pray constantly for his safety and that of our cousins who are in Africa. I've promised to return to the convent when they are safely home."

"You said you were afraid of Mama and him," said Geneva. "Do you mean our stepfather?"

Loretta began crying again. "I didn't do anything, I swear," she said.

Geneva noticed that Maria Elena and some guests were coming toward them.

"Maria Elena," said Geneva, "Loretta's not feeling well. May we take her to the house for a rest?"

"Of course," Maria Elena said. "I'll come to help as soon as I can."

"No, take care of your baby and guests," said Geneva. "Dina and I will take care of Loretta. We just need a quiet place for now."

Maria Elena gave Loretta a gentle hug and kissed her forehead. "You don't look well. Rest as long as you want. Use the bedroom. It's quiet there and no one will disturb you."

Once in the house, Loretta and Dina sat on the edge of the bed while Geneva pulled up a chair near them.

"Loretta, please take your time," said Geneva, "and tell us what has happened."

"Nothing," cried Loretta, "but he is always looking at me, and Mama thinks I'm encouraging him. Why can't she see how uncomfortable I am around her husband?"

"Has he ever really bothered you?" asked Dina. "You know, said something or did something to you?"

"Sometimes he comes up very close to me, looks at me, and smiles or winks. Once he was so close to me, he grabbed my shoulders and pressed himself against me. He laughed and said I was becoming very womanly."

"What did you do?" asked Geneva.

"What could I do? I was cleaning Gloria's room, and it's so small that I fell back against the chest of drawers and froze in shock."

"Why didn't you tell Mama?" said Dina.

"I tried, but she said I was a liar. Then she smacked my face and said I was ungrateful for all she and Umberto had done for us, and that now that I was in America, I think that I can flirt with any man I wanted. But I never…I would never, pay attention to him except as Mama's husband and our stepfather."

"That sounds like Mama," said Geneva. "It's always your fault—never hers or her precious husband or their spoiled-rotten children."

"Did he ever do anything like that to you?" Dina asked Geneva.

"Oh, sometimes he was a little too friendly," said Geneva. "Why do you think I talked Mario into marrying me and getting me out of that house?"

"The worst of it is that Mama blames me," said Loretta. "She sees him staring at me, and she thinks I'm encouraging him. I'm so nervous at dinner I can't eat without feeling like I'll be sick."

"Well, she doesn't entirely blame you," said Dina. "The fighting they do late at night is frightful to me."

"Not just at night," said Geneva. "Sometimes I'd come home from school and Mama was supposed to do something for Umberto, or the time she lost some money, he hit her and shoved her into the stove. She got really hurt and had to stay off her feet for almost a week. I was so scared I hid under the kitchen table and blocked my eyes. I was supposed to help her that week, but I was too scared to go into their room in case he was there, or came in. Ava and Luca ended up taking care of her and the house. Luca hates him too."

"Poor Luca," said Loretta, "he's always the brunt of Umberto's bad temper. The trouble is that he stands up to him and fights back, and Umberto thinks it's disrespectful and always criticizes him."

"Why doesn't he think Lorenzo and Davido are disrespectful?" said Dina. "They're always getting into trouble."

"Because Mama protects them," said Geneva. "She tries to help Luca out once in a while, but God help him if he ever criticizes her precious little princes. Only Gloria is sweet and so shy that nobody pays attention to her. After Anita died, something happened to Mama. She became harder."

"Why did she stay with him?" asked Dina. "She could have come back to Italy. Her family would have helped us."

"I think Mama likes being a rich man's wife, and in some crazy way she loves him. But don't think she doesn't fight back," said Geneva. "Once she took the long pin she uses to roll out the pasta, and she hit him so hard he needed stitches."

"It was never like that when Papa was alive," said Dina. "She had a temper, but he was so kind and gentle he always calmed her down and coaxed her until she laughed."

"If I ever marry," said Loretta, "I'm going to marry a man like Papa— someone who'll make me laugh again."

CHAPTER 77

An Ally—November 1936

"You'll take the job in Boston, Dina," said Umberto.

"Please, don't make me. Loretta has been ill, and she needs me to help her at work and with cleaning the house. If I work in Boston, it will leave her to do all the noontime chores, and I'll be late getting home every night. Besides, I'm afraid to work in Boston. It's a very big city and I might get lost."

"If your father says you will work in Boston, that's where you'll go," said Caterina. "Signor Gallo is his friend, and you are lucky to find a better paying job in a big factory. Both you girls can be so ungrateful."

Dina looked at her sister across the dining room table. Loretta's large eyes were shining with tears. Her dress hung on her thin body and she was shaking. Her dinner was untouched. Dina thought of the days when her youngest sister ate with enthusiasm, savoring every mouthful of the bounty they found in America.

"Loretta, try to eat something," said Dina. "Your food is getting cold. Eat the pasta at least."

Loretta looked down at her plate and shook her head. She then passed her plate to Luca, who hesitated for a moment, then began eating.

"Thanks, Sis," he said. Then, halfway into the meal, he looked at Loretta and said, "Are you sure you're not hungry?"

"I'm sure," she said. "You eat it. You work hard."

Luca smiled at her, gave her a wink, and proceeded to clean the plate.

Caterina, who had been in the kitchen, brought out a plate of lamb chops. "Ma, those look good," said Luca.

"These are for your father and the younger children," said Caterina. "You ate enough."

"Yeah, pasta, bread and greens," said Luca. "How about some meat for a change?"

Davido, followed by Lorenzo, threw their chewed lamb bones at Luca. "Here's some meat for you, Luca." They laughed.

Luca started to rise, and then he heard his father laughing, too. He turned to face Umberto and clenched his fists. Loretta reached over and squeezed his arm, trying to pull him back into his chair. Luca looked at

Loretta, who had begun to shake again, and saw tears streaming down her face as she silently begged him not to fight his father.

Later that evening, when Luca was on the porch smoking, Loretta went outside to talk to him. "Thank you for not fighting him," she said. "They are all *bastardi,* and my mother is not much better. I can't bear all this fighting and arguing. It's difficult to see them not treat us all equally, but please don't give them an excuse to torment you, too."

"You're a good kid, Loretta, and I'm sorry you got mixed up with this crazy family. Ma used to be better, but she's afraid of the old man and has become a little funny in the head sometimes."

"I pray every night that my brother, Paolo, will come. I have terrible dreams that he will be killed and Dina and I will be alone here. I'm so afraid of them, even Mama."

"Don't worry, kid," said Luca. "Maybe we'll get married some day and get out of here."

"No, Luca. I like you, but I'll always think of you as my stepbrother."

"I hope you change your mind someday. You're having a rough time, kid, and I'm sorry because I like you and Dina. She can be a little too holy for me sometimes, but a nice lady. Anyway, keep the thought. I'll ask you again when you feel better," he winked.

Loretta smiled and patted his shoulder. "Good night, Luca. Don't catch cold out here."

CHAPTER 78

The Talking Thief—December 1936

Loretta's nervousness and problems eating and holding down her food continued. The holidays were approaching, and Caterina was busy shopping and preparing for her charity baskets. She kept a locked larder in the basement and wore a key ring on her belt beneath her apron. On a particularly busy day, Caterina asked Loretta to go to the larder and retrieve some food needed for the evening meal and her baking projects.

"Take this key, Loretta, and open the large brown cabinet opposite the canning sink. Use one of the wooden fruit boxes to hold the things on this list. And I want you to talk to me while you are gathering the supplies."

Loretta took the key and climbed down the cellar stairs.

"Are you at the cabinet yet?"

"Almost, Mama. I'm looking for a box to carry back the things on your list."

"All right, but as soon as you open the cabinet, I want you to talk to me."

Loretta stopped and looked back at the stairs. *Why does she want me to talk to her when I reach the cabinet?* she muttered to herself.

"What was that?" asked Caterina. "Talk louder, so I can hear you."

"I didn't say anything, Mama. I was just talking to myself."

"Well, speak up and talk to me, you stupid girl," said Caterina. "Have you opened the cabinet yet?"

"I'm opening it now, Mama. What do you want me to say?"

"Just talk. You can tell me what you are putting in the box from the list."

Loretta opened the cabinet and, seeing all the food, began to gag.

"Are you eating any food? Just talk to me as you put it in the box."

That's it! thought Loretta. *That miser is afraid I'll eat something. She only asked me to do this because she knows I can't eat. I'll just spite you, Mama!*

Loretta kept up a dialogue with her mother as she placed items into the box. Before closing the cabinet, Loretta stuffed four raw eggs and a package of dried figs into her loose dress, tightening the belt securely. She continued talking to her mother as she climbed the stairs carefully carrying the wooden box of food away from her dress. She placed the box on the kitchen table and smiling at Caterina said, "I need to rest a little, Mama."

"All right then, rest a while," said Caterina, "but come back to the kitchen in an hour to help me prepare the bread."

"Yes, Mama."

Loretta left the kitchen, threw on her coat, and carefully walked out to the back shed where Luca was working at polishing a monument. "I brought you a surprise," she said and began fishing out the eggs and figs from her dress.

Luca was delighted. "How did you do it? Mama will give it to you if she finds out."

Loretta laughed. "Can you save one egg and a few figs for Dina? While you eat, I'll tell you the story of the talking thief."

CHAPTER 79

Boston Blues—February 1937

It had been two months since Dina started commuting from Quincy to her new factory job in Boston. For the first few weeks, she traveled with her cousin, Enrico, and Zia Guiseppina. They parted at Boston's South Station train terminal. During those weeks, Enrico would walk her to her new job before leaving her. Crowds and crowds of people were everywhere—on the train, at South Station terminal, and on the Boston streets. Buildings towered over her, and the wind seemed particularly strong, cold, and raw along street corners. She passed cafeteria windows where people were drinking steaming cups of coffee. She often wished she could enjoy that comfort on these wintry days.

"Mama, please talk to Umberto about giving me more money from my paycheck. It's embarrassing not to be able to buy a cup of coffee sometimes. The girls always invite me, and I have to make excuses or pretend I don't understand."

"And what's wrong with bringing coffee from home?" asked Caterina. "Are you too proud, my little nun?"

"Don't call me that! I know you don't want me to fulfill my vocation. Is it because you and Umberto would have to pay a dowry to the Church?"

"A dowry is for girls getting married—not for girls who are throwing away their life for the Church. The Church should pay us for your servitude to them."

"Mama, that's sacrilegious!"

Caterina gave a short laugh. "Go on, get to work. Here is your money for the week. And remember, Umberto now has to pay for the train—that's fifty cents a week."

"Well, if I'd stayed at my old job, he wouldn't have to pay," said Dina. "He made me leave so I would earn more money. He benefited, not me."

"You know, Dina, for someone who wants to be a nun, you crave earthly possessions too much," sniffed Caterina. "Not a healthy trait for a nun, my girl."

Dina hated her daily trips to Boston. Many of the factory women were not Italian or even Sicilian. They were Irish, Jewish, French, Polish, and even Chinese, all of whom spoke their own languages with their own countrywomen. Most spoke a few words of English, but since she still understood little English, it was not a sociable environment. The factory owners were demanding. Signor Gallo and Signor Rothberg were partners who argued constantly. Since the women did piecework, they were paid by the volume produced. A fifteen-minute morning and afternoon break and thirty minutes for lunch were the only times they were allowed to leave their machines, and the times were strictly enforced. All bathroom breaks had to be taken within these time frames. The women were discouraged from talking to each other while they worked. The noise of the sewing machines was deafening, and the air they breathed was heavy with steam from the pressing machines and millions of particles of lint from the fabrics they sewed.

Men ran the pressing machines, and they stood at their task all day. The posture of the women was head bent over the machine, their right hand holding the material to be sewn under the needle, while their left hand pulled the fabric through at the right time and their feet pressed the treadle on the floor to activate the motor. As the piles of completed blouses or skirts mounted, the owners rushed around scooping up the work. Each woman received a bundle of pieces to sew. As she completed her bundle, she retained the count slip on which her final pay would be based. Women who were fast and proficient at their work made the most money. If a piece was not done to the owner's satisfaction, it was returned to the stitcher to rip and re-sew before it was re-counted. By the end of the day, the women were tired, dirty from fabric lint, and sore from the tense work environment.

One Friday night, Dina, exhausted and eager to get home, rushed to the subway station. It had begun to snow earlier, and the streets were crowded with people rushing home. As she entered the station, someone bumped into her and she dropped her nickel for the train. She tried to bend over to look for it, but people were pushing her and someone almost knocked her to the ground. Dina stepped aside, waited for the crowd to thin, and began looking for her nickel again. Three trains had pulled into and out of the station and she still was not able to find the coin. Panic set in, and she began to cry as she continued searching the ground for her precious nickel. Two more trains came and went. She was frantic. She tried to stop someone and tell them she needed help, but people were anxious to leave and no one seemed to understand her. It was almost seven o'clock before the station thinned out.

"Oh, God, I'm all alone! Please help me!" Dina found a bench, sat down, and covered her eyes as her body heaved in fright and frustration.

"Miss, miss, are you all right? Dina is that you? What's the matter?" asked Signor Gallo. "Are you ill?"

"Oh, thanks be to God, Signor Gallo. I'm not ill; I lost my nickel. I can't find it; I can't go home."

"You lost your fare, is that it?"

"Yes, I looked and looked, but I couldn't find it. No one understood me. Can you help me, please?"

"Do you mean to tell me that you only had a nickel in your purse? That's all?"

"Yes, my stepfather will be angry that I lost it. He gives me fifty cents a week for the train."

"Is that all? What about your wages?"

"Oh, well, he helped my sister and me to come to America and he takes care of us, so we give him our pay."

Signor Gallo took Dina's arm. "Come on, I'll take you home. I have a few words to say to your stepfather."

CHAPTER 80

Paolo Leaves the Army — March 1937

My dearest sisters and mother,

By the time you receive this letter, I will be on my way home from Somalia, arriving in Italy sometime in April. The first thing I'll do is find a nice hot bath, get a decent shave and haircut, and put on a clean uniform. Prepare yourselves; if all goes well, I'll be released from the Army in May and on my way to America. Is it as rich and beautiful as people say? Could you ask Papa's relatives if they can ask about a job for me? As long as I don't have to wear a uniform, I'll do any honest work.

By the way, remember that message I got from a soldier in my platoon that someone was asking for me? Well, that someone was our cousin, Antonio. He was stationed about fifteen kilometers from my platoon. Somehow between actions, marching, marching, and marching, we met up. I was never so happy to see anyone. He almost crushed me with his big arms and we danced in circles, laughing and holding each other like two dusty bears. I know we must have looked foolish, but at the time, I didn't care.

I wish I'd have the time after my release to take a trip back to visit our family and see Zia Vittoria and Zio Pietro and all the other relatives before coming to America. To be honest, I have just enough money for the passage, a few clothes—never again a uniform—and a little saved for our life in America.

Dina paused and said to Loretta, "They are not paying for his passage. Is that what it means to you, Loretta?"

"But they paid for us, why not Paolo?"

"Could Mama and Umberto be so mean," said Loretta, "as to not help Paolo come to America?" Loretta's body shook as she began crying. "Please God, he must come! He must come! I will die here if he doesn't come to help us."

"Calm yourself," said Dina. "He is coming. He said so in the letter. He is coming soon, my dear. Don't cry."

Loretta's bouts of sudden crying, nervousness, and despair were getting more frequent. She kept to herself and wouldn't join her friends or Dina for outings. She worked every day at the factory and at home, but she was like a shadow moving about. Gone was the cheerful, spontaneous imp who was always laughing and playing pranks. A naturally petite woman, Loretta had lost so much weight that her dresses draped her skeletal frame. Her large, dark eyes dominated her thin face. Dina could not look at her without pain. She prayed constantly that God would send Paolo to them. He would relieve Loretta's fears and bring her back to health.

"What else does Paolo write?" asked Loretta. "Keep reading."

Dina looked at the next sentence and smiled at Loretta, as she continued reading.

How is my funny little Loretta doing? Do you have American boyfriends banging down the door? I miss your joyful spirit. I want you to know that remembering all your wonderful antics, and your loving generous nature, has helped keep me sane in an insane world.

"See," said Dina. "You must get well for Paolo."

Dina, all those prayers must have helped divert many bullets because I'm still in one piece. I don't often say it, but thank you for your prayers. You must have a special communication with God. I would frankly miss you if you still want to be a nun, but at least I'll know I'll always have someone to put in a good word for me.

I hope Geneva, Mario, and the children are well. I love the idea of being an uncle, so be prepared for me to spoil them when I arrive. Tell my little nieces that Zio Paolo will have a present for them.

Mama and Umberto, I appreciate your taking care of Loretta and Dina. I long to see you again, Mama, and pray that it will be soon. When I have my release papers and can make arrangements for passage, I'll write you.

My best to all the relatives, especially Zio Lorenzo. Tell him to make some wine for my return.

With great affection,
Paolo

CHAPTER 81

Letter to Sister Giovanna — April 1937

My dear friend and sister in Christ, Domenica,

Please forgive me for not addressing you as Sister Giovanna, but to me you will always be my dearest friend, Domenica.

So much has happened since Loretta and I arrived in America and were reunited with my mother and her new family. The most wonderful news is that Paolo is coming to America next month. A petition was made to Il Duce that Paolo be released from his military duty and allowed to obtain a visa for the United States of America based on his past history as a war orphan. With my father's death in the Great War, and Paolo's sixteen years as a military orphan, including twelve years of military service, he successfully petitioned that he be reunited with his mother and sisters in America. He leaves Naples the end of this month, the 26th, and arrives in New York on May 7th. Although Loretta and I begged Umberto to allow us to travel with him and my mother to New York to greet Paolo, he has refused. "…foolish waste of money," he said. "You waited this long, you both can wait a few days more."

Loretta had been ill with a nervous condition since last summer, but is finally looking better and beginning to gain a few pounds. With all of us together again, she is hopeful that life will be better. I pray this will be true. My mother is still adamant that I not return to the convent. She has gone so far as to invite men related to their friends or business acquaintances to the house to meet me. These evenings usually end in my being polite but not giving these men any encouragement. Mama and I usually have an argument the next day. She said that I am haughty and aloof, that I act superior and therefore purposely discourage any further attention from these men of good families and backgrounds.

Perhaps Mama is right about my becoming a nun. I still have a problem with strict obedience and a life of poverty. I can confess to you, my dear friend, that I have always enjoyed beautiful things and craved their possession. Our voyage to America on that magnificent ship was like a fantasy. The gracious manners of the crew, the elegant table settings of porcelain plates, delicate glasses, and fine linens all enveloped me in splendor. I never told anyone—not my sister or even you—because I was ashamed of desiring such grandeur. My destiny is to be a nun; therefore, I must desire an unadorned life of simplicity and poverty. Your little joke when we were students, about my being overly money-conscious by recording every lira spent, is still true. God help me! I am now hiding money from my parents. My boss helps me by paying me in a separate envelope any extra money I earn. He and my stepfather had a terrible argument over my not having enough money to travel to and from work. Now my boss, who has been so kind to me, pays me directly anything over an average week's pay. I opened a savings account in Boston and deposit the money every Friday before going home. Do you think it is a mortal sin not to give my parents all my money? I pray that God will forgive me, but I need to have something to protect my sister and myself, and to help Paolo when he comes.

To bring you up to date on the rest of the Leonardi and Fabrizio families, my sister, Geneva and her husband, Mario, are doing well and have three beautiful daughters—Bonita, Donata, and Vienna. Geneva is so excited about Paolo's arrival that she has been primping, decorating, and shopping to impress him when they finally meet again after sixteen years. She bought a new silk sport dress for $2.99. She said it was originally $8.95. Imagine!

On the Fabrizio side, Ava and her husband, Salvatore, have three boisterous children—Andrew, Michelina and Angelina. Her husband is a very nice, quiet man who is an attentive father. Lena and her husband, Bernardo, have one son, Jimmy. Perhaps it is my imagination, but her husband seems afraid of her. I often wonder if she inherited her father's temper. Umberto, the son we call Berto, is still in the Army and unmarried. He told me he has a woman friend, but no plans to marry as yet. Berto is a pleasant and sociable man. I hope she is a good person too. Luca is still at home and proposes to Loretta almost weekly. She likes him, but he reminds her of our stepfather—argumentative and a drinker. Luca is fond of Loretta who has saved him many times from his father's fist. When she bakes, she always makes him something extra. He has a healthy appetite but is thin and is what his father calls a "scrapper." I wonder what that word means.

Davido and Lorenzo, who are now fifteen and fourteen respectively, are devils! They like sports and have their uniforms and dirty shoes everywhere. They are always jumping on each other or rolling on the floor. More than a few pieces of furniture have been broken in the house. Mama thinks they are funny and high-spirited and treats them like royalty. Gloria, who is almost twelve, is a loving, dainty young girl. She is still a little timid around Mama and Umberto, but Loretta, Geneva, and I have taken her to heart. Loretta makes pretty dresses for Gloria, and I enjoy knitting sweaters, scarves, mittens, and bed slippers for her. She is always so grateful. She loves Geneva's children and visits them often. It's hard to believe she is part of Umberto's family.

Finally, my dear cousin and friend, Maria Elena, is expecting another child. Marianna is now nine months old. I hate to confess it, but I'll tell you my dearest friend about a recent incident. Umberto made a crude remark about Maria Elena's husband and then he winked at me and pinched me! I was never more humiliated in my life. I looked at my mother and expected her to say something to him, but she gave me the coldest look I have ever received. She actually was angry at me!

Please pray with me that when Paolo comes, Loretta and I will not be subjected to any more insults. Sometimes, I wish we never left Italy.

May God bless you my dear friend.

Dina

CHAPTER 82

My Son, My Son—May 1937

Caterina was more nervous about seeing Paolo again than she had felt when Dina and Loretta arrived. Would he remember her? Would he ever forgive her for leaving them and marrying Umberto? Or would he be angry at her and show no forgiveness?

Of all the children of her first marriage, Paolo had been her favorite. She liked his being a perfect blend of both her and Antonio. Paolo was quiet, serious, and very meticulous as she remembered. He resembled Caterina in facial features, but he had his father's nature. He was special looking, too. His beautiful dark eyes were deep and soulful under his shock of bright red hair. "My peacock," that's what he was. That brilliant red hair that shone with gold highlights when Paolo stood in the sun. Paolo possessed the best qualities of her and her first husband, Antonio.

"Caterina, calm down," said Umberto. "You are twitching about like a hummingbird."

"Do you think this is the right pier? Did you ask someone where we should meet him? Umberto, what time is it now? Do you think we missed him?"

"If we missed him, he will find us. He needs us to get through immigration, remember?"

"I wonder how tall he is now. The last photo we received showed him in uniform posing by a pedestal. He looked so grown-up, but his face was still young-looking and serious as always."

"Soldiers are supposed to be serious. Did you expect him to be smiling like some demented fool?"

"Umberto, promise you will be good to my son. Of all the children, he has suffered the most. I never thought he would be made a soldier so young and sent to fight in some foreign country against uncivilized people. His father died for Italy; they should never have sent his son to battle."

"Caterina, you are pretty but very naïve. When there's a war, even a dispute because somebody wants what someone else has, they send men—usually young men—to fight the battles and win the prizes. The bigger the prize, the more men they send. Young men are idealistic. They want to be heroes and true patriots, so they go. If they don't go, they're imprisoned or shot. Not much of a choice."

"Excuse me," said the young man. "Are you Caterina and Umberto Fabrizio?"

Caterina turned and looked at the young man. "Oh, God, is it you, Paolo?"

The man's hands cupped Caterina's face; he looked at her, smiled, and gently kissed her cheeks and forehead. "Mama, still beautiful," he said with tear-filled eyes, "and so healthy-looking too!"

Caterina embraced her son and kissed his face repeatedly while she stroked his hair. "What happened to your red hair? And this full mustache!" she cried as she shook her head in disbelief. "I can't see your face behind this bush."

"Mama, I hated my red hair. I've spent every extra *lira* on hair tonic to darken it. Fortunately, my wonderful mustache, the first one ever, is growing in darker." Paolo hugged his mother again and kissed her. "I've missed you so much," he whispered. "Are you happy? Are you well, Mama?"

Umberto placed his hand on Paolo's shoulder, and mother and son broke their firm embrace. "We must get the papers signed and be on our way. There is a train which leaves for Boston in two hours and twenty minutes. We should be on it. Welcome, Paolo. Your mother has been nervously awaiting your arrival. Your sisters are anxious to see you. If we don't catch that train, we'll be late for the dinner they are preparing for you."

"Yes, sir," he said. "Nice to meet you, too."

CHAPTER 83

Introduction to America—August 1937

Antonio's family found a position for their nephew, Paolo, as an apprentice tailor. Now both Paolo and Dina traveled to Boston with their relatives.

Paolo's arrival did more to improve Loretta's health than any doctor or medicine. The brother and three sisters—Dina, Loretta, and Geneva—were together again.

Perhaps because of Caterina's influence, Umberto did not demand a significant portion of Paolo's pay. He requested a nominal amount, to which Paolo easily agreed, to help the family. Although it was never discussed, both Paolo and Umberto acknowledged the fact that Paolo had paid for his own transportation to America. Like Dina, Paolo was frugal and only spent what was necessary. Perhaps because they were the older children, the days and years of poverty and deprivation clung to them. Both were emotionally strong as well as savers, ready to meet whatever challenges life dealt them.

Geneva and Zio Lorenzo were eager to share the beauty and richness of the region of America they now lived in. Weekends were spent going to the ocean or picnicking. Paolo loved to swim and had spent many enjoyable hours swimming at Anzio Beach when he was stationed near Rome. At first it was difficult not to compare the beauty, charm, and tranquility of Italy, especially the lovely mountainous region they came from, with America. Dina and Loretta liked seeing the ocean and catching its salty breezes, but they rarely ventured above their knees in the surf. Paolo and Geneva were the swimmers; both loved splashing through the strong waves of Nantasket Beach in Hull, Massachusetts. Paolo especially liked playing the big fish that Geneva's two older girls, Bonita and Donata, rode, clinging tightly to Paolo's neck as they crashed into the looming waves. Paolo laughed and playfully covered his ears when the girls shrieked with delight. "More, more…another one, another one!" they begged.

Dina and Loretta organized and served picnic lunches, but Loretta's favorite occupation was chatting with the friends and relatives who accompanied them on their outings. Having all the people she loved all together again and enjoying themselves each weekend brought back Loretta's high spirits and returned her to better health. During the week when Paolo and Dina were at work in Boston and Geneva was home tending to her family, Loretta was quieter and somewhat more guarded in her demeanor in the family home. She enjoyed going to work at the factory each day and had again begun to see friends, many of whom joined them at the beach outings.

On rainy or cool weekends, Paolo, Dina, and Loretta spent time with Zio Lorenzo and with Maria Elena and her family. She was like another sister to them, and her husband, Joe, was a warm, generous, and gregarious man. The men had become good friends and played cards and *bocce* ball, and went bowling on occasion. The women were always in the kitchen or garden, deep in conversation about children, sewing, cooking, and the latest gossip about friends, family, and neighbors. Except for infrequent visits, mostly to Zio Lorenzo's house, Caterina and Umberto spent their free time with their younger children or their own friends and associates.

Zio Lorenzo had remarried. His wife, Bella, was charming and eager to please. As soon as they came to visit, she would clap her hands together and happily kiss them. She then rushed off to the kitchen to get the wine, *biscotti*, and plate of homemade salami and cheeses. She fluttered around, making sure everyone had everything they needed. Although she had a high-pitched, sing-song voice, her sweet, caring nature endeared her to all of them. The only time she would sit down and relax was when Zio Lorenzo got up from his chair, took her arm, and walked Zia Bella to her favorite rocking chair. "There now, sit. Everyone is eating. Everyone has something to drink. Everyone is happy."

At this point, he would turn to the guests and ask, "Are you happy?"

Everyone would laugh, salute with their glasses, and say, "Yes, Zia Bella, we're very happy. Thank you!"

Zia Bella would then take a deep breath, sighing audibly, relax her soft, cushiony body, and smile as she rocked in her chair.

CHAPTER 84

Death of a Dove—September 1937

If there was a honeymoon period, his first four months was it.

Paolo became aware that his mother and stepfather argued behind closed doors on a regular basis. What the arguments were about was difficult to determine. Perhaps they were about money; Caterina liked fine things and seemed generous to friends and neighbors. She was constantly making up a basket or shopping bag of food or used clothes for someone. People in the street, on the rare occasions when they went to church, would come up to her and be very respectful. Some even kissed her hands and called her, *la patrona*—their patron.

It hadn't escaped him that the two young boys, Davido and Lorenzo, were spoiled tyrants who could wheedle anything from their mother. They had a more reserved demeanor with their father, he observed. Those two boys were badly in need of discipline, some responsibilities, and some good manners. Once when he noticed their rudeness to his sisters, Paolo verbally reprimanded them while holding the neck of their shirts. Once free, both boys went to complain to Caterina.

"Paolo, did you hit Davido and Lorenzo?"

"No, I gave them a talking to, but a good paddling on the backside would do them a world of good."

"They're only boys. There is too much fighting in this house. You must never threaten them or hurt them again!"

"Mama, you're raising two tyrants. I only spoke to them. If they are ever disrespectful in my presence, or if I ever find out they were unkind to my sisters or to you, I will deal with it—with or without your permission."

"No! This is Umberto's and my house. You will not interfere in our family. Do you understand?" Paolo had never seen his mother look so fierce. She was obviously trying to restrain herself because her face was scarlet and she was clenching her fists for control.

"You're right, Mama. It's Umberto's and your house. I didn't realize that I'm only a guest. I made the mistake of thinking we were a family again—my error."

Paolo told his sisters, Dina and Loretta, about his encounter with their mother over the boys.

"We should have warned you," said Loretta. "They're the crown princes. They're smart enough to stay out of Umberto's way, but Mama dotes on them—her perfect boys who inherited her own high spirits. I inherited her high spirits, I'm told," said Loretta, "but it hasn't endeared *me* to her."

"I think Mama can't look at us without feeling guilty," said Dina. "She doesn't want to feel guilty, so she's angry with us for making her feel guilty. Does that make sense?"

"More than you know," said Paolo.

"She doesn't seem to treat Gloria the same way," said Loretta. "She is such a nice girl. I sometimes want us to run away and take Gloria with us."

"How is Gloria?" asked Paolo. "Is she still feeling sick? She's been complaining of a stomach ache for three days now. She doesn't eat anything. Why haven't they called the doctor or taken her to see him?"

"Mama says it's cramps," said Dina. "Umberto said it was a woman's thing and not serious enough for a doctor. Do you think we should take her to the doctor? Let's check on her again."

Gloria's tiny room, in the alcove off the living room, had a distinct smell of ammonia. Gloria lay on the cot uttering a soft moan.

"Gloria, my dearest, can we do something for you?" asked Dina. "Did you wet yourself? Don't be embarrassed, it can happen when you're sick."

"I'll go get clean sheets, a blanket, and nightgown for her," said Loretta. "Paolo, could you get a basin of warm water, some soap, a wash cloth, and a clean towel? We'll need your help to lift her, too."

"Of course—don't worry my little dove. Your sisters and I will look after you."

After Dina and Loretta had washed and changed Gloria, Paolo tried to lift her so that they could change the sheets and blanket. Gloria cried out.

"Let's just slip a clean sheet under her," said Dina, "and cover her with the fresh blanket."

"Tonight, I'll talk directly to Umberto at dinner," said Paolo. "He makes all the decisions for Mama and everyone else. I'll try to convince him that Gloria is really sick and needs the doctor."

That evening, Paolo impatiently waited for Umberto to finish his dinner and wine, then addressed the subject of Gloria. "Umberto, I believe Gloria is getting sicker. Her forehead was very hot and she was crying in pain when I saw her just before dinner. I'd be willing to pay for the doctor if it's a question of money. The girl is obviously very sick. Perhaps we should take her to the hospital. In fact, I think that would be the best plan."

"Hospitals, doctors, do you know how much they charge?" said

Umberto. "She's like her mother says, a little hysterical—no more. She's our daughter. It's best you keep out of our family affairs—all of our family affairs. You understand?"

Paolo knew he was referring to the incident with the boys. Paolo had to leave the house, walk, and think of what to do next. He decided to stop at the doctor's house to talk to him.

Dina and Loretta sat with Gloria. They made tea; they applied warm compresses to her stomach; they held her hand and tried to calm her.

Gloria died that night of a perforated appendix. She was twelve years old.

CHAPTER 85

The Mourners—October 1937

When Gloria died, Caterina took to her bed, spending most of her days crying or complaining of violent headaches. Dina and Loretta had taken over the housework as well as the cooking.

Loretta was in the kitchen preparing the evening meal of homemade pasta. Resting her hands on the mixing board, she asked Dina, "Why does Mama have to wait until something terrible happens before she can show her love for someone?"

Dina, who had been at the stove frying meatballs for the tomato sauce, looked up. "Gloria was a shy, sweet girl who was always eager to please. Perhaps Mama didn't notice her much."

"Well, if being loud and wild gets Mama's attention, no wonder the boys are her favorites." Loretta angrily kneaded the dough. "But I've noticed that they've quieted down, too. Their little sister's death has shaken them up and made both of them grow up a little."

"Only Umberto seems unaffected," said Dina. "How can a man be so hard? I don't understand it."

"I don't think Umberto knows how to show his grief," said Loretta. "But you must admit he has been working more, and when he is home, he's with Mama, which is a relief to me. I think he's grieving for Gloria in his own way, and he's also worried about Mama's health."

Dina turned around from the stove and looked at her. "Loretta, he's a hard man. He's probably telling Mama to get over Gloria's death and get back to running his house."

"Yes, I would have said that a few days ago, but now I think Umberto can be kind and thoughtful when he wants to be," said Loretta. "Last week when I was cleaning Gloria's room, I found a candy box under her bed. At first, I smiled to myself, thinking that Gloria had hidden it so she could have a treat whenever she wanted. When I opened the box, I found a stack of drawings made by Umberto and addressed to Gloria. He must have given them to her on different occasions. There was a sweet drawing of rabbits frolicking among spring flowers. Another was a lovely religious scene; some were flowers or animals drinking at a stream. They were beautiful, and all drawn by Umberto and addressed 'To My Gloria from Papa.'"

"I don't believe it," said Dina. "Oh, he can be pleasant and almost charming, but sentimental—never."

"It's true. I'd show you the box and drawings, but I gave them to Mama to make her feel better. Strange, I thought she'd be as surprised as I was, but she wasn't. She took the box, hugged it, and started crying again. I even told Geneva, and she said that Umberto used to draw pretty cards for her when she was a child and even does one occasionally for her little girls."   Later that evening, Loretta repeated the story to Paolo. He didn't seem as surprised or unbelieving as Dina, but responded only with a deep sigh and a shake of his head.   "Well, it's reassuring to know that Umberto has a heart as well as artistic talent and business sense," he said. "He's an artisan after all. You can see it in the wonderful monuments he creates. That takes some heart as well as strong hands. I don't know why Gloria had to die. I thought it was because of money, but she died because of ignorance and fear of doctors and hospitals. Umberto and Mama know that, and I think it will haunt them forever."

CHAPTER 86

The Workers—January 1938

Recriminations, anger, sorrow, and a pervading sense of helplessness began to invade Paolo, Dina, and Loretta. Paolo immersed himself in work. He spent long days and most weekends at the factory trying to make enough money for them to escape his mother and stepfather's house.

With Gloria's death, Dina became more introspective. After work and her daily chores, she would retreat to the local church for prayer and meditation. She prayed that Paolo would help them leave this house that had held so much hurt and sorrow. Dina worried that Gloria's death would create a setback for Loretta and prayed that Loretta's health would not deteriorate again. Her greatest fear was that she would lose her beloved sister, like she lost her dearest half-sister. Her prayers may have been answered, since after an initial period of grief and depression, Loretta became strong in her sorrow and subsequent anger. She was determined to work as hard as Paolo to secure a future for all of them.

Finding herself alone with Dina one afternoon, Loretta decided to share her plans with her sister. "Dina, you'll be pleased to know that I'm following your example of thrift and savings. I've arranged to earn extra money and bank it under my name. I spoke to my boss about making the necessary sample garments—dresses, blouses, and skirts—that are required to win a contract from clothing buyers. He agreed! He said that I am not only a good stitcher but fast. My boss was able to price each piece competitively and said it showed excellent workmanship. He agreed to pay me separately and 'under the table' for all sample work."

Dina contemplating Loretta's plan and realized that the consequence of Loretta's skill would be to set a standard for all the other stitchers if they wanted to earn a good pay. Loretta had confided that some of the women had chided her to slow down when making the samples so that they would be paid a higher piece rate.

Velma had said, "Loretta, you don't have to prove you're a good stitcher. Slow down. You sew like the devil is chasing you. The boss is pricing the stuff based on your output instead of the average stitcher."

Then Carmella had said "You know that it hits us in the pocketbook, kid. Try to take it easy sometimes so we can all make a few extra bucks."

"I tried because I want their friendship," said Loretta, "but it's in my nature to work fast."

Dina listened, but truth be told, Loretta enjoyed her reputation as a top stitcher and the respect it earned her with her employer and the buyers.

Dina, like Paolo, was very methodical, and both had the exasperating trait of perfectionism. Unlike Paolo, who was quick but disciplined, Dina was slower and would spend more time thinking through her projects and redesigned as she went along. With her work habits, Loretta was making as much money as Paolo. This caused some competition between the sisters.

One evening, Dina was setting the table for coffee, and Loretta said, "Dina, you're so slow at everything, and I'm sure that's why you don't make as much money at work. If you want to do piecework, you have to move your hands, feet, and eyes at a faster pace. If your work is not good, believe me, the boss will return it to you to do over. Don't waste time trying to be so perfect. You're not sewing for the Pope you know."

"And you're like a whirlwind with everything. You even talk fast, Loretta. I've watched you at the sewing machine. You go like a demon. Someday you'll sew your fingers together. I may sew a little slower, but I never have work returned to me."

"And I do?" responded Loretta.

"Stop!" said Paolo. "You two should just accept that you are both good at what you do; you just do things differently. You two are like a lion and a cat," he laughed, "both of the same family, but with different habits and temperaments."

"And I suppose Loretta is the lion and I'm the cat? I'm not sure I like that distinction—a lazy cat or a wild lion."

"I'm not a wild lion, but a languid cat fits your description," laughed Loretta.

"Thank you," said Dina sarcastically.

Paolo looked at his sisters. *It's interesting how siblings bond, but are so different in their makeup,* he thought. He and Dina had a lot of similar traits, as did Loretta and Geneva, but each one of them was still unique. Paolo thought about himself for a moment. *I'm an ex-soldier; no girl in my life; in a new country where I can't speak more than a few words; at a job I'm learning to enjoy; living in my stepfather's house at twenty-seven years old and playing peacekeeper between my sisters. God, do I need to get out of here. We all do, and the sooner the better!*

CHAPTER 87

A New Home—May 1938

"I've found us a place to live," said Paolo. "It's close by, so we can still see Mama, Geneva, and the family. It's close to your work, too, Loretta."

"Can we see it now?" asked Loretta. "What's it like? Does it have a porch or yard?"

"Let him finish," said Dina. "Tell us more, Paolo. Where is it? How many rooms? Is it close to the trains? Is it very expensive?"

"Well, rather than describe it, I'll take you both to see it now," he said.

"I need to give the landlord a deposit by tomorrow if we want to rent it. Come on, we can walk to it."

After a twenty-minute walk from Umberto's house, Paolo, Dina, and Loretta stood across the street from a large, grey building. Each sister looked at it, silently forming her own opinion and thoughts.

"The building is on the bus line, and there's an Italian grocery store, barbershop, and general merchandise store nearby," said Paolo, wanting to persuade them.

"It's a big apartment house," said Loretta. "How many people live here? Are they Italian? Do we know anyone?"

"We might meet some people we know," said Paolo. "The landlord is not Italian—American, Irish—something like that. I had a hard time talking to him, but he's learned a few words and gestures. He likes to rub his thumb and index finger a lot to ask about money." Paolo laughed. "Come on, let's go inside. He left the apartment open so I could show you."

They walked around to the back of the square, flat-roofed building. A maze of wooden steps that led to each of the three levels lined the rear of the building. "Don't worry, it's only on the second floor," said Paolo. "Follow me and be careful of the second step; it has a crack in it."

"God help us," muttered Dina.

As they climbed the steps, their noses were assailed by numerous pungent odors—cooked cabbage, fried onions, burnt garlic, and occasionally, the sweet smell of tree blossoms. "Oh, look at those beautiful trees back there!" said Loretta. "The flowers smell so sweet it almost hides the cooking odors."

"Thanks be to God," said Dina.

As they climbed up the stairs, one or two of the apartments had their doors open. Loretta tried to peek inside each apartment to learn more about its occupants. Dina, noticing her sister's curiosity, pushed her along until they reached the second floor.

Paolo led them to the center apartment and they no longer could smell the trees, but other odors intensified. "Well, here we are," he said. "Don't worry, I'll paint the door."

Dina noticed deep scratches in the door. "Are there animals in the building?"

"You're allowed a cat or a bird, but no dogs," said Paolo. "Obviously, the previous tenant either had a dog or a very ferocious cat."

Loretta laughed. "Oh, let's get a cat. I'd love a cat. Please, Paolo, can we get a cat?"

"It's okay with me," he said. "Do you want a cat, Dina?"

"No."

"Don't worry," Paolo whispered to Loretta, "we'll get a cat later when Dina's in a better mood."

The apartment was small, dark, and dirty. "I can smell that dog," said Dina. "We'll be cleaning this place for days."

"Where's the bathroom?" asked Loretta.

"Two doors down on the left is the shared bathroom for this floor," said Paolo. "It's just a toilet—nothing else. You'll need to bring your own paper." He looked back at his sisters. "Not everyone has nice private bathrooms," he said. "You're both spoiled Americans now after Umberto's fine house. Remember, we had a shared toilet in Italy, too."

"But we knew our neighbors; we don't know these people," said Dina. "They may not be very clean."

"Well, we'll just bring bleach every time we need to use it," said Loretta.

Paolo showed them the rest of the apartment—two narrow bedrooms, a small sitting room off a kitchen with a soapstone sink, a coal stove, an icebox, a cold water tap, and a squeaky floor. "Sorry, no heat except for the stove," he said. "We'll also need to heat up any water to wash ourselves or our clothes. This, my dear sisters, is what is called in America a 'cold water flat.'"

CHAPTER 88

The Break—May 1938

Paolo took the apartment, paying the landlord the required two months' rent. Since it would be another two weeks before they would move, Dina and Loretta planned to spend every spare moment cleaning the apartment.

"Let me tell Mama and Umberto about our move tonight," said Paolo. "Hopefully, Mama will not be too upset. I'm sure Umberto will be relieved to be rid of me, but may resent missing the money you both contribute."

The dining room table was crowded that evening. Berto was home on leave from the Army. Luca, the two boys, Lena, her husband and son, along with Paolo, Dina, and Loretta squeezed in along the sides of the table. At the ends were Umberto and Caterina. As usual, the meal was noisy with everyone talking at the same time. Food was passed back and forth and across the table.

"Ma, you're still the best cook," said Berto. "Army grub was the hardest thing I had to get used to, after eating all your great cooking."

"So, when are you coming home?" asked Caterina. "Tell the Army you want to leave. Your father will give you a good job and you can eat good food, sleep in a clean bed, and find a nice wife."

"Thanks, Ma, but I'm thinking of signing up for another stretch. Believe it or not, I kind of like Army life."

"You wouldn't like it so much if someone was shooting at you," said his father. "Tell him, Paolo."

"Being a soldier in America is good," said Paolo. "Be grateful you're here. In Europe, there's always trouble. Friends write me that things are bad and getting worse there. Now people can't be a Jew in Italy. I'm finished with soldiering myself, but if Army life makes you happy, good luck to you."

Umberto gave Paolo a hard look. "A son should help his father, not waste his time weaning young recruits."

"Hey, Pa," said Luca. "I help you. I bust my ass every day working for you."

"Luca, there are children at the table," said Caterina. "Please watch your tongue."

"Ma," said Luca, "those kids could teach me a few new words."

As the adults lingered over coffee, Paolo decided to discuss the new apartment.

"I wanted to tell you again, Umberto and Mama, how much Dina, Loretta, and I appreciate your arranging for us to come to America. We've decided that it's time we moved out and got our own apartment. As a matter of fact, it's only a twenty-minute walk from here."

Simultaneously the stepbrothers and sister said, "Hey, that's nice," "Wonderful," "So close."

"What, what," asked Caterina. "You're leaving our house?" The room became quiet as everyone looked at Caterina and then Paolo.

"Yes, Mama," said Paolo, "we're adults. You have another family that you need to raise."

"Mama, Paolo's right," said Lena. "You and Papa were good to bring them here, but they have jobs now and should find their own place."

Caterina turned angrily at Lena. "You be quiet and mind your own business or go home!"

"Well, I'm sorry," said Lena. "Come on, honey, let's go. Maybe you guys should leave, too."

"Go, all of you, go. I want to talk to my children alone."

"Ma, let them do what they want," said Berto. "You can visit them. They'll be down the street. They're not leaving you forever."

Caterina gave him a hard stare and Berto's face flushed a bright red. He turned to his brother and said, "Come on, Luca. I'll buy you a beer."

Luca, who was disappointed with the news since he had grown fond of Loretta, wanted to say something, but one look at his father made him think better of it, and he left with Berto.

The house was finally quiet. Lena sent her younger brothers off to bed before leaving, and the boys gladly retreated.

"And what do you think people will say when you all move out?" asked Caterina. "They will think we have trouble in the family. It will be a scandal, especially two women living in an apartment."

"I'll be living there too, Mama," said Paolo. "I'll look after them. I don't like your even suggesting anything else."

"What is it? They have boyfriends and you are protecting them?"

"Mama, how can you say that?" asked Dina. "Loretta and I have never given you any reason to say that."

"Oh, you," said Caterina, "so holy, always running to the church. How do I know you're not meeting some men and pretending to be in church?"

"God forgive you, Mama," said Dina.

"And you," said Caterina pointing to Loretta, "I see how you tease Luca—always hiding on the porch or in the back shed. What are you two doing, eh?"

Paolo grabbed his mother's arm and turned her to him. "Mama, stop this sick talk. You know they're good women. They work all day and every free moment they're cleaning, cooking, sewing, and running errands for you. You have no right to say these terrible things to them."

"Let them go, Caterina," said Umberto. "No one will criticize us. We brought them over, gave them a home, and provided for them. People will draw their own conclusions about them."

"No," said Caterina, "it's a scandal. Young women can't leave their home to live in apartments. Everyone will think badly of us." Turning to Loretta and Dina, she said, "You'll be called 'tramps,' and I'll be the first to call you that name. Go, then, but never come back, you ingrates."

"Caterina, calm yourself," said Umberto. "If they want to leave, let them go. I warned you that it would not work out. Everyone would have been happier if you left them in Italy."

"Go, go now!" shouted Caterina. "Don't think you can come back. Even if you starve, I don't want to see or hear from you. You are ungrateful children who were never taught to respect your elders."

Paolo looked at his mother, speechless at her cruel streak. He expected Umberto to be ignorant, but not his mother.

"Well, Mama," said Loretta, "if you had stayed in Italy to raise us, maybe you would have done a better job."

Caterina turned to Loretta, and without warning, slapped her hard across the face. "Get out! Get out!"

Having to leave Umberto's house the evening of the confrontation, Paolo, Loretta and Dina had nowhere to go. They walked with bags in hand to Zio Lorenzo to ask for shelter for the two weeks until they were able to move into the new apartment.

Zio Lorenzo was furious with his sister and her husband. "Caterina always had a spiteful streak, and she did you all a great injustice by leaving you alone in Italy after your father died, but this is her greatest sin ever."

"Poor children, poor children," cried Zia Bella. "You stay here. I'll take care of you. Don't worry."

Loretta hugged her aunt, and Zia Bella enveloped her in her large embrace and gently kissed her bruised face as they both cried.

CHAPTER 89

A New Start—January 1939

Supporting a new apartment during the first few months proved to be a financial challenge for the siblings. Paolo had saved enough money to buy some pieces of used furniture, and Zia Bella supplied much of their linens. Their cousin, Maria Elena, and her husband, Joe, also gave them some dishes, eating utensils, cutlery, pots and pans, as well as a few tools for repairs around the apartment. Geneva frequently invited them for dinner and also supplied some material for curtains and a slipcover for their single stuffed chair.

"Well," said Loretta, as she adjusted the new slipcover, "it doesn't make the chair any more comfortable, but it looks a lot better."

"I wish we could meet more of the neighbors," said Dina, "but working and fixing up the apartment keeps us so busy. I did meet a nice lady at the bus stop. She lives in our building and said there are a lot of Italian families in our building as well as in the neighborhood."

"We know there are a lot of Italian people, especially from our region of Italy," said Loretta, "but most of them know Mama and Umberto and have stayed away from us. Even at church, the priest was very cool to us at the Christmas Midnight Mass."

"Well, I'm happy that the church is still walking distance away, even if the priest is not as friendly," said Dina. "I wonder what Mama has been telling people and if they believe her. She didn't even want to see us or take a present from us at Christmas. She's still very bitter about our moving out."

"Paolo was hurt," said Loretta. "He didn't say much, but for all her meanness, he still loves Mama. How well does she know him or even care? Remember the first week we lived here? That night when I thought someone was in the apartment while we were sleeping? I got up and there was Paolo sleepwalking. The window was open and I thought he would fall out," she said. "I didn't know what to do. People say it's dangerous to wake a sleepwalker. Thank God I got him back on the sofa chair and he went back to sleep. I sat up and watched him all night."

I asked the doctor about Paolo's sleepwalking," said Dina, "and he said it's a sign of stress. I know that the confrontation with Mama upset him deeply."

Do you still love Mama, Dina?"

"I pray for her all the time, and God tells us we must love everyone, even those who hurt us. But I also pray that God will help me to forgive her, because I don't know if I ever will," said Dina. "When she left me at the orphanage, I felt like my heart broke in two and would never mend. I was blessed with some good friends like Domenica and Sister Lauria, but the fear and deprivation of those days will never leave me."

"Then why do you want to become a nun and go back?" asked Loretta.

"Because I found a peace there, too," said Dina. "I could retreat into my prayers and think of Papa and all the wonderful memories I have of him and the childhood I shared with Paolo, Geneva and you. I felt safe in letting God direct my life when Mama abandoned us. I wanted us to all be together again and if that couldn't happen, then I wanted to dedicate my life to serving God. But I had trouble in the convent. I am too attached to things, and money is important to me for security. Those are not good traits for a nun. I'm not sure about anything anymore, but I am happy to be here with you, Paolo, and Geneva again, so who knows the future?"

"I want us to be happy, each find someone we can share our lives with, and all grow old together surrounded by all our children and grandchildren for a hundred years," said Loretta. "That's what I dream our future will be."

CHAPTER 90

The Meeting—February 1939

Dina and Paolo thought the location of the apartment, despite its proximity to their mother, was ideal because it was directly on the bus line. This allowed them to travel together to Boston or do errands. Only Loretta had a longer distance to travel to work. At first she feared she would lose her job, since Umberto was friends with her boss, but fortunately, that did not happen. In fact, she had recently seen Umberto driving his truck. She was waiting for the bus for work when he stopped and parked his truck in front of her. Loretta froze as he approached her.

"How are you, Loretta?" he asked. "Are you, Paolo, and Dina all settled? This is not too bad a place, but I'd advise you to buy some mousetraps."

"We're fine, thank you. We already have mousetraps."

"You look like I'm going to bite you," he said. "Calm yourself. I wish you all well. No hard feelings. It's better this way. You're not children. You need your privacy and your own life. Your mother doesn't understand. She thinks you have disgraced her by moving out. She'll come around."

"I don't think she will ever forgive us," said Loretta. "She wouldn't even see us when we went to Gloria's Memorial Mass or when we came by at Christmas to bring her a gift. No, she can be cruel and unforgiving. But she's the one..." Loretta stopped speaking and looked down to hide her tears.

"Yes, your mother can be a formidable woman. She has a lot of regrets but is too proud to admit them. Don't give up on her. She doesn't show it, but she needs your love and loyalty. The respect and opinions of others mean a lot to her."

"You have to give respect and love before you can receive it," said Loretta. "I'll never forget the things she said. I tried to forgive her because she's my mother, but I'll never forget."

"Feisty women," he said. "I like feisty women, but they turn your hair gray and make you drink."

"There's the bus," said Loretta. "I have to go to work now."

"I'd offer you a ride, but I doubt you'd accept it. Be well, Loretta, and tell your brother and sister I wish them well, too."

CHAPTER 91
Unrest and Uncertainties—July 1939

My dear friend in Christ, Sister Giovanna/Domenica,

I received your letter and am so excited, I could burst with joy! God is so good to send you to America to teach at a school in Wisconsin. I don't know where that is, but I'm sure that Paolo can find out for me. We can finally be together again!

Although I have received no encouragement from my family, and I struggle with my own self-doubts, I have not given up my desire to return to the convent. Now, I have hope that if I take my vows here in America, we can be sisters in Christ again.

I appreciate your words and prayers of encouragement concerning the situation with my mother. She accused Loretta and me of the vilest motives for leaving and getting an apartment together with Paolo. She was not as harsh with Paolo because she knew that Umberto wanted him to leave. After Gloria's death, Umberto and Paolo barely spoke to each other or even looked at each other. It was just a matter of time before Umberto would tell Paolo to leave or Paolo would walk out of the house for good. We have tried to visit my mother, but she refuses to see us.

Geneva and her husband are talking about moving to California. She is expecting their fourth child, and Mario has a friend who promised him a good job. They feel this would be a good opportunity for several reasons. Mario's mother died in April, which was the same time that Mario was laid off by his company. And as usual, Geneva and Mama are still not getting along.

We will miss Geneva, Mario, and the children. Geneva confided in us that she and Mario have always had a troubled marriage, and she is hoping that this move will help them become closer.

So many problems in the world. Paolo received a letter from your brother, Marco. He spoke of all the times they spent together at the orphanage and then in the Italian Army, and how much he misses Paolo and all the good times they had playing soldiers at school. He wrote that he doesn't miss the Army, but there are few jobs in Italy or in most of Europe. Many people are trying to leave because of the rumors of another war. God forgive me, but if you were the bride of a rich man instead of the

Church, perhaps you could have called for your brother and his family, and he would find a job in Wisconsin. A foolish thought, but there is my dilemma of being insecure where money is concerned.

Most of my father's family is now in America, and we have been trying to see them more, to strengthen our family ties. Only Mama's sister, Vittoria, her family and a few cousins are still in Italy, and we worry about them. My aunt is a wonderful correspondent and writes more often to us since we left Mama's house. We miss her, our uncle, and all their loving family.

Paolo and Loretta and I work hard to survive in America, but we are happy to be together and don't mind doing without some of the luxuries we had at Mama's house. Loretta likes to cook, and I like things clean, neat, and orderly, so that's how we divide the work at home. Paolo, you remember, is a very neat, meticulous man and he keeps our few pieces of furniture in good repair. He's very good at catching mice, which has become less of a problem now that we also have a cat named Nina. Paolo has met a few girls, but nobody special yet.

Loretta has always been more social than I am. She has friends from work, and they go on picnics, to the movies when we can afford it, and to the beach. Most of the women are not married, but a few married women join them occasionally if their husbands are busy with clubs or work. A nice man who comes from Gaeta has invited Loretta to the movies a few times, but she always refuses. I admit I have mixed feelings about her meeting someone and getting married. Right now we are taking care of each other, and I am content with that for the present time.

Well, my dearest friend, my head droops in sleep, so I will end this letter. As soon as I find out where Wisconsin is, I will see if we can arrange to see each other again.

Remember me and mine in your prayers, my dear, dear friend, and I will remember you.

With great affection always,
Dina

CHAPTER 92

The Fair of the Future—June 1940

Dina rose to clear the dishes from the table.

"Sit for a while," said Paolo, "I have a surprise for you and Loretta. How would you like to go to New York and see the World's Fair?"

"Oh, Paolo, can we, really?" said Loretta. "When can we go? Do I have time to make some new clothes? I'll need new shoes too!"

"How can we afford such a trip?" said Dina. "We haven't the money or the time to take such an extravagant vacation. Do we?"

Paolo laughed. "Always the practical one, Dina. And Loretta, always the gypsy—grab your tambourine and go! Well, my dear sisters, we all have one week's vacation the first of July. We can take the train to New York on Sunday, June 30th and return on Saturday, July 6th. That way we lose only four days of work but gain a whole week of free time."

"But where will we get the money for the train, a place to stay, food, and everything else?" said Dina. "It must cost a fortune for such a trip."

"We have money saved," said Loretta. "We can work overtime when we get back. When will we ever again go to a World's Fair—a World's Fair in New York City?"

"Well, the Fair is outside of New York City, but close enough for us to visit both," said Paolo. "In fact, the train takes us into the city, and we'll need to find transportation to the Fair. Don't worry, though, I'll work out all the details before we go."

"Spoken like a world traveler," said Dina, "but where will we get the money?"

Paolo got up from the table and went into his room. When he returned, he handed a bankbook to Dina. "This should be enough," he said.

Opening the book, Dina stared at it and tears misted her eyes. "Why have you kept this from us? We scrimp and save and you've had all this money in the bank."

Loretta pulled the book from Dina's hand. "*Deo mia*, did you rob the bank?"

Don't cry, Dina," said Paolo. "I wasn't trying to deceive you. Most of this is back pay from the Army that finally reached me. The rest was money I saved from overtime work. A man has to plan for the future. I didn't mean to be secretive, but wanted to have money saved for a special occasion or an emergency. I'm sorry if I upset you."

"Who cares?" said Loretta. "Now we can go to the Fair and have fun!"

"Isn't this a grand Fair?" said Loretta. "It's like peeking into the future. This must be what heaven is like. Look at the huge white monuments and buildings!"

Paolo positioned his sisters in front of the Perisphere with its moving stairs transporting visitors into visions of the future in transportation, communications, and business systems. An obliging tourist took a photo of Paolo with his sisters in front of the huge Helicline, which was a colossal globe and planetarium. Another friendly man took their photo with the seven-hundred-foot Trylon column in the background.

"This is like touring the world without ever getting on a boat," said Loretta, who particularly enjoyed the exhibits from different countries. "Let's hope the theme of 'For Peace and Freedom' will be true for the poor people in Europe, especially Italy."

"Isn't the American government exhibit impressive?" said Dina. "Our new country is so wonderful and exciting. So many grand inventions like the Futurama! Oh, it was so exciting to sit in a chair and see thousands of future American homes, cars, trucks, beautiful water parks, and so many trees. And the new refrigerators and air boxes to cool you and even science boxes where you can see stories and people amusing you. Oh! It's so amazing! Paolo, do you think it will really happen?"

"Who knows, but if it does all happen," said Paolo, "I want one of those fancy automobiles."

"Wouldn't that be wonderful!" said Loretta. "If you buy a car, can you teach me to drive it?"

"If I ever have enough money to buy an automobile, you'll be the first to learn after me. I promise."

"Let's eat something before we leave," said Loretta. "I vote for ice cream."

"Well, I've eaten my way through many countries," said Paolo, "and I still think you two are the best cooks."

After checking out of their hotel room with its small efficiency kitchen, lumpy couch, and sagging beds, Paolo hailed a taxi to bring them to the train station.

As she took a last look at their impressive surroundings, Dina turned to look at her brother and sister as they sat together waiting for their train at New York City's Grand Central Station. Loretta was clutching a cardboard box that held their souvenirs. Paolo was checking his camera and polishing its lens. "You both look tired, and I know I'm exhausted, but I think I will always remember this week as one of the happiest times in our lives, thanks to you, my dear Paolo."

CHAPTER 93

The Bloomers—July 1940

Loretta placed the large plate of polenta with its generous scoops of marinara sauce on the table.

"This looks and smells wonderful," said Paolo. "I'm lucky to have two lovely sisters who wait on me and stuff me with good food."

"Don't forget the salad," said Dina. "Did you cut up the tomato into thin slices? If you're careful, we'll have enough for the week."

"Dina, Zio Lorenzo gave me almost a dozen tomatoes from his garden, we have plenty. I'm putting them in our lunches tomorrow. Besides, he said to come back for more tomatoes, beans, and Swiss chard on Saturday.

"Well, we don't want to take advantage," said Dina. "He needs vegetables for himself, and for Maria Elena's and Tomaso's families, too. Isn't it wonderful that Tomaso married and now after only six months has a son? Zio Lorenzo's first grandson—such a pretty baby."

"Yes, that Tomaso is a fast worker," replied Loretta as she winked at Paolo.

"Since Mama's speaking to us again," said Paolo, "Zio even brings some vegetables over to her, but they don't need much, since Mama has her own garden."

Loretta sat at the table, joining her brother and sister. "Mama has peppers and eggplant if we want to pick them."

"Let her keep them," said Dina. "We may be speaking again, but I don't want anything from Mama or her husband."

Loretta raised her dark brown eyes to Paolo and shook her head slightly. Paolo smiled and winked at her.

"The funniest thing happened today, Dina, as I waited at South Station for you," said Paolo. "A young lady lost her panties right there on the platform."

"What!" said Dina.

Loretta laughed. "How did she lose her panties? And what did you say? I know. Pardon me, lady, are these your bloomers?"

"No," Paolo chuckled. "I didn't say anything. Poor girl was rushing and all of a sudden, her panties were on the ground. I tried to look away to save any embarrassment, but she just looked around, stepped out of them, and kept walking."

"Oh, poor woman," said Dina. "How shameful. She must have wanted to die."

"Well, I think she handled it very well," Paolo said between chewing his food. "No hysterics, just stepped out of them and walked away as if nothing happened. I almost burst from trying not to laugh."

Loretta, who was laughing at the story, started to choke.

"See," said Dina, "God is punishing you for laughing at that poor woman's misfortune."

Drinking some water to clear the food, and regaining her composure, Loretta asked, "What did she look like? How young was she? Was she pretty or plain?"

"I guess fairly young, maybe twenty or so. I didn't see much of her face, but she had a nice figure and wore pink panties."

"Stop, you two! This is disgraceful. You should have turned away, Paolo. The poor woman must have been in shock."

"You're right. If I wasn't waiting for you, Dina, I would have followed her and returned the panties."

"Oh, you'd never!" said Loretta.

"No, but I wanted to see Dina's reaction. Sorry, my innocent little sister. I'll stop talking. By the way, do you want the panties?"

As Loretta and Paolo burst out laughing, Dina shook her head and made the sign of the cross.

CHAPTER 94

The Chicken Man — August 1940

"Fall cleaning—I hate it!" said Loretta.

"You hate spring cleaning, summer cleaning, and winter cleaning, too," said Dina. "You just hate cleaning, period."

"We agreed that I would cook and wash and you would clean. Remember?"

"Loretta, don't I cook, wash, and mend too? Weekly dusting and cleaning is fine, but when it's time to do deep cleaning, everyone needs to help," said Dina. "Even Paolo does the windows and fixes things around here, and I don't hear him complaining."

"I think he's met someone," said Loretta. "He's always in a happy mood, whistling and humming. He's always so neat and meticulous in his clothes and shoes, but he's even more so, if that's possible. Sometimes I catch him smiling and talking to himself. Do you know anything?"

"No. If Paolo has met a girl and he likes her, he'll tell us in his own time."

"I wonder who she is?" said Loretta. "I hope it's not that homely girl who lives across the street. She's always trying to catch Paolo at the bus stop. She's so funny. She's always giggling and playing with her hair. Paolo couldn't possibly like her. Besides, she bites her fingernails. Ugh, he hates that."

"It's none of your business. He'll tell us when, and if, it becomes serious. Besides," said Dina, "that girl is not even Italian. I've been at the bus stop with Paolo and she chatters on and on. I don't understand most of what she says, and I'm sure Paolo doesn't either."

"Well, you can tell she's flirting with him, and you don't need to understand English to know she's making eyes at him constantly."

"Enough," said Dina. "Finish the floors. I need to do some shopping. I want to cook something special for Paolo's birthday."

Dina decided to try the farmers' market set up in the ball field near the city's high school. As she rode the bus, she tried to think of a menu, but it depended on what she found reasonably priced.

"Eggplants, get your eggplants here," called the burly man whose hands looked like he had been digging dirt all morning.

"Com'ere, lady. Good tomatoes. Nice and ripe, just for you," another vendor called.

Dina collected her purchases and combined them in a sturdy linen bag she had made for shopping. Just one more stop at the butcher shop downtown and I can finally go home, she thought. As she walked toward the main square, she passed a few more vendors. Suddenly she felt someone come up behind her.

"Beautiful lady, please stop," said the man. "You are the most beautiful woman I have seen all day—all week—all summer. Come and see my beautiful chickens. Not beautiful like you, but for chickens, they are beautiful. Come and see, my lovely lady."

Dina stopped and was prepared to tell this man that he could keep his beautiful chickens.

"My apologies, lady, but I mean it. You are a beautiful woman. I wanted to just say that to you."

Dina looked at the man. He was tall, slender and about her age—late twenties. His chin had a deep cleft, his hair was thin and a medium brown color, his eyes were deep, almost hooded, but his voice sounded sincere. *He's nice looking,* she thought, *but too sure of himself.*

She felt him taking her by the arm and directing her to the stacked cages of chickens. The birds cackled incessantly and fluttered around trying to escape their confines.

"Look, beautiful lady. Look at these fine chickens."

"I'm really not sure I want a chicken. I'm on my way to buy some meat at the butcher's."

"Is it for your husband, dear lady?"

"No, for my brother. It's his birthday."

"So, you're not married?"

"No, but that's none of your business."

"You make me happy today, my beautiful lady. These chickens are from my mother's farm in Weymouth, so they haven't been in the cages too long. Take a chicken and cook it for your brother. He'll be happy and you'll make me happy, too. I'll give it to you for a low price because you are a beautiful lady."

Dina felt she could ignore all the charm this handsome man exuded, but the phrase "low price" was the clincher. "All right, I'll buy one of your chickens. Give me a good, fat one."

"For you, my beautiful lady, the fattest."

Dina paid a reasonable price for the chicken, and the man also gave her a lightweight cage to carry it on the bus. Returning home, Dina put the chicken in its cage on the back porch since she would not need to kill, clean, and cook it for another few days. She put a cup of water and some dried bread in the cage for the chicken. The next day, Sunday, she added fresh water and more bread. On Monday, she noticed that the chicken had not eaten the bread. On Tuesday, the day she was to prepare the chicken for dinner, she noticed that it had not only not eaten its bread, but had drunk little water and was unnaturally quiet.

"That thief sold me a diseased chicken," said Dina to Paolo, "and now I can't make the Chicken Fiorentino you like so much."

"Don't worry. I'm sure he didn't know," said Paolo. "The chicken looked fine when you brought it home last Saturday. Maybe it was too hot on the porch."

"No, it was a diseased chicken and this beautiful woman is going to hit that lying thief with his beautiful, sick chicken."

On Saturday morning, Dina took the languishing chicken on the bus and headed for the farmers' market.

"Oh, it's you, beautiful lady," said the chicken man. "You didn't need to return the cage, but you can use it for another chicken."

Dina took the cage and shoved it against the man's chest. "Keep your diseased chicken and give me my money back."

"What's wrong with the chicken?" he asked as he opened the cage. "You're right," he said, "this chicken is bad, but honestly, it was fine. If I gave you a bad chicken, I apologize. Here, take another chicken and your money back, too. I'm an honest businessman. I've never cheated anyone, especially a beautiful lady like you," he smiled. "Please, take the money and the chicken with my sincere apologies. Look, I'm not a farmer. I'm only helping my mother sell her chickens at the market. I build houses, you know, a contractor. I guess I don't know a lot about chickens."

Dina looked at him. He looked and sounded sincere enough. Maybe he didn't know the chicken was sick, or maybe Paolo was right about the heat affecting the poor chicken. "I'll take back my money."

The chicken man took several dollar bills out of his pocket and handed her two.

"No, you only charged me one dollar. I'll take one dollar back."

"Please, beautiful lady. Let me give you another chicken for your brother. If this one is sick, I'll eat it myself. I promise." The chicken man bowed and gave her a beguiling smile.

CHAPTER 95

Luca's Queen—September 1940

"I wonder what she's like?" said Loretta. "Luca said she lives on a large farm in Braintree and called her his *piccola regina italiana*. What does that mean?"

"It means she is queenly, but short," said Dina. "How do I know what he means?"

"Why, Dina, that sounds almost sarcastic for you."

"Well, I didn't mean to be sarcastic, but I have a hard time picturing Luca with anyone who has regal qualities. I mean he's a nice man and a hard worker, but he's illiterate, a drunkard, and he never looks quite clean."

"Luca's rough looking and uneducated, but he has a good heart," said

Loretta. "You know how hard Umberto has always been on him—hitting him, calling him stupid, never encouraging or praising his own son for his long hours and back-breaking work."

"You're right," said Dina, "but what would a girl who has had schooling find appealing in a man who is uneducated?"

"I like Luca. He protected me from Umberto and Mama when I was ill and made the younger boys act respectfully to us," said Loretta. "He gave me money when I needed it and bought me sweets when I was depressed."

"That's because he wanted to marry you. Thank God you had the sense to say no."

"I'll always be grateful to Luca for being my big brother when Paolo wasn't here. Luca just needs a strong woman to polish out his rough edges and clean him up a bit."

Paolo purchased a bottle of wine for dinner to accompany Dina's homemade gnocchi and Loretta's tomato sauce with homemade sausages. Fresh greens, tomatoes and cucumbers were provided by Zio Lorenzo's garden, and Zia Bella gave them fresh baked bread.

Dina had just finished rinsing the bowl of fruit and grapes for dessert when she heard the knocking on the door. "Would you get that, Paolo?" she said.

Opening the door, Paolo saw Luca holding hands with a petite, olive-skinned young woman with lovely, dark eyes fringed with the longest lashes he had ever seen. "Come in, come in, Luca. This must be Jennie. I'm very happy to meet you. Come and meet my sisters."

"My sisters, too," said Luca.

"Our sisters," said Paolo, patting Luca's back. "Luca, you look good. This is a nice suit."

"Jennie helped me pick it out. She chose the tie and shirt, and even my socks match," Luca said.

"Jennie, you have good taste," said Paolo. "I've never seen Luca look so stylish."

"Luca, you look wonderful," said Loretta. "So handsome! Don't you think, Dina?"

"Very nice," said Dina. "Please sit down, Jennie. We've been looking forward to meeting you."

"Luca talks about all of you so much, I was anxious to meet you too, especially you, Loretta," said Jennie. "Luca told me all those stories about how you would steal food for him or save him from a fight with his father. I'm almost jealous knowing how fond he is of you."

Loretta blushed and lowered her head before speaking. "Luca looked

211

out for us while Paolo was still in Italy, in the Army. We helped each other when times were bad, that's all."

Redirecting the conversation, Paolo said, "Tell us about yourself, Jennie. Luca said your family has a nice farm and you're a great help to your parents."

Jennie shrugged, smiled, and began talking about how busy and hard farm work was. She spoke warmly of her parents and siblings, and reflected a happy family life that was based on working and enjoying their times together.

"I go and help her father sometimes," said Luca.

"Yes, you may need a woman's touch to clean you up a bit, my dear, and a strong hand to hold you," Jennie laughed, "but you are a hard worker, I'll say that, and you're so good to me and my parents."

"Oh, you know I like your folks. Your mom is always feeding me and your dad…"

"Yes, my dad is always offering you *grappa*," said Jennie stiffly.

"*Grappa*! That stuff is so strong," said Paolo, "that it dissolves hair from your chest."

Everyone laughed.

Dina called everyone to the dinner table and the evening went quickly and pleasantly.

Loretta served *biscotti* and *espresso* as Paolo apologized for not having any anisette liquor to add to their coffee.

"I'll bring some the next time," said Luca.

"No, we all can do without it," said Jennie. "Remember, you promised to start saving your money."

"Oh, yeah," said Luca, kissing Jennie's cheek, "and this is my pretty little banker."

After Paolo, Dina and Loretta said their good-byes to Luca and Jennie, Dina closed and locked the door. "Good," she said, "Luca has found a nice, no-nonsense Italian girl who has cleaned him up and will shape him into a good husband and provider. Good for her. Good for him."

Paolo smiled, then clicking his heels, saluted and said, "Yes, *signorina*!"

Loretta laughed and said, "I like her, too."

CHAPTER 96

Sicilian Friends—November 1940

Loretta stood at the bus stop and watched the densely falling snow. A few other riders were taking shelter in a door front, but there was little room left for her.

"Where is that bus?" a woman in the shelter asked.

As Loretta was leaning off the sidewalk looking for the bus, a snow-covered car pulled up into the bus stop, making her jump back. A window rolled down, and a woman heavily bundled up leaned out of the back window and called her name.

"Loretta? It's Rosa. Get in. We'll drive you."

Loretta smiled in relief when she recognized Rosa Alongi, one of the Sicilian women who had recently started working with her. Rosa's sister, Sarafina Ianuzzi, sat in the front seat with a young man who seemed to be annoyed with stopping, but didn't say anything.

"You know my sister, Sarafina, and that's my baby brother, Luigi Caramazzo. What a bad day. We saw Lucia at the bus stop down the street, and then I saw you, so I told my brother to stop and pick you both up."

"Oh, thank you so much. I was getting soaked," said Loretta. "It was nice of you to stop, Luigi."

"Yeah, okay," was all he said.

"Do you live near here?" asked Rosa.

"Yes, just across the street in that big gray building."

"We go by your house every day. We can give you a ride whenever we see you. Can't we, Luigi?"

"Yeah, I guess."

It was a relief getting a ride once in a while, but Loretta did not want to take advantage of her new friends. At Christmas time, she gave Rosa and Sarafina hand-crochet bureau scarves and gave their brother a bottle of wine.

"Did your Sicilian friends like their gifts?" asked Dina.

"Yes, I think so. Rosa thanked me profusely, admired my work, and hugged me. Sarafina said it was a very nice design and stitches."

"What about the brother? Did he have enough manners to thank you?"

"Yes," he said, "thanks, that's nice, you didn't have to, but thanks anyways, Merry Christmas!"

"I work with some Sicilians," said Dina. "They keep to themselves. I tried talking to them, but I don't understand their dialect. Do you understand when they talk to you?"

Loretta laughed. "When I first heard them speaking, I thought they were speaking English, but then some words almost sounded Italian. It took me a while before I understood they were speaking Sicilian dialect."

"So now you understand them?" said Dina.

"Sometimes I need to ask someone what they said, or they try to help me understand better. Both women are married to Sicilians and seem to be very close knit with the other Sicilian women, so they are very comfortable in speaking with each other. They are very nice, though, and try to include me and the other Italian women in their conversations. Rosa's husband speaks a little English and they have five children. Sometimes Rosa mixes her Sicilian with a few words in English when she talks. Sarafina speaks mostly Sicilian, and their brother speaks English for the most part."

"Well, be careful being friends with them. Everyone knows that Sicilians have terrible tempers. I've heard that many of them even carry knives."

Loretta clutched her chest and groaned a loud cry before collapsing into her chair, laughing.

CHAPTER 97

Greetings—February 1941

"What should we give Loretta for her birthday?" asked Paolo. "I was thinking of a nice ring with her birth stone. I saw a pretty one last week at the jewelers' building in Boston."

Dina looked at her beloved brother. His face was fuller now and his hated red hair was now a dark reddish brown, no longer full and wavy, but shorter and thinner. His eyes, a deep warm brown, always seemed to hold a smile.

"Loretta doesn't expect such an expensive gift," said Dina. "She'd be happy with a smaller gift like a new blouse or sweater."

"Well, our baby sister is going to be twenty-four," said Paolo, "that's almost a quarter of a century. A special birthday gift is in order. Let's have a nice get-together with the family, too."

"Suppose we have a bad storm," said Dina. "You know that Mama won't leave the house if there's snow on the ground. Zia Bella is afraid of walking on the snow, too, as are the old aunts."

"What a worrier you are," said Paolo. "If it's too much trouble or expense for you, we'll just invite fewer people."

"My sister's birthday is not too much trouble or expense," said Dina hotly. "How can you say that to me? I'm very hurt you could suggest such a thing about me."

"I love Loretta, and I love you, too. I just …"

Dina was suddenly crying into her hands, and a stray strand of her dark brown hair escaped her carefully coiffured hair knot.

"Dina, for God's sake, what's wrong? Are you ill?"

Composing herself, Dina pulled an envelope from her pocket and handed it to Paolo. It had been opened. Paolo read the telegram: "Greetings, the President of the United States and your neighbors have selected you for the draft. You will report to the U.S. Army Recruiting Office, 500 E. Congress Street, Boston, Massachusetts, on Monday, March 19, 1941 at eight in the morning for induction into the United States Army following a satisfactory medical examination."

Paolo looked at his sister, who was quietly crying again. "I'm sorry I opened it," said Dina, but it was a telegram and I thought someone died. How can you go into the American army when we're not even citizens yet?"

"Lucky, I guess," said Paolo.

After dinner, Paolo and Loretta sat in their small parlor area while Dina finished washing dishes. Paolo was holding up the newspaper, but Loretta noticed he seemed distracted, staring over the top of the paper instead of focusing on the print.

"Are you reading or just hiding behind that paper?" She teased.

"Loretta, we need to talk," said Paolo as he folded, then dropped the paper to the floor.

"I knew it," she said. "Something terrible has happened. All night Dina looked like she lost her best friend and you were so deep in thought I knew something was wrong. Did someone in the family die? Tell me. Did you or Dina lose your job?"

Paolo got up from his seat and sat on the floor next to his sister. He reached into his vest pocket and handed the telegram to Loretta. Loretta's face blanched as she read the telegram. Then she said,

"Well, at least no one died, but this is impossible."

"Obviously, it's not impossible," said Paolo. "They started the draft last fall to build up the American army, and my name was picked."

"But why? How?" said Loretta. "We're not citizens; you can't even speak or read English very well," she said as she picked up and shook the Italian newspaper at him. "Tell them they made a mistake. Maybe we need to have Umberto tell them, or the priest. Tell them you can't go. You were a soldier long enough. Tell them."

"Yes, have Umberto or even your boss tell them you are not a citizen yet," said Dina.

"I'll have to go and maybe they'll decide I'm not American enough or young enough to serve in their army," said Paolo.

"At least there is no war in this country," said Loretta. "Maybe because you were a soldier, they want you to train other men."

Paolo thought about the unrest in Europe which filled the news. The last time he heard from his cousins and his friend, Marco, things were bad in Italy and in most of Europe. "At least there is no war here," he repeated. Then putting his arm around Loretta's shoulders, he tried to sound light-hearted as he said, "It will be difficult to train men who only speak English when I can only speak Italian. Besides, the American army must do things their own way. They're not interested in Italian-trained soldiers."

"We need to send someone with you who speaks English and can explain why this is a mistake," said Dina. "Maybe they don't know you're too old for the Army."

"Dina, I'm thirty-one," said Paolo. "Not exactly ancient, but maybe you're right. Most men go into military service as boys, usually under twenty in most countries."

Loretta's birthday was February 18th. Paolo and Dina had a large surprise party on Sunday the 16th and invited all the family. The mood was mixed. For Loretta's sake, the family tried to have a happy celebratory face, but everyone was aware that Paolo might have to serve in the American army.

"To my little sister, Loretta," toasted Paolo. "May you find love, happiness, and a worthy man—not necessarily in that order."

Everyone laughed as they toasted Loretta. Dina and Paolo both kissed her, and Dina handed her their gift. Loretta opened the small, red velvet box and stared at the beautiful large amethyst ring sparkling from a rectangular gold setting.

"It's beautiful!" cried Loretta. "I'll love you both always and will treasure the ring forever."

"I hope so," said Paolo as he winked at her.

CHAPTER 98

The Sleepwalker—March 1941

Tension was palpable among the siblings the night before Paolo was to report to the Draft Board.

"Believe me, the American Army doesn't want old alien soldiers who can't communicate in English. So, stop worrying and go to bed," he reassured Dina and Loretta.

While she made a lunch for him to take the next day, Dina sniffed back her tears.

"Dina, you'll make the bread soggy," Paolo teased. "Stop! It's going to be fine."

"Paolo," said Loretta, "why not ask Umberto to go with you? Maybe he can explain things better."

"For your information, my little sister, I'm a big boy and don't need anyone to hold my hand, especially Umberto. Stop worrying, both of you."

Paolo's father, Antonio, filled his dreams that night.

"Where are we going, Papa?" They were both in a tall tower, and Antonio was letting Paolo climb the high ladder which led to the roof. Paolo began climbing up the narrow ladder, but kept stopping to look down at his father who was encouraging him to keep climbing.

"I want you to come, too, Papa."

"No, you must not stay with me. You need to escape. Keep climbing. Don't stop!"

Halfway up the tower wall, Paolo noticed a window. He was so tired he wanted to rest on its wide ledge. There was fighting below. Bands of men with artillery were shooting at each other.

"Don't stop! Don't look down!" called his father.

But Paolo was only a small boy, and these soldiers might be his father's comrades. Maybe they could help them. He climbed through the window and …

"Oh, my God! Paolo wake up! Wake up!"

It was Loretta's voice. What was she doing here? She wasn't even born yet.

"Paolo! Dina, come quickly!"

217

Dina rushed to the room tying her bathrobe. "Oh, *Dio mia!*" she said, "He's sleepwalking! It started when Papa died. Help me get him back to bed."

Paolo, still asleep, struggled and muttered, "Wait for Papa. Wait for Papa," before he fell into his cot, fast asleep.

"He almost fell out the window again," said Loretta. "If he fell to the street, he could have been killed."

CHAPTER 99

Easter Dinner—April 1941

Contact with their mother, Caterina, and stepfather, Umberto, had been sporadic. Work took up most of Dina and Loretta's time. When they had the opportunity, the sisters would work Saturdays to earn extra money. Weekends and evenings were filled with household chores, shopping, classes for their citizenship papers, and most importantly, writing letters to Paolo, who was stationed in Maine. After being inducted into the American army, Paolo received his American citizenship in Maine during basic training. Although the sisters were constantly busy, it did not prevent them from dwelling on Paolo's absence. Loretta missed the comfort and security of her brother's presence. Dina fretted constantly on the bad luck of Paolo's name being picked for the draft.

With Luca's impending marriage and Paolo's induction into the Army, Caterina decided to gather her family together for Easter dinner. She felt the need to observe Holy Week and attended church services every day, culminating with a glorious High Mass early Easter morning. Umberto, Davido, and Lorenzo even accompanied her on Sunday. She felt happy and hopeful that day as she prayed for her two deceased children, Gloria and Anita, and her missing children, Paolo, and Geneva, who now lived in California.

"Why didn't you go to church today, Luca?" said Caterina. "It's Easter!"

"I'm going now, Ma. I'm picking Jennie up and we're going to her church in Braintree, then we're coming here for dinner. One o'clock, right?"

"*Sempre,* and don't be late. Don't forget the *panettone* I made for her parents."

"Okay, Ma. See you later." Luca gave Caterina a hug and kissed her cheek before leaving.

"Umberto, please chill the wine before you read the paper," said Caterina. "I'm happy that Luca found a nice girl. She'll be good for him."

"She's already made improvements in him," said Umberto. "He doesn't drink as much, he's not getting into fights with the workers, and he takes baths now and primps like woman. That girl has him wound up and standing straighter than a corpse. Maybe she should work on the other two ruffians who live here."

"Davido and Lorenzo are good boys. They work very hard for you," said Caterina. "You're always so hard on the children."

"Teach them to grow up and know what hard work is like. You coddled those boys too long. They needed to be toughened up."

"They're only nineteen and eighteen years old; they're still boys."

"My brother, Davido and I were on our own at their ages. No fancy house, no good food on the table or a coddling mother to baby us. No, the world kicked our asses, so I kick theirs once in a while to teach them to be strong—to be men."

"I'm so afraid they'll leave us like the others," said Caterina, holding back tears.

"Well, if they do, good riddance! They can learn to support themselves like I did. But don't worry, Caterina. Those boys are smart and spoiled. They know they have to put up with me to get the business and the money someday."

"Did I tell you I received a letter from Paolo and an Easter card from Geneva? She sent a picture of the girls." Caterina began to cry. "Beautiful children, all four of them—I wish they were all here."

"Ava and Lena are bringing their children. The house will be noisy enough. Now finish cooking, or there'll be nothing to eat."

Umberto had set up two tables end to end to accommodate the crowd of seventeen people.

Dina and Loretta, wanting to show their mother how well they were doing, and also at Paolo's urging to keep the peace and attend, splurged by bringing a tray of Italian pastries and a ricotta pie. Ava and her husband brought Umberto a bottle of whiskey; Lena's husband brought cigars; Berto, home on leave from the Army, and now a sergeant, brought his mother a lily plant; Luca gave Caterina a tulip plant; and Jennie brought a plate of cookies she had made.

At first, everyone was exceedingly polite, and the atmosphere was quiet and reserved. By the time the third bottle of wine was finished, the mood was lighter and everyone chatted noisily across the tables. Umberto stood and quieted everyone.

"Your mother has given us a wonderful meal and a special day, even though her heart is heavy with the thought of Geneva and Paolo being away from us. I'm glad you are all here and giving her someone to spoil and stuff with her exceptional cooking. "Caterina, you have outdone yourself today, and we salute you, my dear."

Caterina stood up and lifted her glass. "To our families: those who are here with us, those who are far away, and those whom we have loved and lost. *Saluti la famiglia, sempre!*"

Everyone lifted their glass to toast, but the somber mood returned again as each person became lost in their own thoughts and memories.

CHAPTER 100

The Girl in the Straw Hat—May 1941

"I tell you, Ma," said Luigi Caramazzo, "Angelina and I have been engaged for almost two years but she can't decide when we should get married. If she's got cold feet, why not just say so?" Returning from a visit with Angelina and her parents, Luigi waited for his mother to settle herself before starting the car. As he turned the key in the ignition, he looked up and whistled, "Wow! Now that's a beautiful girl," he said.

"You know that girl!" said his mother. "That's Loretta Leonardi. She works with your sisters."

"That's not her! That can't be that little girl I pick up every so often."

"Of course it's her. She's not a little girl. She's in her mid-twenties."

"Gee, Ma, I never realized what a looker she is. That big straw hat might hide her face a little, but what a figure! Great legs, too!"

"She's a pretty girl, but Angelina is a sweet girl and very pretty too," said Mrs. Caramazzo. "Besides, Angelina and her family are Sicilian like us. Your father has known Raimondo since they were boys in Agrigento."

"Who do you think she's visiting?" asked Luigi. "Does she have a boyfriend?"

"I don't think so. That's her cousin, Maria Elena's, house."

"How do you know that?"

"Unlike you, your sisters tell me everything."

"Maybe it's time I talked to them," said Luigi.

Several days later, Luigi handed his mother her sweater and said,

"Come on, Ma, I'm taking you out for an ice cream."

"I have to finish the dishes and my friend, Assunda, is coming over for coffee and to crochet."

"Hey, Melina," said Luigi, "Ma has to go out. Finish the dishes and make some coffee for Ma's friend when she comes."

Before his younger sister, Melina, had time to object, Luigi hastened his mother down the steps and out the door. Luigi drove to the high school and parked the car.

"I thought we were going for ice cream," said his mother. "Why are we sitting here?"

"You'll see," said Luigi. "Wait, there she is." Luigi jumped out of the car and approached Loretta.

"Hi. I was just taking my mother out for some ice cream and saw you. I thought you'd like to go, too, and then I'd drive you home."

Loretta looked cautiously at the car. There was an older woman sitting in the front seat. Loretta waved at her, and she waved back.

"I'm not sure," said Loretta. "My sister might be nervous if I'm late coming home from citizenship classes."

"The ice cream store is on the way to your house," said Luigi. "Come on, I promised my mother and it's a hot night, perfect for ice cream. I'll drive you straight home, and you can eat it on the way."

Loretta got into the back seat and murmured a hello to Luigi's mother. Mrs. Caramazzo nodded her head, and turned and looked at Luigi who was happily starting the car.

CHAPTER 101

First Date—June 1941

Luigi managed to give Loretta a ride home from citizenship classes several times, but always with either his mother or a sister in tow. Although his three older sisters were married, fortunately he had two younger sisters at home to bribe. Finally, Luigi walked Loretta to her door and asked her for a date.

"Well, I'm not sure," she said. "I probably should write my brother."

"I'm not asking your brother out," said Luigi. "I'm asking you. Do you like the movies? There's a new comedy film at the Strand Theatre. Do you want to go on Saturday night?"

"You'll have to come over early to meet my sister," said Loretta. "I've told her about you, but she wants to meet you, too."

"Fine, I'll be over at six-thirty and we can catch the seven o'clock show. Is that okay?"

"Yes, I'll see you on Saturday evening then," said Loretta as she awkwardly offered her hand.

Luigi took her hand into his strong, coarse grip, and shook it enthusiastically. "See you on Saturday."

Loretta wrote her brother Paolo that night to tell him she had accepted a date with Luigi.

"I'm not going to tell you too much about him yet, since I know almost nothing myself. He's a little rough around the edges, but he makes me laugh. He's nice looking, if not handsome; he has a large hooked nose, black hair and hazel eyes. He's not tall and is of average build. He works at the shipyard and is a pipe-fitter, so his hands and nails are not always perfectly clean. If I compare his appearance to you, my dearest brother, you are Ronald Coleman and he is Lou Costello—you are a Tiffany lamp and he's a G.E. light bulb—but there is something very likeable about him."

Dina answered the door after the first knock. "Hello, are you Luigi Caramazzo?"

"Yeah," said Luigi. "You must be Loretta's sister. How are ya?"

"I'm well, thank you," said Dina. "Would you like some coffee?"

"No, thanks. We're going to see the seven o'clock show, so can't stay too long."

"I'm ready," said Loretta, entering the room and looking at both Luigi and her sister. "My sister wants to get to know you, but I told her we need to leave in time for the movie."

"Right after the movie, what, nine o'clock?" said Dina, "I'll have coffee made and some pastries. Please come right back so that we can talk."

"Well, I was going to invite Loretta out to Howard Johnson's for a banana split after the movies," said Luigi. "How about after that?"

"No," said Dina, "That will be too late. Come for coffee instead. I insist," she smiled.

"What would you like to do, Loretta?" asked Luigi.

"It might be best to come back here for coffee and pastries," said Loretta, "if that's all right."

"Sure," said Luigi, "we'll be back around nine, nine-thirty. Okay?"

"That's fine," said Dina. "Have a good time. Don't be late."

When Loretta and Luigi returned from the movies, Dina directed them to the table and began pouring the coffee as she talked. "So, Luigi, were you born in America or in Sicily?"

"I was born in Agrigento, near Palermo," he said, "and came to this country when I was eight."

"Oh, did both your parents come together with all the children?" asked Dina.

"No, my father came a few years earlier with his brother. They found jobs and a place for us to live. Then, like a lot of other families, he sent my mother the money to bring us all here—my three sisters, my mother, and me. We arrived at Ellis Island in October 1920."

"What did your father do in Sicily?" asked Dina.

"He worked as a laborer on a farm. It was hard work and not much money, so he and my mother decided to come to America to do better," said Luigi. "My father is still a very hard- working man. They say that hard work won't kill you, but I'm not too sure."

"Oh," said Dina. "Did you go to school here in America?"

"Yeah, but I wasn't crazy about school," said Luigi, "and we needed the money, so I quit after the eighth grade. Been working ever since."

"Luigi's sisters are always talking about their brother and how hard he works, and how much he does for his family," said Loretta.

"What kind of work have you done?" asked Dina.

"Well, I started out shining shoes, then I worked at a food market, then I apprenticed at the shipyard as a pipefitter, and that's what I do now," said Luigi. "Oh, and before you ask me how much money I make, I need to tell that I give most of my paycheck to my parents."

After Luigi left that evening, Loretta stopped Dina from clearing the table and made her sit down. "Was it necessary to ask him all those questions the first time he asked me out?"

"I wanted to know more about this man and if he was suitable," said Dina, "and I don't think he is right for you. His family are laborers; our family were professional shoemakers and tailors. Remember, one uncle was tailor to Pope Pius XII!" He's just not good enough for you."

"I think I should be the judge of who is good enough for me."

"Well," said Dina, "did you enjoy your evening?"

"Yes, the movie was very funny," said Loretta. "I haven't laughed so much in ages."

"Do you intend going out with this Sicilian again if he asks you?"

"He has asked me, and yes, I'm going out with him next Saturday."

"Are you out of your mind?" asked Dina. "What could possibly attract you to this man? He's not good looking; he has a big nose; he's not well-educated or well-spoken; he doesn't dress well; he's not very clean looking—and he's a Sicilian!"

"I don't know why I like him, but I do," said Loretta. "You're right, he does have a rough exterior, but he's very nice to me, good to his sisters and parents, and I think he has a good heart. I plan to go out with him again and get to know him. If he disappoints me in important things, then I'll stop seeing him. Now if you'll excuse me, I want to write Paolo before I go to bed.

"All right," said Dina, "but if you end up with a Sicilian, don't cry to me when you wake up some day with your throat cut!"

CHAPTER 102

The Proposal—June 1941

"There's a dance tonight at the Armory," said Luigi. "Want to go?"

"Sorry, I can't dance," said Loretta.

"I can teach you. It's wonderful fun. Want to try it?"

"No, I can't. Besides, everyone would look at me and know I can't dance," said Loretta. "It would be so embarrassing."

"Nah, no one would look at your dancing. They might look to see a pretty girl who's stylish and smart, and wonder what's a beautiful dish like you doing with a homely guy like me?"

"Luigi, you're not homely. Your nose is a little big, but you have a nice face. In fact, I'm jealous of your long, black eyelashes, though not of your bushy eyebrows," she laughed.

"You're a sweet girl. You know that?"

"You think that because you don't know me," said Loretta teasingly.

"Here, I have something for you," he said.

"It's not my birthday or anything," said Loretta. "Why a present?"

"Well, it's seven months since we first met," said Luigi. "That snowy day in November when my sister, Rosie, made me stop to pick you up, and seven is my lucky number."

Loretta opened the package and pulled out a snow globe with two snowmen enclosed. "Oh, Luigi, how lovely! I knew you had a good heart, but now I can see that you're also sentimental. Thank you."

Luigi looked at the pretty woman with dark, curly hair which seemed so full and thick, he felt he could bury his face in it. She had a crisp pink dress with white trim, white shoes, and white handbag. There was an electricity about this girl which was almost palpable. She had dark, quick eyes and a soft mouth—not too thin or full, just right. Her hands were long and tapered with slender fingers. Her figure was like one of those Hollywood actresses—full bust, slender waist, and small hips, with the best looking legs he had ever seen. She noticed him looking at her and blushed slightly as she turned her head.

Luigi started up the car. "Let's take a ride to Nantasket Beach, okay?"

"Okay," said Loretta. "It's a perfect evening for a nice drive."

Luigi parked the car near the grandstand. A band was playing and people were dancing, laughing, and sipping cold drinks or licking ice cream. "Let's get a frozen custard and walk for a while," said Luigi. "Okay?"

"Only if I can have chocolate," said Loretta.

"Good! You have chocolate; I'll have frozen pudding."

As they walked and ate their ice cream, Luigi began to tell Loretta about Angelina. "I wanted to tell you that I was engaged to this girl, Angelina Fossi, but I broke it off. We've known each other most of our lives. My dad and her dad grew up together in Sicily. A nice girl from a good family, but I don't think I ever loved her like a man should love the woman he marries."

"Was she heartbroken?" asked Loretta.

"No, I think she was as relieved as I was," said Luigi. "She probably didn't love me enough either. That's why she kept delaying setting a date for the wedding. Our relationship was…hell, we didn't have a relationship. I only saw her alone occasionally, and she spent most of the time telling me how she was praying about her decision to marry and leave her parents."

"Is she pretty?"

"Oh, yeah…blond, nice figure, pretty face, but kind of cool and proper—like your sister," said Luigi. "Sorry, your sister just struck me that way. I don't really know her."

"Don't apologize. Dina is very protective of me, and she is distrustful of Sicilians in general."

"Crazy, hot-tempered people—right?"

"Are you hot-tempered?" asked Loretta.

"I can be, if pushed hard enough," said Luigi, "but I try to let most things roll off my back. It's easier that way. I have a small suspicion that you're probably more hot-tempered than I am."

They talked, laughed, exchanged stories about each other, and finally held hands as they walk along. When Luigi brought Loretta home, he took her arm to keep her from leaving the car.

"Loretta, I'm not a kid. I'm almost twenty-nine years old. I just want to tell you how happy I feel. You're a wonderful, beautiful, smart, young woman who could probably find a nice, educated guy, or at least someone who has softer hands and a better job than me. But I'm falling for you and want you to think about marrying me someday soon. Will you think about it?" Luigi asked. "I know that you're all that I think about every day."

"I…I have to go in now. I had a wonderful evening. I don't know…I like you, but…I have to think. Good night." She turned and gave him a quick kiss, then opened the car door, and ran into the building.

"What happened?" Dina greeted her. "Your face is flushed."

"He asked me to marry him—and on our second date!"

CHAPTER 103

Consternation—June 1941

Luigi's proposal totally unnerved Loretta. "Dina, I didn't know what to say. Do you think he was serious?" said Loretta. "I'm so confused, I can't sleep nights, I can't eat, and I can't concentrate on anything. I just think of Luigi proposing to me on our second date, and he really seems to mean it."

"See, he is making you ill with fright," said Dina. "I told you he was a crazy person. All those Sicilians are a little off-balance. What do you think he will do when you refuse him? You must do it easily so he won't get mad."

"Stop it, Dina! He is not going to kill me if—and I say if—I refuse him. I don't know. I wrote Paolo. I want him to meet Luigi. He's a nice man, really. You just have this bias against anyone who is not from our region."

"That's not true!"

"Yes it is," said Loretta. "Remember when Guido DePescatore asked me out? You said don't go because he's a Calabrese and they are stubborn and always want their own way."

"Well, they are," said Dina. "Besides, Luigi is also an American. His Italian is non-existent, and I barely understand his Sicilian dialect. He speaks English most of the time, in any case."

"Luigi is a true immigrant. He and his family came through Ellis Island in New York. He's told me some wonderful stories of his experiences."

"What about the way he dresses?" Dina persisted. "Always that ugly red sweater. He wears it constantly, even on warm days. His pants are too long, and his hands are thick with short stubby fingers. I know he's a workman because he dresses like one. And Loretta, you must admit that he is not handsome with that big hooked nose."

"It's a Roman nose, for your information."

"No, it's Greek. Everyone knows that Sicilians are more Greek than Italian."

"I need to get the mail to see if Paolo's written us," said Loretta, as she quickly left the apartment.

Dina, who was hemming a skirt, pricked her finger when she heard the shout from Loretta as she burst into the room. "It's here! A letter from Paolo," said Loretta waving the letter.

"Let me read it," said Dina.

"No, it's addressed to me."

"You're not going to let me read it?"

"I might, but I have to read it first."

Dina scowled, but returned to her sewing as Loretta read the letter to herself.

My dear Loretta,

Your Luigi has certainly caused a commotion between you and Dina. She's written telling me he is 'totally unsuitable for our Loretta.' But if I read between the lines of your letters, I think you like this man and Dina's reaction is causing you to doubt your own feelings. My only advice is to always trust your own heart in matters of the heart. I'll be home on leave by Tuesday, July 1st and can stay until the 14th of July. I'm looking forward to meeting your friend, Luigi. Until then, follow your feelings and respect the fact that Dina loves you too and wants only the best for you.

As always, my love to you and Dina,

Paolo

P.S. Did he really propose on the second date? No question about his feelings!

CHAPTER 104

Friends and Foes—July 1941

Although Loretta was anxious to introduce Luigi to her brother, Paolo, the chance to visit together and to allow Paolo to visit their mother, Caterina, and other family and friends took precedence over arranging an evening with Luigi.

On the 5th of July, Maria Elena and her husband Joe invited family and friends to their home for a cookout since they would be able to serve meat on Saturday in observance of meatless Fridays. Loretta invited Luigi, who hesitated at first about attending.

"Don't you want to meet my family?" asked Loretta. "My brother Paolo is home on leave and eager to meet you. My mother, aunt and uncle, and other family and friends want to meet you, too."

They were sitting at Faxon Park on a stone bench that offered an overlook of the cities of Quincy and Braintree, with the Boston skyline in the distance. Luigi quietly sat finishing his ice cream cone.

"Loretta, I want to meet your brother and the rest of your family," said Luigi, "but it's just that your cousin lives next door to Angelina and her family. Is there any chance they'll be at the cookout? I wouldn't want to cause any more hard feelings with Angelina and her parents. They're nice people and good friends of my family."

"Do you still have feelings for her?" asked Loretta.

"Not the way you mean," said Luigi. "I've known her since we were kids. She's a nice girl, a sweet girl, but she lacks your … your hot temper!" he laughed.

"I don't have a hot temper! I saw her shopping last week. She was so *lento-lento*, you know slow and languid. You should see the way she picks something up to look at it—like it took great effort. I like to do things fast, and it irritated me to have to wait for the salesgirl while Angelina moved like a snail. And that pretty blond hair is probably peroxided."

"Well, she's an only child, and her folks always treated her like some fragile flower," said Luigi. "In turn, she sort of became like—you know—quiet, shy, and prettied up like a china doll."

"Well, she is a little pretty with all her nice clothes and bleached curly hair."

"Nah, it's natural." said Luigi.

"What! How do you know that for sure?"

"I told you. I've known her since she was a kid. It's always been blond. Come on, let's go. If they're at the cookout, fine. Just you behave," he laughed. "Remember, I broke off with her and am stuck on you. Let's go meet your big brother and hope he doesn't hate me as much as your sister does."

"She doesn't hate you!"

"Right, she just wishes I'd stayed in Sicily."

When they arrived at the cookout, Loretta found her brother talking to an attractive young woman who was very fashionably dressed and wearing the latest hairstyle.

"Oh, Loretta," said Paolo, "this is Liliana Borelli. She's a friend of Maria Elena. Liliana, this is my youngest sister, Loretta, and I assume this is her friend, Luigi?"

"*Piacere*, pleased to meet you" said Loretta as she took in Liliana's appearance. Liliana stood very straight, and her dark brown hair was thick and shiny. She had a slender figure and a graceful manner. She would have looked like one of those models in fashion magazines except she had too prominent a nose and thick eyebrows for a truly pretty face. But Loretta could not help feeling that this woman and her brother made a very attractive couple who both exuded elegance and style in their dress.

"Oh, I'm sorry," said Loretta, "this is Luigi Caramazzo, my...friend."

The two couples stood and talked for a while. After the men left to get beers, the women joined Dina, Maria Elena and Caterina in the garden.

"What a wonderful *festa*, Maria Elena" said Caterina. "I've always enjoyed cooking food over a grill. It seems to taste better. Loretta, why don't we go and see if the sausages are cooked."

Loretta looked at her sister who raised her eyebrows. "Mama, maybe Dina and Liliana would like something."

Caterina took Loretta's wrist and pulled her out of the chair. "We'll bring some food back for them."

As they walked across the yard, Caterina pulled Loretta toward a small bench. "Well, when were you going to tell me about your boyfriend?"

"Mama, he's not exactly my boyfriend. We're just seeing each other every so often."

"Your brother said he proposed. When a man proposes and you are still seeing him, he's your boyfriend."

"I don't want to argue, Mama. We're just friends."

"What do you know about him? What kind of family does he come from? He's Sicilian, I'm told. Do you know most of them are farmers? Your people were craftsmen and artisans. They didn't live with goats."

"Stop, Mama. You don't know him. He's kind-hearted, sentimental, and has a wonderful sense of humor. He's generous, and for all his rough exterior, he's very patient and considerate. I don't think he would ever hit a woman," said Loretta as she stared into her mother's eyes.

"You have a sharp tongue, my girl."

"Hey, Loretta," said Paolo, "Luigi's looking all over for you. Is everything all right? You both look upset."

"We're fine," said Loretta. "Mama is giving me some motherly advice about Luigi."

"He's a nice guy, Ma," said Paolo. "I like him."

Loretta kissed her brother. "I do, too."

"So, Paolo," said Loretta as she walked away with him, "tell me about Liliana."

"Ah, that's a possible maneuver I might explore," he said.

CHAPTER 105

Love and Loss—September 1941

"What's wrong, Luigi?" asked Loretta. "You've been so quiet and distracted all night. Are you feeling okay?"

"Yeah, I'm okay. My father's been feeling lousy lately, but he won't take it easy. My mother has begged him to see a doctor, but he won't go. He's so damn stubborn."

"Maybe you should call a doctor and have him come to the house. Then your father will have to see him."

"Are you serious? My father would be bullshit! I mean he'd probably throw him out and refuse to pay the bill. I'm sorry, Loretta, but I should get home. When I left, he was complaining of pain in his shoulder and stomach. My mother mixed a stomach tonic for him, but knowing him, he probably didn't drink it."

"Of course," she said. "Let me know how he is feeling. Would your mother mind if I made some soup for him?"

"That would be nice. He likes you, but you know how things have been."

Loretta knew that Luigi's parents and sisters, with the exception of

Rosa, were disappointed that he had broken his engagement to Angelina. Her sister, Dina, was not alone in her bias for being with your own people. Only Rosa had invited them to dinner. In turn, Luigi only had dinner with Dina, Paolo, and Loretta while Paolo was home on leave. Loretta's mother and stepfather had yet to invite him or even to want to get to know him. The next day, Saturday, Luigi called Loretta. "How's your father doing?" asked Loretta.

"My father's in a bad way, honey, so I'm sorry but I won't be coming over tonight." said Luigi.

"I took your advice though, and called the doctor."

"What did he say?"

"Before or after my father told him to go away because he wasn't going to pay him? Well, he wanted my father to go to the hospital. But my stubborn father refused and said he would rather suffer in his own bed than die in a hospital bed."

"My mother is like that," said Loretta. "She is convinced that people die in hospitals. If she had made my stepfather take my stepsister, Gloria, to the hospital, she might be alive today." A feeling of sadness overcame Loretta. It was just four years ago that Gloria had died at home of appendicitis. She would have been sixteen today.

"I'll call you tomorrow, honey." said Luigi. "I've got to go now."

On Monday, September 8th, Luigi's father, Rosario Caramazzo, suffered a massive heart block and died at home surrounded by his wife and children. A wake, attended by Loretta and Dina, was held at the Caramazzo home.

"So many people," said Dina. "I didn't know there were that many Sicilians in Quincy."

"Lots of people came from Waltham and East Boston," whispered Loretta. "Luigi's father had been in America for nearly thirty years and started a social club for Sicilians many years ago. Luigi's a member, too."

"Loretta, Dina, thank you for coming," said Luigi. "Would you like some coffee and something to eat?"

"No, thank you," said Dina. "Don't trouble yourself. We're fine."

"How is your mother, Luigi?" asked Loretta.

"Oh, she's devastated. She and my father have known each other their entire lives. They were neighbors and were betrothed when my mother was only fifteen. They married when she was sixteen and he was twenty."

"She's fortunate to have you and your sisters," said Dina. "You all seem very close."

"We are." said Luigi. "My three older sisters are married and live close by so they see my mother every week. My two younger sisters are still home, of course, and my sisters are always together."

Loretta attended the funeral alone. She took a bus to the church but was able to find a ride to the cemetery. Luigi offered to take her back to his home after the funeral, but she declined. "Go with your mother and sisters. They need you," said Loretta. "I'll find someone to ride with and see you at your home."

Luigi squeezed her hand. "Yeah, thanks. I'll see you later. Be sure to come, okay?"

"I'll be there. You'd better go, your mother is crying so hard she may need help."

Since it was a work day, only relatives and some older friends went back to the Caramazzo apartment. Loretta saw that Luigi was busy greeting people, getting them drinks, and consoling his mother. She found a chair in one of the back rooms and waited to speak to Luigi again. His sisters stopped to speak briefly, but they were also busy with their families and friends. As mourners began to leave, Loretta felt it was time for her to leave as well.

"Loretta, sorry." said Luigi. I didn't mean to leave you alone for so long. Let me take you home."

"Are you sure?" said Loretta. "Would your mother mind?"

"My sisters will look after her for a while. Let's go."

After Luigi parked the car in front of Loretta's apartment house, he turned to Loretta. "Thanks again for coming to my father's wake and funeral. Seeing you helped me get through it."

Loretta took his hand. "I wish I'd known my father. You were blessed to have your father for almost thirty years. You have memories that can never be taken away from you."

Luigi reached over and hugged her. She felt dampness against her head and realized that he was crying. She clutched him closer and tried to comfort him. After a while, he separated himself and seemed embarrassed, turning his head and rubbing his face with his open palms.

"It's natural to grieve, Luigi." said Loretta. "Don't be embarrassed.

Luigi got out of the car and walked to Loretta's door. He opened it and took her hand, helping her out of the car. They walked wordlessly to her apartment.

"Good night," he said.

Loretta hugged him and kissed his eyes as she held his face.

"Good night," she said. "Rest now."

That night she made up her mind. If Luigi asked her to marry him again, she would say yes.

CHAPTER 106

Prelude—November 1941

Luigi again asked Loretta to marry him and she accepted. They set the wedding date for Sunday, June 7, 1942. Paolo and Liliana became regular correspondents, and whenever he was able to get home, he spent considerable time with her. Thoughts of the convent once again began to dominate Dina's thoughts, and she wrote her friend, Domenica.

Dearest friend in Christ,

I'm sorry for not writing sooner. I received your wonderful letter last week, and I have been praying for the courage to make a decision about my vocation. Speaking to my parish priest was not too helpful. He is a good friend of my mother, and his church benefits from my stepfather's contributions. Knowing my mother's strong objection to my entering the convent, he kept assuring me that the Church needs devoted wives and mothers to carry on the life of the faith, and that, considering the circumstances of my leaving my mother, I have an obligation to watch after my sister until she marries.

Loretta and her fiancé, Luigi Caramazzo, plan to get married next June. In earlier letters, I wrote that I was not pleased with her choice. Luigi is the proverbial "bull in the china shop." He is not polished in appearance and manners like Paolo, nor is he well-read or particularly good-looking. He has a large nose—very Greek-looking—thin straight black hair, and he always looks like he needs to shave. Worst of all, he's Sicilian. His clothes are getting better, which is probably Loretta's influence. In fairness, he is a kind, generous man who has always been pleasant to me. He has been a godsend in helping us with repairs around the apartment now that Paolo is in the Army again.

Paolo and this woman, Liliana Borelli, seem to be getting closer, too. She writes him every week. Paolo goes out with her when he is home from the Army, and truthfully, I am a little resentful of the time he spends with her and not with us.

I am in such a quandary. Please pray for me. If both Loretta and Paolo get married, I will be alone. Loretta encourages me to be less reserved with men we know and meet through family and friends. I don't know what to do. I have always felt that I made a promise to God and the Order to become a Sister of Charity and dedicate my life to God and others in His service.

There is one man I see occasionally, who is always asking me out to dinner or a movie. His name is Leonardo Sorrentino. He is a builder and just finished my Zio Franco and Zia Donata Tempesta's house. My aunt is my father's sister. If you remember, their son, Enrico, taught Loretta and me how to use an electric sewing machine and helped me and later, Paolo, find jobs in Boston. This builder was the man I wrote you about who sold me that diseased chicken last year. Actually, I may have contributed to the chicken's malaise, since I left it on our porch during several hot days in August. Of course, I never admitted that to him. He is very handsome, obviously a good worker, and would be a good provider. But I'm not sure whether I am ready to give up my dream of becoming a nun.

Paolo hopes to be home at Christmas time, and I will talk to him and seek his advice. In the meantime, please pray for me, my dearest friend. I know that God listens to you, and at times I'm not sure He wants to hear a constant litany of all my problems and worries.

Your sister in heart,
Dina

CHAPTER 107

Day of Fears and Tears— December 7, 1941

"Dina, is that you?" inquired Loretta. "I'm just lying down for a while. This cold is crushing my head."

"Did you eat the soup I left you?" asked Dina. "No, here it is on the stove. Why didn't you eat it?"

"I tried, but I couldn't keep it down. I'm sorry."

"Well, stay in bed and rest if you plan to go to work tomorrow."

"Where were you?" said Loretta. "It's almost four o'clock. I thought you were coming home after church."

"I stopped by Mama's house to see if they had gotten a letter from Paolo. Then I used their telephone to call Liliana to see if she heard from him."

"Well?"

"No, no one has gotten a letter for weeks. Liliana wanted to come over to see you, but I told her you were ill, and perhaps when you're better she could visit. I think she has set her cap for Paolo and wants to be friendly with us, so that we'll approve."

"I like her, don't you?" said Loretta.

"She's very pretty and stylish, but ..."

Suddenly, they heard a commotion in the building.

"What's happening?" asked Loretta. "Go out and see."

Before Dina could go to the door, there was a furious knock. She opened it and Luigi and a number of neighbors were outside milling around the hall.

"I'm sorry," said Luigi. "Did you hear the news? Hi, honey, how are you feeling? God, everybody's going crazy. Did you hear from your brother?"

From the background, several men were shouting, "It's a war! Are you going to sign up?"

A woman screamed, "You shut up! My boy no go! I don't know no Jap. We *Italiana*. He stay home!"

"What are they talking about, Luigi?" said Loretta. "Signora Fennucci, why are you yelling?"

"Eh, these troublemakers want my son to go to war. I say no!"

Dina began to cry, crossing herself. "Paolo will have to go. The Army will make him go. God, please don't let it be true."

"It's true," said Luigi, who was hugging a tearful Loretta. "The Japs bombed our ships in Hawaii—a place called Pearl Harbor—and the President said it's war. Guys are saying they're going to enlist."

"Do you have to go, too?" asked Loretta.

"I don't know, since I work at the Boston Naval Yard and my mom and sisters have just me. We'll see, but don't go getting worried about me. Your brother is the one already in it."

Liliana, who could drive, borrowed her father's car that evening and visited the sisters. Their stepbrother Luca and his wife also stopped by.

"Ma's pretty bad," said Luca. "She's throwing stuff all over the house and cursing. Pa's trying to calm her down, but she'll probably break every dish before he does."

"Dina, when you asked me if I heard from Paolo," said Liliana, "I got a sick feeling in the pit of my stomach, but I didn't know why. Do you think they'll let him come home before he gets sent somewhere?"

No one answered, but all turned their heads to hide their own emotions and fears.

CHAPTER 108

Serenity Lost—February 1942

Suddenly the world had lost its peace and gentleness. People had a burst of energy about them as if they realized they had slept too late. There was a palpable tension in the air.

"If you're taking the bus," said Loretta, "you'd better hurry. Maria Fennucci said it comes earlier now."

"Don't worry," said Dina. "They still need stitchers. Five more girls left our factory to work at the shipyard. I think it's dangerous for them, but they go to make more money."

"And fill jobs too. Luigi told me that there are a large number of women assemblers, riveters and machine operators at the Naval Yard," said Loretta. "I told him he better not flirt with any of them and he said it was hard getting too friendly with a woman holding a rivet gun."

"You're lucky," said Dina, "that he didn't have to go to the war. Even his nephews, Rosa's three oldest boys, are in that God-forsaken war."

"I thank God every night that Luigi works at the Naval Yard building ships. I know he will do a good job and maybe Paolo and other men will not be hurt because our ships are so strong."

"Well, it doesn't hurt that he supports his mother and sisters, either," said Dina. "Paolo helped support us, so why did he have to go?"

"It was just bad timing. Paolo was already in the Army like Berto. Did you know that Berto was made a sergeant last year?"

Before leaving for work, Dina looked around their small, sparsely-furnished apartment. The stove was off, the table clean and set for the evening dinner, beds made, no dishes in the sink—she was ready to leave. "Loretta, could you buy some potatoes and two onions tonight?" We have three eggs and I want to make a frittata for dinner."

Arriving home that evening, Loretta noticed two letters in their mailbox both addressed to Dina. One was from Naples, Italy, and the other from Dina's friend, Domenica, the nun from Wisconsin.

Opening the door of the apartment, Dina saw Loretta sitting at their small table, with her coat on, and two paper bags in front of her. "Good, you remembered the vegetables. Did they raise the price again? That *ladro* is taking advantage of people because of the war."

"He's not a thief," said Loretta. "He's paying more for food and it's winter, so everything is more expensive. Why can't you understand that?"

"Loretta, why are you shouting at me? And why are you still wearing your coat? Hang it up and let's get dinner started."

Loretta continued to sit at the table. Holding up the two letters, she said, "These came for you."

"Oh, good," said Dina. "I'll read them later, after dinner. Come on, help me with the frittata."

"One is from Naples—a convent; the other from your friend, Domenica. Why is someone from a convent in Italy writing you?"

"Oh, it's probably one of my old friends. Let's not talk about it now."

"It's from the Reverend Mother General of the Sisters of Charity," said Loretta. "One of your old friends has certainly risen high in the Church hierarchy in such a short time."

"We'll talk later after dinner." With that, Dina took the letters from Loretta's hand and stuffed them in her pocket.

CHAPTER 109

The Letters—February 1942

Loretta put the last dish away, folded the dish towel, and poured the coffee for Dina and herself.

"We'll probably need to start cutting back on coffee," said Dina. "Maybe we'll only have it in the morning to save money."

Waving her hand impatiently, Loretta said, "What about the letter from the Mother General?"

"Well, I haven't had time to read it. Why don't we wait until tomorrow night? I'm so tired, I don't really feel like reading it right now."

"I'd be happy to read it to you," said Loretta. "You must be as curious as I am to see what she writes."

"Please, let me read my letters, and we'll talk about it tomorrow." Dina rose from the table, carrying her cup to the sink, and began walking to their small bedroom.

"You're going back to the convent, aren't you?" said Loretta. "You wrote this woman without even telling me, but told your friend, Domenica, and she's helping you. Isn't that right?"

Dina stopped and turned to face her sister. "Yes, but I don't know if I can still go back. I want to join an order here in America, but Domenica said I might have to return to Italy if they accept me. Most women at her Institute have a short postulancy and then return to Italy to make their year of novitiate and take their final vows before returning to America. She gave me the name and address of the Mother General and Mother Superior of the Sisters of Charity in Naples to see if they would accept me again."

"Well, open the letter," said Loretta, "and see what it says." Loretta remained at the kitchen table while Dina sat in their only upholstered chair in the sitting room.

Carefully, Dina tore open the envelope, extracted the letter and read:

Dear Dina, child of Christ,

A long time has passed since you left your vocation to join your family in America. I understand you had many problems and good reasons for not returning to fulfill your destiny. I was very sad to know of your painful state in reuniting with your mother and her intolerance of your wish to return to the convent. I do not remember how old you are, or the age of your sister, who also may have a vocation to the Church. We would welcome you both with open arms to our community.

I will be visiting the United States of America in Milwaukee, Wisconsin for the month of April. I would welcome meeting with you and your sister to discuss your future vocation, and this would allow you to see your friend, Sister Giovanna Domenica Antonelli, who has written me several times about your desire to return to the Sisters of Charity. I know you have suffered greatly because you have not been able to take up your vocation. Have courage, accept the trial that the good Lord sends you, and fight like a good soldier against the attractions of the world. I will pray that one day you will emerge victorious.

Yours in Christ,
Sister Elisabetta Augostino

"What makes her think that I want to be a nun, too?" said Loretta. "I've never considered it."

"You told me once that we could enter the convent together and never be separated again," said Dina.

"Perhaps, but that was years ago. I'm getting married, and I want children and a family life. That's what you should have, too. It hurts me to think I will lose you again to the Church. We'll never see each other. You'll be taken away from Paolo, Zio Lorenzo, Maria Elena, and everyone. Please reconsider if you can. I know this has been burning in you for years, but life is different here. We can be happy together in America. Italy is the past."

"Loretta, you're getting married in a few months. Paolo will probably get married, too. Maybe to Liliana, maybe somebody else, but he will marry. I don't want to be alone!"

"You won't be alone! While Paolo's in the Army, you can come and live with Luigi and me after we get married."

"And then what? Suppose I don't get married. Do I move in with Paolo when he gets married? Or move back with Mama and Umberto?"

"Only you know your own heart," said Loretta. "If being a nun is truly what you want for all the right reasons, you should be a nun. I'm being selfish to want to keep you with me. I dreamed we would both get married, have children, be neighbors, and always be together. When Geneva moved to California, we lost her again. You're the only sister I've known all my life, and I love you the best. I want us always to be together."

"You're getting married. You'll have a husband. He won't want another sister living with him. Besides, I haven't always been kind to him. He will never agree to have me live with you."

"I'll convince him. He loves me." Rising from her chair, Loretta kissed Dina goodnight and left her.

After bidding Loretta good night, she opened the second letter and read it:

Dearest friend in Christ,

You should be hearing from the Mother General soon. She will be visiting us in April. My advice is to be strong. I know that your mother's ideas are not the same as your own, so you must suffer a lot, and ascend Calvary alone. Jesus will be with you, and He will continue to give you strength. Remember that your vocation is an inestimable gift. You are His favorite among thousands. You are especially recommended to the Madonna as are all the sisters. She knows very well all your needs, and like a good mother she will come immediately to your aid.

With much affection, and united in prayer, receive an embrace in the Heart of Jesus.

Sister Giovanna Domenica

Dina folded the letter, lowered her head, and silently prayed that God would direct her heart.

CHAPTER 110
The Winds of Prejudice—March 1942

"**W**hy can't Paolo get permission to be at our wedding?" asked Loretta. "The most important day of my life, and my only brother can't share it!"

Luigi released Loretta's hand and put his arm around her shoulder. Faxon Park's skeletal look was disappearing as trees were budding everywhere. It was hard to imagine a war going on somewhere.

"Let's sit down, honey. Please don't start crying again. You read the letter. Your brother's back in Europe fighting this damn war. He wants to be here, but…"

"But where in Europe do you think he is?" said Loretta. "First they send him to Maine, then Maryland. Oh, did I show you that nice postcard with a picture of the White House? Then we get a letter that he's being put on a ship to the European front, but he can't say where. And now a short letter saying I'd better not count on his being back for the wedding."

"Believe me, honey, if he could come home, he would."

"Luigi, I'm so frightened for him. He wrote Dina and me that most of his platoons are young boys—seventeen, eighteen years old. He said he feels like their father. None of the boys have any experience with Army life, much less war, and most are so scared. A lot of the men in his group are of Italian decent, but most can't speak the language or only know a few words—mostly swears."

"Those kids probably feel better," said Luigi, "knowing they have a guy with them who knows what he's doing."

"The language is still a problem for him," said Loretta. "Sometimes they speak their own dialect, and Paolo doesn't know what they're saying."

"You mean they talk broken English?"

"No, but they say stupid things like 'put a sock in it' when somebody talks too much. You know—stupid expressions that are hard to understand. Some of the new girls at work are like that, too. Then they laugh at you when you don't understand, or call you a dumb guinea."

"Hey, don't worry about it," said Luigi. "They probably just like to tease you because they're dumb kids."

"No, they tease me and maybe Paolo because we're Italian."

Luigi looked out over the view of the city. The sun was dropping and

240

the wind picked up. He felt Loretta give a shudder. "Are you cold?"

"Just a little, but I don't want to leave yet."

Luigi pulled her closer to him and tried to shelter her from the wind. *Prejudice*, he thought, *is an evil thing. Guys at the Naval Yard kid him about all his goombahs fighting them in Italy, and they tease the German guys about being Krauts who might screw up for the fatherland. He didn't know about the German guys, but his only memory of Sicily was as a small boy. He would sometimes play hooky from school, visit his grandmother's farm, and ride her donkey.*

CHAPTER 111

The Last Easter — April 1942

"Easter is early this year," said Dina. "the first Sunday in April."

"I hate going to Mama's without Paolo," said Loretta. "Where do you think he is right now? I lit a candle at Mass today and prayed he was safe."

"Me, too," said Dina. "He's somewhere in Europe, I think."

Loretta looked around the compact apartment. "Where did I put my new scarf?"

Dina went to the sagging chair in the corner. She had recently covered it again in a dark rose print chintz with sprays of gold palm fronds. "Here's your scarf," she said. "Don't forget the pastries and fruit."

Loretta walked to their small ice box and pulled out two boxes and several cans. "Mama will enjoy the layer cake with all its frosting; it was only forty cents. I bought a rhubarb pie for Umberto for thirty cents. Maybe it will give him diarrhea." She laughed.

Dina shook her head. "Do you think Mama will like the canned fruit and mint jelly?"

"She loves fruit, and it's too expensive to buy fresh," said Loretta. "I only paid thirty-five cents for three cans of grapefruit and the Melba peaches were only twenty-five cents for a large can. The mint jelly is homemade and only cost ten cents."

"Well, if Paolo hadn't sent us money to buy something for Mama," said Dina, "I would never spend a dollar and forty cents on sweets."

Both women put on their coats and hats. Loretta adjusted her new scarf, which was bright pink with a background of scattered white tea roses.

"Nina, stay off the chair," said Dina to the cat. As Loretta followed

Dina out the door, she noticed the cat promptly jump on the chair and curl into a big furry ball.

The air was still damp and chilly as they walked to their mother's house. Luca opened the door when Dina and Loretta arrived. "Hey, you girls look cold," he said. "How about a brandy to warm up?"

"We're not that cold!" said Dina.

The house was filled with the aroma of roast lamb, fresh tomato sauce, and fried eggplant and asparagus. Dina and Loretta briefly greeted their stepbrothers, stepsisters and their families before going into the kitchen to greet their mother and give her their gifts.

"Well, you're almost late," said Caterina. "Everybody is here. Put those things down, take off your coats, and go sit down so we can have dinner."

Loretta was about to snap back that it was twelve-forty-five, and Caterina had said to arrive at one o'clock. Dina, sensing that Loretta was going to answer back, squeezed her arm.

Wanting to make conversation at the dinner table, Dina told her mother, "Paolo sends his love, Mama. He asked us to buy some sweets for you and wishes he could join us."

Caterina seemed in a daze. She didn't respond or acknowledge that she had heard Dina.

"Mama, Mama," said Dina. "Are you feeling all right?"

No response.

Everyone looked at Caterina. She was slumped in her chair, staring ahead as if in a trance. Umberto knocked his chair over and rushed to her side. His large strong hands gripped Caterina's shoulders and he shook her.

"Caterina, Caterina," he shouted.

Moments later, she seemed to focus again and said, "What are you doing? Stop shaking me."

"What happened?" asked Dina. "Were you asleep?"

"Yes, I suppose so," said Caterina. "Sometimes I'm so tired."

"Mama, you've got to see a doctor," said Luca and Loretta in unison.

"Doctors, what do they know?" said Caterina. "I work hard and I worry about my family. What pill can a doctor give you for that?"

"Ma, they know a lot today," said Ava. "Tomorrow, make an appointment, and I'll try to go with you if you want."

"Look, the children are upset," said Caterina. "You all frightened them with your words. I'm fine. I just need to rest a little."

Umberto took Caterina's arm and led her into their bedroom. "Go on, finish the dinner," he said. "She'll be all right, just tired from cooking and cleaning all week."

Despite his words, everyone had stopped eating, and a pall hung over the table. After a short while, Loretta rose and started clearing the table. Dina began to help her, and Ava and Lena followed. Luca's wife, Jennie, made a pot of coffee for the men who all sat quietly smoking in the living room. After the food was put away, the dishes done, and the dining room table dressed with a new clean tablecloth, the women joined the men to await their mother's return.

Umberto, who had stayed with Caterina in their room, came out. "You better all go," he said. "She's sleeping. Your mother is a strong woman. Don't worry. Like me, she's just getting old."

"If she's old, it's because you made her old, you bastard!" said Luca.

"And I suppose I made you a drunk!" retorted Umberto. Then he left, returning to the bedroom.

CHAPTER 112

Good-bye Again, Mama—April 1942

I t was Saturday. Dina was dusting and polishing their few pieces of furniture while Loretta washed the floors.

"It's been almost three weeks," said Loretta, "and Mama still has not seen a doctor."

Dina came out of the bedroom and began dusting the sitting room. "They're so stubborn," she said. "Both Mama and Umberto listen only to themselves."

"I stopped by to see how she was and to talk about my wedding. She couldn't have been less interested. When I brought Luigi to meet them last Christmas, she was very cool toward him and wouldn't even invite him to Easter dinner. Sometimes I hate her!" Loretta said as she threw the scrub brush into the wash bucket.

"Hating her is a sin," said Dina. "We must pray for her. I think she's ill and doesn't want anyone to know. When I tried to talk to her about the convent again, she held her hands over her ears and told me to be a normal woman and look for a husband instead of a dream."

"Well, for someone who's ill, she certainly has gotten fat!" said Loretta. "She cooks huge meals for those two wild boys she produced. Davido and Lorenzo didn't even talk to us at Easter."

"They were upset," said Dina. "Their mother is ill. It might have frightened them."

"Nothing would upset those two devils. The 'boys,' as Mama calls them, are men. Davido is twenty and Lorenzo's nineteen. They're carefree, while Mama worries herself sick that they will be sent to the war."

A few days later, Dina was cutting some leftover material to make pillow cases for Loretta, who was at the movies with Luigi. Startled by a pounding on the door, Dina's hand slipped and unevenly cut the material, causing her to curse.

"Signorina Leonardi, a phone call—please hurry!" Signora Fennucci, their neighbor, was holding her hand to her chest and breathing rapidly.

"Calm yourself, Signora," said Dina. "What phone? Who's calling?"

"Your brother," she said. "He called the grocer downstairs. Your mother is in the hospital. Very bad! I'm sorry. Go, go talk to him."

Dina rushed out the door, forgetting to close it, and ran down the stairs to the small grocery store next to the apartment building. "Paolo, this is Dina," she said over the phone.

"No, it's me, Davido. Ma had a stroke, I think, and Pa drove her to the hospital," he said. "I thought I'd better tell you and Loretta."

"Yes, thank you," said Dina. "Davido, is she going to be all right? Did your father tell you anything after the doctors saw her?"

"He said..."

Dina heard a muffled cry and Davido's voice was tight when he resumed. "She had a bad stroke. She can't move or talk. It's bad."

"Pray, Davido," said Dina. "That's all we can do. Thank you for calling us."

Returning to her apartment, Dina looked at the clock radio on the ice box. It was almost seven o'clock. "Please, God, don't let Loretta and Luigi stay out late tonight." Dina nudged the cat out of her newly upholstered chair, sat down, and prayed for her mother. Shortly before nine o'clock, Loretta and Luigi entered the apartment.

"Why are you sitting there in the dark?" said Loretta. "For heaven's sake, put on a light and join us for coffee."

"Mama had a stroke and is in the hospital," said Dina. "Davido called and said it's bad."

"Do you want to go to the hospital?" said Luigi. "I'll drive you now if you want."

"Yes, please," said Dina. "Thank you, Luigi."

Luigi put his arms around Loretta, who was crying softly. "I said I hated her the other day."

At the hospital, Umberto was sitting by Caterina's bed with his head bent. Dina and Loretta were allowed only a few minutes in Caterina's room. Davido and Lorenzo sat with moist eyes on a bench outside the door. Other family members were sitting or standing in a nearby waiting room. Muffled cries and soft whisperings filled the air.

My God, thought Loretta, *it's like they're already having the wake.*

Two days later, Caterina Rossi Leonardi Fabrizio was declared dead of a cerebral hemorrhage, arteriosclerosis and hypertension. She was two weeks shy of her fifty-seventh birthday.

CHAPTER 113

Remembering Caterina—May 1942

Fabrizio—In Quincy, April 30, Caterina (Rossi),beloved wife of Umberto Fabrizio. Funeral from her late home, 317 Luna Street, Saturday, May 2 at 8:30 a.m. Solemn High Mass of Requiem in Santa Lucia Church at 9 a.m. Interment Santa Lucia Cemetery. Relatives and friends are invited to attend.

Loretta sat in the overstuffed chair reading the obituary again to Dina, who was straining to finish their dresses under the small kitchen light. Covering the kitchen table with a towel, Dina warmed the iron and filled the sprinkler bottle with water.

"There, done," said Dina. "I've never made dresses so fast. It took me all night, but they'll do."

"They're nice," said Loretta. "Simple but well-cut and stitched. Mama would be proud of you."

Dina began to cry. "The last time Mama said she was proud of me was after Papa was killed in the war. I looked after you every day because Mama was bedridden with grief. Then dear Graciella helped us, and Mama started to get better. I remember Mama kissing me good night one evening and she said, 'You make me very proud, Dina. You are a brave and helpful girl.' A year later, she left us."

"I was always afraid of Mama," said Loretta. "In Italy, she always wore those long black dresses and constantly seemed angry with me. Remember how I used to hide from her?"

"I remember. You would be under the bed or behind a chair or hiding behind Graciella's skirts. Mama would get so frustrated with you. She called you her 'devil child.'"

"And you, of course, were the 'angel child,'" said Loretta smiling.

"Well, perhaps," said Dina, "but Paolo was her most beloved child. I wish he could be here with us. I wrote him last night, but this terrible war makes it impossible to reach him and have him come home."

"What do you think Geneva was to Mama?" asked Loretta. "By the way, Geneva called Maria Elena and said she would come home for a visit, but naturally she won't be here in time for the funeral."

"I'm glad she's coming. We're losing our California sister. She lives so far away, and I sometimes think she is not a very happy woman. Geneva was Mama's shadow child—always clinging close to Mama and having such a great need to be loved and noticed. That's why Mama ended up bringing Geneva to America instead of you. Geneva used to become hysterical when Mama talked about leaving us for a while. I think Geneva felt as abandoned and betrayed as we did when Mama became more attached to her new husband and their family."

"We should dress," said Loretta. "It's after six. Thank God the next two days will be sunny. I hate funerals in the rain."

Their parents' old friends, Giorgio and Gemma Marini, had rearranged the sitting room of Umberto and Caterina's home for the wake. Caterina's casket filled the small alcove that had once been Geneva's and later Gloria's room. Lit candles lined the wall along her casket, and a spray of white roses draped her from waist to feet. Her hair, still thick, black, and softly curled, framed her smooth olive-complexioned face. A robust woman, she wore a deep maroon print dress trimmed with white lace at the collar and wrists. Small gold and pearl earrings, a gold chain around her neck, and a wide gold wedding band completed her dress.

Loretta stood at the casket and touched her mother's stony hands, which were entwined with pearl rosary beads.

"Your mother was always a beautiful woman," said Umberto "and she had spirit, like you." He stood behind Loretta and placed his hand on her shoulder. She stiffened.

"Yes, she is beautiful, but I always favored my father in looks, if not in temperament. My mother and I were never alike."

Over one hundred people came to pay their respects and praise the 'sainted' woman whom God had claimed too soon. In Caterina's kitchen, Gemma Marini fixed sandwiches and brewed coffee as her husband, Giorgio, was in the dining room offering whiskey to the men who came to pay their respects. Later, he returned to the kitchen to leave the tray of dirty glasses and wait for the sandwiches.

"Why did God take her, Giorgio?" said Gemma. "She was such a good woman—a saint—nobody knows, only me, what she suffered for her family. Nobody knows, poor woman."

"Calm yourself, you're making the bread soggy!" said Giorgio. "I know she suffered a lot, especially when her babies died. She was a good woman, but I always wondered why she left her children."

"He made her!" said Gemma. "She told me. She said she begged him; she fought with him; she tried to please him so he would let her go back; she did everything, but he wouldn't listen."

"Well, he did finally let them come, but nobody was ever at peace in this house," said Giorgio. "His own children seemed to resent him as much as her children resented both of them. A sad family."

Carrying the tray of sandwiches and fresh glasses, Giorgio paused to observe Davido and Lorenzo huddled together in the corner, eyes downcast and pensive. Although all of Umberto's and Caterina's children mourned her, Davido and Lorenzo appeared to be the most shaken with grief. Caterina had loved, pampered, and protected them constantly from Umberto's volatile moods. Now they had to face the world and their father alone.

On Saturday morning, Caterina's casket was closed, and her sons, stepsons, and sons-in-law carried her to the church. Neighbors and friends lined the street with bowed heads; some tossed flowers as the casket passed. Three priests conducted the High Mass, and the pastor gave the final eulogy about Caterina, which Dina tried later to recap in her letter to Paolo. "Signora Fabrizio was a patron of this church...She fed the poor...Helped her fellow countrymen and women...Our community will be much poorer in her death...We shall miss seeing her and admiring her great spirit and generous life...Caterina was a wonderful woman, wife, mother, and friend who was loved by all."

At the conclusion of the Mass and final blessing, the pallbearers carried Caterina out of the church and crossed the street to the adjacent cemetery. Her final resting place was on a hill graced by a large granite monument carved by Umberto. Already buried in the family plot were Umberto's brother, Davido, Umberto's first wife, Maura, and Caterina and Umberto's two daughters, Anita and Gloria.

After the final interment and prayers, Luigi, who had stayed somewhat in the background, joined Loretta and Dina. Taking each woman's arm, he helped them down the hill and into his car.

"I'm so sorry about your mother," he said. "I know she was a hard woman, but she was still your mother."

"Thank you," said Dina who began crying again.

"I wish I'd loved my mother more," said Loretta. "I wish she'd loved me more, but now I feel free of those hopes and somehow at peace with Mama. Crossing herself, Loretta prayed, "May God rest her soul and grant her forgiveness."

CHAPTER 114

Memories—May 1942

Instead of waiting for the Month's Mind Mass as a remembrance of Caterina, Dina suggested to Umberto that they have a Mass on May 15, Caterina's birthday. He agreed. All of the family was reunited. Umberto's son, Berto, had come home from the Army, as had Paolo. Geneva was visiting from California with her eldest daughter, Bonita, now called Bonnie. Greetings and acknowledgements at the church between Umberto's children and Caterina's were strained.

"I can't believe she finally showed up," said Lena, nodding in Geneva's direction.

"Well, she has four kids," said Ava, "and is pregnant again, I hear."

"God," said Lena, "what is she—a baby factory? At least my son has a totally devoted mother."

"You seem to forget, Lena," said Ava, "that I have five children myself."

"Oh, oh, I didn't mean…"said Lena.

"Skip it," said Ava.

After the Remembrance Mass, family and friends convened at Umberto's house.

"I want you all to remember that your mother was a good woman," said Umberto in a toast to Caterina. "Good to you, good to her countrymen, and good to me. We will all miss her; possibly, I will miss her most."

Paolo looked around the room. It seemed as though there were divisional camps. Umberto's children from his first marriage were huddled together by the large sofa. Davido and Lorenzo, the offspring of the marriage of Umberto and Caterina, leaned against the wall that separated the dining room from the living room. The Rossi-Leonardi family—he, Dina, Geneva, Bonita, Loretta, Zio Lorenzo, Maria Elena, and their families—sat on numerous chairs or stood opposite the Fabrizios. Conversation was sparse and strained.

Later that evening over coffee in their apartment, Caterina's first family shared their thoughts.

Never one to contain herself for long, Loretta said to Paolo, "It would have been easier for us if you had attended Mama's funeral. Why didn't you come?"

"I told you," said Paolo, "I was in the hospital having dental surgery, and word didn't reach me until after the funeral. Do you think I wouldn't have come to my own mother's funeral?"

"And why didn't you come, Geneva?" asked Loretta. "We called you the same day that Mama died. You could have come to the funeral. It made us look like we didn't care."

"It would have helped if we were together," said Dina, but …."

"But nothing," said Geneva. "I couldn't leave my family at the drop of a hat."

"Don't describe Mama's death," said Dina, "as the drop of a hat. That's disrespectful. She was our mother, after all."

"Hey, stop arguing," said Paolo. "Why are we fighting among ourselves? Could it be we feel guilty about Mama?"

"I don't feel guilty," said Loretta. "I feel angry. Angry that she left us; angry that we were treated like poor relations when we came and then treated differently from her new family. Not to mention the cruel, hurtful accusations she made when we moved out. And then, there was her coldness to Luigi and my wedding plans. I'm sorry, but there were times I hated her! And then there were times I loved her and wanted her to love me," she cried.

Paolo rose from his chair and walked over to Loretta. Putting his arms around her, he said, "In her own way, I believe she did love you. She loved all of us, but Mama was a complicated woman. She undoubtedly harbored feelings of guilt herself," he said. "You know, once she told me that looking at you caused her heart to ache because she saw Papa in your face. It's true, Loretta, you look just like Papa—same dark, expressive eyes, same hair color, same nose and chin, and same playful, mischievous nature," he said, squeezing her shoulders.

"I thought I was like Mama," said Loretta.

"Yes, same wild, stubborn spirit and practicality as Mama, but you have Papa's sense of humor and warmth."

"I received letters from Zia Vittoria and her family in Italy," said Dina. "Zia thinks we should go back after the war."

"Are you crazy?" said Geneva. "You can't go back. This is your home now. We're all American citizens. Why not move to California? It would be wonderful to be together. It's real nice there. No snow or cold weather in Long Beach where I live. Paolo, after the war, you could find a job and we can start fresh again, together."

"Did you forget that I'm getting married this November?" said Loretta. "I know Luigi would never leave his family, especially his mother, who depends on him for support."

"Oh, Lord," said Geneva. "I hope you're not marrying another Mario. I had to divorce him to get rid of his mother. Even dead, she had a hold on him. Thank God, Phil loves my kids and has no mother."

"Well, after the war," said Dina, "your lives will be settled. Geneva is happy with her family in California, Loretta will be married to Luigi, and Paolo will probably succumb to Liliana's charms and marry her. For me, I'll finally return to the convent as is my destiny."

"Dina, the soothsayer speaks," said Paolo.

Dina began to cry. "Don't make fun of me, Paolo. Everything is changing. I don't know what I'll do or where I'll go after the war."

"Luigi and I have already decided that you'll live with us after we're married," said Loretta. "Who knows, maybe you'll decide to get married too. A few men have expressed interest in you, but you turn them away. Why not go out sometime with someone you like?"

"I don't know," said Dina. "That chicken man seems to keep well-informed about me. His uncle is friends with Papa's relatives. He's in the Army now, but his uncle tells them he asks about me and they obligingly keep him up to date. He even sent me a sympathy card after Mama's death."

"Our little nun has an admirer," teased Paolo.

"Please, Paolo, he's too sure of himself for my taste," said Dina. "No, I have always wanted to return to the convent, and I will someday."

Geneva looked at Loretta. Pressing her hands together in prayer, she raised her eyes to the ceiling. Loretta stifled a laugh and shook her head.

"Yes, I will, Loretta!" said Dina, catching the movement.

"Whatever makes you happy," said Loretta.

"It's getting late," said Paolo. "Geneva, Bonnie's sleeping in my room. Hopefully, there's enough room for you in the bed. I'll take the arm chair."

"Paolo, you've said little about how Mama's death has affected you," said Geneva. "You always seemed the most forgiving of her."

Paolo grew quiet for a few moments before saying, "Yeah, I loved her a lot. Maybe being the oldest, I remember her best and all the good times we had as a family. I wish you girls could remember Mama's wonderful laugh and the playfulness between Mama and Papa. Sometimes when she'd pack me a lunch, she'd write *bacio, figlio mia* on the paper she wrapped around my bread and cheese. When I read it, it was like I could feel her kiss." Paolo's voice broke. He cleared his throat, and quickly wiped his eyes. "That's the Mama I always want to remember."

CHAPTER 115

Aftermath—July–September 1942

"Come on, honey," said Luigi. "The Sons of Italy are having a nice cookout on the fourth. You and your sister should come."

"I don't know, Luigi, it's only been two months since Mama died," said Loretta. "People will talk."

"Talk! You know what my mother says about that? 'If you do something good, people talk for two days; if you do something bad, they talk for two days'—so it don't matter."

"My sister won't go," said Loretta. "She's not comfortable when she doesn't know anyone, and she's a bigger stickler for propriety than I am."

"Who's not to know?" said Luigi. "My family will be there, and lots of the *paesani*."

"Your *paesani*," said Loretta, "not ours."

"That's not true, honey. You'll see. Sons of Italy includes everybody—Calabrese, Lombardi, Romano, Genovese, Siciliani, Sandonatesi, everybody. Even people who married Italians. Come on!"

In the end, Loretta accompanied Luigi while Dina preferred to visit their cousin, Maria Elena. At the picnic, many people knew of Caterina's death and came to offer Loretta their condolences. Some of the older members even cried as they hugged her or kissed her cheeks.

To her surprise, Loretta saw her stepsisters, Lena and Ava, and their families at the cookout.

"Hello, Ava," said Loretta. "I didn't know your husband belonged to the Sons of Italy."

"Oh, Mitty's been a member since we got married," she said.

"I thought his name was Salvatore," said Luigi. "Yeah," said Ava, "but everybody calls him Mitty at work because of his big hands, and it sort of stuck."

"What's the matter with Lena?" said Loretta. "She didn't even say hello to me."

"Yeah, well, she's kind of mad that Pa gave all Ma's stuff to you and Dina," said Ava, "and didn't give anything to us. I mean she was your mother but, you know, she was kind of our mother too."

"Dina and I never got one handkerchief of my mother's, much less anything else," said Loretta, "and neither did Geneva, I'm sure."

"Well, what happened to all her stuff?" asked Ava. "Wait. Hey Lena, come on over here. You got to hear this."

Lena slowly walked over to the group and offered a dour, "Hello."

"Hi, Lena," said Loretta. "You're looking well. I like your blouse and shorts."

"Thanks," said Lena. "You look good too. Hi, Luigi."

"How you doing?" said Luigi.

"Fine," said Lena. "I got to go now; my kid wants to join the softball game."

"Don't go yet, Lena," said Ava. "Loretta and her sister say they never got any of Ma's stuff."

"Well, who did it go to?" asked Lena. "I was over at Pa's house, and most of Ma's stuff—her jewelry, some dresses, her nice dishes, and even her best linens—were all missing."

"Believe me," said Loretta, "we didn't get a thing. We assumed that your father would give everything to you and Ava. We haven't been in the house since the memorial Mass."

"You don't think he gave Ma's stuff to Luca's wife, Jennie?" asked Lena. "He always liked her."

"No," said Ava. "He may have liked Jenny, but you know how he is with Luca—fire and gasoline—they blow up every time they're together."

"Maybe he gave it to Gemma," said Loretta. "She was Ma's best friend, and her husband, Georgio, is probably Umberto's best friend."

"Nope," said Ava. "I see Gemma at the Red Cross sometimes. We roll bandages. She told me that when Ma got sick, she gave her a gold chain. Gemma treasures it and said she hoped we wouldn't mind her keeping Mama's gift."

"She's a nice woman," said Loretta, "honest and always kind to everyone, especially Mama."

"So," said Lena, "where is Mama's stuff?"

"He's your father," said Loretta. "Why don't you ask him?"

"Yeah, right," said Lena. "I may be a married woman, but that wouldn't stop him from cracking me on the head. You ask him."

As they said their good-byes and walked away, Luigi said to Loretta, "Wow! Your stepfather really is a bastard."

That evening, Loretta told Dina about her conversation with their stepsisters. "I thought for sure that those two, especially Lena, went over and took all Mama's things," said Dina. "I'm glad they didn't. It will be easier to get along in the years to come."

"Yes, that's true," said Loretta. "But who took everything? Who did

Umberto give it to and why? It was probably a *paesano* or to a stranger, out of spite. Who knows?"

In September of that year, the mystery was solved. A woman named Lana Piemonte and her four children—two boys and two girls—moved into Umberto's house. He and Lana were married less than five months after Caterina's death. The children seemed to have no problem calling Umberto "Papa."

CHAPTER 116

The Eye of the Beholder—September 1942

World War II was still raging, but fortunately Paolo had not been shipped over as yet, and would be able to attend Loretta and Luigi's wedding and give her away.

As a gift, Paolo insisted on Loretta letting him buy her wedding gown and veil. He wrote,

"No homemade wedding dress for you, my sprite. For once you will have a store bought dress—the best you can find. It's my gift to you."

"Thank you, my dearest brother, but the cost!" Loretta wrote back. "You should be saving your money for your own wedding someday."

"No, I insist," replied Paolo. "My little sister will be like a queen in full regalia. You deserve it."

Loretta looked at the cashier's check for one hundred dollars. She knew she should make her own dress and save the money for her life with Luigi. She would just go out with Dina and look at dresses. Maybe try on a few for ideas and save the money. Dina agreed. "We should go to Boston to look at dresses," said Loretta. "How about this Saturday?"

"That's fine," said Dina. "I know of a few bridal shops I've passed on my way to work."

The Saturday excursion was fun. Loretta and Dina even splurged and had lunch at the Woolworth counter—grilled cheese sandwiches and hot chocolate with whipped cream. After lunch, they decided to visit Casa Bianca to see what their gowns were like. They each explored a rack of dresses, sometimes pulling one out and looking more closely at the design or embellishments. Dina even had a notebook to make quick sketches or note particular fabrics, lace, or beadwork design.

"Look at this one, Dina! I have to try it on."

"It doesn't look like much," said Dina. "Too plain."

"I'll just try it on."

A saleswoman came over to ask if they found something and showed them to a dressing room. Loretta put the dress on with Dina's and the saleswoman's help. It had small fabric-covered buttons and loops down the entire back from neck to lower spine. The sleeves were long and tapered over the fingers. The V-neck accentuated Loretta's full breasts, while the dress tapered and silhouetted her slim figure. At the bottom, the dress flared out and had an eight-foot train. The fabric was white, simple with satin embossed flowers in the material and clean, smooth lines which bespoke elegance.

"You look like a queen in that dress," said Dina.

"Absolutely," said the saleswoman. "It was made for you. I have the perfect veil too."

The saleswoman brought out a veil that seemed to be an armful of tulle attached to a small crown. Placing the crown on Loretta's head, the saleswoman spread out the veil, which was about twelve feet long. The fine tulle was edged in a delicate lace that gave the veil a regal quality.

"You look beautiful," said Dina.

"Just beautiful," said the saleswoman. "Like a queen."

Like a queen, thought Loretta. She had never felt so beautiful in all her life but had always considered herself only a little pretty when she dressed up a bit.

"It's a sign," said Loretta. "Paolo said I would be a queen. I feel like a queen. I even feel beautiful. Dina, I'm going to buy this dress and veil."

"But that will take the full hundred dollars," whispered Dina.

"I don't care. For once in my life, I'm not going to worry about money or saving or sacrificing for the future," she said.

"Excuse us," said Dina to the saleswoman. After the woman left, she said, "You and Luigi will need that money. He is still giving his entire paycheck to his mother. What have you both got to live on? This will give you a start," said Dina.

"Yes, I know we could use the money," said Loretta, "but Luigi wants me to do whatever I want. He thinks that Paolo would be upset if I didn't accept his present—a wedding dress."

"Well, we know that Luigi is not the best person to consult about saving money," said Dina. "He's thirty years old and doesn't have a pot to pee in. You will need to be the saver in the family. Start now."

"You're right," said Loretta. "I'll need to be the saver. Luigi's a wonderful man, but not good with money. He's generous to his family and friends. He works hard, but can't seem to save for tomorrow. He's not a drinker, but he smokes, likes to drive around, and he likes to play the numbers. All that costs money. That's the only thing we ever argue about."

"Well, then, it's settled," said Dina. "You will look every bit as beautiful in the dress and veil I'll make for you, and you can put Paolo's money in the bank."

Loretta looked at herself in the mirror. Standing on a pedestal to show the full effect of the dress and veil, she made up her mind. "Call the woman back," she said. "I'm buying this dress and veil today."

"As you like…Queen Loretta," said Dina. "God help you both."

CHAPTER 117

Happy Days Are Here Again—
November 1942

Saturday, November 29th, was a cold, dreary, rainy day. Loretta hoped that the weather would clear by the afternoon, in time for her wedding. The day had begun with sad and frightening news. Reading the paper this morning had left Loretta in tears and horror. She and Luigi had planned to go to the Coconut Grove Nightclub in Boston the night before to celebrate with friends after the wedding rehearsal. A killing fire had consumed the nightclub, and hundreds of people died. "God grant them eternal rest," Loretta prayed. "Thank you, God, for the car trouble which probably saved our lives. Amen."

Dina tried to take Loretta's mind off the tragedy and focused on the day's weather. "Don't worry, Loretta, rain is grace," said Dina. "Everything will be fine."

"The ground will be wet," cried Loretta, "and the train on my dress and veil will get dirty. Everything will be ruined after all the money spent on this foolish dress."

"I'll help you hold up the train and veil," said Dina. "Don't worry. Just get yourself ready."

Loretta took a deep breath, crossed herself, and prayed for a perfect day. Sitting in front of the mirror, she cursed her tightly curled hair. She tried to comb through her thick curls, but the result looked worse. She took a curling iron to tame her hair back to softer, fuller curls that would frame her face. A little powder, a dab of rouge, and a little lipstick and she'd be ready to dress.

"Oh, I hate my thin lips and my nose. My eyes look too big for my face," she moaned.

"You look fine," said her sister. "Here, I'll help you with your dress."

"Dina, you look beautiful," said Loretta. The soft blue-grey voile dress complimented Dina's fair complexion. Her dark eyes sparkled and she had a sweet, serene look that highlighted her prettiness. "You know," said Loretta, "you look like Mama when she was young."

"No matter how near or far—alive or dead—Mama always fills our thoughts," said Dina. "Hurry now or you're going to be late for your own wedding."

Dina took the wedding gown off the hanger and carefully lowered it over Loretta's head, buttoning the back of the dress. "So many buttons," Dina said. "Couldn't you find a dress with a zipper?"

They both laughed. "I hope you'll be there to help me unbutton all these buttons too," said Loretta.

"*Madonna*, what a job! Sit now while I put on your veil." Dina left the room briefly and returned with the veil and a velvet box. "For you, my dearest sister."

Loretta opened the black velvet box. Inside was the most beautiful string of pearls she had ever seen resting on white satin. "Dina, these are exquisite! They must have cost a fortune. That's the money you were saving for the convent."

"Stop, don't cry!" said Dina who was also crying. "You'll ruin your face."

"They're so lovely. I've never dreamt that I'd have anything…." Loretta sputtered.

"Stop, *bella*. Here let me put them on now, then the veil."

There was a knock on the bedroom door. "Are you two ready yet?" asked Paolo.

"Yes," replied Dina as she opened the door. "The bride is ready."

"My God, Loretta," said Paolo as he took her hands and looked her up and down, "you look like a princess."

"I'm supposed to look like a queen, remember?" Loretta laughed through her tears. "You, my dear brother, look so handsome in your uniform. I'm not sure who will look prettier walking down the aisle."

Neighbors from the apartment building and the block were gathered in the street to see her. "*Buona fortuna!*" shouted Signora Fennucci, their friend and neighbor.

"You look beautiful, kid," said another neighbor.

The rain had stopped, and Paolo and Dina helped Loretta get into Joe's car. "Maria Elena and the kids will meet us at the church," he said. "She's so excited and nervous. This rain upset her. She's been cooking, cleaning, and bossing everyone around, trying to get ready for the wedding reception."

"I'll never be able to thank you both enough for hosting the reception for us," said Loretta. "Luigi and I will be eternally grateful. If it weren't for you, we'd just go home after the wedding for coffee and cake."

"Don't mention it," said Joe. "You know how much my wife and I love you people."

Santa Lucia was a large Romanesque church with a long aisle. The wedding party lined up at the back of the church.

"Paolo," asked Loretta," is Luigi here?"

Paolo made an exaggerated bow and, with military precision, stood erect and gave a long stride to the center of the doorway. He then snapped to attention, formally turned and took another exaggerated step back to Loretta's side. "The groom is present and accounted for, accompanied by the best man," he whispered. "We can proceed and take action."

Loretta nudged him and laughed.

"Oh, look," Paolo said, "the bride has a happy face."

As if on cue, organ music began to fill the church. Four ushers followed by four bridesmaids began marching down the aisle. Dina, the Maid of Honor, followed. As the bridal attendants filed into their respective benches, the music paused and then picked up tempo as Paolo escorted Loretta down the aisle. In the background, Maria Elena was quickly arranging the train and veil to float seamlessly behind the bride. Loretta felt like her breathing had stopped. She kept her eyes straight ahead as she tightly gripped Paolo's arm. As she approached Luigi and the best man, she directed her gaze at Luigi, and for the second time in their relationship, she saw tears in his eyes as he looked at her.

Yes, she thought. *He's a good man and he loves me. Thank you, dear God, for giving me this day.*

CHAPTER 118

A New Beginning—November 1942

"Good luck!" *"Buona fortuna!"* "Happy honeymooning!" cheered their friends and family as they kissed everyone good-bye.

"Maria Elena, Joe, thank you so much for everything," said Loretta. "So much food and wine, I'm a little drunk," she laughed.

"You people are so good to us," said Luigi. "I can't believe all the food, good wishes, and presents. How can we ever repay you?"

"Be good to my little cousin," said Maria Elena. "She's very special to me."

"Be happy," said her husband Joe.

"I'll take good care of her," said Luigi. "Don't worry."

As Luigi and Loretta drove away, a group of Luigi's friends piled into the best man's car and followed the couple.

After checking into their hotel room, Loretta and Luigi had barely enough time to hang up their coats when a loud, persistent knocking on the hotel door startled them. Opening the door, Luigi was almost knocked over by the group of friends who invaded their honeymoon room.

"Don't worry, Loretta," said Carlo, the best man, "we're only here to wish you luck and give you this." He handed Luigi a bottle of champagne tied with a huge red ribbon.

"Okay," said Luigi, "you gave us the champagne. Thanks. You guys can go now. You're scaring Loretta."

"No, that's all right," said Loretta. "We should offer them some champagne."

Luigi looked at her. Loretta was rushing around the bedroom and bathroom. "What are you doing?"

"Looking for glasses," she said.

Luigi walked to the door, opened it, and said, "They're not staying that long."

"Aw, come on, Luigi," said Carlo. "Just a quick toast."

"Good night and good-bye," said Luigi, pushing Carlo out the door. The rest of the group, laughing and hooting, followed him.

"Your friends," said Loretta, "are crazy."

Luigi put his arms around Loretta and kissed her. She seemed to stiffen. He took her hand and led her to a corner chair and crouched down on the floor next to her.

"Hey, we should open our presents," he said. "Want to?"

Loretta smiled and relaxed a little. She found and opened her pocketbook. "There must be over thirty envelopes here," she said. They laughed as they opened the envelopes and read out loud the many special messages.

After opening all the envelopes, Luigi collected the money and counted it. "Wow," he said, "there's about two hundred dollars here. Now we can have a real honeymoon. Let's go to New York."

"Can we go to Niagara Falls?" asked Loretta.

"Sure, we'll go to Niagara Falls first, then see New York City, and maybe visit my cousin, Peter. He lives in Brooklyn."

"We should save some money," said Loretta. "We'll need more furniture for the apartment."

"Hey, we'll have time to save afterward," said Luigi. "Let's have a real honeymoon. We can leave right away. I have a week off."

"It sounds wonderful," said Loretta.

"You're wonderful, and I'm the luckiest guy in the world," he said.

"I love you, Luigi. I even love your big, hooked nose, bushy eyebrows, and..."

CHAPTER 119

Settling In—December 1942

Dina moved in a few days before Christmas. In some ways, Loretta was happy to have Dina's company, since it gave her an ally in the Caramazzo household. Her mother-in-law and two sisters-in-law lived upstairs in the three-family house. Her other three sisters-in-law were married but lived close by. All the sisters met for lunch and gossip every Saturday, but never included Loretta.

When Loretta broached the subject with her mother-in-law, Maria Caramazzo said, "You're busy working and taking care of my son and his house. Besides, you have your sister. My daughters come to see me and help me in the house."

Maria Caramazzo was a good woman, kind and generous, but she had wanted Luigi to marry a Sicilian girl. Several of her friends had eligible daughters who had grown up with Luigi, including Angelina, who had been his fiancée before he met Loretta. He wanted this San Rocco girl. So be it. She had her daughters. "You're not upset with them for not inviting us to join them, are you?" asked Dina. "Look at Ava and Lena. They're our stepsisters, and we don't socialize much with them either. We have each other and we have Maria Elena, who is just like a sister. Who needs those Sicilians?"

"Rosa and I were good friends," said Loretta. "She's responsible for my meeting Luigi. She wanted us to get together."

"Yes, but she's friendly to everyone," said Dina. "Her sister, Maria, is very nice and sweet, and Sarafina is pleasant, but cool to me."

"Sarafina's like that with me too," said Loretta. "Melina is friendly sometimes, but other times she can be spiteful and a back-biter. Sally, the youngest, is self-centered and spoiled. She rarely bothers with me at all unless she wants me to sew something for her."

"Forget them," said Dina. "Tell me, how was the honeymoon? Did you have a good time?"

Loretta blushed. "Yes, we had a wonderful time. I loved Niagara Falls. It was beautiful, but I got soaking wet on the tour boat."

"What did you see in New York City?"

"We only spent two days there," said Loretta, "but we saw the Statue of Liberty, went to a show at Radio City Music Hall, and had a nice dinner at a fancy restaurant." Loretta started to laugh, but then muffled her mouth.

"What? Why are you laughing?" said Dina.

Loretta shook her head. "Luigi wanted to take me to a special restaurant. We had a delicious dinner, but it was more fancy than filling. While we were talking, the waiter took Luigi's plate away before he was finished eating. Luigi turned and whistled at the waiter, waving his hand to get him back. The waiter ignored him. When the waiter came back with the bill, Luigi gave him a twenty cent tip.

The waiter looked at it and said sarcastically, "Thanks for the tip."

Luigi said, "You earned it."

"I was so embarrassed," said Loretta, "but the waiter *was* rude. I was still a little upset with Luigi because, after all the money it cost us, he fell asleep at Radio City during the show. We decided to walk back to the hotel, and after listening to Luigi impersonate the waiter and some of the other people we saw at the show, I laughed so much I couldn't be mad for long. That's what I love the most about him—he makes me laugh."

"So you married a clown," said Dina.

"I married an ordinary man who is hardworking, sentimental, kind-hearted, and honest. He has a wonderful sense of humor and sometimes his teasing and playfulness drive me crazy when I want him to be serious, but he means well."

"Is he still giving money to his mother?" asked Dina.

"No. He gave her his last paycheck before we got married and he helps her sometimes, but I manage the money now."

Loretta did not let Dina know that the first serious fight with Luigi had been over who would manage the money. Thank God, Dina had already left for work that day. At first, Luigi agreed that Loretta could manage all the finances, but his sister Melina, learning of this, taunted him saying that "Loretta wore the pants in the family." The remark ate at him, since

Loretta was always fussing about bills and the money he kept from his pay for his own use.

"Luigi, you're wasting money we need," Loretta said. "Can't you choose between buying cigarettes and playing the numbers? You're not single anymore. We have furniture to pay for, groceries to buy, bills to pay, and the stove needs to be replaced. We need the money. Why not just give me your check and I'll give you an allowance?"

"An allowance," said Melina, "what are you, a kid?"

Loretta turned and noticed that her sister-in-law had overheard their conversation. "We're having a private discussion, Melina. Do you mind?"

"Well, I mind that you have my brother trained like a circus dog," she said as she left.

"We need the money, Luigi," said Loretta resuming the argument.

Luigi, who had been shaving, suddenly turned and slapped Loretta's face. "Don't you ever embarrass me in front of my sister again," he said.

Loretta's rage flared and she attacked Luigi, clawing his face.

Grabbing her wrists, he pushed her away. "I'm sorry," he said. "I didn't mean to hit you."

"You ever hit me again," cried Loretta, "I'll leave you."

Luigi's face was a pallet of shaving cream and blood. "That will never happen," he said, "because I'll never do that again. Who knew I married a wildcat?" He smiled.

He looked like a badly made up *Pagliaccio*. She tried not to laugh, but his clownish face was so comical with that dumb smile. She couldn't help it.

"You're a fool," she said.

"Yeah, you're right," he said, "but I was smart enough to marry you. Wanna kiss and make up?"

Loretta pushed him away, but he drew closer to her with his silly grin. "Stop," she said, "you're getting shaving cream all over me."

CHAPTER 120

Winds of Change—January-April 1943

Luigi, Loretta, and Dina were finally settled in the apartment. Loretta converted the larger front room to her and Luigi's bedroom and gave her sister, Dina, the small bedroom at the opposite end of the apartment. Things were awkward at first for all of them. Dina felt she was intruding and afraid she would be a hindrance to her sister's marriage. She vowed that no matter what, unless Luigi was unkind to her sister, she would not interfere.

For his part, Luigi tried to be friendly and welcoming to Dina, but it took a while before he could relax and not feel she was critiquing his every move—how he ate; how he dressed; how much he lost on the weekly pool. The pressure of living with both families had caused the terrible rage that resulted in his slapping Loretta. She forgave him, but it caused a wariness between them for weeks and, knowing Loretta, she would never forget it.

That night when Dina commented on his scratched face, Loretta said, "Luigi ran into some barbed wire." Luigi looked at her and smiled sheepishly, grateful for the lie.

For Loretta, having her sister live with them held mixed blessings. Since they both worked, they shared chores around the apartment and the extra money that Dina insisted on giving was a benefit. Her sister's pickiness and slight superiority were irritating. After all, this was Loretta's house and she was just as capable a cook, money manager, and housekeeper as her older sister. Petty feelings aside, though, with their brother, Paolo, in the army, the two sisters needed to be close. The times were scary and family gave a sense of security.

"My sister, Maria, and her family are moving to Pennsylvania," said Luigi. "Can you believe that?"

"Why Pennsylvania?" asked Loretta.

"Her husband's family moved there and opened a bar. They wrote and told him to come, so they're moving."

"Maria must be devastated," said Loretta. "She's so close to her own mother and sisters."

"Fred has a job with the railroad waiting for him," said Luigi. "Can you believe it?"

"No," said Loretta. "Poor Maria and the kids! I feel sorry for your mother, too."

"Yeah, she's crying up a storm," said Luigi, "but it's a done deal. They move in six weeks."

Loretta was scrubbing out the big porcelain tub while Luigi shaved. She hated this bathroom. The tub took up almost the entire bathroom. She loved the big tub, but there was less than a foot of space between the side of the wall and the tub. You needed to hold your breath and squeeze along the side to clean it. A small sink and a toilet that protruded almost to the sink completed the room. It had no window for light or ventilation, and was off the kitchen. She simply hated it.

Luigi had finished shaving and rinsing out the sink. He asked, "Have you heard from your brother yet?"

"Oh, I'm sorry," said Loretta. "I forgot to tell you that Dina got a letter yesterday. He's being transferred to a new camp here in Massachusetts for more dental surgery. He has an impacted molar."

"Hey, it keeps him out of the war," said Luigi. "My sister Rosie's three sons are somewhere in Europe. Jimmy and Frank are fighting with the Army, and Lennie's somewhere in the Mediterranean with the Navy."

"My sister and I pray for them, too," said Loretta. "Poor Rosie, she worries about them and tries to put on a happy face for the other kids."

"Coffee is ready, you two," said Dina. "Luigi, I made a fried egg sandwich for you for lunch. Are you having doughnuts at work again?"

"Yes, Dina," said Luigi. "I always have coffee and doughnuts at work. I like them."

"Well, it's not a very healthy breakfast," she said. "I could make you some oatmeal."

"Thank you, but I don't like oatmeal. The doughnuts are what I like. I've been eating them every morning for the past ten years."

"Dina doesn't want you to get fat," teased Loretta.

"Did I say he was getting fat?" said Dina. "I just think it's bad to eat doughnuts every day, and it's expensive."

"I appreciate your concern, Dina," said Luigi, "but the ten cents I spend is worth the pleasure. You ought to eat more sweets. Fatten you up for some nice guy," he laughed.

Loretta kissed Luigi good-bye and gave Dina an exasperated look. "*Basta!* Enough," she said quietly.

For Valentine's Day, Luigi brought home chocolates in a large lace-embellished heart- shaped box. He brought a smaller, simple red box for Dina.

"Oh, honey," said Loretta, "you shouldn't spend the money. It's so beautiful—and big."

"For my sweetheart, I can splurge once in a while," he said. "Here's the card."

Loretta opened the large card and read it. She looked at Luigi and kissed him. *For such a rough, plain talking guy, he had the most sensitive and loving heart,* she thought. "Thank you again, honey."

"You're very nice to think of me," said Dina through moist eyes. "Thank you, Luigi."

"Okay, ladies," said Luigi, "how about a movie and some ice cream later? There's a new Bing Crosby movie at the Strand Theatre."

"You two go," said Dina. "I need to write Paolo back and I have a dress to hem."

Luigi blew out his breath, then caught himself. "Are you sure?" he asked.

"No, no," she said. "You two go. I'm busy tonight."

Loretta kissed her. "Happy Valentine's Day. I'm sorry I don't have anything for either of you. I never think of buying cards or candy."

Dina was about to say, "It's a waste of money, anyway," but caught herself. "Have a nice time and Happy Valentine's Day to both of you. Thanks again, Luigi. You're very kind to think of me."

"It's okay," he said.

After they left, Dina chided herself for all the terrible things she said and considered Luigi. *He may lack polish,* she thought, *and looks like a farmer next to my meticulous brother, Paolo, but he is a nice man who obviously loves my sister. It's enough.*

CHAPTER 121

Easter Surprises — April-June 1943

Easter was late–April 25th. Luigi, Loretta, and Dina, along with several family members and friends, were invited to dinner at Luigi's sister Sarafina's house. Her husband, Francesco, was a formal man who had an arrogant air about him. Having no children, he professed to the "children should not be seen or heard" belief. Therefore, when family or friends brought their children, they were coached with "Don't touch anything," "Don't talk too much," "Don't run," "Don't ask for anything," "Just be good, please."

"Everything was delicious, Sarafina," said Loretta. "I would love to learn how to make the Sicilian *tarno* you served. What kind of cheeses and seasonings did you use? Do you always use the large *rigatoni* pasta? How long do you bake it?"

"It's hard to give the recipe," said Sarafina. "When I make it again, I'll call and you can watch me."

"She'll never give you the recipe," whispered Dina. "Some people are like that. They don't share their recipes or if they give it to you, they leave something out, so it's never as good as theirs."

"She said I could watch her," said Loretta, "and I'll just note what she uses and how much. Luigi really loves the *tarno*, which is only baked pasta and cheeses."

While on work break the following week, Sarafina, true to her word, told Loretta to stop by on Sunday afternoon to watch her make another *tarno*. Loretta happily complied, and while Luigi and Francesco played cards in the living room, the two women mixed eggs, cheeses, pasta, and seasonings to make the *tarno*. Loretta noted the recipe for use next Easter when the spring cheeses were available.

In early May, Paolo was granted a short leave. Although his sisters were delighted he was home, they saw him only briefly—an hour here, a few minutes there—since he rose early and came home late most days. Just before he returned to his base, Dina and Loretta had a special dinner for him, inviting their family and Liliana.

"A toast to my pretty sisters who spoil me and stuff me," said Paolo. "If I stay any longer, I won't be able to fit into my uniform."

"Here! Here! *Saluti!*"

"Another toast to my wonderful family and to the lovely Liliana…"

"*Saluti! Saluti!*"

Paolo continued when the cheering died down, "Who has agreed to marry me."

"What!" sputtered Dina.

Everyone was congratulating the couple with handshakes, kisses, and slaps on Paolo's back. "I hope you will be as happy as Luigi and I," said Loretta.

"When was this decided?" asked Dina. "With the war and everything, should you be rushing into getting married so soon?"

A pall settled over the group.

"They are young and in love," said Zio Lorenzo. "Be happy for him."

"I'm…happy for both of you," said Dina, "but it's such a shock…I mean…surprise."

"Please, Dina, be happy for us," said Paolo. "Life is changing very fast these days. I didn't want to tell you this way, but my unit is going to be shipped out before the end of the month. My teeth are fixed, I'm an American citizen, and a soldier during wartime. It had to happen sooner or later that I'd join the fighting."

"We decided to set a date for January 23rd next year," said Liliana, "and hope the war will be over by then."

"January? If you survive that long!" cried Dina.

Paolo took his sister in his arms. "We live day by day, Dina," he said. "We always have. You know that. Do what you do best," said Paolo, "pray for me, pray for all of us. God listens to you, I'm sure."

In June, they received their first letter from Paolo. He was somewhere in Europe and doing fine, he wrote. Some of his words were blackened out, and the letter reflected a war censor's stamp. It wasn't much, but so far he was still alive.

The shipyard where Luigi worked was going full steam with new shipbuilding contracts. Bills and debts were finally manageable. While Dina was often despondent in her worries over Paolo, Loretta and Luigi were optimistic and glowing with life.

Loretta, who had been experiencing morning sickness for the past two months, finally had her suspicions confirmed by Dr. Orsini. She was pregnant and would have a Christmas baby!

CHAPTER 122

A Letter from Home—July 1943

Dearest Paolo,

I'm ashamed to admit that the war has finally become a reality for us now that you are overseas, possibly in combat. Both Dina and I have dreaded this day since the war began. Selfishly, I was happy you were able to attend my wedding along with Rosie's son Jimmy, both of you so handsome in your uniforms. I had hoped that perhaps the war would end by Christmas and you both could stay home.

I hate going to the movies now. The newsreels talk of bombings and show soldiers marching. I wish all the generals and commanders of the Axis and Allies would just fight among themselves and let the regular soldiers come home to their family and friends.

Dina will be writing you soon. She goes to church every day and prays. I pray too, every morning, every night. My thoughts are with you, my dearest brother and friend.

The baby flutters within me and waits for his godfather to return. Luigi hopes for a boy after all those sisters. Following tradition, we must name the first boy Rosario after Luigi's father, the second boy after our father, Antonio, but the third boy (God help me!), will be named Paolo. I promise.

Please stay well and out of harm's way.

With love,

Your sister, Loretta.

By the way, did I tell you that twins run in Luigi's family? Maybe you won't have to wait too long.

CHAPTER 123
Thoughts of a Soldier — August 1943

My dearest sisters, Dina and Loretta,

I've received both of your letters and am grateful for your thoughts and prayers. You will be happy to know that the only serious injury I have sustained so far is poison ivy. It covered the only exposed skin I have—my face, neck and hands. The itching and redness lasted about four days. The medics here are good men. They treated me well.

How are Luigi, the baby, and all our family and friends? I've received several letters from Liliana who writes weekly from the dates on the letters. Hopefully she will not tire of waiting for me or be charmed by some *diavolo* at one of those USO dances."

Paolo paused in his writing and thought of Liliana—her smiling face—her eagerness to please him when they were together. Liliana was a proud woman and could be a little haughty at times, especially with people she wanted to impress. This was just a mask she wore to hide her insecurities. She always tried so hard to reflect the style and confidence of the glamorous women in her magazines. He smiled to himself and, shrugging his shoulders, returned to his letter writing.

I'm not doing any tailoring like I did at the base, but am stitching up ripped jackets, pants and shirts for the guys sometimes. They kid me, but I get cigarettes for my work. I worry about getting my job back after the war though. Have you seen or talked to any of my former bosses or workers? Tell Luigi thanks for offering to send cigarettes, but I get them here occasionally and after the war I plan to stop smoking. It bothers Liliana anyways.

I wish you could send some soap and shaving cream. I'm so dirty most of the time.

While you're thinking of things to send, how about *manicotti*, meatballs, *braciole* with your special *prosciutto* and egg stuffing, and a sweet *ricotta* pie? Just teasing. After this war is over, I plan to have the longest, hottest shower on record, buy a new suit, shirt, and tie, marry Liliana, have babies, and eat until I burst.

Have to say good-bye for now. Remember me to everyone. Keep writing those letters—and praying.

Your brother, Paolo.

"Writing another letter?" asked Charlie Paratore. "Hey, I'm your best buddy, right? I'd like to meet one of your sisters. Maybe she'd write me, too."

"Only one is unmarried, and she wants to be a nun," said Paolo.

"A nun? Forget it!"

"Leonardi, Paratore, move up to Cosgrove's platoon," shouted their CO. The men were sitting in an underground bunker that had been previously occupied by the Germans. It was meticulously crafted with tunnels and barracks. Paolo's platoon sustained considerable injuries and casualties gaining the bunker. The Germans were a tough enemy. In his life, Paolo had only met a few Germans, and they were a proud, obstinate, sometimes arrogant people. The few he encountered while in the Italian military were stubborn and opinionated, but hard working, which he respected. Everything was either good or bad, black or white—no middle ground. You were either with them or against them.

Perhaps that's why Mussolini and the Italian government joined the Axis. Modern day Italians, at heart, were pacifists. Mussolini probably felt it was better to join Hitler than to lose Italy. Another arrogant buffoon, thought Paolo of Mussolini. Now the Germans were firmly entrenched in Italy and Sicily and the fighting was fierce and bloody. It pained Paolo that his country of birth was being systematically destroyed by a ruthless dictator—Adolph Hitler. Paolo had heard news from other American soldiers that the Germans had captured his hometown of San Rocco, and many of the townspeople had either died or were living in desperate conditions without food or water—some burrowing in underground dirt cellars, attempting to hide from the German soldiers.

Occasionally, the men in the platoon got letters from home complaining of rationing, curfews, women being obligated to do men's work, and the general sacrifices required during wartime. How blessed his new countrymen were that they had food to eat, a shelter to call home, and were not living under the constant threat of annihilation that the Europeans were experiencing. People at home cry because they have no butter; people in Europe cry because they have no food, no home, no family—only hope.

CHAPTER 124

A Harvest of Stones—September 1943

Tracers and mortars shingled the sky. "Incoming! Incoming!" someone shouted. Paolo heard the screaming high-pitched whistle of a mortar and felt the ground quake under him. Dirt and debris showered him. Shells hit the dirt and ricocheted everywhere. "Down!" Lt. Cosgrove ordered. "Mackey, get your fat head down or the Krauts will aerate it for you." Paolo gave a quick look back to check on his buddies, especially Charlie Paratore, who had become his best friend. "You good, Charlie?"

"Yeah, I'm dusty, but in one piece, I think."

Off and on, dive bombers from both sides flew over, strafing and bombing the men below. Men scrambled along the trench, trying to get in position to shelter themselves from the constant barrage and gain an opening to retaliate. The fighting went on sporadically most of the day. By the time Paolo was relieved to get some sleep, he was both physically and emotionally exhausted. Before resting on a formerly German cot left in the bunker, he tried brushing off the dirt that covered him. Wetting a scrap of cloth he found with a bit of water, he gave himself a quick face and hand wash, but it made him feel gritty and dirtier, if that was possible. "Ah *che' la miseria*," he muttered and collapsed on the cot.

"Papa, wait for me," said Paolo. "Don't walk so fast; wait!"

Antonio stopped for his son, and turning, put out his hand for the child. "Where are we going, Papa?"

"Up the mountain to San Lorenzo to see my friend," said his father. "He lives in a nice villa and has a very beautiful garden. We will talk with him, enjoy the day together, and bring some spring flowers back for your beautiful mama."

"Papa, will the flowers make Mama happy again? She is always crying. Why does she cry so much?"

Antonio stopped again and picked up the seven-year-old. "Oh, you are getting heavy, my boy," he laughed. "Look, there's a nice rock. Let's rest for a while and talk like men." Antonio placed Paolo on the rock and sat leaning against it. "Papa is going to be a soldier for a little while," he said. "Mama is not happy that I must go, that's why she cries so much. I know you are little, but…"

"I'm not little, Papa! I'm big!" shouted Paolo.

"Yes." Antonio reached up and tousled his son's shock of red hair. "I need you to be big and brave for Mama, and help with your sisters while I'm away. This friend we are visiting, he is an important man and he will help look after all of you." Paolo watched from the garden as his father and the man drank wine and smoked cigarettes. Suddenly, his father fell back and collapsed on the ground. Paolo ran to his father. Papa lay on the ground covered in dirt with a large bleeding hole in his chest as his hand still held the cigarette. "Papa!" Paolo rose so fast that his head hit the upper bunk causing a large welt. "Papa," he cried.

CHAPTER 125

Liliana's Letter—October 1943

My dearest, dearest, Paolo,

Here I am writing you again. I hope you've been receiving all my letters. Each day is such a struggle without you. I want you home with me so much that the yearning hurts. You are in my thoughts and in my dreams always. The pain of missing you racks my body from head to toe. You are the heart of my heart—my destiny—my first and forever love.

Are you safe? The theme of all my prayers is that you not get wounded, that the war end today, and that we will be married and be together forever very soon. Sometimes I torture myself thinking you will meet some flirty European woman and in your loneliness forget me. When these thoughts invade my mind and heart, I cry. But, my dearest love, I try hard not to lose hope—to guard myself against these invasions of my heart, mind, and spirit.

When I feel sad, I splurge and buy something pretty that I can wear for you. Sometimes, I buy something for our future home. My mother and your sister, Dina, chide me I am "wasting money" that we will need. I know you like me to look pretty and I like pretty things. We will have a wonderful, beautiful life and home together.

Your sister Loretta is getting quite a big tummy with the baby. Sometimes I wonder if she is having twins, which she said runs in Luigi's family. She has such a great sense of humor and is always making jokes about her rotund figure.

Maria Elena is her same sweet, giving self. She is so creative and has fabulous ideas about my wedding dress. I know that Maria Elena and Loretta will always be my best friends.

I like Dina, but you know how serious and severe she can be. Honestly, she does have the perfect personality for a nun. She keeps saying that she will join her friend in the convent after we are married. Don't you agree that would be good for her? I think she'll be happy as a nun. From what Loretta and Maria Elena tell me, this has always been her dream. I hope she finally joins the convent. It's what she wants.

Well, my dearest Paolo, I'm going to be late for work again. The autumn weather should invigorate me, but I get dreamy looking at the glorious leaves of rust, gold, and scarlet. A wonderful bright blue sky with cottony clouds shines through my window. I make myself happy by thinking that you too see the same glorious sky and autumn leaves wherever you are.

I love you and miss you, my dearest heart.

Liliana

CHAPTER 126

The Reunion—December 1943

"Luigi, please, no more decorations," said Loretta. "The tree is drooping to the floor."

"Ah, honey, it looks great! The more ornaments, the better!"

"Look at this place," said Loretta. "There are so many Christmas decorations, presents, and that big droopy tree, that I can barely cross the room."

"With the baby coming any day now," said Luigi, "I wanted everything to be ready. Look, I even made a small space with a pillow under the tree for the baby."

Loretta started to laugh, then placed both her hands on her large, protruding abdomen and made a painful grimace. "This is not the Christ Child; we are not putting the baby under that tree."

"No, no, honey," Luigi said as he put his arm around her, "it'll make a great picture of the baby."

"Enough please, dear. With all this stuff and a drooping tree, we might never find the baby again if you place him under the tree."

"Are you still decorating that tree?" asked Dina. "It's almost time to go to Boston, Luigi, and bring Paolo home."

"Don't worry, there's plenty of time."

"What if the train comes in early?" said Dina. "What if traffic is bad? What if there are so many people at the station that we miss him?"

"Okay, okay, I'm going."

"I'm coming with you," said Dina. "My heart is bursting to see Paolo again—to be sure he's fine."

"I think you should stay with your sister," said Luigi, "in case she needs you. Besides, I'm taking Liliana with me to meet him. You know, give them some time together before you two smother him."

Dina, looking at Loretta, let out a huge sigh, but said nothing.

South Station was crowded with people—some shoppers, some who were meeting family and friends for the holidays.

"How do I look?"

"Liliana, you look great," said Luigi. "How many more times are you going to ask me? He'll think you look beautiful. Don't worry."

"Thanks, Luigi. I'm so nervous. Does my hair look okay?"

Luigi nodded his head up and down. "Perfect! You look great!"

Paolo's train finally arrived in the station. Liliana and Luigi kept looking at all the arrivals. A group of soldiers and sailors got off and they scanned the crowd to see if Paolo was among the group.

"Look! Look!" said Liliana. "That's him!"

Luigi held back as Liliana ran into Paolo's arms. She literally enfolded him in her arms, repeatedly kissing his face, covering him with red lipstick prints.

Paolo laughed, dropped his bag, and returned her embrace. "You look wonderful—like a shining Christmas present!"

As they walked arm and arm back to the car, Liliana caught a reflection of herself in the glass door. Her hat was askew, her hair had escaped her hairpins, and her red mouth was smeared with jungle red lipstick. *Oh,* she thought, *I look like a Christmas present all right—one that's been opened!*

Reunited with their brother, Loretta and Dina relished every minute with Paolo. However, precious time with Paolo had to be interrupted with preparations for a sumptuous Christmas dinner. While the women cooked and prepared each dish, they were not above giving orders to Luigi for his assistance. He ran errands, opened tomato cans, and chopped vegetables. Paolo offered to help, but Loretta and Dina wanted him to rest or spend his time talking to them.

They prepared special meals for Christmas Eve and Day. Christmas Eve's menu included a traditional Italian feast of fried fish, stuffed calamari, baked razor clams, and homemade angel hair pasta with a rich tuna sauce. On Christmas Day they managed a fairly complete *antipasto,* *manicotti* with feather-light crepes, and a mix of homemade sausages, pork pieces, and meatballs cooked in a fragrant, rich tomato sauce. Liliana brought Paolo's favorite dessert—*cannoli* stuffed with sweet ricotta cream and sprinkled with chopped pistachio nuts.

"Where did you ever find all this heavenly food?" asked Paolo. "I heard there is a war and everything is rationed. You lovely ladies are not part of the black market, are you?"

Dina was indignant. "How can you even ask such a question? We've scraped and saved and bartered with friends to make this Christmas extra special for you."

Everyone laughed. "Paolo is just teasing us, Dina," said Loretta.

Dina blushed, shook her head, and finally was able to laugh at herself.

"Paolo and I may have a small ceremony in late January," said Liliana, "and if he's stationed in Maryland to finish out the war, I'll join him. When the war is over, we'll come home and have a big, formal wedding. You both must be my bridesmaids."

"Thank God you're home now," said Dina. "You promise you'll come back from Maryland and live nearby?"

"I promise," said Paolo. "Besides, Liliana's family would hunt me down if I took their daughter away for good."

Paolo's two-week leave ended early—just after New Year's Day. "I'm to report to a base in New York," he said. "That's all I know."

"Liliana must be terribly disappointed that you can't get married first," said Loretta. "I had hoped you'd be here for the baby, too, but this baby is in no hurry to be born."

On Paolo's last evening, he and Loretta were up past midnight, restless and apprehensive about their immediate futures. Loretta made some warm milk to calm the unborn baby that ferociously kicked her. Paolo opted for a cup of coffee. They sat together at the small, dimly lit kitchen table.

"Ouch! Please, baby, stop kicking and concentrate on being born." Loretta took her brother's hand and placed it on her abdomen. "Feel how strongly this child fights to be released. Believe me, no one wants this baby out more than I do."

Paolo laughed. "Patience, little one," he said. "The world is not a very nice place right now. Stay protected within your mama until it's safe to come out."

Loretta held her brother's hand and looked at him. He looked so pensive. She noticed that his hairline was receding and he had a slight stoop instead of his normal ramrod posture. *He looks older than his years,* she thought.

"The war should end soon. You and Liliana will marry, and before you know it you'll be counseling your own child."

"Loretta," said Paolo quietly, "if I get sent over again, I know I won't come back."

CHAPTER 127

Anytime Now—January 1944

Loretta waddled gingerly to the front door and checked the mailbox. She retrieved a few bills, a circular from the Capitol Market and, happily, a letter from Paolo.

My dear sisters,

Sorry this is so brief, but wanted to let you know I'm being shipped overseas again. Don't know where, but I may be gone for a while. I've written Liliana to explain that we need to postpone the wedding. She'll be upset, so please look after her. You can write me at the above post office address and tell me how Liliana is doing and all about the baby, too.

With affection,

Paolo

Oh, God, thought Loretta, *please watch over my brother and bring him home soon.* Then aloud she emphatically said, "And please, God, could you push this baby to be born soon, Amen."

"Loretta, did you realize last Sunday was January 23rd?" said Dina. "It was supposed to be Paolo and Liliana's wedding day. Why don't we invite her for dinner tonight? Are you feeling well enough to cook a few vegetables and a chicken?"

"I guess so," said Loretta. "I didn't sleep well again. I couldn't move all night, I'm so big, and my back is killing me."

"Never mind," said Dina. "I'll call her from the train station and arrange to visit her before I come home from work. You rest today and I'll make a simple dinner tonight, maybe a *frittata*."

With Luigi and Dina at work, Loretta thought about her day. Like most Thursday mornings, she would make dough for Friday night's pizza.

After that, she planned to rest in the afternoon.

"Aaah!" Loretta screamed, gripping the table. As she clung to the table's edge, her face grimaced in pain. In desperation she called her mother-in-law who lived upstairs. "Maria, Maria, help me!" Loretta heard a loud banging on the back door.

"Loretta, are you all right?"

It was Laura. "Laura, help me," cried Loretta. "The baby's coming."

Laura Graceffa was her neighbor and friend. The middle-aged woman ran to support Loretta before she fell onto the floor. "Don't worry," Laura said. "First babies take their time. My husband is home. He'll drive you to the hospital and I'll stay with you until your husband comes."

At the hospital Loretta was admitted to the labor ward. "The pain is terrible," she told the nurse.

"The doctor may prescribe an anesthetic," the nurse said, "but we need to wait for the order. Take deep breaths and try to relax."

Loretta's labor continued all night and well into the next day and evening. Since Loretta's uterus was not contracting effectively, Dr. Orsini decided to induce her and use forceps to deliver the baby. The obstetrical forceps had two wide, blunt blades that would fit around the baby's head. After an intravenous infusion of medication to stimulate the uterine muscles, Dr. Orsini carefully inserted the forceps into the birth canal, and as gently as possible, lifted the baby out.

A few hours later, when Loretta was awake, the nurse brought her the baby. Luigi, who had been sitting in the visitor's chair while Loretta slept, jumped up and took his wife's hand.

"You have a sweet little girl," said the nurse as she placed the infant in Loretta's arm.

Loretta uncovered the baby, which caused the infant to cry.

"She looks like a funny little monkey," said Luigi. "What are those marks on her head?"

The nurse came over and began massaging the baby's head. "Don't worry, eventually she'll have a nice round head," she said. "Those marks are from the delivery, but they'll fade soon."

Loretta examined her baby. Ten fingers, ten toes, two eyes, a small nose, two ears, and a square head.

She gently touched the forceps marks and brushed her fingers over the baby's downy head.

"Well, my little *bambina*," murmured Loretta, "you may not be a classical beauty, but you look perfect to me."

"You both look beautiful to me," said Luigi.

CHAPTER 128

Paolo's Letters—February 1944

Returning from the hospital, Loretta found a packet of letters from Paolo. They were written earlier in the month, except for the last, which was dated January 15. She quickly opened them to read.

Maryland, January 1, 1944

My very dearest sister,

Today I received your letter and wanted to tell you not to worry about me.

I didn't want to upset you with all my ignorant talk of possibly going overseas again and not returning.

I'm at a training camp in Maryland. We don't have much spare time, but there is talk we may sit here for a while.

I've written Liliana. Tell her I treasure all her letters. I hope she and Dina are getting on better. Please do what you can to smooth ruffled feathers. Give my warmest regards to the family, especially Zio Lorenzo, Maria Elena, Joe, and Papa's sisters and brother. A letter from Zia Vittoria got through to me once. I've often wondered how Mama and her sister could be so different.

Have you had the baby yet? Don't write again until I can give you my new address.

With love,

Your brother, Paolo

Maryland, January 6, 1944

My very dearest sister,

How are you? Hopefully you and all the family are well. We are training hard, climbing, running, rifle practice, and so on. Most of my infantry are young boys. An old man of 35 years has a hard time keeping up. I'm exhausted at night and find I'm too tired to even dream.

How is Luigi doing? Is he still working overtime at the shipyard?

Dina wrote me and said she called Liliana and invited her to visit but that she didn't come. Liliana's letter said that Dina invited her on her regular club night when she sees her friends, so she couldn't go. Why is it that the women I love the most and who love me can't get along? Fortunately, you and Maria Elena are good friends with Liliana. Hopefully, she and Dina will learn to like each other, too.

Did I tell you that a letter finally reached me from our cousin, Antonio, who's fighting in Africa? Same area I fought in when I was in the Italian army. He said it's rough there, but he is well. Say hello to Luigi's family, especially his mother, Maria. She's a good woman and mother.

With love,
Your brother, Paolo.

Washington, D.C., January 9, 1944—a postcard
Dear sister,
I have a 24-hour leave, and two of my friends and I are visiting Washington, D.C. This is a picture of the White House where the President lives.

Best wishes,
Your brother, Paolo.

The last letter was from Paolo, but written in a different hand.

January 15, 1944
Dear sister,
This is to let you know that, for the present, I cannot write to you in Italian. I have to tell one of my friends what to write. When I get a few details straightened out, I will be able to write to five people in Italian—one letter per week to each person. By looking at this new address, you would think I am in New York, but I'm somewhere along the East Coast. We are under strict censorship here, so I can't tell you anything about my Army life. Don't worry about me. I'm happy here because I'm with a lot of boys from my old company, and the new fellows are a good bunch, too.

I asked you before to stop writing until I received my new address. You can now start writing me again, although this new address will not be permanent. But I will receive your letters and will let you know as soon as possible when the address changes again. I received five letters tonight from Liliana that made me very happy. They were written to my old address and forwarded here to me. Tell Dina to visit Liliana when she has a chance. Tell her to forget everything that happened in the past. Now that I'm away, I want them to be friends.

Yesterday, I went to church and made my confession. It's too bad I can't write my own letters to you. There are so many things I would like to say to you. In case some of my friends want to know why I don't write them, please tell them the reason. When I get a chance, I will. Please tell me about Luigi. Is he going to be drafted? I hope not because I would feel better if he were home with you and Dina.

I sent you a package of clothes. It includes the sweater you made for me, photos, a pen that Zio Lorenzo gave me, and other stuff I can't take with me. When I get back home, I'll want them. Then again, I might want you to send some of them back to me if I need them.

Hope you are feeling well. Don't forget to let me know when the baby arrives.

My best regards to all the family and friends,
Your brother, Paolo.

Luigi found Loretta crying. "What's the matter, honey?"

Loretta held out the letters to Luigi. "Here, you can read this one. It's in English. My brother can wear a uniform and fight for this country, but he can't write in his own language. It's not fair!"

"Nothing's fair in war, honey."

CHAPTER 129

Home of My Fathers—February 1944

As he sat in the belly of the transport ship, Paolo's thoughts ran through an endless series of past memories.

"Hey," said Charlie Paratore, Paolo's buddy, "are you dreaming or what?"

Startled, Paolo replied, "Just thinking about when I lived in Italy. Rumor has it we're being shipped there."

"Yeah, my Pa always talked about the old country," said Charlie. "What do you regret most?"

"Regret?" said Paolo. "It was a hard life, especially after my father died in the first war. My mother left to find us a new and better life in America, and it took me 17 years to get there. Hey, I would have probably stayed in Italy if my sisters had stayed. I had some good friends, some family in the north, and a career as a soldier."

"Are you kidding?" said Charlie. "If you'd stayed, I might be aiming this rifle at you instead of us being buddies."

"That's true," laughed Paolo. "Fortunately, Italy surrendered last

September." Then, turning serious, he said,

"You've been a good friend, Charlie. If I don't get back, I want you to write Liliana and my sisters, okay?"

"What are ya talking about? I'll probably get my fool head blown off…and Paolo, if I do, would you tell my folks that, uh, I, uh, think they're great…you know."

"Yeah, I know."

On February 6, Paolo, Charlie, and the Third Division of the Seventh Infantry landed at Natousa, Italy. They were to join the Fifth Army fighting against German counterattacks at Nettuno and Anzio beaches. Despite the German artillery of 15cm guns which gave accurate fire, American and British troops took many German prisoners on February 7th, but the loss of Allied soldiers was heavy. Front line infantrymen of the Allies like Paolo were not allowed to carry anything on their person that might give any information to the enemy in case they were captured.

Paolo never remembered such a cold, damp, raw February. The guys fighting in Cassino had to deal with snow along with frigid, bitter weather. When their American transport ships tried to land, the 'Anzio Express'—Germany's 28cm guns mounted on railway cars, opened fire on Anzio harbor and the ships. Landing beaches became targets for the German medium artillery. These guns smashed the harbor of Nettuno and Anzio to pieces. Even the trucks transporting them to their assignments were frequently dodging bullets and grenades. Day after day, the fighting continued. Torrential rains covered roads and paths skirting the Pontine marshes in the beachhead area with a soapy layer of clay. In the foxholes and shell craters, muddy water gurgled and sucked in the unfortunate soldiers. In some places, soldiers waded knee-deep in glutinous filth. At every impact of shells, fountains of earth gushed high into the sky. Large fragments of stone whirled through the air after each shattering explosion. The air mixed with smoke from smoldering fires of bombed houses rebounding in a thunderous roar.

From the soggy trench, Paolo watched other soldiers attempt to dig out a field gun from the thick mud, which was greatly hampering the Allied operations in these low lying areas. Frequent thick fogs helped each side to carry out surprise attacks, which kept the infantry on both sides on the alert.

"God, what a hellhole," said Charlie as he darted down, hugging the makeshift barrier.

"Stay down!" said Paolo. "Would you believe that Anzio is a resort town dating back to the early Romans? When I was stationed in Rome years ago, I used to come here to swim with a pretty girl."

"Not Liliana was it?"

"No, her name was Valeria," said Paolo. "She was very special to me."

"What happened? You break up when you came to America?"

"No, before that. Her father didn't like soldiers—smart man."

A barrage of bullets whistled over their heads again. In the distance they could see flares and bursting shells.

"Shit, it's raining again," said Charlie. "Man, everything I own is wet—my shoes, my pants, my jacket, my blanket—damn! It feels like there's a rainspout going down my back to my ass. On top of that, I'm freezing into a goddamn icicle."

"I don't know what's worse," said Paolo, "sitting and sinking in the mud, or trying to run knee-deep in it."

"Yeah, know what's almost worse?" said Charlie. "At night it's so damn dark, ya gotta reach out and hold the guy in front of you to make sure you don't lose each other. God, stumbling blindly around here hoping you're going in the right direction is awful."

"Feels like we're losing a lot of guys," said Paolo as he slowly shook his head. He looked at the young men of his platoon—scared boys with frightened faces, older guys with lonely eyes.

"Well," said Charlie, "let's hope if we get shot, it's a 'million dollar wound'—ya know, not too serious, but bad enough to get us out of here."

"We should be so lucky," said Paolo.

Early dawn of Friday, February 18th, Paolo and his comrades were again fighting off an enemy counter-attack.

"God, no," murmured Paolo as bullets pierced the left side of his body and then in rapid succession, his chest. As he lay bleeding, a medic from the Fifth Army began to pull him out with another soldier assisting. Paolo was bleeding so much it was hard for him to focus. They carried him into the hospital tent.

Someone was talking to him. What was he saying? I don't know. God help me get through this. He prayed. I'm moving again. Where are they taking me? Don't leave me, Papa, don't leave me. Paolo remembered being transported into an ambulance before losing consciousness.

CHAPTER 130

The Tides of Life—March 1944

As she nursed the baby, Loretta could hear her sister moving about in the kitchen. Having her sister live with them had been difficult at times. Dina had her own way of doing everything; she was meticulous and organized while Loretta was more relaxed and spontaneous. Dina was quiet and serious; Loretta was garrulous and fun-loving. They had different attitudes about housekeeping and although each was an excellent cook, Dina seasoned lightly while Loretta loved garlic and pepper.

"Dina, what are you doing?" asked Loretta. "I can hear you moving about and it's only six a.m."

"Luigi just left for work, so I'm cleaning before I start the pasta dough." *God bless Luigi,* thought Loretta. *What a patient guy. Knowing Dina, she was following after him to clean and hurry him out to work.*

Living together in a small apartment with Luigi's family upstairs had been a challenge. Luigi grumbled at times, but he was used to living with women, having grown up with five sisters. Often he was the peacemaker, which was peculiar, since he and Dina hadn't liked each other when Loretta first started seeing him. But Luigi respected Dina and thought she was, in his words, "a good woman."

Dina for her part tried to give Loretta and Luigi privacy as often as possible, sometimes retreating to her room to read or sew, and allowing Luigi and Loretta to have the living room to themselves in the evening. With the arrival of the baby, things became a little tense again, since each woman and Nonna upstairs had very definite ideas about caring for a baby.

"Well, at least nursing you," whispered Loretta to the baby, "is something only I can do."

By nine the pasta was made and laid out to dry before cutting. Loretta made the beds and washed the breakfast cups before it was time to feed and change the baby again.

"I'll clean up," said Dina. "You take a rest. You look tired."

"I'm fine," said Loretta. "This baby is a night owl. She's wide awake all night and I hate to leave her in the bassinet if she's not asleep."

"Babies adjust. Don't worry. You could wake me and I'd take care of her if you need to sleep."

"Thank you, but she's my baby and I'll take care of her."

Dina dropped her head. "Of course she's your baby. I just wanted to help."

"Oh Dina, don't be mad. It's just everything is so new and everyone is always trying to see the baby, rock the baby, hold the baby, that I only get her to myself when I'm nursing her. You're a wonderful help—really, I don't know if I could run a house, cook, and take care of a baby without you."

"Well, you're my baby sister, and I want to help. Right now I'm going to clean up all this flour and concentrate on cutting my pasta."

Both women were startled by a knock on the door. "I'll get it," said Dina. "You check on the baby. I think I hear her."

Opening the door, Dina saw a young, good-looking soldier. She smiled and asked him to come in.

"Miss Dina Leonardi?" he asked.

"Yes, that's me. Are you a friend of my brother, Paolo? Is he all right?"

The young soldier stood erect, took a deep breath and said, "At the request of the President of the United States, it is with deep sympathy and regret that I inform you that your brother, Private First Class Paolo Leonardi, died nineteen February in Italy as a result of wounds received in action."

She stared at him, stunned for a moment. Then his last words echoed in her head.

"No, no," screamed Dina as she beat her floury hands on the young soldier's chest.

"What is it?" said Loretta, carrying the baby to the door.

Dina was leaning against the soldier's chest, crying and hitting him with small ineffectual fists.

The soldier's eyes were glassy, his uniform covered with flour as he worked to maintain a stiff, professional stance.

"My God, no, not Paolo, not Paolo!" cried Loretta, who was squeezing the baby so hard that the baby's shrieking joined that of the weeping sisters.

"I'm sorry, I'm sorry, I'm sorry," the young soldier kept repeating as Loretta pulled Dina off him and the two sisters and baby held each other, crying.

Late morning the next day, a sallow-looking young boy delivered the Western Union telegram from the Adjutant General advising them that "the Secretary of War assures them of his deep sympathy in the loss of their brother. Letter to follow."

Loretta, still in shock, sat rocking the baby most of the day until her mother-in-law took the child.

Dina, overcome with grief, took to her bed. It was up to Luigi to visit Paolo's fiancée, Liliana, and tell her the sad news.

"I'm sorry, but I don't believe it," said Liliana. "I just got a letter today from him. He said he was fine. He said it rains a lot where he is and it's cold, but he's fine. He's fine!"

Liliana's mother and sister took her arm and lead her to a chair. They stood protectively over her, while Luigi shifted from foot to foot, not knowing what to say.

Finally he said, "We can write the President and the Army to make sure they didn't make a mistake. Sometimes people make mistakes, you know—maybe there's another guy with the same name, you know. We can hope."

CHAPTER 131

Devastation and Denial— April–May 1944

"It's not true," said Dina. "Liliana and I both received letters from Paolo last week. It's a mistake! A mistake, I tell you."

Loretta sighed heavily and shook her head as tears fell on her baby's nursing head. "They must know," she said. "They must make sure. It would be beyond cruelty to tell people that their relative died if it wasn't true."

"So many men, they do make mistakes," said Dina. "Remember our neighbor in San Rocco, Costanzo Quintilliani? They told his family he died in the Great War from gas poisoning. Didn't he come home after the war?"

"Dina," said Loretta, "I was three years old when we left San Rocco. I barely remember anyone."

"Well, I've written to the government again and so has Liliana. God has not abandoned us. Paolo may be hurt or fighting somewhere else—maybe in Germany or France—but he has not returned to Italy to die. God is with him."

With Luigi's help, Dina wrote letters to the War Department, the

President, and in hopes of a reply, another letter to Paolo.

Two weeks later, a reply from the War Department's Adjutant General arrived and confirmed Paolo's death. He was "not able to provide additional information at present, but further details as received will be promptly communicated to you." He ended with "the nation's gratitude, and that this thought may give you strength and courage in your sorrow."

More letters and cards followed. General Marshall extended his sympathy; a letter from the President notified them that Paolo had been awarded the Purple Heart posthumously; the Division Chaplain wrote that Paolo had been given a Catholic burial and was laid to rest with full military honors in a beautifully located cemetery, but he couldn't say where at present; and finally, a letter from Roberto, the son of Dina's friend, Marietta Caldarone, also serving abroad, who wrote he would try to find out more about Paolo, but would she keep praying for him, too.

Liliana was also beseeching the War Department for more information about Paolo's death. She received letters of sympathy, but limited information, since "active theatres of operation can only provide brief communications."

She opened the large red velvet jewelry box given to her by Paolo on her last birthday, where she kept his letters, photos, and small souvenirs of their times together. The photo of herself in her new rabbit fur jacket, dyed a rich brown, stared back at her from the inside lid of the box. "To my sweetheart in the service with love," she read, remembering the inscription she wrote on Paolo's copy almost two years ago. "You'll always be my sweetheart, the love of my life, until the day I die." It was a promise she would always keep. Weeping, she hugged her box of memories.

CHAPTER 132

Conflict and Consolation —
June-August 1944

Black became the color of their life. Both Dina and Loretta wore black dresses, black stockings, and black shoes daily. Dina's mood became dark and she suffered from depression. She received a final answer to her letters from the War Department. They informed her that Paolo had "died on 19 February 1944 from shell fragment wounds received on 18

February 1944 (Loretta's birthday) while performing his duties as a rifleman with his company when repulsing an enemy counterattack. He died near Nettuno, Italy. Location of the grave should be addressed to the Quartermaster General in Washington, D.C." However, after writing this official, Dina was told that this information could not be released as yet. It would be nearly two more years before all details of Paolo's place of burial were disclosed.

"Have you responded to your convent friends' letters as yet?" asked Loretta.

"No. All their letters tell me that I should place my trust in God and accept that Paolo is with Him."

"Well, that's what we believe, isn't it?" said Loretta.

"I asked God to protect Paolo, to return him to us. God has betrayed us. He let Paolo die. God abandoned Paolo, and now, I'm abandoning Him."

Shocked, Loretta looked at her sister. "Don't talk like that," she said. "Men start wars. They are the ones who kill each other. Why blame God for war's madness?"

"Don't you understand that first our father had to die in a war, and now Paolo—both at the same age. Wasn't that God's cruel joke? Paolo was sent back to Italy to die at thirty-five years of age, like Papa."

"Dina," said Loretta, "you worry me when you talk like that. God didn't plan their deaths. It was bad luck—blame the people who sent them to war, if you want to blame someone. Papa had to leave a wife and four children, and Paolo wasn't even an American citizen when he was drafted. I found his alien registration card last week, and it almost broke my heart to realize his misfortune. But Dina, Paolo could have fought the draft because of this and his age, but he didn't. It was his choice to accept military service for this country because he was grateful for being here."

Despite Loretta's pleas, Dina closed herself off from family and friends. The exception was Loretta's and Luigi's baby, Maria, whom she loved to distraction. Dina shared a room with the baby and constantly usurped Loretta's care.

"Let me change her."

"I'll put her to bed."

"Here, let me bathe her."

"Don't let her cry, I'll get her."

Dina used her embroidery skills to add designs to dresses that Loretta made for the baby. When the baby was christened, she insisted on making the dress, slip, and bonnet, incorporating a pretty design among the tiny stitches.

285

At times, Loretta felt displaced, but she realized that the baby gave Dina a purpose and someone to love and pamper. "Thank God only I can nurse the baby," she laughed to herself.

In early August, Loretta realized that she was pregnant again. Luigi was delighted and she felt that this baby would add to healing the loss of Paolo.

"Luigi," said Loretta, "if the baby is a boy, can we name him after my brother?"

"Gee, my mother will expect us to name him after my father," said Luigi.

"Please, it would mean a lot to me and Dina."

"Yeah, okay," said Luigi. "We'll name the next one after my father."

"You're the best! Thank you," said Loretta.

After confirming her pregnancy with the doctor, Loretta told Dina.

"How could you do such things when your brother just died," cried Dina.

Loretta was taken aback. "What?"

"You and Luigi, to do those things when your brother just died. What a scandal! You should be ashamed of yourself."

Taking a deep breath, Loretta hissed, "We are married. He is my husband; I am his wife. We love each other. My brother is not disrespected, and you can go to the convent or you can go to hell!"

CHAPTER 133
Traditions Tested—December 1944

"Why have you stopped going to church?" asked Loretta. "The Church means so much to you."

"My prayers seem to go unheard," said Dina. "I don't have the strength to fight anymore."

"Dina, you can't fight the War Department for sending Paolo to serve the country, or God for allowing him to die."

"They did send him and God did let Paolo die. Why can't I blame them?"

Work at the shipyard was in full force, and Luigi was putting in overtime. Dina and Loretta had dinner early and were cleaning up the kitchen. Loretta, trying to address Dina's depression, said, "All those letters you write to the government, to Paolo's friends, to the Army Chaplain—what more can they tell you?"

Dina, who had been drying dishes as Loretta washed, threw the towel down and cried, "I want them to tell me why!"

Loretta embraced her sister. "There is no answer to that question, *bella mia.*"

The women retired to the small living room, and while Loretta knitted a blanket for the baby she was expecting, Dina picked up her embroidery and resumed making the trim for baby Maria's Christmas dress.

Loretta's baby continued to be the balm that soothed Dina's heart. She never tired of attending to little Maria. Dina would make little dresses, slips, and caps for the baby. She embroidered intricate designs on sheets and pillowcases for Maria's crib. Loretta claimed her time with the baby while Dina was at work, but each evening, Dina would hover over Maria, eager to meet her needs and demands now that she was off the breast and on the bottle. Occasionally, she did have to defer to Luigi and his mother, who also doted on the baby.

"Hey, anybody awake?" said Luigi as he opened the back door. "You two are up late. Any supper left? I could eat a horse."

Loretta put down her knitting and headed for the kitchen. "We had polenta tonight, and I saved a big dish for you. Would you like a salad, too?"

"Okay," said Luigi. "One good thing about polenta, it fills you up like cement. Wish we could afford a nice thick steak once in a while."

"I know, honey," said Loretta, "but even if we had the ration stamps, it's hard to find a nice thick steak at the market."

Dina came into the kitchen while Luigi was hunched over his plate shoveling the sauce-topped polenta into his waiting mouth.

"I'll say good night," she said. "Don't worry about getting up early, Loretta. I'll tend to the baby and make the coffee."

"Oh, thank you," said Loretta, "but try to get some extra sleep, and if I hear the baby, I'll get up."

After Dina closed her bedroom door, Luigi asked Loretta, "How's she doing?"

"Oh, the same. Now she hates God and the government."

"Poor woman," said Luigi.

"Poor woman! What about me? He was my brother, too. Everyone rushes to comfort my sister, but no one remembers that Paolo was my brother too."

"I know, honey, but they were so close. You were like their kid."

"No, it's just that my sister is protective and possessive of her family.

287

For a while there was just Paolo and me, but now it includes the baby. In fact, I think she's spoiling the baby."

"Cool down," said Luigi, "she'll hear you. As far as spoiling the baby, she and my mother are in a race to do just that."

"Sometimes I wish we could live far away from everybody," said Loretta.

"You don't mean that. Your sister is good to you and she helps you a lot."

"Yes, but she gets upset when I want to see my friends or if the neighbors stop over too often. She thinks we should bar the doors and sit grieving alone. I miss my brother, but I want to see people and go out sometimes to a movie or to visit friends. She thinks that's not proper during the first year of a death in the family. Damn! I'm tired of wearing black, too."

"Then wear something else," said Luigi. "It's been almost ten months."

"Sure, and have both my sister and your mother making comments to me."

"Tomorrow," said Luigi, "go out and buy yourself some pink or red underwear. They'll never know, and you'll be happy."

"You're a genius! I'm going to do it!"

"I was just kidding!" said Luigi.

CHAPTER 134

The Wounded Heart—January 1945

"Liliana, please, it's been a year," said her mother. "You'll never meet anyone if you always dress like a widow. I know you loved Paolo, but he wasn't your husband. He would want you to get on with your life."

"I don't care," said Liliana. "If I must attend the war bond rally, I'm wearing this dress."

"Black dress, black stockings, black shoes, hat, and coat," said Mrs. Borelli. "It's too much."

"Then I won't go if I have to change. I don't want to go anyway."

"Please, you must come. Your father is treasurer at the Sons of Italy. It's his big fundraiser. How would it look if we didn't go and support our boys? Don't do it for me; do it for your father and Paolo."

"I'll go," conceded Liliana, "but I'm not changing."

Having gone to few public functions since Paolo died, Liliana was anxious about people talking to her about Paolo's death, especially today. A few came up to her, offered condolences, and asked how she was doing. Others, less diplomatic but more pragmatic, suggested, "You're such a pretty girl, I'm sure you'll find someone special again. You should go to some dances. There are a lot of nice young men there."

Not able to leave without her parents and their car, she retreated to the ladies' lounge. Thankfully, it was not busy, and Liliana found a comfortable chair in the corner. The band in the hall was playing 'God Bless America' and, closing her eyes, Liliana remembered the first time she met Paolo at Maria Elena's and Joe's Fourth of July party in 1941.

As soon as she touched his hand in greeting, a spark ignited her heart and it was love at first sight. With Maria Elena's help, she was able to see him at several family functions. The night before he was to return to his base, Liliana found Paolo sitting alone on Maria Elena's porch smoking a cigarette. Well it's now or never, she thought.

"Paolo, I'd like to write you, and maybe you could write me too."

He smiled at her and got up to offer her a seat on the porch swing. "I was going to ask if I could hear from you once in a while," he said.

"Oh, Paolo, of course."

From the living room she could hear the phonograph playing 'As Time Goes By,' and she did the most brazen thing—she kissed him.

He kissed her back.

Riding the wave of her euphoria, Liliana wrote Paolo every day until he replied that, as grateful as he was for her letters, he would be hard pressed to write her as often.

There were only six Army leaves, six occasions to be together before Paolo's platoon was sent to Italy, to Anzio, to die.

Easter 1942, he teased me about my hat, she remembered.

"Pardon me miss, but I think a fat pink cat is sitting on your head."

"What?" I said. "I spent days shopping for the perfect hat—something soft, feminine and I'd hoped attractive—and now you're laughing at me?" *I couldn't help myself, I felt tears filling my eyes.*

"Hey, don't cry. I'm sorry. It's a beautiful hat. I'm a clod for teasing you. Please, Liliana, don't cry. You look so pretty and I like cats."

Despite myself, I laughed.

"You look so regal, I don't know if I can afford such an elegant girl."

Elegant? Paolo was the elegant one. He was always clean-shaven, meticulously dressed with polished shoes and shiny buttons on his uniform. Her heart raced when she looked at his deep brown eyes and dark rusty hair. His facial features were symmetrical, not like her pointy face and large hooked nose. He had beautiful hands, long tapered fingers, and clean nails. He wasn't very tall, about five feet eight inches, but well-proportioned with strong shoulders and narrow waist and hips. Elegant... yes, he was the elegant one.

His mother died in May of that year. He wrote about her in his letters. His sisters had a love/hate relationship with their mother, but he always loved her and forgave her for abandoning them when they were children. Paolo remembered how much his father had loved her, and her passion for her husband who died in the First World War.

He was home again for his thirty-third birthday in August. "Do me a favor, please," he asked. "My sisters gave me this ring for my birthday. I don't want to hurt their feelings, but could you hold on to it for me?" It was a broad gold band set with a square cut red stone. A ruby? Probably not. It reminded me of the college ring men wear but without a school name or year. "I'll guard it with my life," I said.

"I hope not," Paolo said, "but if anything happens, I want you to keep it so you won't forget me."

"Forget you? Forget you? Never!" Liliana could still feel that kiss and his buttons pressing between her breasts.

We saw each other again on Thanksgiving weekend in 1942, and he accompanied his sister, Loretta, down the aisle on her wedding day that last Sunday in November. The reception was at his cousin, Maria Elena's, house. I convinced him to dance with me on the back porch where we first kissed. It had rained earlier that day, and the porch was strewn with wet, slippery leaves. I slipped a few times, but Paolo always caught me and held me close to him.

"I always feel safe with you," I said.

"Well, that's an inviting compliment to give a man when he's holding you in the dark."

I laughed and we almost had our lips together when his sister Dina appeared.

"Are you crazy?" she said. "It's freezing out here and it's going to rain again. Paolo, you'll catch pneumonia. You too, Liliana," she said, though not as emphatically to me.

I remembered how I hated that woman sometimes. She seemed determined to keep us apart. She almost fainted during his next leave in May '43 when Paolo announced our engagement.

He proposed on May 8. Knowing I love flowers, he borrowed Luigi's car and took me to the Arnold Arboretum in Boston. We walked; we talked about family, friends, and our dreams. In front of a pungent lilac bush, festive with lush purple blossoms, Paolo stopped and pulled a red velvet box from his pocket.

"I hope you'll accept this ring and me as a promise of a life together."

"Together forever," I cried. "Yes, I accept, yes!"

The newspapers were filled with engagement and wedding announcements during those war years. Our engagement notice didn't appear until late July. I bought twenty newspapers and sent copies to Paolo and all our family and friends. With hopes that the war would end soon, we planned our wedding for late January 1944.

Paolo's last leave was Christmas 1943. He seemed tired when I met him at the train station, but anxious to spend time with me and his sister, Loretta, who was expecting her first child at any time. Paolo was told he might be sent to a base in Maryland upon his return. We decided that we would go ahead with the wedding on January 23rd, and then I would return with him to Maryland and wait out the rest of the war before returning to Massachusetts.

His last days home he was melancholic, but as he kissed me good-bye at the station, he gave me a big smile and a wink.

"Get that dress and wedding veil ready. I'll see you next month to change your name to mine—Liliana Leonardi. Hey, it sounds good."

"It sounds wonderful, my dearest Paolo," I said. "I can't wait. I love you. Come back soon and safe."

"I'll try," he said.

"Are you all right?" A woman was offering her a handkerchief. Liliana hadn't realized she was sobbing and frantically gulping air to catch her breath. Today was January 23rd. A year ago, this was to have been her wedding day.

CHAPTER 135

Caterina the Second's Arrival— April 1945

"I'm so big I can't walk without waddling from side to side like Maria's roly-poly toy. When is this baby coming?"

"I don't understand," said Dina. "The doctor told you March, and you're late again."

"Are you saying it's my fault that the doctor is wrong?" said Loretta. "First he told me Maria was going to be a Christmas baby and she was born five weeks later. Now this baby is already two weeks overdue."

Luigi's mother laughed. "Babies come when they're ready—not when you or the doctor says. When he's ready, he'll come—not before."

"Ma, do you think it will really be a boy this time?" said Luigi.

"Yes," said Nonna Maria. "The needle test stayed straight over Loretta's belly; it's a boy."

Loretta was clearing the dishes after dinner. She had invited Luigi's mother to join them. She groaned as she struggled to get around the table and chairs. The kitchen was never very roomy and now she felt she dominated the room with her huge belly.

"Well," said Dina, "when I did the needle test, it moved from side to side, which means a girl."

"Stop, please," said Loretta. "I don't care if it's a donkey. I just want this baby to be born. I'm even willing to go through another twenty-four-hour delivery, I'm so desperate."

"Go sit down, honey," said Luigi. "We'll clean up."

The next morning, Friday, April 6th, a letter arrived addressed to Caterina Leonardi Fabrizio—Dina and Loretta's deceased mother. It was from the U.S. Government's Kansas City Quartermaster Depot, Army Effects Bureau. Loretta wanted to open it, but knowing Dina, she decided to wait until her sister got home from work.

Luigi's mother came downstairs from her apartment while Loretta was making pasta and a quick marinara sauce for the weekend, in case she had to retreat to the hospital. Nonna Maria played with baby Maria for a while until Loretta put the baby in for a nap. When Loretta returned, she found Nonna Maria sitting at the kitchen table crocheting a doily.

Maneuvering around the kitchen and her mother-in-law, Loretta said, "Maria, some coffee?"

"Later, later, after you've finished with the pasta."

Loretta got along well with her mother-in-law but sometimes resented Luigi's devotion. *Devotion? Yes, that's what it is. Devotion to his mother and family,* she thought. Maybe because she hadn't had a good relationship with her own mother, she occasionally resented Luigi's jumping every time his mother called for something. A few arguments had centered on this theme, but Luigi was adamant that his mother was alone, old, and not very well. *Well,* thought Loretta, *she does complain about her failing health a lot, but she seems pretty healthy and strong to me. She may love her daughters, but she relies on her only son. Besides, she's not alone—Melina and Sally live with her right upstairs."*

"What?" asked Loretta. "I'm sorry, Maria, I was thinking about something. What did you say?"

"I said that the baby should be named after Luigi's father, of course. That's our way."

"Yes, I know," said Loretta. "That's our way too."

Before returning upstairs, Maria accepted a plate of fresh homemade pasta, which she insisted she would "cook with my own sauce, thank you."

Returning from work, Dina opened the kitchen door. Loretta was not there and dinner was not cooked. Where was she? Where's baby Maria? Dina checked on the baby first and smiled, hearing her gurgling away. Maria was in her crib entertaining herself with her chubby feet. Then she went to Loretta and Luigi's bedroom and saw Loretta on the bed.

"Loretta," Dina said shaking her, "are you all right?"

"Oh, I must have drifted off to sleep," said a yawning Loretta. "What time is it? I haven't cooked the pasta or even made a salad yet. Maria, where is she?"

"Calm down, she's fine; content in her crib for now. Just rest," said Dina. "I'll get dinner. Any mail today?"

"Yes, there's a letter from the government, but it's addressed to Ma," said Loretta. "Why would they send a letter to her attention?"

"Well, they probably meant to send it to me," said Dina. "Where is it?"

"Why just you? Why are you the only one to be sent information about Paolo?" asked Loretta. "You should include my name when writing or filling out forms. I'm his sister, too."

"Loretta, why must we have the same discussion?" said Dina. "Paolo had to give one contact, and being the older sister, he named me."

"Open the letter," said Loretta, "and read what it says, older sister."

"'Dear Mrs. Leonardi Fabrizio, The Army Effects Bureau has received certain funds which belong to your son, Private Paolo Leonardi,'" read Dina.

"They want to know about Paolo's family; whether he was married and if Papa's alive. They also want to know if Paolo left a will and want all papers returned to them before his money will be released."

"I wonder how much money it is," said Loretta.

"Don't worry," said Dina. "I'll take care of it. You have enough to worry about with a family and a new baby coming."

"Okay, but please keep me up to date. Don't forget," she said meaningfully.

"Anybody home?" called Luigi. "I cashed my check with Joe the Greek in case we need any money this weekend."

"Dinner will be a little late," said Dina. "Loretta, you rest and I'll get it ready."

Loretta was happy to oblige. She was so tired and her body ached. She longed to stay in bed.

"Do you mind if I skip dinner?" she said. "I need to lie down again. Luigi, you don't mind if I just stay in bed, do you?"

"No, honey. You okay? Should I call the doctor?"

"No, I just want to rest. Making the pasta must have worn me out."

"Okay, honey. You rest."

Dina gave her a hug and then turned to the kitchen and proceeded to fill a large pot with water for the pasta. She noted that Loretta hadn't cleaned up all the flour from the kitchen floor, and while the water was heating, she grabbed the broom and dust pan. Baby Maria started crying, and Dina left the broom to change her, feed her, and change her again before she finished making the dinner. Just before sitting down, Dina and Luigi checked on Loretta, who was fast asleep. They sat down to eat and midway through, they heard Loretta screaming. Luigi and Dina rushed to the bedroom. Loretta's water had broken and she was wincing in pain.

"The baby's coming! Take me to the hospital, now! Oh, my God, hurry!"

Luigi grabbed the car keys while Dina got Loretta's coat and personal bag from the closet. She tried to get the coat on Loretta, but Loretta was not cooperating, so Dina just threw it over Loretta's shoulders. Both she and Luigi started to go out the door, when Loretta screamed again.

"Maria, don't leave her!"

"No, no, I'll call her grandmother to watch her," said Dina. "Luigi, you take Loretta to the car; I'll call your mother and be right back."

"No, no. I can't wait," said Loretta. "You stay with Maria. Please Luigi, let's go now."

Luigi sped to the hospital and stopped at the emergency room. Leaving the car at the entrance door, he helped Loretta into the hospital.

"Help us," he said. "My wife's having a baby."

A nurse rushed over with a wheelchair and took Loretta. "Don't worry," she said. "Who's your doctor?"

"Dr. Rosenberg," said Luigi. "Can you call him?"

"You take care of your car," said the nurse. "We'll take care of your wife."

The nurse began to ask Loretta questions, wanting to fill out the admission forms. Loretta kept shaking her head and said, "Call the doctor. The baby is coming, now!"

"Now, dear, don't worry. We'll get you upstairs for an exam and see where you are." As the nurse wheeled Loretta into the elevator, Loretta's contractions were coming fast and furious.

"Hurry, hurry," cried Loretta.

"Hold on, dear," said the nurse.

Thirty minutes later, Loretta delivered a robust baby girl—eight pounds and four ounces. The baby's pretty red face was crowned with an abundance of black, curly hair; so much so, the nurses had tied a white silk ribbon on the top of her head when they presented the baby to her parents.

Luigi was delighted with his new daughter, though mildly disappointed she wasn't a boy. She was beautiful with silky black hair and dark eyes. When she grabbed his finger, she won him over completely.

When Dina came the next day, she looked at the baby and then gave Loretta a wry smile. In unison they said, "Caterina."

The baby looked just like her maternal grandmother and namesake.

CHAPTER 136

A Full House—September 1945

Men and women were returning from the war. Many, whether single or married, were forced to move in with family due to a housing shortage. Luigi's nephew, Jimmy, and his bride, Margie, took residence upstairs with Luigi's mother and sisters. Jimmy was Rosa's eldest son—the same age as his aunt, Melina.

Rosa's household was bulging with family. Her three oldest sons had served in the war. All had sustained injuries, but Jimmy was the most fortunate, coming home fairly well healed from his wounds.

"It's because I'm short that I'm alive today," Jimmy said. "While I was in France patrolling some bombed out areas, a Kraut shot me in the head. Luckily the bullet went right through my helmet and missed my brains. I got that bastard though, killed him with my knife."

"Once a Sicilian, always a Sicilian," murmured Dina to her sister.

Loretta pursed her lips together trying, not to laugh. Two of Rosa's other sons had worse luck. Lennie suffered shell shock while seeing action in Sicily. Frank came home with a leg wound from serving in the Pacific. Completing the family along with Rosa's husband, Salvatore, and his sister, Teresa, a spinster, was Michael, the youngest, a preteen of twelve, and Marianne, who was sixteen years old and the only girl.

As she entered their apartment door, Jimmy's wife, Margie, called out, "Hi, Loretta. Do you mind if I take little Maria upstairs for a while? Mamarani said you wouldn't, and it'll give you more time to spend with the baby."

This 'open door' policy of the upstairs occupants was sometimes irritating to Loretta and Dina.

"No, that's fine," said Loretta. "She just woke up and I want to change her. I need to wash some diapers before Rina wakes up from her nap."

Margie and Jimmy often took Maria upstairs to play with them. Occasionally, it was their idea, but more often *Mamarani*, who doted on this grandchild, would ask that Maria spend time upstairs.

Mamarani, thought Loretta—*what a strange word. They probably are saying mamagrandi—a blended version of grand and mother, and in their Sicilian dialect it comes out 'mamarani.'* She laughed. *Of course, the Italian word for grandmother is nonna.* Loretta sighed, thinking of all the strange words that her husband and his Sicilian family and friends used that sounded Italian, but were totally foreign to her ear. She and Dina would laugh and shrug their shoulders trying to decipher words like *carruzza*, which was dialect for girl. Like so many of their words and expressions, it was far from the Italian word—*ragazza*. Loretta tried to learn the words and would sometimes sprinkle them in her conversations with her mother-in-law and other Sicilian family members and friends. Dina refused to speak Sicilian. She was pleasant and patient, but the Italian language was so pure and melodic to her that she stubbornly spoke, refusing to learn a corrupt version.

Margie carried Maria to the door. "Oh, I almost forgot. *Mamarani* is making bread and everyone is coming over soon. She said to tell you."

"Thank you," said Loretta. "Luigi will be home in an hour. I'll send him up."

Every Saturday morning, Maria made wonderful crusty bread, and her daughters faithfully came to eat the bread and to gossip. They drizzled olive oil, pepper, and grated Parmesan or Romano cheese over the hot slices and carefully raised the dripping, oily bread to their mouths. Then they talked about everyone they knew—who was getting married; who lost a job; who died; who had a baby; what so-and-so was wearing at church; and so on, stopping only to chew bread and listen intently for any juicy news.

Although Loretta had previously worked with some of these women and was married to their only brother, she was not totally accepted in the group. Yes, they would be polite, but the mood was restrained when Loretta joined them. They rarely sought her out or invited her and Dina to join them on Saturday for their socializing. Besides, then they wouldn't be able to talk about them. Loretta could see them all now, standing or sitting around the kitchen table.

In contrast with Luigi and Loretta's small four-room apartment, Maria's apartment had six large rooms and one small bathroom off the kitchen. On either side of the kitchen was a bedroom, Maria's on the right, Melina's and Sally's on the left. Across the entry from the one exit door was the dining room which was flanked by another bedroom, now occupied by Jimmy and Margie. A black pot-bellied stove stood nestled along the wall between the dining room and the linoleum-floored living room, which included an upright piano and a radio. Every Christmas Eve, members of the Caramazzo family filled the dining and living rooms for holiday dinner. A small coffee table and the piano bench served as dining tables for the children, and all the adults squeezed around the massive round walnut table in the dining room.

"Hey, wake up," said Luigi. "You almost dropped the baby."

Loretta had drifted off while nursing Rina. Her mind was filled with the activity upstairs, as she thought about what the sisters had to say this week.

"Your mother made bread and wants you upstairs," said Loretta.

"Good. Want to come?"

"No, I need to finish nursing the baby," said Loretta. "You go."

"I'll bring down a loaf," he said and kissed her head and the baby's.

Loretta heard the front door close, and let the tears fall.

CHAPTER 137

Living After Loss—December 1945

"Hey, honey, where are you?" called Luigi. "Loretta?"

"I'm here, in the bedroom."

Luigi came into the room and found Loretta kneeling on the floor beside her opened hope chest. Baby clothes were scattered on the bed, on the floor, and hanging off the top of the chest lid.

"What are you doing?" he said.

"I'm sorting through Maria's old clothes to find outfits for the baby. There are lots of little dresses, but not many crawling outfits that are still in good shape."

"So put dresses on Rina. Girls wear dresses don't they?"

"Yes, but I want to have her legs covered for warmth and to make it easier for Rina to crawl; leggings also cushion her knees."

"So make some. Anyway, I have a surprise for you and your sister—tickets to the Palermo Society banquet. Everybody's going. I was lucky to get tickets, so plan on getting dolled up."

"Luigi, we can't go. It's too early. What will people think? Besides, my sister would never go. You know how she is since Paolo died. In fact, I'm still wearing black because she does. I'm sorry, honey, we can't go. Can you get the money back?"

"No, we're going with or without your sister. Hey, I liked your brother too, but we got to live. All our *paesani* will be there. Lots of guys back from the war and their families. It's Christmas. Let's go have a good time. We need it. *You* need it."

"Honestly, I want to go, but my sister…"

"We're going. Try to get your sister to go, but if she wants to stay home, fine. She can watch the kids, but we're going."

Loretta decided to approach Dina the next morning while Luigi was out running an errand for his mother.

"When I went shopping this week, I saw several of our friends, and they all asked about you. It was nice to see them. I miss going out together and the social events we use to attend. Remember how Paolo was always shooing us out of the house to meet people? It was Paolo who took the time to get to know Luigi's Sicilian relatives and friends and encouraged

298

us not to be afraid of the Sicilians. He even charmed Luigi's mother and especially his sister, Melina. I think she had a little crush on him."

"Loretta, what are you babbling about?" said Dina. "Say what's on your mind before I turn gray."

Heaving a sigh, Loretta got to the point.

"We need to see people again. The Palermo Society's having a banquet to celebrate the end of the war and the return of the veterans. We should go."

"Our brother didn't come back. I can't go and celebrate that fact."

"Yes, Paolo died, but other relatives and friends did come back. We should celebrate that miracle. Paolo would want us to go on. You know it. We should go and acknowledge those who fought beside him. They deserve that, at least. If Paolo had survived and people avoided him because he was lucky enough to come back, how would that make you feel?"

"I don't know if I can see other soldiers and not cry—to see their happiness and not feel my own grief."

Loretta put her arms around her sister whose eyes were welling with tears. "We must believe that Paolo will always be with us."

"I don't know...I don't know."

After many tears and protestations, Dina finally agreed to go.

CHAPTER 138

Return of the Chicken Man— December 1945

Dina's agreement did not include leaving the "widow's weeds" behind. She and Loretta made new dresses, but they were black. Loretta's dress had black beads and sequins that were sewn into a feather pattern off her shoulder and neck. Dina added a lovely embroidered white lace collar to her own dress, which Loretta heartily approved as very becoming. It softened Dina's face and accentuated her slender neck.

"*Wow*, I'm going with the two prettiest ladies in the city," said Luigi. "Grab your coats and let's go, so we get good seats."

Their neighbor, Laura, sent her teenage daughter to babysit. Connie was a good kid and very responsible. Loretta gave her last minute instructions. "Don't let Maria stay up if she wakes up. She's such a night owl. Make sure you put her back to bed even if she fusses. Rina will sleep for you. She's a quiet baby and should be fine for the night." Loretta kissed the babies goodnight and rushed out the door and into the car. Luigi had already started the motor.

Loretta felt a thrill seeing the banquet hall. American flags, Italian banners, festive Christmas wreaths, garlands of holly, gold stars, and an enormous glowing Christmas tree decorated the great hall. Attractive young men in their military uniforms sat next to women adorned in their finest dresses and hairstyles, and wearing holiday corsages. Everyone looked happy, and the air filled with loud chatter and Christmas music.

Luigi, who loved a good party, was caught up in the celebration. Knowing the majority of the attendees, who were Sicilians, he greeted the men with a strong handshake and the women with "Merry Christmas" or "looking beautiful tonight."

"Are you running for mayor, or what?" asked Loretta. "Sit down or people will think you're drunk."

"Okay, okay," he said. As Luigi pulled out his chair, he felt a hand on his back. Turning, he recognized the contractor friend of Loretta's relatives. "Hey, how are you?" said Luigi. "Out of the service yet?" Many of the servicemen were encouraged to wear their uniforms, although most were home for good.

"Yup, I'm out," he said. "I came by to say hello to you, your wife, and your beautiful sister-in-law."

Hearing herself mentioned, Dina turned around and looked at the tall, handsome man. It couldn't be, she thought. Her mind raced back to when she first met this man who sold her a chicken so many years ago.

"Hello lovely lady. Remember me?"

"Oh, my God, it's the chicken man," she blustered. "I'm sorry, I mean Mr. Sorrentino. How are you?"

"Good, I'm doing okay," he said. "I'm sorry about your brother."

"Sit down," said Luigi. "Let me get you a drink. What do you want? How about a shot of whiskey or brandy?"

"I'll take a brandy, thanks."

"Are you going back into construction?" asked Loretta.

"Yeah, I'm joining my uncle's crew until I get back on my feet," he said. "Then I'll be on my own again."

"Did you hurt your eye in the war?" asked Loretta.

"Loretta, don't be so nosy," said Dina. "That's Mr. Sorrentino's business." Dina had noticed his half-closed left eye too, but thought he was still very good looking.

"I collected a couple of German bullets, but I'm doing okay now."

Luigi arrived with the drinks, and after thanking him, Leonardo Sorrentino directed his attention to Dina.

"I tried to write you after your aunts gave me your address, but I never heard from you."

"Yes, they told me, and I did receive your letter, but it came shortly after Paolo was killed. I couldn't write. I had to concentrate on what happened to my brother. The government is not very free with information. I wrote them constantly and they replied telling me almost nothing for the longest time."

"Maybe if you know his Division and Platoon numbers," said Leonardo, "I could help you get in touch with other guys who knew him. Perhaps they can tell you what you want to know."

"Could you do that?" asked Dina. "I would be so grateful."

"Grateful enough to go out with me?"

Dina pulled back. "I don't know. I'm still in mourning over my brother."

"Well, you're here having dinner. How about just having dinner with me some Sunday? We can talk about your brother if you want."

"I don't know," Dina said.

Leonardo downed his brandy. "I'll call you soon," he said. Nodding his head at Loretta, he shook Luigi's hand and thanked him again for the drink. He left, but not before giving Dina a big smile.

"That guy is very sure of himself," said Loretta.

"He's brash," said Dina, "but he may be able to help us get in touch with some of Paolo's friends. I'd eat with the devil if I could learn more about Paolo's last few days."

"You just may be doing that," said Loretta.

CHAPTER 139

Family News—March 1946

With the end of the war, letters from relatives in Italy were finally able to get through again. Zia Vittoria, Mama's younger sister, had been a faithful correspondent before the war. Her letter was full of news.

Cara mia, are you both well? My heart is overjoyed with the news that Loretta has two children—girls who will care for her in her old age. I give thanks every day for my children and grandchildren. This war has brought so much heartbreak. Your Paolo and my son, Pietro, both dead. Antonio is still in a prisoner of war camp in Africa, but coming home soon.

Loretta stopped reading, and went into her bedroom. Kneeling over her hope chest, she searched for the red satin box which held her special letters and cards. The first year they were married, Luigi had given her chocolates in the elaborate box, and although she wasn't a hoarder like Dina, she couldn't bear to throw it out. Leafing through the contents, she pulled out the letter she was looking for. She remembered how her heart lurched when it arrived. It was a prisoner of war letter from her cousin, Antonio, stamped from Africa. The address was barely legible, covered by censorship stamps from France and the United States. Loretta held the letter again to her chest then reread it. Antonio's name, rank as a sergeant, and prisoner number were on one side of the letter. The other side listed the return address as Prisoners of War, Krygegevangene, Union of South Africa, and was in both Italian and English. Under the return address and across the top was printed "*Corrispondenza—Prigionieri di Guerra—*Prisoners of War—P.O.W. 9." The camp and block numbers were blacked out. Antonio had used a pencil and the writing was barely legible. It was dated Monday, 29 January, 1945, almost a year after Paolo's death and on Maria's first birthday. He had written:

"Sad news finally reached me in my mother's letter that Paolo was killed in Italy. Such ugly misfortune and a cruel fate of destiny that he had to return to his homeland to die. I have been a prisoner of war for almost two years, and recent developments now make it possible to receive mail as well as write. Although I was wounded, thanks to my mother's prayers, I'm much stronger and hope to return home soon. My memories of all the happy days at home and especially of your visits keep me strong as the days, months, and years pass. God willing we will see each other again. Please write if you can. Don't forget to write my mother and tell her I am well. Antonio"

Loretta brushed the tears off the letter and returned it to her special box inside the hope chest. Returning to the kitchen table, she resumed reading her aunt's letter.

Antonio was wounded before being captured and put in the camp. My heart aches imagining the pain and deprivation he suffered. The few letters we received were always full of encouragement, telling his father and me not to worry. Not worry? From the moment your child stirs in your womb to the last breath you take, a mother never stops worrying. Thanks be to God my other sons are now home recovering from injuries. Your uncle is no longer strong and active. The anxiety over his sons, Pietro's death, and the ravages of the war caused him to suffer a heart attack. Life has been difficult with little food, no work, and the struggle to just survive each day, but hope lives.

Thank you for the package of fabrics, flour and coffee. These are luxuries that we are most grateful for receiving. I have not had a new dress since before the war. My wonderful daughter-in-law, Cesira, takes care of us now and has already started making me a dress. I fear I will need it when my beloved leaves me.

Now that I am old, all my thoughts are of the past. I think of your mother, my only sister. Caterina had such spirit and determination. She was such a lively girl, and your father adored her. When Paolo was born, she wouldn't leave him, not for a moment. She carried him everywhere, holding him like a valuable jewel. His fiery red hair delighted her. He was her treasure. What an ugly misfortune that Paolo, after being reunited with his mother and finding a woman to love, had to return to Italy and die. Perhaps his destiny was always here in Italy. Antonio said that if Paolo had married his first love, Valeria, then perhaps he would have stayed in Italy and had a different destiny. But only God knows what our true destiny is meant to be. We are free to choose, and perhaps our choice sets our fate.

My family think of you and Dina often and remember happier times before you went to America. Oh, to capture that time again when those we love were together. Perhaps again in heaven. Please write me when you can, and God bless you for your generous heart.

Zia Vittoria

CHAPTER 140

A New Destiny—July 1946

"I think Peppino, Melina's new boyfriend, is very handsome and funny," said Loretta to her sister as they folded clothes.

"He does seem like a nice man," said Dina, "and he has certainly improved her disposition."

"Well, speaking about men," said Loretta, "are you getting serious about Leo? You're seeing him quite a lot."

"I'm not sure yet. He seems to have so many strong opinions about things and I find we clash on many subjects."

"Like what?"

"Well, he wasn't a churchgoer and didn't sympathize with my thoughts of becoming a nun," said Dina, "and he feels I should be over the loss of our brother and wear brighter clothes. He can be cynical and has a dark, moody side which can be a little frightening at times."

"Well, if you want my opinion, I don't like him either."

"I didn't say I don't like him! He's very intelligent and good look-ing. He can be very generous and flattering. He has his own construction company, and he's good to his mother. He even built her a beautiful brick house."

"She won't let him not be good to her," said Loretta. "Concetta is a very strong-willed woman. You will see it when you meet her."

"Well, I've given up on the convent. I tried to understand why God took Paolo, but I can't. My friend, Sister Giovanna—you remember her, Domenica Antonelli, we were in the convent together—still writes me saying that God has a plan for each of us and that Paolo died a noble death, and so on. All we know is that he is dead, but we don't know where he's buried or if he's buried in holy ground."

Leonardo Sorrentino continued his courtship of Dina and a month later, on August 22nd, Paolo's birthday, he proposed to her and she accepted. Loretta and Luigi invited the two families to a celebration din-ner in early September.

"We're going to be married next year on January 23rd," said Dina.

"Dina, January is a terrible month. It might snow," said Loretta, "and for sure it will be cold."

"That's the day I want. It's the same date that Paolo was to have been married."

Loretta looked at Leo. "What do you say?"

"Let her have her own way now," said Leo. "I'll have my way later."

CHAPTER 141

The Wedding Clown — January–February 1947

"It was a nice wedding, wasn't it?" said Luigi.

"Yes, my sister looked beautiful and with the exception of Maria's antics," said Loretta, "everything went well."

"She was funny!" said Luigi. "All dressed up like a beautiful doll. She came down the church aisle all smiles and confidence, greeting people and throwing flowers from her basket. Gee, she was cute."

"Cute! She almost ruined my sister's wedding. Everybody was looking at Maria and laughing; no one was looking at my sister, the bride. I wanted to wring Maria's neck. Then she saw your mother and ran over to her and asked for gum! When we got to the photographer's studio, he had to take flowers from the bridesmaids' bouquets to refill Maria's basket for the pictures. Then she ran around the hall and almost knocked over the wedding cake. Cute! I may kill her."

"Honey, she's barely three years old," said Luigi. "Besides, your sister thought she was funny too."

"My sister was so nervous," said Loretta, "that Maria was comic relief. Wait until she's a flower girl for your sister Melina's wedding in June. Then I'll think she's cute."

Luigi put his arms around Loretta. "Hey, kid, you looked pretty good yourself. In fact, you were beautiful," he said kissing her.

"You looked almost as handsome as the day I married you, and this time your pants fit."

"Okay, okay. I'm never going to live down wearing the best man's pants. All during the ceremony, I was afraid they'd fall down and you'd leave the altar when your sister said, "I told you so.""

Loretta laughed and gave Luigi a playful punch. "Don't change the subject. Maria should be punished for her antics."

"I don't agree, but it's your job to punish the girls in the family. When we have boys, I'll punish them."

"What?"

"Come on, honey. She's just a baby. Everybody loved her."

A few days later, Loretta received a postcard from Florida. Dina and Leo said the weather was warm and there were orange trees everywhere. They'd have lots of photographs to show them.

"That's where we'll go on our next honeymoon," said Luigi.

"Sure," said Loretta. "You'll be in a wheelchair and I'll have to push you by then."

CHAPTER 142

Closure—February-March 1947

On the anniversary of Paolo's death, February 19th, a letter arrived from the War Department. It read:

"Enclosed herewith is a picture of the United States Military Cemetery Nettuno, Italy, in which your brother, the late Private First Class Paolo Leonardi, is buried. It is my sincere hope that you may gain some solace from this view of the surroundings in which your loved one rests. As you can see, this is a place of simple dignity, neat and well cared for. Here, assured of continual care, now rest the remains of a few of those heroic dead who fell together in the service of our country. This cemetery will be maintained as a temporary resting place until, in accordance with the wishes of the next of kin, all remains are either placed in permanent American cemeteries overseas or returned to the Homeland for final burial. Sincerely yours, A.G. Holmes Brigadier General, QMC Assistant."

Loretta looked at the attached picture. It showed a sea of plots with tiny crosses. She counted the crosses on one plot—144. There was nothing else to identify the picture, a town in the background, and a sea of plots with white crosses.

"Well, now we know where Paolo's buried," she cried. She remembered the letter the Army chaplain wrote when Paolo died. He said he received a Catholic burial and was placed in a beautiful cemetery among his fallen comrades.

In March, Dina received papers regarding the disposition of Paolo's body. Families were given an opportunity to have their loved one's remains shipped back to the United States for final burial, if desired. At first, Loretta was hesitant about disturbing her brother's body, but she finally agreed with Dina that they wanted Paolo home. With their husbands' financial help and blessings, they purchased a cemetery plot nearby that would accommodate Paolo for now, and they and their husbands in the future.

"We'll finally have our brother back," said Dina.

In March, a package with Paolo's belongings arrived. It contained a brown cardigan sweater that Loretta had knitted, a chain and St. Michael medal given by Dina, a pen, a pocket knife, a cigarette lighter with Paolo's initials given by Liliana, a picture of Liliana, and a small black address book with names and addresses of family and friends—so little for 35 years of life.

CHAPTER 143

A Rough Start—Spring-Summer 1947

Dina and Leo had returned from their honeymoon on Valentine's Day and moved in with his mother. Leo was Concetta's son from her first marriage. When Dina first met her, she thought Concetta must have been a very beautiful woman when she was young, because was she still a handsome woman with lovely features and a robust figure. Unfortunately, Dina was to find her a domineering, forceful, and spiteful mother-in-law.

Living with her mother-in-law made Dina determined to win her over. She cooked and cleaned and tried to appease Concetta whenever possible. Concetta treated her like a servant and made snide remarks about her time in the convent.

When Dina was soon pregnant, Concetta quipped, "Well, I can see that our little nun knows how to open her legs for a man."

Dina was appalled. This woman was cruder than her stepfather. She appealed to Leo about his mother's constant unkindness to her.

"She's an old woman," he said. "You need to be patient with her. This is her house; she's not used to sharing it with another woman."

"Another woman? I'm your wife and I'm carrying your child. You built this house. It's your house, and as your wife, it's also my house."

"I built it for my mother," he said. "I gave it to her."

"Then please build one for us. I can't live here much longer."

"Be patient," Leo said. "Try to get along with my mother at least until after the baby's born."

In the end, Leo rented and moved Dina back into a second-floor cold water flat in her former apartment building.

CHAPTER 144

A Son Is Born—November 1947

Dina was not unhappy living in her old neighborhood, although now that she was enormous with her pregnancy, the stairs were a challenge, especially when she had to carry groceries and other bundles up the narrow back steps. For the past three months, since Loretta had returned to work, she cared for her godchild Maria during the day. Her godmother, Maria Elena, cared for the baby, Rina.

Work at the shipyard slowed down after the war, and the unions were frequently calling strikes. With two children to support and bills to pay, Loretta wanted to work and hoped to be able to buy a house.

Leo was busy building several new houses and duplexes less than two miles from their apartment. When he wasn't working, it seemed he had projects to complete for his mother. Often she insisted that he come from work and have supper with her before attacking her latest work assignment. He was even helping her sell her chickens and eggs again.

Frequently, Dina sat waiting for Leo's return with the kitchen table set and food overcooked. More times than not, when Dina had a doctor's appointment, Luigi took her because Leo was busy or forgot the appointment. When Leo was home for dinner, he was quiet and usually read the newspaper while he ate.

Leo never seemed to mind Dina caring for Maria each weekday, and she was usually gone by the time he came home in the evening. Maria adapted well to staying with her aunt, whom she loved. Dina would give into Maria's every whim. She met Maria's frequent requests for candy or ice cream by wrapping two nickels in paper with an elastic band, so that Maria could buy her treats down at the corner store.

In late November when Luigi was picking up Maria, Dina asked if he could drive her to the hospital.

"You okay?" he said. "It's not the baby is it?"

"Yes, maybe. Can we go now?"

"Oh, boy! You want to call your husband?"

"You call him after. I need to get to the hospital now."

Luigi drove Dina to the hospital and then drove home to get Loretta. She had walked to Maria Elena's house earlier to pick up Rina, and now they returned both children to Maria Elena's for safekeeping before driving to the hospital.

"I'll stay with my sister," said Loretta. "You go find that jerk of a brother-in-law and tell him his wife is in the hospital. Check with his mother first; he's probably at the old bitch's house."

Concetta didn't seem too concerned about Dina being ready to deliver her baby at any time. "No rush. Leo's working in Braintree. Babies take their time. Dina's strong as a cow. She'll be fine."

Luigi finally found Leo at the job site and drove him to the hospital. When Loretta saw him, she was about to lash out when Luigi caught her eye and shook his head, no.

"Well," said Loretta, "you're still in time. She was in heavy labor and the doctor just put her to sleep."

An hour later, Leo was looking at his new son in the nursery. He had bought flowers and candy at the hospital's gift shop while waiting and brought them to Dina.

"He's a good-looking boy" said Leo. "Your sister thinks he looks like me. We'll call him Antonio after my father and yours."

"No," said Dina. "We'll call him Paolo. That's all I ask of you."

Leo gave her a hard look. "That's all you'll get from me, too."

CHAPTER 145

Joy, then Disaster—January 1949

A year later, Loretta and Luigi welcomed their third daughter, Alexandra—Sandy for short. If possible, this baby came even faster than Rina. Shorter in length but fuller in form, Sandy was a bright-eyed charmer from day one.

Loretta had a difficult time returning to good health after the birth. She felt lethargic and unable to keep from drifting off as soon as she had the children settled in for their naps. She found her breathing labored and noticed she bruised easily. Even her gums bled profusely at times when she brushed her teeth.

Her physician, Dr. Orsini, diagnosed her as anemic and advised her to settle for these three children and avoid getting pregnant again. "Try to add more iron to your diet," he advised.

"Loretta, wake up, wake up," said Luigi.

"No, leave me alone. I want to sleep."

"You can't sleep any longer," he said. "The kids are screaming, and I'm late for work. You have to get up, now!"

"I can't. I can't get up. I feel so weak."

Luigi, who was rarely late for work, was in a dilemma. "Should I call the doctor? Do you want to go to the hospital? Do you want me to call your sister?"

"Call the doctor," Loretta said, "then change and feed the kids."

Luigi called Dr. Orsini, who had delivered Sandy, and who agreed to make a house call that afternoon.

Luigi heard a knock on the kitchen door. Looking through the glass, he saw their neighbor, Laura.

"I noticed your car in the yard. Is everything all right? You're not sick, I hope."

"No, I'm not sick, but Loretta is feeling weak today. Laura, any chance you could stay with her and the kids while I go to work? Things are getting bad at the shipyard, and I'm afraid we might be going on strike soon. I really need to get to work today if I can."

"Of course, what's a neighbor for? I'll take care of Loretta and the kids; you get to work."

"Thanks. You're a good friend, Laura, and a good neighbor," said Luigi. "I'll call you this afternoon. Dr. Orsini is supposed to come by to see Loretta. If you need me, call the main number at the shipyard. There's a secretary there, Barbara; she'll know how to reach me."

After examining Loretta, Dr. Orsini gave her a prescription for iron tablets. "I want you to come to the office tomorrow for some blood tests."

A week later, Loretta, accompanied by her cousin, Maria Elena, visited Dr. Orsini's office again. "I looked at the results of all your tests," he said, "and I think your anemia is more severe than we first suspected. I'd like to have you see a hematologist—a blood specialist—in Boston. I'll set up the appointment for as soon as possible."

Three days later, Dr. Orsini called them. "We're lucky to get an appointment with Dr. Saul Brodsky for January 14th at two o'clock. He's a world-renowned specialist on blood disorders and has written many articles for the medical journals as well as published a book on the subject. We're fortunate he will see you so soon."

When the day of Loretta's appointment arrived, Maria Elena offered to accompany her by taxicab to Boston. Her neighbor, Laura, agreed to stay with the two younger children while Maria was left with Dina, who was home with her own baby.

Loretta was upset with the five-dollar cost each way for the taxi ride to Boston. She and Maria Elena sat and waited almost two hours to see the famous hematologist. When the secretary showed them in, Dr. Brodsky was sitting at his desk reading through some papers. It was a full ten minutes before he looked up and spoke to them.

"Your blood tests indicate a reduction of red blood cells, white blood cells, and platelet cells, which indicates a failure to produce stem cells. From your symptoms, I would venture that you have either aplastic anemia or possibly acute leukemia. We will need to do a bone marrow test as soon as possible. Any questions?"

Loretta and Maria Elena sat stunned. Dr. Brodsky had recited his diagnosis as if he were giving a lecture to some objective, uninvolved medical students.

Finally, Loretta found her voice. "Doctor, I have three children. How long will it take to have this bone marrow test? Can my local hospital do it?"

"No, you must return here," he said. "It will save time if we have all your tests in-house."

"But if it *is* leukemia, that's a cancer of the blood; will I die soon?"

"We'll run more tests and do the bone marrow. Then we can discuss your prognosis more accurately. I'll see you again next week. You can pay the twenty-dollar office charge to my secretary before leaving."

"Can I pay you something, maybe five or ten dollars a week? The taxi cost me ten dollars and I'm also paying Dr. Orsini. My husband only makes forty-five dollars a week, and the medicines are so expensive."

Brodsky gave them an intense stare and then said, "Mrs. Caramazzo, I came to this country as a refugee. I slept on loading docks and behind buildings to scrimp and save so that I could go to medical school. I do not take charity cases, and if you wish to have me treat you, you must pay for each visit and procedure in full upon completion. Thank you for coming. See the secretary before leaving."

CHAPTER 146

The Darkest Days—February–June 1949

Loretta had the bone marrow biopsy, which was excruciatingly painful for her. Her next few appointments under Dr. Brodsky's care were for blood transfusions and medications to fight possible infections. Brodsky diagnosed Loretta as having acute leukemia and predicted she had about six months before the blood cancer would claim her life.

At home, Loretta spent most days in bed, too weak and nauseous to care for her children and home. Maria, now five, acted the little mother to Rina, now four, and entertained Sandy, who was only six months and still in her bassinette.

Fortunately, Luigi would help with dinner each night and romp around with the children, trying his best to help whenever and wherever he could. In order to keep up with the bills, he found a job on weekends cleaning restaurants and offices, as well as working as a dishwasher for a dollar an hour. Their neighbor Laura Graceffa took pity on them and helped too.

"How are we today?" asked Laura.

"Oh, Laura," said Loretta, "the kids could use some milk and bread. The baby started crying a few minutes ago. Could you change her and give her a bottle?"

"Sure, my dear—don't worry. I'll feed and change them. Do you want me to sit with you afterwards?"

"No, you already do so much for us. I hope your family doesn't mind," said Loretta. "My mother-in-law will be down soon. She sits with me and does her crocheting."

Laura heard a knock on the kitchen door.

"Hello, anybody home?"

Laura left the bedroom and went to the door. Johnny Belmonte, who ran a produce and grocery business out of his truck, greeted her.

"Hey, Mrs. Graceffa, how's she doing? Does she need anything today?"

"I'll see," said Laura. "Can you wait a minute?"

"Sure, take your time," he said.

Returning to the bedroom, Laura said, "Loretta, Johnny Belmonte is here. What do you need this week?"

Loretta slowly lifted herself and rested on her elbow. "Luigi left a list and ten dollars on the fridge."

"I found it," said Laura.

"Johnny," called Loretta, "the ten dollars is toward our bill. Is that okay for now?"

"It's fine," he shouted back. "Don't worry. Do what you can and get better soon."

A short time later, Johnny was at the door again with a box of food. Laura took the slip of paper with the account balance and put it on the top of the refrigerator for Luigi. She noted that there were several other bills from Superior Baking for their bread, White Brothers Milk, and Dr.

Orsini, all of them willing to be paid in installments.

Loretta could hear Laura bustling around the kitchen, feeding the children, putting food away, washing dishes and baby bottles, sweeping the floor, and finally, running the tub where she was soaking the diapers before washing them. Tears filled Loretta's eyes. *This wonderful neighbor was like a mother to her. Luigi's two sisters lived upstairs. Melina, now married, had two babies of her own and washed diapers daily but never came down to help, not even to change Sandy's diapers. Sally worked and spent her free time going to dances. Her mother-in-law, Maria, would sit with Loretta, but that was the extent of her help. Well,* thought Loretta, *in fairness, she was also watching the children, and kept them from getting into mischief. But she seemed to favor Maria whenever there was a squabble between little Maria and Rina. Maria, in return, loved her grandmother and enjoyed the attention. Rina was a very shy, timid child, and often when anyone addressed her she would burst into tears and cling to her sister Maria. And Sandy, my sweet baby, would gurgle away and kick at her blankets.* Loretta's eyes filled with tears thinking about her children.

Luigi will probably get married again. Those Maggio sisters down the street have known him since they were children, and Maria had always hoped he would marry one of them. They are Sicilian. Thank God that, in addition to Laura, I have Maria Elena's help. She takes me to all my medical appointments and bakes treats for the children. Dina, who's in a difficult marriage, uses some of her household allowance to take a taxi twice a week to see me, and spends the day cleaning, cooking, and doing laundry while her own baby plays with his cousins.

Luigi's sister, Maria, who lived in Pennsylvania, was kind and wrote her a card once in a while. His sister, Rosa, was busy with her large family and wasn't able to visit too often. Sarafina worked but would drop in on Saturdays when she and her sisters got together upstairs. Occasionally she would bring a bottle of wine or a pound of coffee.

Once when things were bad financially, and Luigi was getting overwhelmed with bills and the reality of his wife's illness, Loretta suggested that he ask Sarafina's husband for a loan. Both Francesco and Sarafina worked, he owned his own business, and they had no children— perhaps they could help. Luigi didn't want to ask, but Loretta urged him to do it. They were getting desperate about being able to pay everyone and felt ashamed that they owed money to so many creditors, so Luigi approached his brother-in-law.

"Well, did you ask him?" said Loretta. "What did he say? How much can he loan us?"

"Never ask me to go to him for money again," said Luigi. "He actually asked me what I do with my money. I said to him, 'I make forty-five bucks a week; my wife's medical bills are more than triple that. I have three kids to feed, rent to pay, run a home, and help my mother. Where the hell do you think my pay goes? I told him that I'm washing dishes in restaurants and cleaning toilets in offices for a lousy buck an hour. So help me God, I wanted to kill him. Never ask me to beg for money again.'"

Loretta started to cry, and then hearing their father shouting and their mother crying, all the children started to cry too.

"Hey, hey, don't worry, honey," said Luigi. "We'll get through this somehow. I'm sorry, I didn't mean to yell at you, but I felt like shit asking him, and then having that superior, arrogant bastard ask me what I did with my money. No more! We'll figure it out, don't you worry. I'll do it!"

Loretta was in constant anguish, not only because she was afraid to die, but because she felt useless and a burden to Luigi and helpless in the care of her children and husband. Whenever one of the girls called out for her or crawled onto her bed, looking at her with confused, melancholy eyes, her heart felt a rip through it.

"God watch over these children," she would pray, clutching them to her.

CHAPTER 147

Anguish and Anger — August 1949

Loretta found it difficult discussing her impending death with Luigi, who was in denial himself. He found the subject too painful, and believed that if you didn't talk about sickness and death, it wouldn't happen. Her sister was having her own problems with a distant husband and an antagonistic mother-in-law. Only with Maria Elena could Loretta talk openly of her fears and anger at her terminal illness. She found Dr. Brodsky intimidating; he always seemed busy, and when she tried to talk to him, he would reply, "We're doing what we can."

Dr. Orsini, her family doctor, would spend time listening to her as he held her hand. Loretta saw him weekly, and he gave her a fatherly hug at the end of each visit.

"Thank God I can be home with Luigi and the children," Loretta said to Maria Elena. "I would die sooner if I was isolated in some hospital or nursing home. Not being able to be a full-time mother, wife, and homemaker for my family is depressing. Watching kind strangers come in and out of the house helping us when I should be attending to them shames me."

"Don't talk like that," said Maria Elena. "You do what you can for your family. Everyone understands. Seeing you every day gives hope to Luigi and the kids. It should give hope to you, too."

On sleepless nights, Loretta felt deeply discouraged about her life and being robbed of a future. She was no longer independent, and the emotional pain of leaving her family overwhelmed her with anger, depression, and feelings of helplessness. She felt the loss of her personal dignity, relying on others to help her bathe and use the toilet at times. The women who assisted her loved her as she loved them, but she was ashamed of her condition.

It pleased her when Luigi would consult her about family matters and ask her opinion so they could plan for the future, but his denial of the situation also frustrated her. Still, she did appreciate his confidence that everything would work out.

Loretta's greatest fear was that she would die in front of the children and possibly scar them for life. She also feared she would die alone, possibly while Luigi was at work, or during the night when everyone was asleep.

By early August 1949, Loretta had been seeing Dr. Brodsky for seven months.

"Well, Mrs. Caramazzo, we may have better news for you today. It seems you do not have acute leukemia, but a rare type of anemia which affects people of Mediterranean descent. We will continue with treatments and your medications until your blood count stabilizes and is satisfactory, although you will always be somewhat anemic. Well, good news, yes?"

Maria Elena grabbed Loretta's hand, squeezing it, crying, "Thanks, God!"

Loretta was stunned. Finding her voice, she said, "Seven months of agony, taking all those tests, transfusions, medicines that made me sick; those painful bone marrow treatments, the terrible financial hardship on my family, not to mention my anguish thinking I would die and leave my husband, my children and all my family, everyone..."

"I can appreciate your feelings," said Dr. Brodsky, "but you should focus on the fact that you will get better and stronger."

"I felt like a guinea pig," cried Loretta. "Maybe I should have had another opinion, but you're supposed to be the best. But you have no heart. To you I was an immigrant housewife who would put all her trust in you because you are such a big specialist. Well, Dr. Brodsky, only God is perfect. You, big doctor, can make a mistake, but worse, you have no heart or sympathy for another immigrant who is struggling and sick. I thank God you were wrong."

"Please, Mrs. Caramazzo, calm yourself."

"I admit I was afraid of you because I needed to put my life in your hands, and you always seemed so cold and distant. All those expensive tests almost killed me. You nearly put us in the poor house."

"Mrs. Caramazzo, I gave you the best treatment available. Yes, you did suffer some discomfort because the transfusions of blood and platelets, and the anti-cancer drugs used to kill the disease also made you more prone to infections. When we treated you with antibiotics, unfortunately you had an adverse reaction which caused most of the vomiting and diarrhea. In short, you were allergic to penicillin and other drugs. The treatments you received have been beneficial and have helped cure you. No, Mrs. Caramazzo, doctors are not perfect, but we do our best to heal."

CHAPTER 148

The Road to Recovery—December 1949

Loretta had lived past the six month death sentence given by Dr. Brodsky. He continued to see her, administered blood transfusions, and prescribed medication for what he had finally concluded was a rare form of anemia occasionally striking people of Mediterranean descent.

Bobby McInnis, the White Brothers milkman, was still leaving three quarts of milk a day in the refrigerator and taking a dollar or two on account when the Caramazzo family could manage it. Johnny Belmonte came every Saturday and filled a carton or two with produce and staples to get them through the week, trusting they would pay as they could. Even Steve from Superior Baking Company left two loaves of bread twice a week and checked the top of the kitchen table for an installment payment. Loretta and Luigi were grateful to these peddlers who trusted them with credit. Most of all, they were grateful to Dr. Orsini, who always told them to take care of Dr. Brodsky first. They didn't know how they would ever get out of debt, but they were determined to pay all their bills with their own labor and sacrifice.

"You going to be all right, honey?" asked Luigi. "Gary, the restaurant owner, has a banquet tonight and after I work in the restaurant, he's having me stay and clean up. I could be gone about ten hours."

"Ten hours," said Loretta, "that means you'll be home around two in the morning. How can you go to work tomorrow?"

"Don't worry. I don't need much sleep. Besides, Gary promised me a bonus tonight and if there's any roast beef left, he said I can take some home for you and the kids."

After Luigi left, Loretta made dinner for the children, gave them a bath, and put them to bed. These activities exhausted her. Retreating to the kitchen, she sat at the table and covered her face with her hands. "God help me; Mother of God, give me the strength I need to help my husband and kids," she prayed aloud. "I have to get stronger and go back to work. Please, dear God, please."

Luigi continued working two and sometimes three jobs several nights a week. Loretta noticed that he never complained or was too tired to play "horsey" with the girls when he was home. She often marveled when she looked at this rough, unkempt, poorly-educated, simple man with the generous spirit and hard-working, never-quit attitude. Sometimes she would playfully tease him saying, "You know, for a Sicilian, you're really a nice guy." This always spurred him into trying to embrace and kiss her as she coyly protested, "Not in front of the kids."

By December, Loretta felt well enough to contact her friends who were factory stitchers to see if their shop was looking for help. Two weeks before Christmas, she found a job and began working at home so that she would not have to leave the children. Sandy was a year old, Rina was four, and Maria, nearly six, had started school.

Loretta's sewing machine was set up in the kitchen in front of the only full window. One of the factory foremen would drop off work, return to retrieve the finished work, and drop off an additional bundle to be sewn. Loretta did the piecework and was paid anywhere from fifteen to twenty-five cents a garment. She was working again—earning money and paying off creditors. She was satisfied.

CHAPTER 149

A New Birth—January 1950

"Your wife is as big as a cow," said Concetta. "What are you saving that baby for? Christmas is over. Leo, take her for a ride in your truck. It will loosen the baby."

Leo looked at his mother and then at his wife, shook his head, and retreated to the living room to read his paper.

"Well," said Concetta, "are you finally happy? My son has bought this beautiful big house for you."

"I like the house," said Dina, "but we have two tenants –one above us and one below. Besides, I would have preferred to live closer to my sister, especially since Loretta had been so ill. Now we are miles away, and neither she nor I can drive a car."

"With a husband, two children, a big house, and a garden to care for, you'll be too busy for visiting, my little nun."

Dina tried to hold back the tears of anger and frustration. Leo's mother was a sharp-tongued, possessive woman who had never forgiven Dina for marrying her son. Once, Concetta said that Dina had "seduced" her son, but Dina didn't know what that meant. Another time, she talked of young women today who were like prostitutes. That was another word that Dina didn't understand. Even when her mother-in-law said it in Italian, she had never heard the term. When she told Loretta and asked her what the words meant, Loretta laughed at her.

"I can't believe that you're a married woman and still so naïve about so many things."

"Well, what do those words mean?" asked Dina again.

"They mean that Concetta is a cruel, dirty-minded witch. That's what they mean, my big sister. If the stories are true, she was the seductress in her day. Maybe that's why her second husband left her."

Several days later, Dina's water broke, and she looked for Leo to take her to the hospital. Fortunately, Leo was working on a truck in the large lot adjacent to their house. Dina gathered her hospital bag, put on her coat, hat, and gloves, and walked gingerly down the long stairs in the back hall to retrieve Leo. She wanted to cry when he said, "Are you sure?"

"I'm soaked and I'm starting to have labor pains; I'm sure you can leave your truck and take me to the hospital."

"Where's the kid?" he said.

"Dina took a deep breath and said, "Paolo is downstairs with the Fasanos."

A few hours later, Dina was delivered of a strong baby boy whose lusty cry filled the delivery room. The following day, as Dina cradled her baby, Leo looked at his wife, who was nursing their new son. Hoping to please him, she said, "We'll name him Antonio after your father and mine."

"It's about time," he said, as he turned around, sat in the visitor's chair and unfolded his newspaper.

CHAPTER 150

On the Move—June 1952

It took over two years of scrimping and saving with Luigi and Loretta working every waking hour, but they finally were able to pay off their debts and begin saving a few dollars a week.

Luigi's family was growing, as were the children of his sister Melina and brother-in-law, Peppino, who lived upstairs with Luigi's mother and sister, Sally. One Sunday morning after church, he told Loretta and the children they were taking a ride before going home.

"Where are we going?" said Loretta. "The girls are going to be hungry soon."

"Don't worry," Luigi said. "I'll buy them each a doughnut. That'll keep them happy for a while."

"Three doughnuts? That's fifteen cents! And they'll get sugar and cream all over their dresses."

"Ah, come on, honey. It's a special treat. Besides, I have a surprise for you."

"Your surprises always cost us money," she said.

"Hey, you can't take it with you!" He winked.

"I don't want to take it with me; I just want to have enough to pay each week's bills while we're here."

"You worry too much."

"I need to worry because you never worry about anything."

After buying the doughnuts, Luigi set off on their mystery ride. They drove for about ten minutes before he stopped the car and said, "Look at that."

"Look at what? Luigi are you crazy? We're down the street from my old apartment."

"See that big, beautiful, brown house? It's for sale. A four-family, and it's not too much money."

Loretta, Luigi, and the girls got out of the car and walked across the street for a closer look. "We can't afford this big house," Loretta said.

"Yes, we can. Three apartments are rented, and we can fix up the house and the fourth apartment for ourselves. The owner died and his kids want to get rid of it. It's a great chance."

"Luigi, this street has businesses and a cold-water flat across the street; it's not a family neighborhood."

"Sure it is, honey. Look, the people next door are real nice. She's a Spanish lady and her daughter lives downstairs."

"It's a rough neighborhood and the house and yard need a lot of work. If it looks this bad on the outside, what does the inside look like?"

"Well, come on, I'll show you. One of the sons is here to show us the house."

Loretta scooped up her toddler and carried her into the house. Sandy was covered in sugar and had a sticky red glaze over her mouth, cheeks, and fingers.

"You had to buy her a jelly doughnut." Loretta scowled.

The empty apartment had five rooms with a butler's pantry off the kitchen and a built-in china cabinet in the dining room. The two bedrooms were both larger than the one bedroom in their current apartment. Loretta was immediately impressed with the three main rooms—the kitchen, dining, and living rooms were large, bright, and had nice woodworking details. The floors, however, were badly scuffed. The owner took them to view the other three apartments which were identical in layout, but like the original, needed serious freshening up and new plumbing in the kitchens and baths as well as new fixtures and floor refinishing.

Outside again, Loretta noted that the yard was adequate for the girls to play in. There was also room for a long clothesline. Looking over the fence into the Spanish woman's yard, she saw a lovely oasis of plants, flowers, and a pretty birdbath. It gave Loretta a warm sense of pleasure just looking at this well-kept garden.

"*Buenos dias. Mirar el casa?*"

Loretta looked up. On the second floor porch stood the elderly Spanish woman who was talking to her.

"*Buon giorno. Si, cercare il casa.*"

Loretta automatically answered the woman in Italian, confirming that they were looking at the house.

The woman smiled at Loretta and pointing to the girls said, "*bonitas.*"

Loretta thanked the woman for the compliment saying, "*Grazie mille.*"

Luigi joined her and the girls, waving at the Spanish woman. "So, talking to the neighbors? You must like the house."

"She seems very kind. She spoke to me in Spanish and I answered her in Italian, and we understood each other pretty well."

"So, what about the house? The guy wants twenty-nine thousand dollars. I think I can get him down. The place needs a lot of work, but I can do it."

"It's such a big gamble," said Loretta. "If we can scrape up the down payment, we'll be carrying a mortgage for thirty years. We'll be in our sixties. We should wait and save more money—maybe in another year or two."

"You're the one going crazy in my mother's house, remember? It's too small, you don't want to live there anymore, and my mother is hinting that Melina and her family need an apartment of their own. Did you forget all the arguments you gave me? Well, here's our chance."

"What about that house down the street from us? It has four apartments too, is in better shape for about the same money, and it's in a better neighborhood."

Luigi looked down at the ground. "I told my sister Sarafina about it. She said to wait until she and her husband looked at it for us."

"And did they like it?"

"Yeah, they liked it. They put an offer on it and bought it from under us. They said we'd never be able to afford it anyway."

Looking at the children, Loretta silently mouthed "Those bastards!" Aloud she said, "Let's talk to this guy and try to get the house for twenty-five thousand dollars."

CHAPTER 151

Maintaining the Homestead—
June 1952-August 1954

Moving into their new home created mixed feelings for the new occupants. Loretta and Luigi were excited about purchasing their first house, although the work needed to rehabilitate the four-family was daunting. Maria, now seven, hated the move. She had left her beloved grandmother and all her friends. Rina, now six, liked the new house and quickly made friends with Linda, a little blond girl from the apartments across the street. Sandy's first few nights in the new house upset the two-year-old, but she finally adjusted and happily ran from room to room, trying to open drawers and cabinets.

Luigi, lacking sons, recruited Maria as his helper. He picked a peach-colored paint to refresh the hallways and front door entrance. To dress it up a bit, Loretta picked out a soft creamy yellow as a painted overlay with a floral print. This was accomplished with a patterned roller.

"Okay, Maria," said Luigi, "you take this sandpaper, and everywhere you see a white patch, you rub it to get a nice smooth wall. You're my 'number one son,' so do a good job."

Maria concentrated on one patch and kept rubbing it with the sandpaper until she created a hole again.

"What are you doing?" said Luigi, who had been distracted painting up and down the hallway. "No, no, not too hard and long in one spot; just a little. Never mind, here, use this paint brush and paint that section of wall. Nice and smooth, up and down, just like Daddy's doing."

Eager to please her dad, and enjoying the attention, she said, "Okay, Daddy, nice and smooth, up and down."

Luigi handed Maria a paintbrush. "Nice and smooth, up and down, up and down, okay?"

"Okay, Daddy."

Luigi went back up the stairs to paint the top landing. When he finished the upstairs hall, he decided to check on Maria.

"Maria! You were supposed to use the peach color for the walls, not the yellow." Luigi gave a huge sigh, took the brush from Maria's paint-spattered hands and arms, and said, "Go ahead, go help your mother."

Disappointed that she wouldn't be working with her dad, Maria left but would follow him on other occasions when he worked around the house. Luigi often recruited Maria, but his calling her his "number one son" did not improve Maria's handyman abilities. Holding fence pickets for him to hammer, she would put her hand too close to the nails; sent to fetch a tool, she often brought back the wrong one. With a frustrated headshake, Luigi would eventually say, "Go help your mother."

Working hard and persistently, Luigi rehabilitated the house, doing all the carpentry, plumbing, painting, and yard work, under Loretta's directions and supervision, of course. Maria was permanently assigned to be mother's helper, caring for her younger sisters, learning to cook and keep house. Luigi, however, never stopped jokingly introducing her as his "number one son."

CHAPTER 152

And the Waters Rose—
August 31, 1954

All summer, Loretta, Dina, and Maria visited farms and bought fruits and vegetables for canning. The shelves in their basements held a bounty of canned tomatoes, peaches, pears, grape jelly, and a Sicilian appetizer specialty called *caponatina*, made with eggplant, celery, green olives, tomato sauce, and capers.

The heat of July and August was oppressive, but in late August, heavy rains developed, and the neighborhood children were out jumping, splashing, and shouting in the rain as the streets flooded.

"Freddie, dear, please come up on the porch," called their tenant, Mrs. Lacosta. "Maria, you and the other children should get out of the street. My Freddie follows you."

Freddie was actually dragging Maria and Linda, a neighborhood child, into the middle of the street and trying to push them down into the water.

"Stop it, Freddie! Your mother's calling you," said Maria. "You're such a creep."

Soon Loretta came on the porch. Seeing her mother, Maria broke away and said, "I'm coming, Ma," before Loretta could chastise her.

"Maria, what's the matter with you? You could get polio splashing in that dirty water. Look at you; you're soaked. Go change, now!"

The rains and high winds continued mercilessly; the news reported that Southern New England was experiencing Hurricane Carol, and the town of Braintree's dam had ruptured. Water rose faster and faster, flooding the street until it was up to their first floor landing on both the outside porches and in the Caramazzos' basement. When water had begun flooding the basement, Maria went down to try and retrieve the laundry off the makeshift clotheslines as well as taking boxed and the canning food off the storage shelves.

"Come up here," shouted Loretta. "Do you want to get sick? Let it go. Come upstairs now!"

Luigi, coming from work, left his car several blocks away on higher ground, and walked home. By the time he got home, the water was one basement step below their living room's entry closet.

"Everything is gone!" cried Loretta. "All our food, our laundry, your tools, the washing machine—everything." As they watched from the landing, Loretta's trunk which she had brought from Italy floated by.

"Oh, my God! Our winter blankets, my good linens, and my wedding dress!" she cried.

"Don't cry, honey," said Luigi. "We'll get it all when the water goes down. Right now, they want us out of the house. There are boats picking people up. We can stay with my mother."

"I'm not leaving my house!"

"Honey, you have to go with the kids. I'll stay here. The oil burner's busted, and the water in the cellar is full of oil. It's safer for you to leave."

"You take the kids to your mother. I'm staying—no argument. I'm staying with my house."

Loretta packed a bag of clean clothes and toothbrushes. Luigi and the three girls stood on their front porch and waited for a boat to pick them up.

Luigi hugged Loretta and said, "You sure you want to stay?"

"Yes, I have to stay."

"Okay," he kissed her, then smiled and winked. "I'll be back as soon as I can. Stay away from the cellar stairs."

Loretta started to cry again. "All our work—all your work on the house—gone!"

"Hey, don't worry, we did it before. We just need a bigger mop this time. When I get back, we'll have some *espresso*, a couple of your *biscotti*, and take a vacation for a few days until the water goes down. Then we'll pull this place back together again."

"What about all our things in the basement—the washing machine, furnace, all my canning, our linens, and our groceries—all gone."

"Loretta, we can't go back. We need to just go ahead. You fix your face. I'll be back soon."

Loretta waved to them as they sat in the rowboat heading up their street to dryer land.

Later, after the clean-up, the girls salvaged Loretta's wedding gown, veil, and some of her pretty trousseau, and paraded around, playing, "Here comes the bride."

CHAPTER 153

A Family's Pain—June 1956

The flooding from Hurricane Carol had set them back, but Loretta and Luigi continued taking on extra work at their jobs as well as cleaning and repairing the house. All the girls were in school, and Maria was put in charge of caring for her two younger sisters and their home after school.

The Caramazzos were in debt again. They had to replace their wringer washing machine, two furnaces, two oil tanks, and numerous personal and household possessions. They were also faced with the task of cleaning, repairing, and repainting the first floor apartments' entries, stairwells, and basements. Fortunately, their tenants had few personal possessions in the second basement, and their homeowner's insurance gave some compensation for claims by one tenant, the Lacosta family.

Along with their financial problems, a far greater emotional burden was the discovery that Rina had a serious heart defect. She needed a complicated heart valve replacement, which was accomplished at Children's Hospital in Boston when she was nine years old.

Loretta agonized over the bills. She was often tense and anxiously worried about getting back to managing—and hopefully saving—some money each month.

"That refrigerator doesn't feel cold enough," Loretta told Luigi at breakfast.

"Well, we'll need to call somebody to look at it," he said with a huge sigh.

Loretta asked for a recommendation of a repairman while at work. At lunchtime, the parochial school the three girls attended sent the children home for lunch. The Caramazzo girls always carried their lunch to their mother's factory and joined her at noon.

"Maria, a repairman for the refrigerator is coming this afternoon. Let him in to fix it, okay?"

"Okay, Ma."

The repairman came, inspected the refrigerator and gave the bill and diagnosis to Maria. When Loretta and Luigi came home from work, Maria was busy setting the table and heating up the minestrone soup for dinner.

"Well, did the man come?" asked Loretta.

Maria took the slip of paper from her apron pocket and handed it to her mother.

"Twenty dollars!" said Loretta reading the bill. "Well, it couldn't be avoided."

"Ma," said Maria timidly, "he said the refrigerator is gone. We need a new one."

Loretta stared at Maria for a moment, then turned, pulled out a kitchen chair, and sat down. Suddenly, she put her head down on the table, buried it in her arms, and began to cry so forcefully that Maria was startled. Rina and Sandy, who were playing in the living room, came in and ran to their mother.

"I'm sorry, Mummy," said Maria, now also crying. "I'm sorry."

Luigi, who was in the bathroom washing up, came out still wet and tried to question his wife, then Maria.

That evening, Loretta began hemorrhaging. Luigi took her to the hospital. She had been pregnant—a boy, a miscarriage. Loretta's physician said her childbearing years were over; she needed a hysterectomy.

While at the hospital, Loretta had the misfortune to have a rough and sadistic nurse. When she tried to complain, the nurse cautioned her, "If you tell anyone, you'll be sorry." Loretta was terrified, but felt she needed to tell Luigi so that he would get her transferred to another hospital, or at least to a different nurse.

Luigi's generally quiet, compliant nature found its Sicilian temper. He not only spoke to the nurse, he followed the chain of command all the way to the administrator of the hospital to have the nurse fired. Since the wheels of most organizations turn slowly, Luigi hired a private-duty nurse to care for Loretta.

The loss of a son was painful for both of them, but taking inventory of what they had together created a stronger bond with their girls and with each other. But the loss of a baby brother weighed heavily on Maria. For years she blamed herself for the loss. After all, she was the one who told her mother they needed a new refrigerator, which had caused her mother to cry so hard that she lost the baby.

CHAPTER 154

Working the Dream—1957-1959

After a short recuperation, Loretta was back to working full time and managing their finances. Luigi had kept his second job in a large restaurant and banquet facility, as well as cleaning the owner's offices and private residence.

Only Maria remained in parochial school. Both Rina and Sandy wanted to transfer to public school, which added to the savings in the family budget.

Loretta made clothes for all the girls and herself. With the exception of socks, shoes, underwear, and Easter bonnets, they never had to shop for clothes. An accomplished needlewoman, Loretta made beautiful coats and sweaters as well as dresses, skirts, blouses, nightgowns, pajamas, play clothes, and slips.

"Is that a homemade dress?" asked Judy Shea, Maria's classmate at St. John's School.

Maria's face colored. "Yes, it is." She was embarrassed that most of the girls had store-bought clothes, and hers were homemade. Their dads were lawyers, doctors, or businessmen. Judy's dad was a Superior Court judge.

"It's very pretty," said Judy.

"Thanks," said Maria, wishing that just once her mom would buy her a dress at the store.

Maria, being the oldest, was well aware of her parents' financial limitations. She was always trying to find little jobs—selling salve and greeting cards door to door, babysitting, shucking clams, and even doing light housework and laundry on Wednesday afternoons and Saturday mornings for two couples. After school and on non-school days, she would run for coffee and doughnuts for the people who worked with her mom. Some people gave her a nickel or dime tip. One woman occasionally bought her a doughnut. Some just thanked her. She took pride in helping her family, but her parents' dependence on her to care for her sisters and the home was a weighty responsibility. Often they spoke with her about purchasing decisions and took her along when buying appliances or furnishings. They trusted her opinion. This caused some anxiety in Maria, who was afraid of giving the wrong advice.

But these were busy and happy years. In the summer, the family joined other family members and friends every Sunday for sumptuous picnics at Nantasket Beach. The women cooked, served, and cleaned up the ceramic dishware, glasses, pots and pans; the men took naps, read the newspaper, and listened to the baseball games; and the children played at the beach and amusement park before and after dinner. Family and friends visited each other frequently. Holiday dinners were shared with family—Christmas at Grandma Maria's house, Easter with either Aunt Sarafina or Aunt Melina, and Thanksgiving at Loretta and Luigi's house.

Loretta's cousins, aunts, and uncle were also frequent dinner guests. Her cousin Bruno, his wife, Anita, and their five sons often visited. Likewise, Loretta, Luigi and their three daughters spent many wonderful get-togethers eating and playing games with these much loved relatives who lived in Newton, Massachusetts. Life seemed contented and secure in those happy growth years.

CHAPTER 155

A New Challenge, a New Opportunity—1959-1963

In April 1959, Luigi and Loretta had an opportunity to buy a three-family house that abutted their present home's back yard. It had a huge barn filled with trash, and the house was not much of an improvement. The owner was an elderly woman who, it was rumored, lived on peanut butter and stale bread donated by a local bakery. Her representative, a prominent attorney from Boston, would handle the sale of the property.

"Let's take a chance," said Luigi. "We can tear down the fence and barn, and have plenty of parking for the tenants. The owner's apartment needs a lot of work, but the other two apartments are rented."

"Can you handle another house?" said Loretta. "What does the lawyer want for it?"

"Well, we haven't settled on a price. He wants time to go through the house and barn before selling."

"The woman was poor; does he think she hid money under the mattress or in the barn?"

"Who knows, but we can sign a paper that gives us temporary

ownership until after the barn's cleaned out and torn down, and the lawyer goes through the papers and stuff in the apartment."

"I don't know. Maybe we should let it go," said Loretta.

"But honey, the location and land are perfect. Plus, I won't be too far away to do work on both houses. I think we should buy it. We'll set a date for transferring the house and land with the lawyer—say September first. What do you think?"

Finally they agreed with the terms set by the attorney.

Cleaning out the barn was a major undertaking. Highlights included broken farm equipment, horse harnesses, and a variety of dirty, broken furniture. Once Luigi started cleaning out debris, rats scurried everywhere and the neighborhood was infested for months.

The contents of the barn fascinated people. Occasionally, someone would ask for a piece of furniture or a stack of old magazines. Luigi was glad to get rid of it. Each night he came in filthy with dirt and dust. Loretta and the girls were curious about the barn, but Luigi insisted they stay out of it.

The attorney found what he suspected. Stacks of money were hoarded in cookie jars, old cigar boxes, cereal boxes, pillow cases, and every conceivable cubby hole. The tenants watched armed men carry out boxes of the worn, wrinkled bills.

"I can't believe that old woman lived like a rat herself and begged food from the neighbors when she had all that money," said Loretta. "Maybe if we're lucky the attorney didn't find it all."

"Don't kid yourself," said Luigi. "They tore the place apart and removed all the furnishings to be on the safe side. All that's left is dirt. They even took her half-empty peanut butter jar."

As he had done with their first house, Luigi rehabilitated the empty apartment, land, and exterior of the house. His two tenants were willing to have no renovations at present if the rent could remain the same for the remainder of the year. Luigi liked the tenants and agreed.

Luigi put considerable effort and expense into updating the former owner's apartment. He put in a modern tile bathroom and cabinet kitchen, and sanded and polished the hardwood floors, bringing them back to their original quality and gleam.

A local minister responded to the rental ad for the apartment. He explained that the apartment was not for himself, but for a man recently released from prison and his family. The minister, pleading for the family, assured Luigi that they would be good tenants and able to pay the rent. Unfortunately, the man proved to be a nightmare for Luigi and Loretta.

Returning to his bad habits of drinking and brawling, the tenant's family left him shortly after they moved in. Soon he began trashing the apartment—defecating into the toilet, bathtub and anywhere else it suited him. He punched holes in the walls and broke all the light fixtures.

When Luigi tried to evict him, the tenant called the Board of Health and claimed the plumbing was faulty. He terrorized the elderly couple in the upstairs apartment who were too fearful to talk to the police or health officials. It took Luigi four months and thousands of dollars to get him out and repair the damage in the apartment.

Luigi's tenants were not always easy to deal with, but fortunately Luigi was easy-going and able to handle complaints quickly and satisfactorily. In most cases, he and Loretta enjoyed a good relationship with their tenants for all the years they owned the two houses. In time, the gamble and hard work brought success, and the houses became a good investment for them.

CHAPTER 156

A Home of Our Own — February 1963

Valentine's Day 1963, and the excitement in the Caramazzo family was overflowing.

"The bedroom on the right is mine," said Maria. "Rina, you and Sandy can have the one on the left of the hall."

"Is yours bigger?" asked Sandy. "Why do Rina and I have to share? Why can't I have my own room?"

"Because I'm the oldest and in college. I've never had a room all to myself, and you, my baby sister, will need to wait until I get my own apartment or house someday."

"I think our room is bigger, anyway," said Rina.

Claiming a specific bedroom, however, became moot over the years since the girls traded bedrooms every few years.

Luigi and Loretta's hard work and ability to manage their finances, while sacrificing when necessary and saving when possible, had finally paid off. They were able to purchase a large newly-built house near the ocean. Loretta threw her heart into decorating this, her first new house—no relatives, no tenants—just her husband and children. She and Maria traveled to Boston on several occasions to select satin brocades and fine, embroidered sheers for drapes and curtains.

Luigi gave her full rein in selecting the furniture, carpeting, and lighting. Loretta chose elegant Italian Provincial furniture throughout the house. The living room set had rich silk sage green and gold upholstery. For the dining room, she had formal chairs with gold velvet-covered seats. Both rooms had thick gold carpeting, and crystal tear-drop chandeliers graced the dining room and entry hall.

Loretta and Luigi's Italian Provincial bedroom was inviting and comfortable. Their original bedroom set, heavy and fashioned of a wood finish with a waterfall pattern, was moved into Rina and Sandy's room. Maria got a new mattress and headboard and inherited the girls' old bedroom frame, bureau, and wardrobe closet.

The lower level of the house had a wood-paneled family room which extended the entire length and breadth of the house—a perfect party room which was used to its full capacity over the years. Pajama parties, birthdays, holidays, and graduation celebrations evolved into bridal and baby showers as well as wedding anniversary parties. To allow for all the extra cooking and refrigeration, they added a small kitchen off the garage.

Loretta even converted a small portion of the family room as her sewing corner, eventually using it for a little business during her retirement. Happy to employ her skills and socialize with neighbors and customers, she rarely charged much, especially if they were elderly, policemen, clergy, widows, or students. Maria often chided her that she was supposed to be running a business, but Loretta was happy to be of service to these people. Once, she even made a dress in one afternoon for a mother who had just lost her son and couldn't bear going to the stores to shop for a dress for the wake and funeral—no charge, of course.

If the house was Loretta's and the girls' domain, the yard, garage, and shed were Luigi's. Every spare hour he had, he worked in his flower and vegetable gardens. The land rewarded his efforts with an abundant harvest of tomatoes, string beans, and other vegetables, as well as herbs like parsley and basil. Luigi would share his bounty with anyone who stopped by the fence to talk. His thick verdant lawns framed a floral display that was attractive enough to be photographed and merchandised by a local businessman. As payment, Luigi was given a framed copy of the photo. He and Loretta kept that photo for the rest of their lives. It was proof that they had achieved the American dream.

CHAPTER 157

Dina's Lot—1964-1975

Dina and her husband Leo endured their turbulent marriage, which was exacerbated by their eldest son's schizophrenia. Paolo, now wanting to be called Paul, was a tall, handsome young man with a photographic mind and genius I.Q. For most of his life he had been a very meticulous, extremely neat, studious individual. When he, his brother, and Loretta's children played together, Paul would have his books carefully stored away. His toys were perfectly placed in formation to create a war or cowboy ranch scene. He always knew when one of the other kids moved a piece or disturbed his possessions. This would anger him, and he would scoop up his toys, put them in a labeled shoebox, and retreat to his room.

Although Dina suffered from ill health due to severe deprivation in her early years, she constantly sheltered and protected Paul, particularly since her husband favored their younger son, Tony. Leo was a very intelligent man, but found it difficult to understand and bond with Paul. Tony, his rough-and tumble-younger son, who shared Leo's passion for mechanics, was his kind of boy. Tony was a man's boy; he was messy, funny, liked playing on the construction trucks, and got into scraps with other boys at school.

In contrast, Paul was a quiet, high-achieving young man all through school. Because of his outstanding grades, a local politician wanted to recommend Paul for West Point. Paul enjoyed the art of conversation and debate. He could speak on a variety of subjects like art, politics, religion, and history, as well as world events. He and Maria always engaged in small discussions until she felt out of her league to argue a subject further or felt Paul was becoming too heated in the debate.

Paul was not interested in West Point. He harbored a distrust of the military and government officials. He started college, but found some of his professors' teachings intolerable and socialistic. Eventually, he dropped out of college and began his intervals of dropping out of society.

Every few weeks, he would leave home for days without telling anyone where he was going. When he returned, he was unshaven and slovenly dressed. He would shower using Ajax cleanser and then burn all his clothes, even his shoes. This went on for a year or so, until his parents had

332

him committed to a psychiatric hospital for observation. After four days of therapy, Paul walked out of the facility and hitchhiked.

"Never send me there again, or I'll kill somebody," he said. "That weirdo doctor was the crazy one. You should have seen him, Ma. He had long hair like a girl, and it was tied in a ponytail with a red ribbon. He even had a beard and was a complete homo jerk."

Paul's mystery trips subsided for a while, but his brooding around the house only caused arguments with his father and brother. His departures began again, only now he wanted to shower and change his clothes before returning home. After disappearing for three or more days, he would call his mother collect and ask for money for a hotel room and a change of clothes and shoes.

"Maria, *bella*, you must help me," said Dina.

"Zia, are you all right?" Maria looked at the clock next to her bed. It was 1:20 in the morning.

"Paul is in Boston, and he needs some clothes and money," said Dina. "Please, *gioia*, I have a bag ready and some money. Come now and then bring it to him. I'll give you the address when you come. Come quietly, please. We can't wake up your uncle."

Maria got dressed and drove to her aunt's house and collected the bag of clothes, shoes, food, and money. The address was in one of the worst sections of Boston—dark, dirty streets sheltering drunks, addicts, homeless people, and lost souls like Paul. Driving around these streets frightened Maria, who was frantically searching for her cousin. After driving around for about fifteen minutes—her watch said 2:55 a.m.—she finally saw a man standing on a corner, waving to her.

"God, please let it be him."

"Thanks for coming," said Paul. "Do you have my stuff?"

"Yes, and some money. Paul, let's go home." Maria looked at her cousin. He was extremely dirty from head to foot. What was he doing here? Where had he been to get so dirty?

"Did you bring some food?"

"Yes, your mother packed this bag for you. There are sandwiches and some fruit. I grabbed a bottle of soda from the fridge."

"Great," he said, as he hungrily ate the sandwich.

"Paul, let's get out of here. It's creepy."

"Okay, drive to Somerville. There's a Best Western there where you can rent a room long enough to take a shower."

Maria did what he asked and waited in the parking lot while he got a room to shower and change. When he returned, he was clean-shaven, neatly dressed, and resembled himself again. As Paul got back in the car,

333

Maria asked, "Where are your old clothes?"

"Forget about them," he said. "I ditched them."

"Even your boots? Paul, your mother just bought those for you. Couldn't you keep them?"

"They're dirty."

"Well, everything can be cleaned," said Maria. "They could be stored for a while or donated. Your mother buys all these new clothes and shoes and pays for hotels without your father knowing. She's desperate to help you, but she's not well, you know that."

Paul didn't reply, but closed his eyes and turned toward the passenger door with his back to Maria.

God, I know I should be afraid to anger him, but I'm not. Please, God, help him and help my aunt, Maria silently prayed as she drove Paul home.

The situation continued, and Maria would frequently drive to Boston, or occasionally to Rhode Island, to bring her cousin home.

"If anything happens to me, Maria," said Dina, "promise me you'll take care of Paul."

"Zia, you know how much I love you," said Maria, "but I don't know if I can promise you that. I'll do what I can, but Paul needs professional help. He's a very disturbed man who seems to hate himself."

Just before his twenty-fifth birthday, this troubled young man committed suicide by jumping off the roof of a Boston hotel. His death in some way formed a truce between Dina and her husband, Leo. Their son, Tony, had married and had a beautiful baby girl, and this seemed to offer a healing balm to these two life-worn people. But in many ways, Dina had lost her will to persevere. She died two years later at the age of sixty-four, of heart disease. Her husband, who survived her, spent the next twenty-one years bemoaning the loss of his *sweet angel*, a term he adopted after her death.

CHAPTER 158

The Homeland Revisited—May 1968

Having celebrated their twenty-fifth wedding anniversary, Luigi and Loretta decided to visit Italy and Sicily. They invited Maria, the oldest, to accompany them on their first trip back to their homeland.

"I've studied this travel book backwards and forwards," said Maria. "There are so many wonderful places to visit when we get to Rome! Dad, did you know there are some fantastic Greek temples in Agrigento, which is near your hometown? And Ma, we should see Monte Cassino while we're visiting your towns."

"Okay," said Loretta, "I'll show you my two little towns, San Rocco and San Lorenzo, your father will show us his village near Agrigento, my cousins in Belforti will show us their town, and you can show us the rest of Italy and Sicily, okay?"

"Ma, please, aren't you excited about seeing Rome, Siena, Naples, Pompeii, Capri, Florence, Pisa, Venice, Milan, and even the Italian Riviera? I've even spent a lot of time talking with Nonna Maria so that I could speak a little Italian when we're there."

"Good, you can talk for me," said Luigi. "I've forgotten a lot of my Italian."

"Ha!" said Loretta. "What you speak, and your mother, especially, is not Italian, but Sicilian dialect. Only the goats in Sicily will understand you." She laughed and tweaked his prominent Greek nose.

"Never mind," Luigi said. "You talk. I'll eat and drink the wine."

Luigi and Loretta's first plane ride was an adventure for her and a terror for him. A rare drinker, Luigi fortified himself with two shots of brandy before leaving for the airport. He insisted on sitting in the aisle seat while Loretta took the window. Maria, sitting in the middle seat, tried to reassure her father that flying was safe and enjoyable. When the stewardess came with dinner and wine, Luigi drank two glasses. The ride was fairly smooth as they flew through the clear, dark night, and Luigi seemed to relax a little. But when they reached the European continent, the plane hit a squall and the ride became bumpy.

"It's okay, Dad. We're just hitting a few air pockets; we'll be out of them soon," Maria said with a grimace. Luigi was crushing her hand, trying to steel himself from his fears. Finally, the plane was flying smoothly again, and Luigi released Maria's left hand.

"Thank God I'm right-handed," she murmured to her mother, who was looking ashen herself.

In Rome, Luigi's cousin, Raimondo, who worked in the city, met the trio and collected their luggage after a series of bear hugs and cheek kisses. He then escorted them to his tiny automobile, and they all crammed in, ready for their Italian homecoming in San Lorenzo. Raimondo drove them to his high-rise apartment in the older quarter of Rome, where they were greeted by his wife, Aida, and three children, Alessia, Mondo, and Fo-Fo, short for Alfonzo.

Aida had cooked up a banquet and set a table on the balcony. They could see St. Peter's Basilica in the distance. The apartment was small, with four rooms and a balcony which served as the dining room and sleeping quarters for sultry summer nights. The couple insisted that Luigi and Loretta take their bedroom for an afternoon siesta, and Maria could rest on the couch. They would use the children's room, which was equipped with bunk beds and a small cot. After much discussion about whether the Caramazzos would go to a hotel for the night, Aida and Raimondo convinced them to stay with them, and Raimondo would drive them to San Lorenzo in the morning. "*Noi sono famiglia!*"

CHAPTER 159

Going Home Again—May–June 1968

Happiness and nostalgia consumed Loretta as she returned to her little mountain town of San Lorenzo. Her childhood friend, Guiliana, now living in France, had arranged to visit their town at the same time, and both families were able to stay with Guiliana's mother.

Fausto, Guiliana's husband, had served in the Resistance during the war. Twice in the night, Maria heard him crying out.

In the morning, when she mentioned it to her mother, Loretta said, "Yes, I heard him too. Guiliana told me that he has nightmares from being captured and tortured by the Germans during the war. Did you notice his hands? They smashed his fingers and did terrible things to him. Guiliana says he never talks about his experiences, but he still has nightmares."

During their stay, Loretta and her friend were young again, giggling and telling stories of their adventures.

"Remember when you stole the figs and hid them in my father's umbrella?" The two women regaled each other with stories of playing hooky from school and other Loretta-inspired pranks.

Maria was astounded when she was introduced to Loretta and Guiliana's former school chums. They all looked so much older than her mother. She proudly saw that her mother was a very pretty, vibrant, and well-dressed woman who loved to laugh, tell stories, and seemed to have been popular with her friends. Somehow, her mother, despite all she had gone through, was able to retain her attractiveness and vivacity while the years had taken their toll on her friends and classmates.

"I still have cousins and an aunt in San Rocco," said Loretta. "I was born there and left when I was three years old. Tomorrow, we'll visit them."

Zia Anina, her father's sister, was a sweet, tiny woman, still dressed as a widow. She showered Loretta, Maria, and Luigi with moist kisses and gentle hugs. Her long dress was a faded black with a large shawl collar, and fitted sleeves, and an apron. Maria imagined that this was the way women dressed perhaps sixty years ago. Zia Anina's coarse, grey hair was knotted and partially covered by a black scarf. Her gentle, weathered face was a life map with lines around her small mouth and twinkly eyes. Zia Anina smiled constantly. While rushing to provide refreshments, she often paused to hug Loretta. Of Zia Anina's children, one daughter, Fulvia, still lived in San Rocco, and her other children, Antonio and Bruno, had immigrated to the United States. Loretta explained to Luigi and Maria that Zia Anina was her dear cousin, Bruno's, mother, and Anita's mother-in-law.

After a lunch of minestrone soup, *espresso,* and almond *biscotti,* they visited Anina's daughter Fulvia, and her family. When she met Fulvia's twins, Loretta burst into tears. Both the boy and girl had bright red hair and dark brown eyes. The boy was the image of her brother, Paolo, when he was a very young man.

Bidding her aunt and cousins good-bye, Loretta, Luigi, and Maria walked around the ancient, picturesque town which, with the exception of electrical wires draped here and there, had not changed for centuries.

Residing on the side of a mountain, the town had numerous stone steps to climb. People still drew water from the town square's fountain. Occasionally, women balancing a stack of bread or a jug of water on their head passed them.

In the middle of the square was a war memorial with a black wreath listing all those who perished in the First World War. Loretta's father, Antonio Leonardi, was among the names. Almost diagonally across the street was a small lane where the Leonardis' former house and cobbler's shop still stood. In the distance, you could see the groves of fruit trees and gardens which lay at the base of the town. From this height, you could look at the old cemetery crowded with family tombs, graves, and wall plaques which held fresh flowers from visitors.

"Oh, look," said Loretta. Coming down the hill was an elderly man leading a scrawny goat. He carried a dented metal cup. He tipped his hat to Loretta and Maria as he passed. "*Attesa, attesa,*" called Loretta. The man stopped and retraced his steps waiting for Loretta to speak again.

"You must have some fresh goat milk, Maria," said Loretta. "It's delicious."

Loretta spoke to the man again and he proceeded to milk the dusty goat in the middle of the lane. The milk squirted into the tarnished, dented cup and Maria could hear a plishing sound.

He offered the cup to Maria, who smiled at him and said to her mother, "I can't drink that! It's not pasteurized, homogenized, or even sterilized. God knows how many people have already used that cup. Besides, the goat doesn't look clean or well. Sorry, Ma, I can't."

The old man was smiling, nodding his head, and repeatedly handed the cup to Maria.

"Go ahead, it's good," said Loretta. "You'll like it. Don't hurt his feelings."

"Ma, I don't…" was all Maria said before taking the cup and sipping the goat milk. It tasted warm and sweet—similar to cream. Maria handed the cup to her father, but Luigi refused.

"I hate milk," he said.

Raising her eyes, Loretta took the cup and finished the milk in one gulp. She paid the man, who took out a dingy cloth and dried the cup before tipping his hat again and leading his goat home.

"Wasn't that lucky?" said Loretta. "Nothing is better than warm milk right from the goat."

CHAPTER 160

Sicilia, Bella Sicilia—June 1968

When Luigi, Loretta, and Maria visited Sicily, Maria was anxious to see her great-grandmother's farm. She had heard all the stories about what a wonderful place it was and how her dad would skip school to visit his favorite grandmother, Nonna Rosa, and ride her donkey. A small stone and mud cottage with a straw roof in great disrepair is what she found. On the positive side, there were many pistachio trees and prickly pear bushes on this arid piece of land. Maria conceded that her dad still saw this land through the eyes of a seven-year-old who had loved his grandmother and cherished his time with her.

Before traveling to Sicily, Luigi learned that he had inherited some land from his father. Since his uncles were still farming, he decided to give his share to them and his cousins. To his dismay, once the cousins had the land, they had sold it to developers who built apartments and condominiums. Despite this disappointment, Luigi relished being among his relatives and back in his homeland. He proudly reacquainted himself with family and friends throughout Sicily, Naples, and Rome.

Maria had to admit that her father had a colorful family. Three cousins all shared his name. Of the Sicilian cousins, one was the superintendent of schools and the second, a teacher. His American cousin was a talented engineer and inventor. Among his Sicilian cousins, two were policemen in Palermo and Naples, one worked for the telephone company in Rome, one was a businessman, and one was the lawyer for the local Mafia. Unfortunately, the attorney had serious gambling problems which kept him tied to this nefarious organization.

Although she found her father's homeland beautiful and the people friendly and hospitable, Maria appeared to be allergic to her father's hometown and was extremely ill while visiting there. Bouts of nausea, vomiting, and diarrhea happened each time she visited. She experienced these symptoms from the hour she arrived to the hour she left the small town. This proved embarrassing, since all her relatives were very generous with their hospitality, and whenever she refused to eat or rushed to the nearest toilet with her body retching, the female relatives would crowd outside the door calling to her and asking if they could help. On those occasions, Maria wanted to be left alone, sorry that she might be offending her father's family, but wishing she could suffer in peace.

Fortunately, Maria never got ill when they toured the Greek temple in Agrigento, Mount Etna, Palermo, Taormina, Messina, Catania, Victoria, where Luigi's Zia Lucia lived, or Siracusa with its famous fountain, or Monreale where a moving mosaic of the staring Christ follows the visitor around the majestic cathedral. It remained a mystery why she experienced such ill health in her father's village.

Back home in America, Nonna Maria offered an explanation for her grandchild's reaction to their hometown. "Your Aunt Sarafina was always a sickly child before we immigrated to America. People warned me that she was too weak to survive the boat trip to America. Surprisingly, Sarafina not only survived the trip, but never had a sick day most of her life once here."

Maria recalled that her aunt, who eventually died in her seventies of congestive heart failure, never took anything medicinal except Alka Seltzer for her aches, pains, and indigestion.

"Well," said the younger Maria, "there must be a strain of bacteria in the air and water that I'm highly susceptible. I've traveled to quite a few countries, including Mexico, and have never gotten ill. It's a good thing you gave our land away, Dad, or I'd be buried in Sicily."

CHAPTER 161

Geneva's Final Farewell—1986-1988

Several years after Dina's death, Geneva returned to Massachusetts for a family reunion with her five daughters and grandchildren. She and Mario had been divorced for more than thirty years, and Geneva had remarried twice while living in California.

Geneva, who rarely corresponded with her siblings, took the opportunity to visit Loretta.

"You look so young," said Geneva, "not a grey hair on your head."

"Oh, thank you," said Loretta. "You look good. Have you been feeling okay?"

"Well, you know, old lady illnesses—arthritis, a bad stomach, high blood pressure—enough to remind me I'm not young anymore."

Maria, who was meeting her aunt for the first time, noticed that although Geneva's hair was colored a sandy blond shade, she had an easy friendliness and resembled her late sister, Dina. But Geneva was more worldly-wise than Dina could ever have been. She dressed in a modern style, wore make-up, spoke only English, and had been married and divorced three times.

The visit with Loretta was pleasant and gave some closure to the sisters, but years of absence made the reunion more reminiscent of friendly acquaintances than cherished sisters.

News reached Loretta two years later that Geneva had died. The loss of her last family member saddened her, particularly since they had suffered two major separations in their lives. Loretta mourned the lost years of closeness—of growing up together, and growing old together.

CHAPTER 162

The Later Years—1989-1992

While they enjoyed their retirement, Loretta and Luigi watched their daughters create their own futures. Maria pursued a business career, was active in numerous volunteer activities, and traveled extensively. The love of her ancestral history infected Maria, who visited her parent's homeland many times before settling down to motherhood through the adoption of two children. In their later years, she cared for her parents for the remainder of their lives.

Rina married first and lived in the Caramazzos' old apartment for a few years until the birth of her first child and the sale of the two apartment houses. After the birth of her second child, Rina's husband moved his family to California, where they lived for ten turbulent years before divorcing. Rina and her children returned to Massachusetts where she found work in the health care field.

Sandy, always a popular, spirited girl—like her mother—married a local boy and moved to the country to raise her two children. Although her husband had good prospects through a family business, he lacked the necessary ambition and drive to make it successful. Bad eating habits, excessive drinking, and smoking finally took their toll. Her husband died at fifty-three. After being widowed, Sandy pursued her own career in secretarial and administrative work.

Loretta and Luigi relished their growing family, especially all their grandchildren and great-grandchildren. They traveled together extensively over the years, visiting most European countries, including seven trips to Italy and Sicily. While in Italy, they often visited Zia Vittoria's sons and their families, as well as Luigi's uncles and many cousins.

After celebrating their forty-fifth wedding anniversary, Loretta suffered a massive cerebral hemorrhage at the age of seventy-one, similar to that which claimed her mother's life at age fifty-seven. The stroke left her severely disabled. Permanent damage to her left brain caused paralysis and loss of speech. Loretta, the talkative, became silent; Loretta, the energetic worker, became passive; Loretta, the independent spirit, became dependent; and Loretta, the wife, mother, grandmother, became like a child herself. But that indomitable spirit fought on.

Although Loretta had lost her ability to speak, her eloquent eyes and bright smile welcomed those who gave her their attention. Her boundless faith and love of God, her family, and friends gave her life a new inner strength. Following extensive rehabilitation, Loretta was able to return home under Maria's care. Luigi, now seventy-six, was himself struggling with health problems and had difficulty accepting Loretta's disabilities. His strong, vibrant, gregarious wife was now a tiny, weak, child-like invalid who looked at him with large, confused eyes.

Luigi began his daily mantra to Maria to "make her better; make her talk." The added anxiety over Loretta further compromised his health. Maria and her sisters watched their strong bear of a father begin to lose weight, become weaker in his responses, and finally succumb to a heart attack at age seventy-nine.

Although Loretta never regained coherent speech, she did learn to walk again. After Luigi's death, a weight seemed to lift off of Loretta's shoulders. She had constantly worried about her beloved husband, wanting to please him so he would stop fretting over her. After nearly fifty years of marriage, Loretta missed Luigi terribly, and whenever he was spoken of, or if she looked at their photographs, she would cry quietly, make the sign of the cross, and nod her head in thought.

With time and determination, Loretta's irrepressible spirit met and conquered her disabilities. Intensive physical therapy and exercise helped her to walk again. Once walking, the gypsy in her soul took over. Loretta attended daily church services, sometimes walking to church and returning by way of the local neighboring streets. She loved walking around Luigi's gardens, particularly when they were in flower. Always ready for a car ride, she accompanied Maria on all errands and enjoyed the weekly get-togethers with Sandy and Rina and her grandchildren. Often when Maria thought out loud about the possibility of going somewhere, Loretta would put on her coat and wait in the car, sometimes causing Maria to look for her. She never passed up the opportunity to go places, see people, and experience new attractions.

Maria, a lover of travel herself, took her two children and Loretta on yearly vacation trips. Florida was a popular and frequent destination. Loretta and the children loved Disney World. Other vacations included road trips to Pennsylvania's Amish country, New York City, Newport, Rhode Island, the Berkshire Mountains of Massachusetts, and every other New England state. If there was a wedding in Pennsylvania or a funeral in West Virginia, Loretta was ready to go.

CHAPTER 163

Liliana's Tale—1992-2003

In old age, death becomes a part of life. Every day, Loretta would scan the newspaper for the obituary page and bring it to Maria for review. In September 2003, an old friend, Liliana Borelli Polaski, who had been engaged to Loretta's brother, Paolo, died at age eighty-six. Loretta and Maria had not seen Liliana for several years, but wanted to attend her wake and funeral.

After Paolo's death at Anzio during World War II, Liliana had waited ten years before marrying a widower with two sons. Together, they had a third son, William.

Liliana remained close friends with Maria Elena and often saw Loretta and Dina. After Loretta's stroke, Liliana would visit occasionally and, to give Luigi some respite and sometimes at his suggestion, she would take Loretta for a drive. Appreciating the kindness, Luigi began giving money to Liliana to compensate her for gasoline—usually ten or twenty dollars each time. Eventually he proposed that Liliana become a regular companion for Loretta, and he would compensate her. Liliana agree, but insisted she would like at least ten dollars an hour.

Friendship aside, Luigi felt this was outrageous and, never known for his tact, told Liliana so. Following this confrontation, Liliana rarely visited for the next eight years until Luigi's death, when she came to offer her condolences to Loretta.

In time the women became friendly again, largely due to Maria Elena's closeness to both women. The friendship lasted another eleven years until the beloved Maria Elena passed away at age ninety, just a few months before Liliana's death.

Looking around the funeral parlor, Loretta and Maria noticed many of the photographs displayed were of Liliana and Paolo—not of her deceased husband. Other mementos of Paolo were also evident to them. Maria remembered an earlier visit to Liliana's apartment. A large photo album had dominated the coffee table. Liliana had opened the book to show Maria photos of Paolo and herself. Maria also noticed that Paolo's image in various picture frames surrounded the room—Paolo as a civilian; Paolo as a soldier; Paolo and Liliana together in happier times— these were the only photos with the exception of an old high school picture of her son, William. Remembering Paolo, Liliana's eyes had filled with tears and her grief seemed still fresh.

Maria had been deeply moved at the time, thinking how passionately Liliana must have loved her uncle, and still did. She also couldn't help but reflect how difficult it must have been for Liliana's husband to live in Paolo's shadow. That thought returned now—that Paolo was still a dominant force at Liliana's wake.

William, Liliana's son, greeted Loretta warmly and told her and Maria of his mother's request that all jewelry and mementos she shared with Paolo be buried with her. Not wanting to contradict the dead, he asked their advice.

Maria suggested that he keep Paolo's ring to remember his mother, and all the jewelry could someday be given to William's new granddaughter as a gift from Liliana.

Loretta and Maria saw William again on Christmas Eve. His surprise visit caught Maria in the middle of baking and arranging the dining room table for her family's dinner.

As Maria gathered up a bag of Italian cookies for him, William took Loretta's hand and gave her Paolo's ruby ring. Loretta wore the ring every day, proudly showing it to everyone. Later, she gave the ring to Sandy's son, her eyes reflecting the joy of her brother's memory.

Maria wished she had known the man who earned so much love and devotion from these women.

CHAPTER 164

Christmas Angel—December 2006

On another Christmas Eve, three years later, Loretta's last day was taken up with what she relished most—spending time surrounded by her family.

Loretta, who appeared weak and ashen grey, insisted she wanted to participate in the festive Christmas Eve dinner. Though she ate almost nothing except a little chicken broth and a fork full of pasta with sips of water, her eyes glowed as she watched her children, grandchildren, and great-grandchildren relish the homemade Italian wedding soup, pasta with tuna sauce, shrimp, roast beef, mashed potatoes, salad, and numerous desserts and pastries.

Somehow she managed to stay alert while the children opened their Christmas gifts. After the last present was opened, she retired to rest in her bedroom.

Maria, Sandy, and Rina, sensing she was failing rapidly, called an ambulance to rush Loretta to the hospital where, surrounded by her entire family, she died on Christmas morning.

She had attained the age of ninety and left this earth the way she lived—ninety percent angel and ten percent devil. At her mother's funeral, Maria shared the advice Loretta had given her children to "look at those better than you and do what they do."

Maria reflected that it had taken her a few years to turn around and look at her mother and father to see that they were the best people she could ever emulate—and always would be.

The End

11/14
gift